WILD

-Slave

By Randi Darren

Special Thanks:

The one and only Miss N.
Leta K. You're never on time and always late, but you never fail.

Chapter 1

Vince looked at the board while his face screwed up into a frown. His eyes swept from one notice to another, finding nothing that really suited his skillset.

Escort, escort, escort, escort, escort. Nothing but escorts. I'm no caravan guard. No simple sword to defend a wagon of goods.

Sighing in defeat, he looked to the tag in his hand. It was the only one that even came close.

The money promised was good, though. Almost too good. It would've been equivalent to nearly three years of normal wages if he'd had a normal job.

I'd never last as a farmer.

Like all the other tags on the board, it was an escort mission. At least for this one the clients were moving on foot. No wagon or horses.

No goods.

Moving on foot meant he could take some of his personal detours. He could account for them, and know they were safe.

At least as safe as the Wastes could be.

The roads through the Wastes were perilous in the best of times. Patrols through the Wastes did little more than lose soldiers and waste money on gear and training.

Shaking his head, Vince turned around and cast an eye up one side of the street and then down the other.

Speaking of patrols…

Across the street, in front of the old United States postal office, a squad of pike-wielding men in various pieces of mismatched armor marched along.

They looked far too proud for a group of people who collectively probably had less experience than the newest Ranger on their first day.

Vince felt his face twitch at the sight of it. They were the same people he found more often than not as half-chewed corpses under a bush out in the Wastes.

They stomped past two men Vince had marked earlier as people of note. Of interest.

He'd only been at the Ranger board for a few minutes before these two had wandered over and set up near an alley, watching everyone walking by.

They kept to themselves and their speech didn't drift or carry.

He'd taken notice of them simply due to the sheer amount of hate they were putting out whenever a non-human passed by.

Those men were like a smoldering bed of coals waiting for a stick of wood.

Grumbling to himself, he picked up his feet and headed over to the inn. He'd rather get this contract moving than sit around cooling his heels.

Winter would be coming soon, and trying to get through what used to be the Rockies during a Wastes winter would be suicide.

Keeping his pace sure and steady, his long strides carried him swiftly along.

With a glance to the side as he passed a window, he caught a quick reflection of himself.

He hadn't seen himself in a mirror for a few days and was surprised by the clear reflection in the window.

Light brown hair, bordering on moving towards being an actual blond, framed an average face. He kept his hair rather short. No longer than three or so inches. Longer than that and he felt like he was always pushing it out of his blue eyes. His height made him look scrawnier than he actually was. Being six foot had advantages, but not always.

Big-ass scarecrow.

Snorting at the idle thoughts, he turned his head to the path ahead of him, then to the watch on his wrist. It was an antique. A very old antique. He didn't wear it when he was out and about often, though when he had a timetable to keep, it was invaluable.

His father had called it an Eh-Eleven, but that didn't mean much to Vince.

It only took him a minute to enter and find the potential clients.

Both were older than he was, perhaps in their late thirties. Nondescript and looking no better or worse than anyone else in this border town, they were very average.

Vince didn't bother to attach any value to the way they looked, but instead looked at their clothes.

Lightly worn, no patches, no dirt or dust, boots that were new and unbroken. The cuffs of their long-sleeved shirts were the only part that didn't look immaculate, really. To his eyes, they looked as if they'd been bleached repeatedly.

It was their nails that gave up their profession, which then explained their cuffs. The cuticles of their nails were black. Ink-stained.

Scholars.

Vince plastered a placating smile on his face and took a seat in front of the two men.

"Name's Vince, I pulled your tag. Was hoping to discuss it with you," the Ranger said, laying the request on the table.

"Ah! Splendid, splendid. We only put that up this morning," said the man on the left. He was a little heavier than his fellow.

"Indeed, indeed. I'm Marcus, this is Gator," Marcus said, motioning to the man who spoke first.

"Your marker says thirty gold standards. Ten in advance, twenty on completion." Vince didn't really want to hear their life story. People seemed to think he gave a shit.

He didn't.

"Uh, ah. Yes. That's correct. We're looking to cross so we can—"

"It also says you'll be carrying only packs. No wagons or anything like that," Vince confirmed, interrupting Gator.

"Indeed. We'll be carrying—"

"Good. We can get started tonight. The sooner we can get over the Rockies, the better I'll feel. Wastes winters are good for no one. Not even the Wasters themselves," Vince explained.

"Oh, I see. Yes, well. In that case, could we see your Ranger's license?" Marcus asked.

Vince nodded his head. It was a reasonable request and he'd expected it. Reaching into his vest, he pulled out the wooden license card.

It had his basic information and confirmed his qualification as a Ranger. Someone who could cross the Wastes professionally.

The backside of it was his successful mission tally, which would show he'd completed thirty some odd missions for the Ranger guild already.

If he managed to make it to fifty, they'd change the card out with a new one that had a different design.

"Is this a lot?" Gator asked, tapping the back of the wooden card.

"For my age, it's far more than one could expect. I'm also rated as a single notch below a master swordsman. I have no taste for firearms, way too much cost in upkeep. I do have a proficiency" — Vince said, reaching over to turn the card over and tap the listed weapons — "with crossbows and field medicine."

The vast majority of his crossings he'd done by himself. Nearly at a sprint from one side of the continent to the other as an armored courier. Not to mention one could do multiple courier jobs in one circuit.

Escorts just take too long.

"Mm, mm. I see, I see. Yes, yes," Gator said.

"Fantastic, here's the ten standards in advance. We look forward to working with you," Marcus enthused, dropping a coin pouch onto the table.

Vince picked it up and held it in his hand. He needed to clarify one more point with them. "Know this: while we're out there, you do as I say, and you listen to what I say. This isn't a democracy and it isn't a consensus decision. You do what I tell you to. My goal is to get you safely to the eastern seaboard. Is that acceptable?"

Both men nodded their heads absently, Gator returning the guild card.

"Then we've a deal. Thank you, gentlemen," Vince said with a genuine smile.

It had taken the better part of two months just to cross into what used to be Colorado. They'd just barely slipped through before ice and snow made the passes too treacherous.

Even out in the vast plains of the Wastes, it'd be hard going.

Vince kept them moving along the old roads, which had long since been deserted and ravaged by the merciless touch of time and environment.

They'd help move them along, though, and keep them on track, even if half of these roads, highways, and freeways were wrecked.

"Goodness. Is that a city?" Marcus asked, pointing to what could distantly be seen.

Vince glanced over and then nodded his head.

"Never been. Cities like that tend to collect things that you're better off not dealing with. Most notably undead. We'll be fine out here in the plains." Vince looked back to the road, his eyes sweeping back and forth for dangers.

"It's hard to believe the entirety of the Wastes is all from a couple of experiments by the old United States," Marcus said.

"Indeed, indeed. Now the world lies in ruins. Ruins! The sky's full of creatures that tear planes out of the clouds, the sea's full of monsters that devour boats, and the Wastes are as big as they were to begin with. There's been no retreat in any way, shape, or form. Even after the crusades," replied Gator.

Vince listened in, interested in the conversation. His reading skills weren't great, but even he'd read a couple of books about the pre-Wastes world.

"Well of course it's big, it split the continent in two. Apparently, some of the worst of the Wastes is from what used to be Mexico up to…well, here, actually," Marcus said thoughtfully. "Now it's all overrun by fairytale creatures. It's almost like something out of a bad play."

"They're not fairytale creatures. They exist. They live. They want nothing more than to play with your skull. While you're still using it," Vince murmured. "Even when you can't see them, they're there. Listening."

The conversation died after that. They kept marching along and the day wore on. An hour or so before the sun would hit the mountains behind them, Vince took them off the road and to the side.

The roads had different occupants at night. It was better to simply not be on it when that happened.

They pitched their camp under a ridgeline that had a smattering of trees. That and the scrub brush all around them did a fair job of obscuring their location.

He'd managed to guide them into a shallow depression between two ridges, which meant they might even be able to have a fire.

Which was great news, since Vince had managed to catch several hares. He'd skinned, gutted, and drained them moments after catching them. He'd butchered them on the walk, and the results were all gathered in a sack on his hip.

The sun had barely graced the edge of the mountaintops when Marcus started screaming.

Vince unslung his saber from his hip and cleared the distance of their camp to the scholar in a breath.

"I saw it! I saw it. Behind that brush there!" screamed the hysterical man.

Vince ground his teeth in frustration. Half the time, these situations resolved themselves without interaction between the two parties. Providing that one didn't discover the other one. Watchers would watch unless they had no alternative. Some would simply attack due to the confrontation.

A lone Orc charged out of the brush, straight for Vince.

Strange. Only one.

It was average size for an Orc. Maybe a touch on the taller side, but not as wide. As tall as Vince was, though, and the light green skin visible on muscular arms and legs was unmistakable; it could only be an Orc.

Dressed in a fur vest and what looked a lot like a loincloth, the attacker had a savage look to it.

Long black hair flowed back from the Orc's head, bound behind its skull in a warrior's knot.

Snarling as it closed the distance, it kept its long two-handed war sword held out behind it.

Can't block that thing. Dodging it is.

While the Orc was big, Vince had an advantage over him. He had quite a bit of experience fighting in the Wastes. Humans and non-humans alike.

Impressively, the greenskin brought the weapon around in a vicious arc as it slid to a halt.

Whipping around faster than Vince had originally given the Orc credit for, it nearly caught Vince in the middle of his torso.

Dancing backwards and then diving immediately forwards after the blade passed, Vince went on the attack.

His blade came around in a circular swish that was targeted at the Orc's waist.

Moving with his blade, the Orc brought the big piece of steel around and held it vertically with both hands, stopping Vince's strike cold.

Raising his eyebrows in surprise, Vince pressed up against the Orc and slammed his knee up into the Orc's stomach to buy himself a few precious seconds.

Connecting with the rock-hard abs, Vince only gained a chance to disengage easily instead of a follow-up attack.

The Orc pressed a hand to its stomach and then looked at Vince with renewed heat. Bringing the huge two-hander around itself with ease, the Orc impressed Vince. It wielded the big blade as if it were nothing more than a longsword. There was also the fact that this fellow definitely had some experience in combat, too.

Vince would have to wait for another opening. He was outmatched on reach and strength.

The Orc gave him a leer and grunted at him.

Then the two-hander came forward in a lunge. An incredibly fast lunge that Vince had to turn sideways to dodge, and practically bend himself into a knot.

Not wanting to miss whatever opportunity he could, the Ranger kept moving down and swept low with one leg at the Orc's forward foot.

Unfortunately, Vince was surprised by the Orc again. He lifted up his leading foot and simply stepped over Vince's attack, then smashed a wicked hook into the side of Vince's head.

Stumbling under the force of the strike, Vince took several steps away and shook his head to clear it.

His blood began to sing, his ears rang, and his body felt lighter by the moment. Vince could feel his control slipping as he got worked up.

He'd always walked a delicate line between the savagery of his own nature and the control his personality demanded.

In his heart of hearts, Vince knew he wasn't actually completely human.

Not entirely.

The Orc tilted its head to the side, watching Vince for a moment, before dashing forward. The big sword came out in a sideways slice.

Without a thought, Vince took a step forwards and then kicked off the ground, spinning himself out horizontally over the blade. The big sword passed harmlessly underneath him.

Vince landed on his feet and used the rotation of the move to bring his saber around.

The blade caught the Orc's forearm and stopped dead on the bone, going no further.

Orcs were sturdy creatures. Very sturdy.

The momentum of the attack did more than the edge of the blade. The weight of his blow was heavy, and though it stopped cutting at the bone, the weapon kept moving.

With a cry of pain, the Orc lost its grip on its weapon. It spun end over end into the trees and scrub nearby. It made a deep clanging sound as it rebounded off a tree.

Scrambling after it, the Orc darted into the foliage, one hand pressed to its forearm.

Chasing after it, Vince loped along; he felt confident he could catch the Orc as it reached its weapon, or right before.

Sliding to its knees, the Orc's hands scrabbled amongst the grass, trying to get a hold of the hilt.

Vince stepped down firmly on the flat of the blade as the Orc got purchase on it. He turned his sword around and aimed it downward. It pointed straight into the center of the Orc's ribcage, right into its heart and lungs.

With a sudden jerk on the hilt by the Orc, Vince's attack didn't go as planned as he was thrown off balance.

He only managed to get the tip of his blade wedged into the thigh of the Orc. The edge itself was pressed up to the Orc's throat, however, which left Vince staring into the eyes of the Orc who was kneeling before him.

Unintentionally, one of Vince's gifts decided it was a good moment to wake up.

One of the biggest reasons Vince knew he wasn't entirely human was he had a number of what he called gifts. Gifts that would mark him more of a Wastelander than a human.

A mutant.

As his empathic senses opened up, time for Vince stood still. He was inside of the emotions of the Orc before him. Empathically entrenched in its feelings and psyche.

Hunger. Overwhelming hunger. Fear. Resignation. Acceptance.

Along with that came the context behind it. Knowledge without reading the subject's mind.

It was a female. A young Orc female. She'd been driven from her tribe when she refused to submit to a young male. She'd bested him, then the Orc's father, then the father's brother, in single combat.

With none left willing to challenge her, and none earning her favor, she was shunned by her tribe. They'd been driven her out completely after that.

Orcish pride was a prickly thing.

Her choice had been between only two possibilities: To accept that banishment, or fight them to the death to claim her place as the leader.

She'd allowed herself to accept the banishment. Taking what few possessions she had with her, she'd set out.

Unfortunately, she'd met nothing but misfortune. Water had come to her easily, and she'd always been able to find it readily enough. Food had been another matter altogether. She had no formal hunting experience.

By the point that she'd gotten the basics down from trial and error, she hadn't the strength or time to spare anymore.

Gathering fruits, berries, and wild vegetables didn't fill her stomach, either. It left her wanting more. Craving protein.

She was an Orc warrior with an athletic body.

She had a need for meat that she couldn't ignore at a racial level.

Her plan had been to steal their meat when they fell asleep. It wasn't until Marcus had spotted her, and Vince had sprung over with weapon in hand, that she'd changed her plans.

Giving his head a shake, Vince returned to his own mind. Dark black eyes gazed up at him, waiting. They were large eyes, to the point that she nearly had no whites.

Willing his arm to move, he wanted to separate her head from her neck and be done with it.

And he couldn't.

He'd killed quite a few Wasters. No small number of Orcs.

And he couldn't.

Gritting his teeth, he felt his heart deny him the ability to kill her.

She was too human now.

He knew her.

Her skin was green, she had a set of tusks, her strength was greater than a human's, and she sported a pair of pointed ears, but other than that, as a race, they shared more than they differed.

Instead of letting his thinking go further, or killing her, he untied the pouch of rabbit meat on his hip and dropped it into her lap.

Dislodging the sword from her flesh, he carefully slid the edge from her throat. He watched her for a few seconds without really seeing her.

Slowly, he lifted his sword up and wiped the blade clean on the edge of his tunic. Her blood smeared the fabric in a bright red streak.

Deliberately, he sheathed his sword and then began to take slow, cautious steps back from her.

Her eyes darted from him to the sack and then back to him.

Holding up his hands, empty hands, he took another step, and then turned around. Putting his back to her.

Calmly, slowly, he walked out of the trees and back to his companions. They had a number of months to go. He'd have to catch more wild game tomorrow.

They had more than enough dried rations for a bland but filling meal.

Most of all, he knew without a doubt the Orc woman wouldn't trouble them further.

Chapter 2

They spent longer in the central Wastes than he would have wanted. Marcus managed to hurt himself climbing a ruin foolishly. It forced them to a much slower pace for far too long.

Their destination was Jacksonville, down in what was once called Florida.

Whatever Jacksonville had been in its past life, it was more of a fort now. A city perched on a shore that they didn't dare leave. The fear of the monsters that inhabited the deep waters kept humanity land-based.

Vince and his wards had yet to cross the Mississippi River, but they were only a few hours from one of the few maintained outposts in the Wastes.

The Wastelanders were on both sides of the river, of course, but for whatever reason, their presence on the eastern side of the river was diminished. The Wasters that could be found past the river were typically far closer to human in appearance and temperament.

Vince was on high alert because they were so close to the river. The few times he'd had a true brush with death had almost always been near the river. Local Wasters had figured out a long time ago that humans would cross the river. And only in certain places.

Many had begun treating it as a predator would a watering hole.

Wait, watch, ambush.

Marcus and Gator were chatting amicably as they walked along the dirt path. Vince hadn't wanted to risk much, and so he had them taking a back-brush path rather than the patrolled and more frequently traveled road.

He'd already tried to hush the two men several times and had finally given up. They spoke in hushed voices, but seemed unable to remain silent for any length of time.

Drop 'em off, get our pay, get to the board, pick up several courier messages, get back home.

Vince couldn't deny he was looking forward to a return to his little home on the edges of wasteland territory.

In fact, he'd privately cursed himself almost every step of the way on this agonizing escort job. He'd promised himself over and over again he'd never do another one after this.

At least until I can't get a courier job. Again.

It wasn't the first time he'd promised himself such a thing. Nor did he doubt it to be the last.

Vince's ears picked up the sounds of someone, or something, crashing through the bushes off to their right. Heading right for them.

Only thing off in that direction is swamp.

At that moment, a group of reptile-men burst out of the brush, growling and hissing. They were on the nastier side of the Waster population.

Wasters could be anything, really. From undead to elementals. Creatures that more resembled humans with animal traits, and monsters that looked more like animals on two legs.

These were the monsters-on-two-legs version. They truly looked like alligators on two legs.

And to Vince, they looked as if they knew what they planned to do before having even seen the humans. All six of them were already moving straight for Marcus and Gator.

Unsheathing his saber, Vince stepped off the path and into the way of the six assailants.

"Make for the crossing. Don't wait. Go," Vince hissed, bringing his blade up. Marcus and Gator took to flight, their booted feet pounding at the dirt as they listened immediately.

If they could have listened when I told them to shut up, that would have been great. This is why I don't do escort missions. I could outrun these damn things.

The alligator-men clutched small, crude weapons in their scaly paws. The lead attacker leapt at him, forgetting the weapon in his hand and looking to try and clamp his massive jaws around Vince.

Stepping to one side, Vince flourished his blade, separating from its neck. The gator-man's head tumbled to the ground, its body slapping into the ground.

The second gator in line tracked Vince and came in swinging. It was a low swipe, aimed for Vince's knee.

Sliding back a step and then darting forward, Vince unleashed a piercing strike. After he skewered the reptile between the eyes, it went limp and nearly took Vince's sword with it.

Unfortunately, the third opponent attacked Vince before he could recover from slaying the second.

An obsidian dagger was slammed into his shoulder above the line of his leather armor chest guard. Then it was ripped out of his shoulder with a vicious jerk.

Before Vince could respond, the fourth leaned in and clamped its wide mouth around Vince's forearm protector.

Growling, Vince managed to get his saber up and run it through the throat of the biter.

Pushing off from the slumping dead weight of the dying gator, Vince felt the knife sink into the side of his stomach.

His foe had angled up under the edge of the leather armor. It sank in a few inches from his navel.

Stumbling backwards, Vince got his saber up into position again. The three remaining gators looked to him and then to their dead on the ground.

Vince fell to a knee as his body started to give out underneath him. He wasn't sure if the bastard had nicked something, but he knew he was in trouble. He was sure he'd been in worse scenarios, but none came to mind.

Pressing a hand to his side for a moment, he pulled it away to check his palm. It was coated in bright blood.

Damn.

He pushed his hand back into place to try and stanch the blood, and then Vince started to rise. A pulse of blackness washed over him and threatened to put him back to the dirt.

A forearm came over the top of his head and clamped down around his chest from behind. A light green hand gripped tightly to his wrist, locking his weapon in place, and began dragging him backwards.

Looking over his shoulder, he saw the profile of an Orc as the edges of his vision continued to darken.

Damn, damn.

Looking straight ahead as his chin began to feel far too heavy for his neck, he watched as the living gator-men fell on their dead and dying companions for a feast.

As the last of his strength fled him, he realized the Orc was dragging him deep into the bushes.

Damn, damn, damn.

Vince's eyes creaked open, then closed again.

Alive?

Slowly, determinedly, he managed to pry his eyelids apart.

Up above him, the foliage of trees danced to and fro, leaves spinning in a gentle breeze. Far beyond that was the blue sky.

Screwing his eyes up in pain, Vince started to go through a checklist of body parts.

Head, shoulders, elbows, hands. *Okay, good.* Chest, stomach... specialized manly gear that he couldn't imagine living without... knees, feet.

Everything was accounted for.

Tilting his head, he tried to get a look at his shoulder. That gator had punched a hole deep into the muscle.

The wound was sutured closed and smeared liberally with... something. Something that stank.

Turning his attention down south and discovering that he was naked, he found his stomach had had similar work done.

That, and apparently his specialized equipment was giving him a proud and strong salute.

Can't be too much wrong with me if the little soldier is standing at attention.

Looking around, he did a surroundings check.

Wedged into a clump of bushes, he was laid out in the dead center of them. To his eyes, it looked like an animal had denned here for a while and then left. It was a small enclosure, protected from prying eyes and the wind, which might even help obscure his scent.

Then he noticed the motionless Orc. It was crouched low in one of the walls of bushes.

A second after noticing it, he realized it was the same one he'd come across months previously. She was staring back at him with those large, dark eyes.

Blinking once, he strained to look at her, wanting to make sure it really was the same Orc.

Long black hair pulled back behind her long-tipped ears. Where her arms and legs had been exposed previously, she now had roughly cured and tanned hides covering her limbs.

Her face was smooth, lacking all emotion. As if she were studying him as he studied her.

Her lips were generous, her nose straight and slim, her cheekbones high, her jaw sleek and trim.

In terms of beauty, he found her oddly disconcerting. She had a face that would actually be considered cute, perhaps bordering on being a little pretty.

Then again, when was the last time I really looked at an Orc like this? When was the last time I didn't kill them simply out of hand?

The Orc move forward, her eyes settling on his torso.

Her lips peeled back as she sniffed twice at him. She had tusks, as all members of her race did. But they tucked cleanly into her upper lip. They looked like large canines more than anything.

Unable to move or do much of anything, Vince watched, wondering what the hell she was up to. Orcs didn't patch humans up. They didn't drag them off from a fight they were losing to save them.

Then she wrapped a green hand around his member. Her hands were callused, but the touch was soft. Light. Hesitant.

Betraying Vince's own desires, his little soldier simply continued to direct all attention skyward.

Vince's eyes had gone wide at the suddenness of her action.

Giving him a thoughtful tug, she sniffed again at the air. The pull had been cautious, a curious testing.

He got the impression she wasn't sure about his genitalia. Then again, he could have been the first human she'd seen in person. Let alone naked.

Much to his embarrassment, he felt his heartrate speed up. Though on second thought, he couldn't tell if it was fear of what the fuck she was doing or excitement at what the fuck she could do.

After a heartbeat of nothing further from her, she turned her head to stare into his eyes.

The Orc warrior murmured something in a feminine yet low, rumbling voice. He swore it had a question attached to the end of it.

"I'm-I'm sorry I don't speak your language. Ah…" Vince said unhelpfully.

The Orc repeated the same phrase, though this time the question sounded more like a statement. He only made out the last word that sounded a lot like Fes.

"Fes," Vince said aloud, nodding his head. At this point, he'd repeat whatever the hell she wanted like a parrot so long as she didn't tear his member clean off.

The Orc's eyebrows came together over her dark black eyes. With her free hand, she reached out and tapped his chest with her fingers and said something.

Then she touched her own chest, and repeated "Fes."

It's her name?

"Fes," Vince parroted.

At that, the Orc grunted, her eyebrows smoothing again. Apparently she was satisfied with that response.

Dismissing him, her eyes turned back down to his private part held in her hand. Speaking quietly to what he assumed was herself, she waggled him a little. Her words sounded like she was speaking her thoughts aloud.

Finally, she released him. Much to his great joy and secret shame. Then she gently pressed her fingers to his side. She pushed at the wound, dragging her thumb along the stitches. Then she repeated the process for his shoulder.

Now that he thought about it, they looked markedly healed. Far more than they should have been.

Actually, how long have I been out?

Content with whatever she saw there, she reached to his side.

He recognized his canteen in her hand at the same time his mouth told him he was as parched as a desert.

Unscrewing the cap with long green fingers, she held it over his mouth.

He opened it in mute acceptance for her, and she began to pour its contents into his mouth.

It had a slight woody taste to it, but the sweet wetness of it on his dry tongue nearly brought him to tears.

She paused at times, allowing him to swallow. All too soon, she re-stoppered the canteen and set it to one side.

His head started to tingle, and his hands and feet went numb within minutes.

Oh. I see.

It was the only thought he managed before he was swept into the nothing that was a medicated sleep.

Vince's eyes snapped open. He recognized the leaves above him, even though it was night now. The air had a bite to it, but he didn't feel cold. He caught the twinkle of a star or two between the branches.

Feeling weak all over, sore, and tender at the same time, he realized he wasn't going to be getting himself to safety anytime soon. He doubted he could wrestle a kitten right now.

His eyes began to take in the small amount of light available. He'd always had better than normal night vision, and for once felt thankful for those non-normal gifts of his.

Inspecting his surroundings again, his eyes found he was unmoved from where he'd awoken last.

He couldn't even assume this was the same day from when he was last awake.

Well, that wasn't quite right. He'd clearly been moved an inch or two, but he imagined that had been probably to check either his wounds or… well, to clean him up if he'd had an accident while he slept.

Being forced to sleep didn't preclude his body from relieving itself of waste, after all.

Looking down to himself, he found the Orc woman pressed up into his side, her knee draped over his hips and one hand on his shoulder, her head on the grass next to his injured shoulder.

Not being cold made a bit more sense now. That and the fact that the woman felt like a damn furnace. She put out enough body heat for her and him.

Belatedly, he realized she was awake. Awake and watching him from inches away.

Clearing his throat softly, he tried the only word he knew, the one he assumed was her name.

"Fes?" he asked.

She nodded once at that, lifting her head fractionally from the grass.

Again came a stream of words, none of which he knew. He swore he could pick out a few in there that he'd heard before.

Unable to appropriately ask what she'd done to treat his wounds, he decided to try pointing. She'd clearly attempted the same method to him earlier.

Pointing at his shoulder in front of her nose, he waited a second. Her eyes focused on his finger before looking back to him.

Moving his hand again, he pointed at the wound on his stomach.

Her eyes followed his finger towards the wound.

"What did you do?" Vince asked, moving his pointing finger to his shoulder and then back to his stomach. "Infection is easy to get out here. Oh hell, she won't know what I'm saying, what am I doing?"

Dropping his hand to his side and laying his head back down on the grass, he stared up at the tree canopy above him.

Check it in the morning.

Beside him, the warrior shifted to an upright sitting position, withdrawing her hand and knee both. His skin felt cold as she drew back. Letting his eyes move to his apparent savior, he watched her.

Her eyebrows were drawn together and her lips were pursed. She looked like she was contemplating something.

"Fes?" Vince asked, hoping that nothing was wrong.

Blinking rapidly at the question, the Orc looked to his face.

"Fes," she said with a nod of her head.

Her right hand snaked down along his stomach. Her fingers brushed over the wound gently and then straight down to his privates.

Her fingers immediately curled around his girth and gave him a light squeeze. Soft, callused fingers with a careful grip. She cradled him in her palm and brushed a thumb over his tip.

The whisper of the touch made his skin prickle. Vince's breath caught between his teeth as his heart lurched.

Reaching out with his left hand to stop her, he encountered her free hand. She lightly swatted his hand back and then pointedly looked into his eyes.

Her fingers gently squeezed him, the firm flesh of her hand sliding upwards before releasing him. For a warrior, her touch was surprisingly gentle.

Her nails, a little longer than a man's, grazed up and down along the underside of his length. The simple unexpectedness of the touch made it jerk in response.

Again, his body betrayed him, immediately responding to the soft, sensuous touch of the warrior woman.

Her hand closed around him once more and with another squeeze of her hand, he'd gone to full attention.

Releasing him, she swung a leg over his hips. As if it were the most natural thing in the world, she pressed her knees into his sides. She then set one hand down beside his head and caught his eyes with her own.

Distracted by the intensity of her gaze, he missed it when she reached down between her legs with her left hand.

Staring into her large black eyes, he felt himself at a loss. It wasn't until he felt the heated touch of her fingers on him again that his brain shifted gears.

Her fingers stopped moving and instead pulled at him with gentle tugs.

Tender fingertips pulled him upwards and he felt the tip press to the soft opening between her legs. Unerringly, she guided him into her channel and then slid herself down onto it in a single fluid motion.

Vince felt the tightness of her as she squeezed him. The give of her flesh as she impaled herself.

He caught a momentary flash of pain crossing her features as she settled herself onto his lap at the end of her journey.

Fes took in a shuddering breath, putting her other hand beside his head now.

The incredible warmth of her skin was nothing in comparison to the crackling heat of her core.

Vince stared into those inhuman eyes for several heartbeats as she stared back into him. Then the warrior woman began to move herself back and forth atop him, working him slowly in and out of herself.

Physically unable to respond, Vince lay there as she did the work for the both of them. He could feel his heart pounding in his chest as his body responded to her determined yet inexperienced ministrations.

Her breath started as slow, easy exhalations, washing over his face and neck. Her lips parted to reveal her tongue and teeth. It didn't take long before the intensity of rolling her hips brought her to deep, heaving breaths.

With each and every undulation, he could feel her tightening as she got closer to release.

Despite her inexperience, she brought herself to a dead pant in only minutes. Her hips worked furiously now as she found the rhythm she wanted.

Vince noticed when her big black eyes went wide and started to glaze over as she stared down at him.

Laying his hands on the sides of her thighs with a light touch, he gave her what guidance and encouragement his numbed mind offered up.

Unexpectedly to him, she sat down heavily on his hips, burying himself up to the hilt. Her waist grinded back and forth as if trying to drive it deeper.

Then her entire body came to a shuddering halt. She held her breath, before letting out a slow, raspy exhalation.

Collapsing atop him, she closed her eyes and immediately fell off to sleep.

Leaving him hard up, wide awake, and about as deep as he could be in her molten insides.

Staring up at the sky above him again, Vince wasn't quite sure how to take what had happened.

For the time being, all he could do was go along with it.

It's not like it didn't feel good. I'm only a man, after all. But... with an Orc? That's... yeah.

Shit, wish I finished.

Chapter 3

Vince spent the next two nights being cared for by Fes. It took that long before he could even stand without feeling like he'd pass out.

After that, he started his long journey back west through the Wastes. To his surprise, and yet not really, Fes joined him.

There was no point in heading east to see if his clients had made it. If they had, they could leave with a patrol. If they hadn't, it was irrelevant.

West it was, then.

During the day, he rested and tried to conserve his strength as they traveled. He checked his wounds frequently and always found them healing quite well. More so than he would've had any right to expect them to if he were a simple human.

At times, Fes would leave for a while and return with food, both wild game and anything she could forage.

In the short time since their first encounter, she'd clearly come light years ahead in her survival skills.

As they trekked west, they talked to each other in their own languages. Sometimes for the sake of simply speaking to another person, even if they didn't understand one another, and other times to begin teaching the other.

They started to pick up various words here and there, though Fes clearly had a better grasp of English than he did of Orcish. The simplest way, of course, was pointing at items and things and then naming them.

Most surprising was when they settled in for the night.

Each and every evening, Fes mounted him until she dropped, sleeping atop him. Vince wasn't quite sure what to make of the situation, but felt no need to try and stop it.

Why should he? It was pleasurable and his only real concern was... well, he hadn't gotten off. Yet.

Sexual pleasure without a release was its own torture.

As to her motivations, from what he could tell, they were genuine. The brief flashes from his empathic gift, when he couldn't control it, only returned emotions of honesty and concern to him from Fes. Or desire.

Whole lot of desire, actually.

Enough to make a brothel seem tame. For such a stern and thoughtful warrior woman, she seemed internally driven to distraction by her own sexual wants.

He'd have never guessed.

They made slow progress despite neither of them having much in the way of baggage.

Vince had his sword, a knife, canteen, and an empty rucksack.

Fes had her own gigantic sword, of course, some implements for skinning and tanning, and the sackcloth he'd given her.

It didn't help their speed when Vince was paranoid of any encounter, no matter how small it might appear or remote. He'd drag Fes into whatever cover was nearby whenever he felt like there might be a danger nearby.

Diving into the foliage, he'd pull her in close and wait for whatever perceived danger to pass. Or for his paranoia to pass.

Either or.

She seemed content enough when he did so, letting him dictate their direction and movements.

The only time she became insistent was right before they'd try to get some sleep. For obvious reasons that he didn't argue with, she always got her way.

And just like that, they passed through the Rocky Mountain Range as winter released its grip without incident.

Vince had a quiet thought in his mind about the fact that this single trip had cost him half a year already. The return trip was almost so quiet that he feared what he'd find upon returning home.

He didn't voice it, of course, since it would only jinx the whole damn thing.

Once they were out of the mountains, things got easier. Wasters were in short numbers this far out.

It became more of a matter of dodging humans out past the mountainous divide. Those humans would happily avoid you as you avoided them, which suited both he and Fes just fine.

The world had never been truly kind, but now it wasn't even cordial.

Fes had the look of a warrior facing their doom, though, as they went.

Every day they traveled further into the human lands and closer to the edge of the Wastes, the more she looked troubled.

It also showed at night. Her lovemaking became more and more frantic at night.

Their destination was Vince's family home, so he shared none of her concern or fear. It was actually inside the edge of what was considered by most as being the Wastes.

It was in what used to be a national forest in California, to be exact.

His parents had made sure to keep the wild animal and Wasteland animal population alive and well populated. They encouraged those creatures to propagate freely.

A forest full of Wastes creatures kept other humans out, after all.

He'd grown up in this forest. Knew it inside and out. Leading Fes straight to the two-story home through the thick woods and over shallow streams was as simple as if there had been a giant, glowing arrow in the sky above it.

Not bothering to show Fes around, or even strip his clothes off other than his leather armor, Vince had slumped into his bed and passed out without a word when they finally arrived.

Waking up the next morning, he knew it was pre-dawn. One of the unfortunate side effects of his gifts was a predisposition to wake before the sun.

Looking to his side, he found Fes sleeping in his bed with him. She hadn't woken him up the previous night and had been content to simply join him.

It'd been the first time there'd been no coupling the night before.

Looking around his room, he felt a little strange. Once he'd turned eighteen, he'd built the additional room himself. With his father's help, of course. "Odd" was the only way he could describe his feelings now.

No one else had been in this home since his parents had left something like six years ago.

Except now he had a woman here.

In his home.

In his bed.

An Orc woman.

An Orc warrior woman.

One that seemed intent to ride him like a cheap date every night.

Fes snorted and then let out a loud, ripping snore, one tusk peeking out from her lower lip.

Vince watched the sleeping Orc for a second before he gently brushed loose strands of hair back from her eyes.

In response to his touch, she tucked her head under his shoulder and snuffled before resuming her dedicated battle against the silence, snoring deeply and loudly.

No delicate princess here.

Getting out of the bed quietly with a small grin, he pulled the covers up over Fes. Then, using his best impression of a ninja, he slipped out of the bedroom.

Entering what could be called the living room, he found Fes's equipment in the corner. A quick glance provided him with confirmation that nothing else had changed.

At all.

Haven't made it home, have ya?

Vince dismissed thoughts of his parents and went to the basement trapdoor. He opened it and looked inside.

"Breakfast won't make itself," Vince muttered. Clambering down the wooden steps into the cellar, he sighed.

He walked past the jars upon jars of pickled and preserved food and headed straight to the back.

Opening another door, he stepped into a room that seemed more like something from a horror story.

Racks upon racks of cured meat, still on the bone, hung from hooks.

His parents had discovered early on that Vince had a number of things that set him apart from normal humans.

The most unusual trait was his ability to take anything he ate and make it a part of himself.

In fact, that was how he'd developed his ability to see in the dark so well. His parents were nothing if not proficient hunters. They'd brought back any number of animals for supper, many of which had incredible night vision, or simply better vision in general.

His mother, ever the scientist, had noticed that her little boy wasn't developing in normal ways. Through trial and error, hypothesis and testing, she'd eventually narrowed it down to his diet.

In the end, his mother had begun feeding him various things to bring about changes. Changes she could track, such as vision, regeneration from damage, resistance to toxins — anything that she could attribute to a specific animal, catch, and then feed him.

Not faulting her for curiosity, but instead praising her for helping him to develop his gift, Vince now had a room full of cured meat.

As well as a very healthy and stronger-than-normal body.

He trained that body with the sword, his mind with the knowledge his parents had passed down to him, and his... whatever it was, with the genetic sampling of other creatures.

Settling down to his "breakfast" routine, he began carving out chunks of each and every type of meat in his cellar, and ate it right there.

Eating more than his fill, Vince managed to pull himself out of the cellar before he made himself sick.

He pulled out enough from the larder for a breakfast for Fes when she got up, and set it out on the table. There was no way she could miss the sight of it, let alone not smell it.

Her sense of smell is almost better than my own.

He left his home quietly after collecting his "bathroom kit." No reason to look like a wild bushman if you didn't have to. Today would be a good day to get rid of the facial hair that had sprung up during the trip.

The kit also contained soap, which he hadn't taken with him, a hand towel to scrub the grit and dirt out, and a large bath towel to dry himself with.

He walked in the silence of the dawn to the nearby creek. He hadn't been able to wash himself in weeks, and was starting to feel more like an animal than a man.

Fresh and safe water wasn't bountiful in the Wastes.

Not to mention he'd need to check the condition of the creek and make sure the water was flowing cleanly. Stagnant water was the quickest way to setting himself up for a future failure.

He heard the water long before he saw it. The sound of it assured him that nothing had changed.

One less thing to fix before we have to head into town and register the partial success.

The guild of Rangers would be expecting to hear from him. Their ability to negotiate contracts was built on dependability and transparency.

He'd catch a five-gold standard fine for not completing his mission, but it would be refunded if the East Coast arm of the guild reported the arrival of the clients.

Vince felt the anger building in his chest for his mission choice. He berated himself for taking an escort mission.

They never worked out for him and he knew it.

Pulling his shirt up over his head, he immediately worked to clear his head.

He dropped his pants, ripped his socks off, and wriggled himself out of his boots. Dropping his shaver atop his pants, he clutched the soap and hand towel. He was ready. And to clear his head instantly, he dove into the frigid water.

It wasn't ice water, really, but it wasn't far from it.

Spluttering as he surfaced, he began to lather himself up. He was a Ranger, not a polar bear.

Dirty polar bear. With an Orc... girlfriend? Slave? Sex buddy?

Thankfully, the cold water did its job—both to keep his mind clear of anger and other distractions. Like the Orc he'd started thinking about.

What do I do with her? I have to go into town and check in with the guild. Does she wait here? Do I take her with me? If I do, she'll have to wear a collar. Would she wear one?

Law for both the West and East Coasts was that all non-humans needed to be wearing a slave collar. The magic inherent to them prevented the wearer from doing anything outside of the rules placed on them by the owner of the collar.

He'd found a number of broken collars in the woods. Unfortunately, many an owner would send a slave to simply... die in the woods. He'd encountered a few as they died, even.

Trying to render them any aid at all would force them to turn violent.

They were under orders to die, after all.

Most of the collars had had the appearance of being whole and intact. Functioning.

Except they weren't. Since the order was carried out successfully, the collar would show a positive result, but no longer have any power or spelled rules.

Frowning at the thoughts and coming to no answer, Vince set it aside for now. Taking a deep, bracing breath, he dunked himself under the icy water, washing off the soap and lingering trail dirt.

Popping back up above the water after several seconds, Vince let out an explosive breath.

"Good. No stink. Clean," Fes said from the bank. She was squatting down next to his clothes, her fingers moving through them disinterestedly.

Vince was awful at Orcish, apparently. Fes had told him so many times. Truth of the matter was he had no ear or tongue for it.

He was awful at it. Truly awful.

Thankfully, she seemed well suited to learning English. Her vocabulary expanded every day, and he thought she'd have it mastered relatively quickly at the rate she was moving.

"Being wounded does tend to make one stink," Vince agreed. Splashing over to the bank, he set down his hand towel on a flat rock, the soap going down atop it.

Fes grunted and watched him. Her eyes trailed down his body and then back up with a carnivorous eye.

"Wound good. Look good," Fes claimed. She reached out with two fingers and brushed them along the healing skin. His skin prickled quickly at her gentle touch.

The wound itself looked far more like an angry scar by now, and it pulled at his skin when he moved.

That'd fade with time, though.

"Glad you approve," Vince said, picking up the towel and starting to dry himself off.

Fes nodded her head and then stood up. In a few quick movements, she was naked.

The entire time they had traveled, she'd never once removed her clothing. She'd been insistent that he strip for her, but he'd never forced the same stipulation on her. During their sexual romps or otherwise.

In fact, they'd never even kissed or spoken of their nightly sessions.

Picking up the soap and used washcloth with her right hand, she unbound her hair with the left.

Blue-black hair fell around her shoulders and face in a shower.

Vince couldn't help but inspect her green body with a touch of admiration.

And regret that he'd waited this long to get the view he was now afforded.

Despite knowing she was an Orc, he could only see a woman with green skin. Everything about her was more or less human. She only happened to be stronger, green, and have a few extra teeth.

That green muscular body was dirty, stained with the road, and the world.

And sexy as hell. An alpha predator in her prime. Lean and fit.

She didn't have an hourglass figure or an impressive bust, but she was put together in a lovely way. Slim but with a decent waist, athletic and incredibly toned, but still a bit more than a handful in the chest.

Letting his eyes roll over her like a starved wolf eying a steak, he felt the heat return to him quickly.

Fes didn't notice the visual assault he launched at her. Or if she did, she didn't care.

Instead, she set about washing herself clean, mimicking the same things he'd been doing but minutes ago.

She was watching.

"I need to head into town. City. Village. I have to tell the guild what happened with my clients. Tell them the result of my mission. Let them know what happened," Vince said, taking the opportunity to watch her bathe.

He'd developed a tendency of overexplaining things to her. It'd help her vocabulary, he was sure, but it would create problems further down the road if he didn't keep it from becoming a long-term habit.

"I understand. Fes go with Vince."

Fes turned around, watching him as he watched her. His eyes immediately moved to her hands as they lathered up her underarms and chest.

"Okay. You'll have to wear a fake collar. All non-humans have to wear a collar," Vince said apologetically.

"No collar. No slave. Fes," declared the woman. Her eyes hardened a bit, and she turned to the side as if contemplating putting her back to him.

"No collar. Fake collar. Fes not a slave. Fes is Fes," Vince agreed.

"Fake collar?"

"Lie collar," Vince tried instead.

Fes blinked at that, her mind probably sorting through the words she knew. Suddenly she looked at him and gave him a small smile.

"Lie collar, yes. Fes is Fes. Fes go with Vince," Fes agreed.

"Great. We'll pick it up when we're done here," Vince answered, his eyes roaming down her body again.

Fes apparently had noticed by this point and flicked water at him. She gave him a smirk when his eyes finally returned to her face.

"Sorry, look good," Vince apologized, imitating her earlier proclamation over his healing wound.

"Fes look good?"

"Yep, Fes look good. Very good."

Unbelievably, the warrior woman's face became a darker shade of green. Turning her back to him, she went about her business.

Fuck it.

Standing up, Vince dropped the towel in a dry spot on the bank and waited.

Fes finished up and made her way back to her clothes. She eyed him warily now after the way he'd watched her.

Her eyes were tracking his midsection, as if they were about to start fighting and she wanted to be able to react accordingly.

"Fes," Vince said softly when she came close.

Her eyes jumped from his torso to his eyes.

Not waiting for an invitation — or to give her one, because she probably wouldn't understand it anyways — he finally made a move of his own.

Reaching out, he placed one hand on the side of her jaw and then leaned in close to her.

Her response was no response. She froze rock solid. Still as a statue as he pressed his lips to hers.

Her lips were warm and soft, a little cracked, and one corner had a cut, but the feeling of her mouth was wonderful.

Slipping an arm around her hips, he kissed her deeply, before tilting her backwards towards the towel he'd laid out.

Firm hands came up to clutch his shoulders as he eased her down into the fabric. Settling gently atop her, he continued to kiss her.

Moving his hands gently, slowly, he started to explore her body, caressing and flowing over her smooth skin like the wind.

Turning his head an inch to the side, he caught her pointed ear and bit into it carefully. The soft flesh was warm between his lips as he tugged at it.

"Vince, Fes. Fes. Fes is…" panted the Orc.

Breathing out heavily into her ear, he lifted his knees and tried to spread her legs apart.

Fes shivered, her strong fingers digging into his shoulders. She allowed her legs to spread wide after a moment of hesitation, her ankles coming up to rest behind his thighs and pull him in closer.

Angling his shaft, he managed to find her slit on the first try. Taking in a breath, he bit at her ear again. Moving his hips forward, he plunged himself into her in one smooth stroke.

Fes took in a quick breath. Her ankles pulled at him even as she turned her head to press her face into his neck.

Vince held himself up with his forearms resting on either side of her head. Giving the tip of her pointed green ear a nibble, he started to work himself in and out of her.

Slow and cautious, he could only bask in the roaring heat of her insides. Her body as a whole was rapidly heating up, despite having been in the snow runoff only minutes before.

Truthfully, he had to fight against Fes more than his own desires. She seemed as if she wanted to drive him straight into sexual abandon. Her teeth and lips worked furiously at his throat and neck. Her heels and ankles pulled on his legs when he moved forward. As if she wanted him to move faster and harder.

To take her.

Growling a little under his breath, he turned his face into hers and kissed her fiercely, keeping his own rhythm and pace.

Fes responded immediately, her mouth opening and her teeth and tusks biting at his lips. She gouged her fingers into his back, dragging them down forcefully.

Vince only kissed her in the same way he had earlier, refused to change speed, and pressed in closer to her.

Fucking wasn't his goal right now. He'd done that plenty enough to know the difference between that and what he wanted.

She calmed down, albeit slowly. Apparently it finally sank in when he didn't respond in the way she expected to her actions. Instead, she began moving in time with him.

She started to move in sync with his body.

Her hips slid forward and back as he thrust into her.

Callused and tender hands pressed into his back without the urgency that they had previously. Now they held him.

Her thighs and ankles were glued to him now, instead of pulling at him.

Strong limbs melded to him instead of trying to dictate a pace.

Pulling back from her face, he switched his weight to his hands instead of his forearms.

Slowly, he built up his momentum, his speed, his strength. Fes's cheeks darkened as her eyes began to lose focus as he worked.

Letting his control slip as he got closer to release, his empathic gift got away from him.

Shocking in its intensity, he felt every emotion that poured out of the woman beneath him. Most of it flew by him before he could identify it, but there was one overwhelming feeling he couldn't overlook.

A feeling of acceptance and completion.

Grinding his hips into her, Vince felt himself spill his seed into her fiery depths.

The empathic link shut off at the same time Fes smashed her face into his, kissing him with a passion he hadn't expected.

Grunting, he collapsed atop her, kissing her hungrily.

In time, and after his loins were done filling her, he pulled back from her face. Gasping for breath, he pressed his forehead to hers.

With a quick kiss to her lips, he rolled off of her. He reached out to his side and rested a hand on her hip and stared up at the blue sky.

Gotta wash up again.

Chapter 4

It took five days to get to Knight's Ferry from Vince's home, most of which was trail hiking.

The trip, normally dull and boring, wasn't unpleasant in the least with Fes as his companion.

Days were spent talking, building on Fes's vocabulary, and giving her the right set of expectations for where they were going.

Evenings were interesting with the change that had occurred down at the creek. Sometimes she'd be on top, other times he'd be on top. It was a tossup of who managed to wrestle the other one to the ground first.

Knight's Ferry was as close to the big cities as Vince ever really wanted to get. The location acted as a perfect outpost for him to purchase supplies, make sales, and pick up contracts sent from the local Ranger headquarters.

When the Wastes had been created, it had been at the height of the war in Europe. This had left a serious population gap between men and women, as well as fracturing what control the military could have provided during such a catastrophe.

All of this had led to the simple fact that the big cities became sprawling slums and neighborhood turf wars were dominated by women.

Eventually, the cities became deserted or became more feudal-like, as it was clear much of the world was reverting to an earlier place on the technological timeline.

There wasn't really a need for bankers, scientists, or artists. Guns fell out of favor when ammunition ran dry in the first several years. As technology collapsed, no one was making new guns or ammunition.

Swords, polearms, axes, all the old accoutrements of war made a rapid comeback.

In that first decade, the world had turned itself into an appalling approximation of medieval territories reporting up to a neighborhood "baron."

From these barons eventually rose the government that loosely governed the West Coast. A collection of barons or baronesses who answered to a count or countess, who in turn reported to a council of dukes or duchesses. From Baja all the way to Alaska, that was how it was ruled.

They'd called themselves "The Government of the Western States" with a complete lack of creativity. Most called it The West or The Government.

A similar and separate situation had occurred in and on the eastern seaboard. They'd ended up with a king rather than a council, however.

Eventually people had begun making the long-distance journeys between the two would-be kingdoms. The Rangers had been born from that need.

Membership was voluntary and required a certification. On top of that, there were examinations and tests to determine if you were fit for membership.

No training was provided by the guild. Membership in the guild came at a contracted percentage of every mission being handed over.

The guild kept their people in line while providing contracts. They were also swift in distributing justice to their members.

For these reasons, the Rangers were trusted completely to be employed.

Trying to hire someone outside of the guild was a sure way to get your throat slit in the Wastes during the night.

Or so the guild would have you believe.

Fes stayed at his side when they entered Knight's Ferry, her head moving on a swivel to track everyone and take in everything at the same time.

Unthinkingly, she reached up and adjusted the thick silver slave collar that rested on her collarbones. It wrapped around her neck in a way that would deprive her of oxygen if she disobeyed.

Well, that was what it would have done, if it had been a working collar. Which it wasn't.

Vince motioned to the large two-story building to one side of the cracked pavement road.

"We're in there for a few minutes. I need to report in, and then we'll go hit the merchants' square," Vince whispered.

Fes followed the direction of his fingers and nodded her head. "Fes will remain at your side."

Nodding to that, Vince walked in through the front door and stopped for the door guard.

Holding out his Ranger license, Vince only had to wait a few seconds. Then he was ushered in without a word.

Ignoring the common room, the bar, and job board, as well as everyone inside, Vince went straight to the service counter.

An older man of perhaps forty winters sat with an open ledger in front of him.

Withdrawing two stacks of five standards each from the pouch at his waist, he set it down atop the ledger along with his license.

"Partial completion. Clients made it to the Mississippi River fort. I was wounded by an ambush of gators. Took one Orc warrior woman as a slave on the return trip. Registering her as mine," Vince said.

Five coins were a penalty for a non-completion of his contract, and the over five coins were to register Fes.

"Name?" the man said, flipping over Vince's license.

"Fes."

The clerk grunted and reached down beneath the counter. Then his hands came back up with a small iron stamp. Popping open a container to his left, the clerk pressed the iron into the sponge inside and then pressed it to Vince's license.

Closing the container, the man dropped the iron back into whatever he'd pulled it out of below the counter.

Sliding the wooden license to one side, the clerk pulled out a paper from a folder and then rapidly filled it out.

Spinning the paper around, he slid it in front of Vince.

A quick signature on Vince's part and Fes was registered.

The clerk then picked up the Ranger license and wiped a piece of cloth over the wood. A symbol had appeared on the back. Exactly where the clerk had pressed the iron. A big letter O with a small S next to it.

"You'll be notified if the clients report in and the penalty will be refunded. Anything else?" the clerk asked, looking up at Vince.

"Nope, thank you."

Turning on his heel, Vince left as quickly as he'd come in. He didn't really want to look at contracts right now. His body didn't quite feel at one hundred percent even though he knew he was healed.

Exiting the building, they stood on the cracked and broken sidewalk.

"What now?" Fes asked, her eyes sweeping up one side of the street and then the other.

"Clothes and armor for you. Maybe get something a bit more… balanced than that I-beam of yours. You handled it well, but I I'm betting you'd be better with a weapon that required less work," Vince answered. Turning to the right, he began walking down the street towards the merchant quarter.

Fes scrunched up her nose in obvious distaste.

"Small sword for small people."

"No, a big sword. Larger variant of the longsword. Trust me. Clothes and armor first."

Fes only nodded her head, falling in beside him.

Vince kept himself on alert as they walked along the boulevard. Violence in Knight's Ferry was rare, but not unheard of.

Everyone was an enemy until proved otherwise. This world wasn't for the faint of heart.

The short time it took them to get to the tailor was thankfully uneventful. A few people took in an eyeful of Fes, but that wasn't completely unexpected.

Orcs were a little uncommon. Orc women more so.

Clothes shopping with Fes was blessedly swift. She accepted everything he set out to purchase for her with barely a nod.

Four sets of clothing and a few coins later and they were on their way back into the street.

"Next up, armor. Can't have you running around in just clothes," Vince said, indicating the blacksmith several doors down from the tailor.

"Why? Armor not right. If I get hit, I lose," Fes grumbled.

"Because I don't want you to get hit? Honor is for the dead and pride is a commodity."

"You don't want Fes to lose."

"No, I don't. I want Fes to grow old and die when her heart gives out," Vince said, shaking his head.

Fes said nothing more, following Vince into the blacksmith shop.

A Dwarf with a slave collar stepped out from behind a counter and peered up at him.

"Vinny, come to finally get some real armor, eh? None of that stupid cow skin? Didn't help the cow none, why would it help you?" shouted the dwarf.

"Deskil. Good to see you. Loud as ever. How's Minnie?" Vince asked, holding out his hand to the diminutive blacksmith.

"Speaking of her, I'm not nearly half as loud as the ol' ball and chain. Just the other night I had her squealing for hours until the—"

A door banged open along the back wall, and a woman stepped out in the common room.

She was on the plump side, and the hard work she put in was starting to show in her face and hair.

"Another word, Deskil, and I'll have you making pots and pans for months," she threatened with a warm smile.

"Oh, love, my honey bunch, buttercup, sweetums, you know I'm only bragging," Deskil responded, beaming up at the woman.

As a pair, they seemed ill fit at first glance.

Minnie had to be in her mid-thirties, and Deskil, only he knew. Dwarves lived considerably longer than humans.

Vince smiled, watching them get wound up. "Minnie bought him about a decade ago at the auction. She runs the shop, he makes the equipment," Vince said under his breath to Fes.

Fes grunted at his explanation.

Minnie suddenly looked to Vince and gave him a bright smile. "Who's this?"

"This is Fes. I... picked her up in the Wastes," Vince explained, stepping to the side, one hand held up towards Fes.

"Fes?" Deskil rumbled. His bushy eyebrows came down over his eyes. It looked like he wanted to say more but held his tongue.

The Orc woman nodded her head once at the two, silent.

"She, uh, she doesn't talk much, but she's picking up the language quick. Came in to pick up some armor for her. Can't have her running around with me without protection, after all."

Vince walked over to one of the wooden mannequins that lined the wall. Reaching out, he fingered the chainmail that it wore.

"With her strength, I was thinking a mail hauberk. Wrists to knees. Matching gambeson, of course."

"Course. Makes sense. I've got something in mind. One adjustment, probably. Her chest is a bit bigger. Could walk out with the mail today in a few hours, or come back before you head out for the evening. Anything else?" Deskil asked, his mind having made a choice and setting it aside.

"Need a longsword just shy of being a great sword. Preferably one that she can wield one-handed but not hit the ground from a guard pose," Vince offered up, his eyes moving to the side wall where the swords were.

"Oh, we can definitely do that. Again, I think I have something you can take home with ya today. She'll be a force to be reckoned with. I take it you won't need that... thing anymore?" Deskil asked, pointing at the freakish sword strapped to Fes's back.

Fes looked to him but said nothing. She was letting him make the choice.

He knew, knew it without using his empathic gift, that even if she never swung it again, she'd still wish to keep it.

"We'll be keeping it. All in price?" Vince said turning to the dwarf.

"Call it twelve for the whole thing and you've got a deal."

Damn. That's... quite a bit.

Then again, he knew that Deskil was probably already giving him a low price.

He also knew he had a surplus of captured prize weapons from things he'd killed in the Wastes. He'd have to pack up a good portion of them and bring them in and get his money back.

It wasn't as if he were poor, though. His parents had left him with near five thousand standards. And that was what they had buried under a cement block in his home. In the local bank, his parents had two thousand standards available to him.

He'd added another three thousand to that number in the bank through his various contracts and being frugal with selling his prizes.

Just collecting dust anyways. Too many swords for one man.

Unless someone wanted to contract the purchase of, say, werewolf teeth, he had no reason to sell any from his giant bag of werewolf teeth that was in his trophy room.

"Done," Vince said, not wanting to haggle. Pulling the coins out of a flat purse strapped to the inside of his armor, he set them down on the counter. "We'll be around to pick it up later. We won't be st—"

"Staying the night, I know. You never did, never will. Right, no time like the present," chuckled the dwarf. Stumping towards a table, he began rubbing his hands together.

Minnie watched the Dwarf with a smile before turning back to Vince.

She mouthed a silent 'thank you' and then went back to the office in the back.

Vince turned and left the blacksmith shop, pulling Fes along with him.

"They don't get as much business as they should. People seem to think Deskil makes inferior equipment. Contrary to that belief, I think his work is phenomenal."

Fes once more said nothing. She had nothing to add, so she said nothing.

"That leaves us with some time to kill. Anything you want to see?" Vince asked the Orc, looking over to her.

"Auction," came the immediate response.

"We could do that. Never really been to one. I've seen them in passing, but... it's one thing to kill a Wastelander in the Wastes. It's another to sell them into slavery," Vince said, shaking his head. Turning to the left, they set off down the boulevard again.

"You don't sell or buy?" Fes asked.

"No. I don't."

Silence settled down between them. Comfortably so.

As the road turned a bit, Vince could see the auction square up ahead. It was placed next to the river since a lot of slavers shipped everything by boat. Knight's Ferry had a large auction for a town that wasn't that big.

Mostly because the slavers didn't want to risk trying to get their merchandise into a bigger town. The auction guild invested here instead.

When the government had failed, all the dams and agriculture siphons on the river had collapsed. The Stanislaus River was now very much a deep and free-flowing river. All the way to the San Joaquin.

The slaves would be unloaded from the boats and lined up on the platform right there, then sold.

The auction began the same time every day and would go until every slave had been up on the auction block. Sometimes there were only a few, sometimes there would be a large number.

All depended on what they caught and brought in.

Fresh catch of the day, Vince mused bitterly as his eyes took in the slaves.

Having started sometime earlier, the auction was well past the halfway point.

There would only be a few slaves that would catch high prices at the start. Most of the valued or noteworthy ones would be in the last twenty-five percent.

It kept people around from start to finish that way.

Even now, the specimen being sold looked little more than what could be used for housework with how malnourished it was.

"Sold!" bellowed the auctioneer. The gavel clacked twice and the slave disappeared from sight before Vince had even gotten a good look at them.

"So many," Fes said quietly. At least thirty more slaves were lined up waiting for their turn.

"Yeah, the Wastes are huge. You wouldn't think it, but there's some proof out there that humankind might actually be outnumbered. Some of these could be non-sales from other cities. On top of that, they could be resales. The auction doesn't act as an intermediary. They purchase everything outright and then work to sell it at a profit. If they don't see a sale here today, it gets shipped elsewhere to try again," Vince explained.

"It?" Fes sneered, her eyes latching to his face.

Vince sighed and pressed a hand to his forehead. "Them. They."

Fes nodded to that and she visibly relaxed. She wore her emotions on her sleeve.

"Next on auction is a Dryad. While we can't confirm this, we believe she's an ash Dryad. A Meliae," the auctioneer called to the crowd.

A nude woman was dragged forward from the line to stand before the crowd front and center.

"She was caught only this morning. In fact, we believe she's never planted a tree. If you can get her to plant a tree, she'll be yours for as long as the tree lives. I guarantee she's untouched as well, as she was picked up by a well-established acquisition agent. Plant your seed and have her make it grow," crooned the seller.

All around him, the people who had seemed interested were no longer so.

"Like that'd happen—"

"—dead in the week. Waste of money, I s—"

"Good for a fuck, and then bury it—"

"—move on already. It's garbage—"

Vince frowned and looked up to the Dryad.

She was pretty, as were all of her kind. High cheekbones with a full mouth and soft green eyes. Her face had a tenderness that invited kindness.

The bruises and cuts from what he could only assume came from her capture diminished the wonder in the world.

She had a skin tone that ran towards being a light tan. As the sun hit her at certain angles, her flesh almost shimmered green.

Her pale white hair was cut short, hanging limply at the sides of her face. Topping out at five foot one, her bust size was impressive for her build. It would've been impressive on a six-foot woman, in truth. A thin waist and rounded hips gave her an hourglass figure that only a fantasy could produce.

Much as everyone had said, they'd be willing to buy her if to bed her, only to bury her when she refused to plant her tree.

A Dryad without a tree was a plant without soil. They were already dying.

"As a reminder, don't attempt to use the slave collar to force a tree planting. The tree dies within the hour, followed by the Dryad. Starting bid at ten standards." With a clack of the gavel, the auction began.

"Fifteen."

"Twenty."

"Twenty-five."

"Twenty-six."

"Thirty."

Vince felt a pang of regret for the little thing. Her life would be a short, ugly thing.

Fes pulled at his forearm.

Turning to the Orc woman, he raised his eyebrows.

"Seed?" asked Fes.

"Thirty-two—"

"Ah, yeah. Seed. Have her grow the seed," Vince said with a vague hand gesture at the ground, his eyes moving back to the auction.

"Seed. Grow seed," murmured Fes. "Buy her. Buy the seed grower, Vince," Fes grumbled at him, her hand gripping his forearm more firmly.

"Thirty-five—"

"Err, what?" Vince asked, confused.

"Forty—"

"Buy the seed grower. Vince no regret," Fes promised.

Sighing, Vince looked back to the auction once more.

The bids had stopped. Forty standards for a week of time with a Dryad.

"Going once—"

Vince hesitated. He didn't want to buy the Dryad, and wasn't sure what he would do with her even if he did buy her.

"Twice —"

The green eyes of the Dryad found his through the crowd. Before he could stop it, his empathic gift leapt free of him and enveloped the creature.

Fear, pain, humiliation, hopelessness. An insurmountable wave of despair.

"Vince... for Fes?" asked the Orc.

Fes's question snapped him free. The way she posed that question and his glimpse into the mind of the Dryad had him raise his hand immediately. "Forty-five."

"Fif —"

"Sixty," Vince said, interrupting the other man mid bid.

There was no counter to that. In acting the way he did, he gave the impression that he would be willing to keep going.

"Once. Twice. Sold!" shouted the auctioneer.

Vince pressed his lips into a thin line and left the crowd. He'd have to use one of the few bank notes he kept on his person. He mostly used them for trade in towns and cities. He'd have to use one to purchase the Dryad. Sixty standards was more than he had on him in hard currency.

He moved towards the pickup and payment table to complete the transaction for the Dryad.

Fingering out a bank note from an inside fold of his armor, he glanced over it. It was set for one-hundred standards, which meant they'd be paying him forty in return, minus a tendering fee.

The Dryad he'd bought stood next to the table, her eyes downcast towards the ground.

Vince flipped the bank note and his Ranger's license onto the table before the auction clerk could say a word.

"Forty in return," Vince stated.

"Hmph." The clerk picked up the note and Vince's license, then checked the authorizations. Meeting whatever requirements he had, he then picked up two sheets of paper. "Five standards in fees. Five more for the services. Registration will be set without a name. Be sure to update it if she lives through the week. One moment."

Fes had stepped up to the Dryad and immediately unchained her.

"Hey, you can't —" started one of the guards.

"Can't what? Can't take over my property? I've already paid," Vince hissed at the man.

Not used to having someone question him, the guard fell silent. Fes pulled the Dryad off to the side, placing it between Vince and herself.

Vince noted two men off to one side. He vaguely remembered them from another visit.

They'd been around the last time he was here, scowling and throwing dirty looks at every non-human they could see.

Now they were a group of five, sequestered at the back of the auction. Even now, one was watching Vince.

Before he could focus in on the watcher, they turned their head away.

"Here." The clerk shoved the license back into Vince's hand, jarring him back into his current situation.

An uppercase D and a lowercase S were now burned into it next to the mark for Fes. Then the man slid five rows of standards across the table to Vince. Not bothering to count it, he simply opened his waist purse and swept them inside. "Paperwork will be filed this evening with the registrar and the Ranger guild. Thank you. Next!"

Turning on his heel, Vince slid an arm around the Dryad and escorted her back towards the clothing shop.

"Just... tolerate this for a little bit longer. We'll get you some clothes from the tailor and be on our way," Vince whispered under his breath.

The Dryad lifted her eyes and looked into his soul with that gaze. Eyes the color of fresh leaves weighed him.

Just as quickly, the Dryad looked back down to ground. Dismissing his words.

"Tailor, blacksmith, general store, home. Thinking our return trip may go a bit slower now, Fes," Vince said, listing out the best plan he could come up.

"No regret, Vince. Fes promises it," soothed the warrior.

"It's fine, Fes. It's fine. I'm sure it'll be fine."

Hopefully.

Chapter 5

Three days into the return journey and they were barely past the halfway mark. It'd be another three or four assuming the Dryad could keep her current pace. Vince didn't figure that would be likely, since she'd probably fall down and die in a day or two.

An unplanted Dryad didn't have long and only withered as time went on.

Her bright white hair had faded to a dull gray, her skin becoming ashen, and her eyes turning sunken.

Vince felt pity welling up inside him as he watched the Dryad across the faint warmth of the campfire. It was morning of their fourth day and they'd be setting a similar pace to previous days.

She didn't move much. She just sat there listlessly, her eyes staring into the dying coals of the fire.

"Feel like you could eat something? Anything? Maybe a little water?" Vince asked her.

Not looking up at him, she shook her head woodenly.

"If you feel like you can hold something down, let me know."

Vince kept himself from sighing. Barely.

Watching her wither into nothing. What a messed-up situation.

Fes patted the Dryad on the head as she went about getting into her new clothes and armor. The warrior woman had been dubious about the armor at first, but then had immediately grown comfortable in it.

That like had only grown again when she'd realized she lost little to no movement. Especially so when she began working with her new blade. Vince couldn't help but feel a touch nervous with how quick Fes could rip the sword through the air with maximum force.

He was still pretty sure he could take her in a fight, but it wouldn't be so easy now. At all.

The part he personally wasn't used to was the fact that Fes still wanted to have their nightly fun. Despite the Dryad being there. And watching.

The entire time.

The first night, the little tree spirit had been shocked when Fes had mauled him and then mounted him. She'd watched wide-eyed and unmoving.

Vince had to wonder if she thought it would have been her on her back instead of him. Especially since that was the expectation of what she had been bought for by almost everyone else there.

The second night, he'd managed to pin Fes to the ground. It'd been awkward with the Dryad there, but he'd gotten over it. It was that or get mounted again.

By the third night, the Dryad either didn't care or was too weak to care.

As tactless as it sounds, I could always eat her. I'm sure there's something unique about her that would help me.

The thought didn't appeal to him. In truth, it rather unnerved him. But his efficient personality wanted to assuage what little it could of the money it had cost to buy her.

Distancing himself from the thought, he made his final preparations to leave. The road waited. Eating her would be a last resort, and he'd cross that bridge when it came.

Once everything was good and ready, he slipped a hand under the Dryad's arm and eased her to her feet.

"Come along, little tree. It's time for us to away. Hopefully we can make it home before... well, before."

Vince could only regret the fact that he didn't have the means to break the slave collar off of her. It would restrict her from escaping, and at a certain distance begin to choke the life out of her.

Many a slave had simply run to the extreme edge of the boundary and committed suicide in that fashion before an order could be given to not do that.

Until he got her home, there'd be no way to get the collar off. As it was, he was pretty sure he'd signed her death warrant by buying her. Though at least if she died on the way, she could do it far from human civilization, unviolated, and in relative peace.

With a little encouragement, the Dryad started to put one foot in front of the other. Fes nodded to Vince and fell in a few steps behind the Dryad. Vince moved up to take point.

They'd only progressed maybe an hour down the road when Vince had a strange feeling creeping over him.

Looking over his shoulder, he checked and found Fes and the Dryad marching along behind him. Focusing on the path in front of him, he let his eyes unfocus, trying to pick out anything that didn't fit the pattern of the road.

The same moment he caught sight of someone in the foliage next to the road, an attractive woman stepped out within arm's reach of him.

There was no reason for someone to be out this far. Especially to make an entrance like she did.

His actions from Knight's Ferry came back to him. He'd flashed money in a public fashion. This was all his fault.

He made a purchase that would have put a dent in anyone's pocket. Did so with a bank note and asked for change.

Careless.

Grasping the hilt of his saber, Vince unsheathed and swung in the same motion. The speed of the attack caught the woman off guard.

So much so, that it wasn't until his blade exited the left side of her neck with a wet swish that she realized her error.

"To the rear!" Vince called out, taking several steps backwards. Putting himself close to the Dryad.

The headless corpse of the woman fell to its knees and then lay still. Blood spurted from the stump with each beat of her heart.

Three men rushed at him, materializing from the same area the woman had stepped out from. They were all wearing brown leathers and had their swords out.

A deep-throated yell from behind was his only indicator that Fes was engaged as well.

"Dryad, get out of here, keep yourself safe. Come back when it's over," Vince called out.

Stepping forward, Vince skewered one of the men through the throat. Backpedaling once more, he was left with two attackers. Both seemed very unsure about the whole thing now that they'd already suffered two causalities.

Not wasting the time for witty banter or anything else so cliché, Vince went on the attack.

Flashing his saber out in a feint at the man on the right, Vince stepped to the left and brought his sword back around towards the man on the left.

The man on the right fell backwards while Vince's sword slammed into the man on the left's forward leg.

Crossing his feet one over the other to move with the strike, Vince drove his left hand into the now wounded man's side.

Dropping to his unwounded knee, the would-be bandit tried to lift his weapon to defend himself.

Stepping in close, Vince wrapped his arm around the man's head and leaned it backwards, sliding his saber forward at the same time.

Skin parted and the sound of a whistling windpipe gurgling filled the air as Vince's saber slid through the man's stretched neck.

Dropping the dying man, Vince moved towards the last attacker in front of him.

Apparently, the bandit had suddenly realized the error of his ways and started to turn around.

Unsheathing a throwing knife from his belt, Vince swept his left hand forward. The blade flipped end over end to embed itself in the back of the man's knee. The strength of the throw buried it into flesh up to the handle.

Collapsing to his hands and knees, the man turned his head to see Vince closing in on him.

"Please, ha —" the man started, before Vince's blade speared through his heart. Pulling the blade back out, Vince turned to see what was going on with Fes and the Dryad.

The edge of a blade slid along his hardened leather breastplate and then slammed into his collarbone. Skittering off the bone, the blade burrowed underneath it and then into him.

Reaching up, Vince struck the blade from the hand of the man who had tried to stab him in the back and brought his saber around.

Catching the man in the armpit, Vince's saber tore through the joint and came out the top, severing the arm entirely.

Screaming, the bandit fell to his knees, his right hand clasping at the missing limb.

Vince smashed the hilt of his blade into the man's windpipe, crushing it. He'd die either from the blood loss or the inability to breathe.

Reaching up, he unhooked a strap of his armor and exposed the upper part of his chest. Vince frowned at the bloody gash, then pressed his hand to the wound firmly and turned his gaze on Fes. He saw three dead bandits around the warrior. Two nearly split in half.

She was in the process of withdrawing her blade from the third's sternum. Her eyes were blazing when she unstuck the blade and turned to find Vince watching her.

"Fourth go—" she nearly shouted, before her eyes fell on the armless dying man on the ground in front of Vince. "Ah, good."

Vince nodded once and then looked to the surrounding flora. "Dryad? Damn, we really need to get her to tell us her name. Errr, Meliae?" Vince tried.

Creeping out of a low bush, the Dryad came into view. Unharmed and whole. *Whole as a dying Dryad can be, at least.*

"Vince, you wounded," Fes stated, coming up to him. She'd re-sheathed her blade and her hands immediately came up to his chest.

"Yeah, he got me. Would have put it in my spine if I hadn't turned around," Vince explained. Lifting one hand to look at the wound, he was shocked at the amount of blood that flowed out. "Damn."

Pressing his hand as firmly to the wound as he possible could, Vince sat himself down on the ground. He wasn't sure if he could keep himself standing if it got worse, despite wanting to keep the wound much higher than his feet. "Get a dressing out for me, Fes? I'm not a master of anatomy, but I'm fairly sure there's a vein in there somewhere. So long as it didn't get nicked, this'll be fine in no time. If it did… bury me somewhere nice."

Fes pulled her pack from her shoulder and bent over it, rooting around for the requested bandage.

Vince looked to the Dryad as she sidled closer to him. She had a curious look. Almost like he imagined someone would look if they'd been caught doing something wrong.

He gave her a weary smile.

Maybe she blames herself.

"Don't blame yourself for me catching that sword," Vince said. "I could have handled the auction better and not been so flashy. I let my anger over the situation get the better of me."

Blood started to seep from between his fingers, though it didn't seem to be as bad as when he'd pulled his hand away. Dropping his saber at his side, Vince flexed his free hand.

Maybe we got lucky after all and this is just a bleeder. Getting too many new scars as of late, though.

Not paying attention, Vince was startled to realize the Dryad was nearly atop him. Her green eyes were staring into his face, her small hands halfway between her chest and his.

Unable to stop himself, he felt his empathic power rise up and link into the Dryad.

Curiosity, fear, shame, and guilt. Determination.

Vince wanted to tell her it wasn't her fault again. Instead, he felt his tongue stick to the roof of his mouth.

In her right hand was a softly glowing seed pod. He'd seen them often enough in the wild to know what it was.

Her eyes watched him, green and awake. The haze that had been hanging over her had dissipated.

Tender, pale fingers picked at the hand covering the wound in his chest. Deciding to see what she'd do, he lifted his hand to give her access to it.

Blood pumped out and flowed from the gash. He couldn't tell if it was any better or worse, but he doubted releasing the pressure was helpful.

Then the Dryad reached forward with her right hand and stuffed the seed pod into the wound. Using her left hand, she dragged the ball of her palm against his saber and then pushed her bloody palm atop his wound.

Pushing firmly, she looked into his eyes and gave him a cautious smile.

Nothing happened at first, and the only thing he could hear was Fes rooting around in her pack, muttering to herself. To him, it sounded like the contents of her pack had shifted around in the fracas and she was having a hard time finding anything.

A warmth came into his arms and legs. In retrospect, he hadn't even noticed it earlier, but he'd actually started to get cold. Never a good sign. Certainly not a sign of a fatal injury, but not a good one.

Oddly enough, Vince felt like something was moving around inside him.

"My tree grows," the Dryad whispered, her eyes still staring into him unrelentingly.

"Did... did you plant your tree in me?" Vince asked her.

Before his very eyes, he watched as her skin gained a healthy glow. Her eyes cleared completely, her cheeks coloring.

The brown-and-green shimmer to her coloring came back nearly immediately.

"I did. Your blood reeks of strength. It empowers me. My tree can breathe through your veins. You are now my tree's home." Her voice was smooth, rich, strong. It was deeper than he'd expected for such a small frame.

"I see. So... why? And also, you're feeling talkative now?"

"Your wound looked bad. You treated me kindly and didn't use me as many would have. You have a relationship with your Orc that I don't understand. Now that I can feel you..." The Dryad paused at that. A ticklish feeling in his brain came over him for a second. "I can tell that you're a good person. Your body is different as well. You're not completely human." The Dryad tilted her head to the side.

"I speak now because I choose to. Before you ask, I have no given name. I am me. I am Meliae."

Vince digested all that and found himself mostly at a loss.

Then Fes was there, her face between himself and the Dryad, looking from him to her and back.

"Seed grower safe, good. Good job, Vince. Seed grower healed Vince?" asked the Orc, seemingly unconcerned with the situation.

"Yes, Fes. Vince is healed." As if to demonstrate, Meliae lifted her hand from the bloody mess only to reveal smooth, clean skin.

"Ah, good. Seed grower is healed, too. Good Meliae," Fes said, giving Meliae a big smile and patting her on the head.

Vince frowned as he felt things continue to shift around in his chest, stomach, and head. He wasn't quite sure about having a tree growing inside him, or if it was even possible, but he couldn't deny it'd happened. There was no mistaking that seed pod as anything but a seed pod.

"Thanks, Meliae," Vince said, patting the Dryad on the shoulder. "Alright, Fes. Let's strip the bodies of anything of worth and dump them off to the side. The wolves will feast on their corpses and we'll make coin on their belongings. As Father always said, waste not, want not."

Home was around the bend, so to speak. They'd picked up the pace since Meliae had recovered. What had looked like it might end up taking an extra three days to get home ended up being only one. They were even arriving as the sun rose.

Meliae had really come alive in the days since. Her appetite had skyrocketed, and she'd started to vanish on occasion, only to show up with nuts, fruits, and wild vegetables.

Meliae isn't her name. She doesn't have one.

And yet they called her Meliae.

In the days following her recovery, she'd become equally parts silent and talkative. Small talk and chitchat weren't in her repertoire.

Fes remained unrelenting in their nightly activities. Meliae never shied away from watching, yet never commented or spoke of it, either.

Other than that, nothing changed that Vince could identify.

Except the fact that he had a tree growing in him. At times, he could feel it when it shifted or twisted itself around. He could only assume it was expanding. It would need as much space as it could wring out of a human torso, and was contorting itself to do so.

At least it caused him no discomfort. Well, he wasn't sure about that. He couldn't tell if the Dryad was blocking discomfort or if it really didn't bother him.

Meliae had been a little thin and gaunt-looking when they had set out. Now she had a full-bodied figure and face that was a little distracting at times. The change had been completed in a single day.

Finally, Vince could see the two-story house through the trees. Fes and Meliae were already walking up to the front door as Vince circled around the front of the house.

"Everything appears as it should be," Vince said, inspecting the dirt track that led up to the entryway. "No tracks, prints, or marks. Good. There's a room I've been using to store 'prizes' in. We'll drop this junk off there. I'll be removing Meliae's collar after that.

The Dryad looked at him sharply. Vince ignored it. He didn't feel like answering her insistent questioning when she got chatty right now.

Fes grunted and looked down. She'd apparently forgotten her collar and now took a moment to strip it off. Holding it in one hand, she opened the front door and disappeared inside, Meliae following her in.

Taking the steps leading up to the porch, Vince stepped inside and closed the door behind him.

Fes waited in the entry hall for him. Pointing at a side room, he moved to join her.

The warrior woman opened the indicated door. Looking inside, she hesitated and then dropped the loot they'd taken from the bandits.

Turning around, she walked towards their bedroom, her hands already working at stripping her armor and gear off.

Shaking his head with a grin, Vince collected the gear Fes had dropped and stepped into his prize room.

Assorted through the room were racks, stands, and dressers. Everywhere was loot from the dead and ruins of the Wastes. He'd organized it and laid it out according to his own mental plan for it.

It took Vince only a few minutes to put away all the additions and step back out of the room. Fes passed by him, dressed in her normal clothes.

"Going to go stretch. Relax. Train. Be back for lunch," Fes said, stopping in front of him.

"Mm, alrighty. Don't wander off too far. While it sounds fun hunting you down in the woods, I'm not sure this is the right time for play." Vince grinned at her, putting a hand on his hip.

Fes guffawed at that and gave him an appraising eye. "Already caught. No need to hunt me." Reaching up, she gently patted his cheek with her callused fingers.

Opening the front door, Fes left the home and closed the door behind her.

"So, Meliae, how do you—" Vince stopped talking as he turned his head to find the Dryad. She stood in the middle of the hallway, her fingers clutched around the collar.

"Yeah, let's take care of that first. Have a seat at the table. I'll go get the battery." Vince pointed vaguely at the dining room off beyond the far end of the hall.

Vince stripped off his gear as he moved. Flipping his saber onto the bed, he shucked his armor off in front of the door as he passed.

He moved to another door and popped it open. It served as a storage room for tools and other things he needed, but not regularly. Included among the tools was a battery his father had found somewhere.

It had a simple function: Drain whatever item the contact point touched of energy when activated. This included magical energy. It would then retain the charge for a period of time or until used.

Exactly like an old-tech battery.

Picking up the strange bucket-looking thing, Vince went to the dining room.

Sitting in a chair, Meliae was looking around the room. Her fingers were still flexing around the collar around her neck.

"Alright. Hands tight on your collar, Meliae. When this goes off, I need you to grab hold of that collar and pull as hard as you can. It's going to drain all the magical energy from it in one go. The collar recharges itself pretty quick. My dad figured out that this little doohickey does a solid job of giving you about a single second to pull it off. After that, the collar won't come off. It actually adapts, frighteningly enough," Vince explained.

Stepping in front of the little Dryad, he upended the battery and pressed it to his forearm. Hitting the discharge stud, he felt the leftover charge from the battery pass into him.

Normally, it energized him and gave him a little flutter of nerves. This time, it… vanished. Like it never even happened.

"Oh. That was lovely," Meliae said. Vince looked down to find the Dryad staring up at him, her green eyes had a faint sheen to them. "Will you do that again after you drain the collar?"

"Uhm, sure. Did it… did the tree take it? Take the energy?" Vince asked, placing the contact point to the collar.

"Yes. It was very tasty. I'd say my tree jumped ahead at least a month in its growth. Very helpful."

"Good to know." Fingering the trigger, he gave the Dryad a small smile. "Ready?"

"Yes. Though I value my freedom, I have to ask, why? Why free a living eternal slave to you?" Her voice was quiet, as if she were afraid of her own question. Or the answer.

"Don't need slaves. Don't want them, either." Vince activated the battery. A crackling filled the room as the collar was drained instantly.

Quick as lightning, Meliae gripped the collar and snapped it free from her neck. Her little hands dropped it to the ground as if it might leap at her and reattach itself on its own.

Panting, Meliae looked up at him, her eyes triumphant.

"Yeah, it can wind you when it gets deactivated. The damnable thing takes a bite out of you as it tries to refill itself." Picking up the collar, Vince flipped it over his shoulder to hang on himself. Turning the battery over again, he pressed the contact point to his forearm again.

"You sure? This won't hurt me? Never tried a full battery charge."

Meliae kept panting, her green eyes plastered to his face. She gave him a sharp nod of her head.

Without another word, Vince activated the discharge function. Fully expecting to get turned into a fried squirrel.

Except nothing happened. To him, at least.

Meliae's eyes, on the other hand, glowed a bright green for a few seconds before the light died away.

Vince could actually feel whatever it was inside his chest rapidly expanding. Coiling itself tighter. In fact, he could make out what looked like light brown veins crawling up his arms, before settling into the skin and disappearing.

"That was like an entire year. We should get more slave collars," said Meliae. Looking back to the Dryad, he was momentarily caught off guard. She was staring hard at him. Almost with a hungry glint to her eyes and eager cast to her mouth.

"Uh-huh. Not every slave is so casual after being freed, you know. Quite a few attack afterwards. Not that I blame them. I'm just a human to them, after all," Vince said with a grin.

"You're far from a normal human. Far from it," whispered Meliae.

Chapter 6

Vince woke up slowly through the fog of dreams. Blearily, he cracked open his eyes to find Fes sprawled out on her back next to him.

One of her strong forearms was laid out on his chest and one of her legs over his hips. Grinning, he gingerly folded her arm in, and then her leg. Carefully, he pulled the covers over her and slipped out of bed.

She snorted once but otherwise fell back asleep, drool trailing down her cheek.

Trying not to laugh at his very Orc bedmate, he slunk from their bedroom, closing the door behind him.

Ghosting along the hallway to the dining room and attached kitchen, Vince let his mind wander. He started cataloging what he'd need to take care of, both around the house and the forest.

Population check, secure the house and surrounding areas. Check the fringes for humans or sign of them. Secure and make sure all caches are intact. Go look for mo —

Vince's brain hit a wall when he looked into his kitchen to find Meliae seated at the table. She had a low bowl full of dried berries, nuts, and a small chunk of cured meat.

Her eyes flitted to him as he entered and she gave him a wide smile.

"Morning to you, Vince. Your cellars are well stocked," said the Dryad. Her voice sounded more vibrant today. While she had looked visibly improved in the last day, maybe she had still been recovering.

"Thank you. I strive to have as much food on hand as I possibly can. You never know when a storm will come through," Vince said, forcing one foot in front of the other again.

She'd taken up residence in one of the bedrooms that had never been anything more than... empty. His parents had planned to have more children but hadn't done so. He'd never asked them, but it seemed after having him they had changed their minds.

"Wise. I'd like to build a house of glass attached to the side of the house. I was... caught... while I was inspecting such a marvel. Everything inside was protected from the elements and warm." Meliae turned back to her meal.

Bending low, he opened a cabinet and peered in.

In the kitchen, he kept all the nonperishable goods. Tin and glass jars lined the cabinet, labeled by a wax crayon.

He'd salvaged tin storage containers and glass jars with watertight lids.

They were worth their weight in gold. There really weren't too many comparative alternatives for food storage.

Many a home and house had been ransacked by Vince in the Wastes for all his pickling jars in the basement.

Vince settled for a near-identical meal as Meliae's and another that looked like it could be described as a "meat plate."

Vince sat down at the table along with the two plates.

He put the one similar to the Dryad's in front of himself and the other to the side of it. Dropping two water skins down next to the plates, he looked to Meliae.

"I take it you've decided to remain for a time?" Vince asked casually as he picked up a handful of dried blueberries.

"I have. I could leave easily enough and simply replant elsewhere. I choose not to. My freedom is mine. Besides, your body is providing more nutrients than my tree would ever receive in natural soil. Not a big tree, but a very strong tree," said the Dryad, nodding her head.

"As you like," Vince said, not really wanting to talk about trees growing in him and how strong they were. "That would be a greenhouse, by the way. The house of glass. We could probably do that. Won't be easy, though. Glass isn't the easiest thing in the world to bring all the way out here. We can make a special trip to Knight's Ferry during next summer though for it. Will probably have some glass blowers trying to offload product." Vince took a big bite of a dried apple slice and shrugged his shoulders.

"That'll be fine. We can set about creating my garden ahead of that. It'll be harder to keep it alive during the winter, but... doable," said the Dryad.

Meliae hesitated, munching on a few nuts. She clearly had more to ask or say.

Vince didn't pressure her; she'd speak when she was ready, and only then.

Instead, he focused on his meal.

Why is snake meat so strange when cured? He really didn't care for snake meat, but he knew their reflexes and speed would only continue to help him. Especially with how often he kept getting hurt lately.

"Why do you agree so easily? You eat with me as if it were nothing. You keep a warrior Orc as a—" Meliae stopped. Vince had to wonder if she was searching for a word she liked. "Mate. It's abnormal."

Vince shrugged his shoulders. "I would agree with you. Up until Fes, I honestly killed any Waster that I came across that was hostile. Then I met her and... well, things change, I guess."

"Waster?" Meliae asked.

"Err, inhabitant of the Wastes. Wastelanders. Wasters."

"Wastes. Was it not always as it is today?"

"No, not at all. In fact, it was part of a fairly large human country. Your kind, and all of the Wastelanders, didn't even exist one hundred years ago."

Meliae frowned, her brow furrowing. "I had no idea. Well, I'm glad for your recent change. How exactly did you take... Fes... for a mate?"

"Hm. Honestly, it's a little odd. She was starving out in the plains. She had originally planned to steal our meat supply. One of my clients noticed her. We ended up fighting. I won. Then... I realized what her problem was. I gave her all the game I'd caught that day and... left her there."

Vince picked up a flask of water and took a sip.

Meliae nodded her head slowly.

"After that, she didn't show up again until I was ambushed by six crocs. I think it was six? Anyways. Crocs ambushed me. I killed a number of them but was simply over run. Fes showed up, threatened them, and dragged me away as I blacked out. And there's the story."

Meliae chuckled throatily. She tilted her head to the side, white hair fanning out. "You realize how unlikely that all is?" asked the Dryad.

Vince shrugged yet again. "Doesn't change how it happened."

From down the hallway, he heard Fes stumble out of bed. She wasn't a quiet morning person.

The door opened and Fes's heavy footfalls came towards them.

Smirking, Vince watched as the Orc woman looked first to the Dryad, then him. Her dark eyes were coming to life from the land of her dreams.

He gestured to the meat plate set at his side, then pushed a skin of water next to it.

Fes gave him a broad, sleepy grin and sat into the chair next to him taking the proffered plate and skin.

"Vince, thank you," murmured the Orc. A green hand reached across the table and patted his forearm.

"Course, Fes. Need anything else?"

"No. Good. Happy." Fes picked up a section of meat and started in on it.

The warrior woman's eyes closed and she rested her elbows on the table, eating her breakfast while practically dozing.

"Any other surprises? Other than taming one of the fiercest Orc women I've ever seen, living in a... Waster-inhabited forest, and purchasing and freeing slaves?" Meliae asked, her full lips curling up into a bright smile.

Vince said nothing, not wanting to admit anything further about how different he was.

Instead, he tried changing the subject.

Turning to Fes, he reached over and laid a hand on her wrist.

Two sleepy black eyes opened and focused on him at the touch.

"I need to travel the forest for a few days. Will probably head out after breakfast. Check on everything. Make sure we don't have anyone else around, check in on the populations and confirm they're in balance, and that the forest is healthy. I've never had anyone ever make it to the house, but that's no guarantee."

Fes nodded her head, her hand patting his own.

"Take Meliae with you. Her forest eventually. Plant seed with her. Will defend home while Vince away. Need to train and build anyways," Fes said softly.

"Will do. Thanks, Fes, I appreciate it."

"Duty of Fes. Vince won't regret Fes," said the Orc, brushing aside the concern physically with her left hand in a wiping motion, her right hand resting on his left hand.

"You willing to come along, Meliae? It'll be a few nights out there. We'll need to plan accordingly," Vince asked, looking to the Dryad.

Her cheeks were a deep red, contrasting sharply with the color of her hair. She nodded her head slowly. Apparently the idea of exploring a forest excited her.

Can't blame her. How many Dryads get to claim a forest for themselves, I wonder.

Vince brushed his fingers over the trail. He couldn't explain it, but he had the feeling the game trail hadn't been used in a while. The print under his fingers had long ago dried, and the edges of it were cracking and fading.

The animals of the forest ran it freely. Vince made it a point to keep the predator population low. Acting accordingly, he took more prey animals so that their population wouldn't strip the forest.

In this way, he had managed to always have more meat on hand than he'd ever need. Cured, smoked, salted, enough meat to get him through a winter or two if he became wounded and unable to hunt.

That, and when the snow really dumped and he got trapped indoors for a while.

Lifting his head up, he sniffed deeply, willing the scents nearby to tell him the story.

There.

It was faint. Almost to the point where he wouldn't have noticed it. Death.

Standing up, Vince brushed his hands over his pants. "Trail is dormant. Need to track into the woods over yonder," Vince said, pointing towards where he felt the smell was coming from.

Meliae nodded her head, staring up at him.

She'd been quiet for most of the day. They'd left immediately after finishing their meal. Fes had been dozing at the table as the door shut behind them.

The Dryad had said barely more than a handful of words since then.

Dismissing the problem, since it wasn't one, Vince set off after the scent he'd picked up on. It was a unique smell he'd never be unable to forget.

As they picked their way through plants, bushes, and small saplings, Vince kept his eyes moving, trying to pick it out before he found himself drowning in the stench.

Unfortunately, he wasn't successful. One moment it was only a trace smell, the next, the nauseating, gut-wrenching mess of a rotting corpse hit him.

"Ugh," Meliae whispered.

"Yeah. Something died out this way that isn't normal for these parts. Critters in this forest are a skittish type to abnormal smells. Death is normal; whatever died doesn't belong here."

Then Vince was suddenly on top of it.

Laid out before him were the festering remains of a humanoid. A slave collar lay in the moldering throat of the body.

"They send slaves they don't want out here to die. I've buried or burned my fair share. It's where all those slave collars come from," Vince explained. Reaching down, he fished out the collar and set it to one side.

"I see. I can help with this," Meliae said.

"Oh? I'd be much obliged. Digging takes a while, and this isn't the best part of the woods to be lighting a possibly uncontrolled fire in. That, and the stink of a burning body is awful."

Meliae didn't respond, and instead lifted her left hand. All around the corpse, the dirt shifted. Cracks and rifts formed in the soil and the corpse was pulled down, into the earth.

As quickly as it had all started, the dirt mounded itself up over where the corpse had been and ceased moving.

"There, the roots will feed on her. She shall serve in her death to grow nature."

"She?" Vince asked. He hadn't been able to identify the gender. The clothes had been nondescript, and the corpse too far gone to figure out.

"The trees told me. She was an Elf. She lay down and died right here."

"Ah. Probably killed herself. Go far enough away from the owner of the collar and it'll start strangling you. Depends on the allowed range. Take too long to turn around and you'll end up dying. Thanks for the assist, by the way, it was blessedly quick," Vince said, grinning at the tiny Dryad.

Her eyes were pinned to his own. She blinked twice, her small hands pressed to her stomach. She finally gave a small nod of her head. "Of course. The trees speak of you. That you wander often. Even as a young boy."

Vince tilted his head. He'd heard tales of Dryads from his parents and that they were far different than the physical world. That they had powers over nature and woodlands.

"You protect the woods. You drive away those who would harvest the trees for lumber and keep everything healthy. The animals do not fear you. They view you as a natural predator. That you come and collect the weak or sick."

The Dryad's voice had taken on a strange quality during her speech. Vince simply waited for her to finish, wondering if she was communing with them.

"I try. This wood is in my care, as per my father's wish. Though I do think it could easily foster a village or a town here. Would do well, too. I limit the population, but it's still a very large population. I'm constantly trying to cut down the numbers with the speed at which they reproduce. They're Wastes beasts. They eat anything. Leaves, pine needles, bark, poisonous plants."

Vince sighed and rubbed two fingers to a temple. "Alright. We should probably head north. This is all hilly, rocky mountain country and it's slow going."

Setting off in the direction he wanted, Vince let his mind start to wander.

"What are you looking for in the north?" Meliae asked him.

Vince stopped dead in his tracks at her question and looked over his shoulder at her.

"Same thing as here. Corpses. Sickness. Anything that would cause a problem for the health of the area. Why?" he asked after a moment.

Meliae closed her eyes and held still. Vince turned around and watched her, waiting. Several minutes passed in silence.

Then her green eyes slid open. "There is a problem with a water source west of here. Nothing is wrong in the north. East and south are equally without problems."

"Handy. Remind me to take you with me on my forest walks," Vince said, giving her a smile.

"Mm. I will."

"West, you said? There's a creek west of here. Blocked?"

"I'm not sure what the problem is. Just that there is one. That's what the trees told me."

"Off we go, then."

Vince dropped his pack down in the small clearing. The problem Meliae had directed them to had ended up being minor and yet horribly annoying at the same time. The creek had indeed been blocked, by a minor rockslide from the surrounding area. It'd clear eventually, though it'd create problems for everything downstream until then.

He'd chosen a spot that managed to provide shelter as well as a windbreak for them, the trees having grown up close to one another and a small dip in the land providing the protection.

Meliae sat down on a rock nearby. Her fingers picked at her clothes as if they bothered her.

"Something wrong with the fabric? We can try washing it to see if it was something we picked up on the way," Vince offered. Kneeling down, he struck a flint stick to the side of his hunting knife.

With a handful of strikes, he caught a spark and then blew gently into the kindling as it started to smoke.

"I'll adjust in time. Dryads don't wear much, and when we do wear clothes, it's skins or furs. Nudity doesn't embarrass us."

"Oh?" Vince immediately thought of when she was on the auction block. Standing there nude for the whole world to see. Taking a deep breath, he blew into the smoking bundle of moss, bark shavings, and small twigs.

It leapt into flame and he slid it under his pile of small sticks and branches. Leaning in, he blew on the whole thing, feeding more dried moss in on top of it.

"Being looked at like a piece of meat to be devoured is entirely different than being nude." Apparently her own mind had gone straight back to the auction as well.

Setting larger branches atop the now burning smaller ones, Vince built up the fire. "Understandable."

"When you're done with that, I'm ready," Meliae muttered.

"What, for sleep? Hit the sack, then. There's little out here that would bother us, so there's no need for a watch."

Vince opened his pack and pulled out a piece of dried jerky. He couldn't remember what kind of meat it was, but at this point he didn't really care.

Meliae said nothing to that. Vince looked up to find her hunched over the pack between her knees. Her eyes were watching him. Curious and with a hint of concern.

"What do you know about the Fes's culture?" Meliae asked him.

"The Fes?" Vince asked around a mouthful of jerky.

"I suppose that answers that," Meliae said with a sigh. "Fes isn't her name. Her name is Berenga."

Vince felt his face turn into a frown. There'd been a number of times when Fes — or Berenga, he supposed — had spoken quietly with Meliae.

"Fes is a title. Before we get into that, what do you know of Orc culture?"

"Nothing. Except they're warlike and tribal." He had no problem admitting ignorance.

Meliae tilted her head to one side and then nodded. "Unflattering, but accurate. Orc culture is tribal at its lowest level. Nomadic, almost. As it moves upwards, it gets larger until it's clan sized. The clans can be very large. These clans are measured and evaluated on the strength of their leaders. Their leaders are always men."

Vince nodded, taking another large bite of his unappealing dinner.

Unsurprising. Backwards society.

Vince was of the opinion that man or woman could easily be... well, whatever. There really weren't limitations on the sex in this world. You weren't going to complain if a woman merchant smashed you into the ground because you were too stupid to get your prices correct. Or if a woman leader outdid you on the political scene.

Though the numbers between men and women were starting to rebalance, the vast majority of his own leadership was women.

Strong survive, weak die. Regardless of sex.

Meliae opened her pack and pulled out a small pouch. Closing the flap, she set the pouch on her knees. "Most of this I know from my mother, who dealt with the Orc clans often. She made deals with both humans and Orcs. Dryads are keepers of nature and fertility. She taught me many things. I've learned some of their culture from Fes herself. Men are measured in a number of ways."

Taking a nut from the pouch, she placed it in her mouth.

"The first is obvious. Their strength and combat prowess," she continued, crunching up the small morsel. "Another is the number of wives he has, and their comparable strength. Orc men want strong wives. Though not as strong as them."

"Figures." Vince wrinkled his nose. Meliae popped a handful of seeds and nuts in her mouth as he continued. "Fes is stronger than I am; doesn't bother me in the least. If anything, I feel more assured by it."

"She would argue that you are stronger. Back to the discussion at hand, though. For her, this is actually a big problem. She's stronger, smarter, and faster than those in her tribe. She defeated all the prime marriage candidates handily. She would have needed to go to a clan-meet to seek out a future. Even there, it's unlikely she would have found someone who could match her that wouldn't be much older than her.

"I imagine she would have beaten everyone suitable easily. Which would have only left older males with a great deal more experience. The problem there is their wives would be intimidated by a younger, stronger wife. Fes would have been disparaged by the older generation, and unable to find a place in the younger.

"Then you came along. She says you defeated her in single combat, spared her, and then gave her what she had challenged you for anyways. Taking and asking nothing of her." Meliae stuck a finger in her mouth and dislodged something from between her teeth.

Vince shrugged at that. "And? She was hungry."

"Yes. Then she intervened when you attempted to protect two non-combatants from a group of six... gator men, you called them?"

"Big lizard men. Look like alligators."

"Yes, those. You killed half before the other half overwhelmed you?"

"Something like that."

"Then after rescuing you, you called her Fes."

"Mm. She asked a question, if I remember correct. Fes was the only word I could make out. I thought it was her name."

"I see. If I had to guess, she was asking you if you wanted her to be your First Wife."

"I... I don't —" Vince stopped, his face screwing up in a grimace.

"You don't speak her language, I know. She realized that much later herself. Fes means First Wife. Apparently you labeled her that, and then indicated for her to mount you."

"What? No! I... this is all a little too much to believe. She told you this?"

"Yes. She did. She also said how happy you make her. You treat her as an equal and dote on her. That was not her expectation going into a relationship with a human male."

Vince scratched at his cheek and turned his eyes away from the Dryad. Vince was feeling embarrassed and a little off balance.

"My parents acted that way. I've seen others act similarly. Seems only natural to act that way to your..." Vince trailed off. He wasn't quite sure what to call her. Apparently she viewed herself as his First Wife, as it were.

"Call her Fes. It makes her happy. Using her name would only confuse her." Meliae's hand was there suddenly, pressing into his chest. Vince looked up in surprise as she pushed him down to the ground.

In the time he'd looked from her, she'd managed to remove her pants. Small hands began pulling at his belt.

"Meliae, w-what are you doing?" Vince asked, his hands moving to fend off her own.

"Stop," said the Dryad in a firm voice. "Fes and I already spoke about this and I'll be second. Meliae is fine, I need no title." Somehow, she managed to avoid his defending hands and slipped his belt free of the loops.

Root tendrils snuck out from the ground beneath him and caught the loops of his pants. With a single jerk, Vince was pantless and exposed from the waist down. As quickly as it happened, the roots vanished.

He felt once again betrayed by the fact that his body was responding to the fact that a woman was taking advantage of him

"Whoa there, Meliae, I think you've got the wrong—"

Meliae interrupted him by taking his semi-erect self into her mouth. The wet warmth of her caught him off guard and he froze.

Surrendering immediately to her soft lips and writhing tongue, Vince relaxed into the ground.

Meliae worked her head back and forth slowly, her lips and tongue doing all of the work. Her right hand reached under and lightly cupped him in one hand as her left slid up under his armor.

The Dryad released him and then threw a leg over his hips. He felt more than saw her diminutive hand grab his slick, erect length and angle it upwards.

"Mother always said that'd work. I didn't believe her," Meliae whispered, her green eyes watching him. They were full of fear and longing in equal measure.

Her fingers were tiny and soft, supple. Her skin smooth and pale, exactly as he remembered. Exactly as he had dreamed of. Restraint was only possible during the waking hours since his subconscious had dwelled on her naked form repeatedly.

Then she managed to fit the tip of him into her narrow opening. Placing her hands on his shoulders, she looked into his face.

Then, not sparing herself the luxury of going slowly, as if waiting might cause her to lose her nerve, she slammed herself down on him.

Her saliva let him slide into her tight crevice easily, tearing past the resistance her body held at his invader.

Her hips and bottom were warm against his thighs and lap, the soft skin pressing to him as she grinded hard into him.

Meliae's breath caught and she closed her eyes tight in pain. In that single thrust, she'd committed herself. Now she held perfectly still from the waist down.

Turning her head to one side, it was obvious to him she'd cracked her virginity on him in that push.

Not trusting his voice, Vince pressed his hands to her hips and held her there. Slowly, his fingers let her go after a few seconds and began to gently run up and down her hips and lower back.

He wasn't going to fight her off, but neither was he going to let her make her first time a painful experience.

She'd taken the choice from him, but in reality, it was a choice he'd have made anyways.

Eventually, the Dryad let out a shuddering breath. Her head slowly turned back to him. She slit her eyes and peeked up at him through her lashes.

Vince gave her an encouraging smile, his fingers ghosting along her lower back and spine.

Shivering at his touch, Meliae let go of his shoulders to grab the hem of her tunic and under shirt. In one smooth motion, she pulled it off and tossed it to one side.

Taking the opportunity for what it was, Vince reached up and grabbed her sides. In one smooth motion, he rolled her onto her back and positioned himself atop her.

"Ah! Vince, ah, wait—" Meliae started, her legs being spread apart by his movement. Her knees trembled as they were pushed outward.

"Okay, you let me know when to continue," he said softly. He slid his hands down to rest on each side of her, his forearms pressed to her wide hips.

"I... alright. Thank you," Meliae looked everywhere but him for a few seconds. Eventually, with nowhere else to go, her eyes returned to his. "I think I'm ready. Just... slowly, please. I'm not Fes."

"No, you're not. You're Meliae. A very different woman entirely," Vince said with a grin. Leaning down, he kissed her tenderly as he pulled his hips back and then pushed forward.

Her small body shuddered as he reentered her. Her knees pressed into his sides while her hands clutched at his lower back.

Vince kept his pace steady, and slow. He plied her warm skin with soft kisses and gentle nuzzles, traveling back and forth along her neck and shoulders. Coupled with a few grazing bites and light touches of his fingers, he could feel her embarrassment fading.

The Dryad's knees sunk down to each side, opening herself up to him completely without a hint of resistance. Her arms circled around his neck and pulled him down to her, kissing him fiercely.

Her hips started to move as she figured out his rhythm. Rising and falling as he moved. She devoured his face, kissing him repeatedly, never stopping. Practically taking his breath away with her demand to keep her lips to his.

Taking the subtle unspoken encouragement, Vince continued, building up more speed and force as he went.

When Meliae started panting, she finally let him free of her hungry mouth. She rested her head on the grass, her body bucking with each thrust of his hips. Her green eyes were partially unfocused as she gazed up at him.

A small smile lit her face even as her whole body tightened up around him, her skin flushing as she experienced her first orgasm. Her pupils contracted until they were little more than pinpricks, and the green of her eyes looked almost like they were glowing.

Unable to resist the look of her face or the sensation of her channel pulling at him, urging him, Vince hit his own climax.

Pushing up firmly against her, he unloaded his seed. Digging deep into her, he felt his shaft swell. His forearms locked to her hips and kept her still. He held her there against the grass as he ground his hips into her thighs.

Two more solid pumps and Vince felt his peak end. Lowering his head, he rested it on her bare shoulder.

Meliae lifted a hand and ran her fingers through his hair, her fingernails tickling the back of his head.

Vince felt her full, moist lips press into his ear, her tongue snaking out to flick at his earlobe.

"That was wonderful. Again?" whispered the Dryad huskily.

Isn't another name for a Dryad a Nymph?

Chapter 7

Vince's brain drew a blank. Slowing his approach to the house, Vince watched as Fes lifted a giant block of stone and set it in front of another.

They'd only been gone three days, in the end. Admittedly, it was closer to four days, since evening was settling over them, but it hadn't been long.

In that time, Fes had started building a heavy stone wall forty feet out from the house. She'd managed to complete several circuits all the way around, the height of it coming up to her thighs.

The green muscular, shirtless Orc dragged a forearm across her brow before shifting the stone around a touch.

Vince couldn't help but appreciate the view of the lovely half-naked woman. Despite being sweaty and dirty, she still had that natural feral charm to her.

Strange tastes there, Vinny.

He wasn't sure what to label his feelings for Fes as. He definitely cared for her. Enjoyed her company at night immensely. Did he love her, though?

What exactly is love? Is it a deeper form of care?

Suddenly, Vince wished his parents were around. His interactions with women up to this point had been casual sex. Only a few minor relationships. Right up until Fes.

Setting the whole thing aside for now, he corrected his course to head straight for Fes.

"Hey there, beautiful. Now, I admit I don't mind the view, but maybe I'd be jealous if anyone else saw you?" Vince asked in a teasing voice.

Fes's head whipped around at his voice. Her face nearly split in two at the smile she gifted him with, her small tusks slipping free of her lips. She had no embarrassment at his comments or his wandering gaze.

Her black eyes shifted from him to the Dryad at his side.

"Done?" the Orc asked.

"Done. All is taken care of," Meliae answered. She strode up to the warrior nonchalantly, a smile curling her lips.

"Good." Fes leaned down and hugged Meliae warmly. Meliae hugged her in return and then kissed Fes's cheek, before walking off towards the front of the house.

Vince shook his head, figuring it for some strange custom he'd have to figure out later. Stepping up to Fes, he tilted his head to the side, indicating the wall.

"A wall, huh?" Vince asked, looking from the interlocking rocks. He hadn't noticed it at first, but it looked like Fes had shaped them and even put a paste between the rocks.

"Good defense. Will protect our home. Always expect an attack and plan. Vince... is okay with a wall?" asked the warrior. Her black eyes watched him.

"Sure. You're not wrong. My father would agree with you completely. It's a good idea, Berenga," Vince said, stepping in close to her.

The use of her name froze her in place, her lips coming together and her spine stiffening.

Vince gently placed his left hand on her strong jaw and kissed her. "Relax, Fes. Fes Berenga. All is well. In the future, I'd like to be consulted on taking more wives, though? I always considered myself a one-woman kind of man, but apparently I now have two."

Fes's cheeks colored a dark green and she nodded her head a fraction.

"Good." Vince pressed a kiss to her lips. Running a thumb along the line of her cheekbone, he pressed his forehead to hers. "Woods are fine. Meliae was a big help. You were right on picking her up. Thank you, Berenga, my Fes."

Fes only managed the barest of head nods, her black eyes wide.

"Come on. Let's clean you up and have dinner together. I'll scrub you down if you promise to behave."

Fes only nodded again, seemingly unable to speak.

"Meliae, we're heading to the creek to clean up. Want to come?"

"No. I'll start in on the evening meal," called back the Dryad from the open door. "Take your time."

"Well. If the Nymph says take our time, maybe we don't have to behave after all."

A week later, and Vince found himself on the outside of his house looking at the trail west again.

"For as little time as I get to spend here, I sure do miss it," he muttered, looking at the building over his shoulder.

"It's because it's home," Meliae said, adjusting the fake slave collar around her throat. "We'll return shortly, as you said. We really do need to sell off this... stuff you've been collecting. You yourself said this is mostly the castoffs that wouldn't be worth holding on to."

Vince could only nod his head, looking towards the path ahead of them.

"Yeah, I know. It'll also give us a chance to put in a request for a glass merchant. Summer is right around the corner. Still."

"I understand, Vince," Fes said, placing a strong hand on his shoulder. "Home for us, too. Come, we go." Fes put her hand back to the handle of the two-wheeled cart they'd constructed behind her and set off ahead of them.

Inside of the cart was a jumble of armor, weapons, and odds and ends that Vince had been simply collecting with no plan.

Meliae had taken one look at it all and then cataloged everything that needed to be gotten rid of.

Off to sell my junk. Being a bachelor was a lot easier.

Putting one foot in front of the other, Vince took up a pace behind the cart. Meliae slid in next to him, her green eyes peering at him as if to decipher his odd mood.

It was slow going with the cart. The trails and mountain paths weren't meant for it. Nights had gotten interesting, though. Fes and Meliae had worked out some type of agreement or plan. He couldn't quite figure out a pattern to who ended up in his bed with him, but he quickly realized he didn't care.

With Fes, it was the same as always, a wrestling match followed by one of them surrendering to the other.

For Meliae, it was very different. The Dryad rarely wanted anything different than him mounting her. That and always initiating the whole thing with her mouth.

Fes had looked confused the first time she saw Meliae perform in that way. Each time after that, she'd watched intensely when Meliae started them off.

For Vince, it was a test of his mental fortitude. He hadn't thought of himself of shy, but this was something entirely different.

By the time they reached Knight's Ferry, he was honestly looking forward to a break, if only to give his battered mental strength a breather.

After arriving, Vince had noticed they were getting far more scrutiny than he remembered last time. Or any time previously. He wasn't sure if it was the fact that he had two non-humans with him this time or if it was him.

He hadn't seen the men he'd noticed the last two times, but Vince had a thought that they were involved or directly responsible with the atmospheric change. One or the other.

As they walked along the road towards Deskil's place, he noticed that he wasn't alone in the increased scrutiny. Anyone with a non-human was being given a second or third look.

Either slavery is on the way out… which seems unlikely, given the profit involved. Or non-human sentiment is falling further.

An older man glared at Fes and then Meliae in turn, ignoring Vince entirely.

That answers that.

Vince couldn't remember clearly the last time it had gotten like this. Only that his parents hadn't traveled to Knight's Ferry for a year after something similar had started.

Apparently this was a normal ebb and flow type of situation. Something would happen, they'd blame non-humans, take "revenge," then feel satisfied for a while.

"This'll be our last trip for a bit. Or at least the three of us together. Make sure you pick up anything you think you might need," Vince muttered barely loud enough for his companions to hear.

Fes grunted from up ahead. Vince noticed Meliae nod her head out of the corner of his eye.

Stopping outside of Deskil's shop, Vince stepped up to Fes and laid a hand on her forearm. "Get the cart up near the door, Fes. If someone challenges you, call out. I'll see if we can get Deskil out here quick like," Vince said. Letting go of Fes, he motioned to Meliae and stepped up to the door.

Without a sound, the door glided inward and Vince stepped in. A soft thumping from the backroom told him where Deskil was. And Minnie.

"Oh," murmured the Dryad.

"Yeah. They're like teenagers. Bored and little else to do." Vince walked up to the counter. Sitting there was a corroded service bell. Setting his hand down next to it, he put his finger on it and pressed it down twice. Two dings rang out clearly, despite the metal looking rather uncared for.

He didn't like interrupting them, but he liked leaving Fes alone out front even less.

A bed creaked audibly, followed by the flop of bare feet. The back door jerked open that Minnie had appeared out of last time. This time, Deskil appeared, fastening his pants.

"Oi! Vinny. Didn't you hear me working back there?" Deskil complained, catching sight of Vince at the counter. His eyes flicked from him to the Dryad and then back. "Heard you'd bought yourself another one."

"I did hear you back there, but I have Fes out front with things to sell you and the locals seem… different. And… yeah, Fes and I bought Meliae."

Deskil ran his hands down the sides of his pants as he thumped his way over to Vince.

"Hmph. As to the locals… some… thugs went missing. Happy to see them go, but people are claiming they were jumped by a raiding party."

"Huh. Was it a pretty woman with a bunch of men? Dark leather armor?" Vince asked, a pit forming in his stomach.

Deskil reached Vince and looked up at him. "I take it you met them, then?"

"Yeah, tried to rob me. Killed them all. Stripped them and dumped their bodies into the bushes."

"You're not trying to sell me their equipment, are you?" Deskil asked warily.

"No, no. We kept it for now. We didn't want to raise suspicion if we didn't have to. Come, we'll —" Vince paused, staring at Deskil again.

"What is it, Vinny? Never seen a Dwarf wanting to go finish off his woman?"

"You know I'm a friend, right, Deskil?" Vince asked, wanting to prep the Dwarf first.

"I don't approve of your recent purchases, but you're a friend, sure."

Vince gave the Dwarf a tight smile and then tapped his own throat.

Deskil blanched, his skin turning a pale paper white. One hand came up to touch his bare neck. A neck that should have been wearing a collar.

Vince and Deskil stared at one another. Vince wasn't quite sure what to say or do. A slave without a collar was to be immediately "put down" without question.

"Uhm, Meliae?" Vince asked, turning his head to the Dryad a few steps behind him. She had been looking at something and hadn't really been paying attention to the men's exchange.

"Yes?"

"Could you… could you pull off your collar real quick?"

Meliae's head came around and she eyed him questioningly. She knew what a collarless non-humanoid meant. Then she noticed Deskil, and his hand pressed to his neck.

"Oh." Meliae lifted a hand and unfastened the collar with a click. "Is that suitable, husband?"

"Mm. Thank you, Meliae." Vince didn't feel like fighting her on the term she used right now. She'd used it the entire way here whenever she wanted to prod at him.

She'd already gotten too much of a response out of him on the trip here to want to give it up easily. She seemed to enjoy taunting and teasing him.

The Dryad replaced the collar with a smile and turned back to the wooden staff she'd been looking at.

Deskil let out a breath and then gave Vince a lopsided smile.

"I should have known. No Orc woman would willingly allow herself to be called Fes."

As Deskil finished talking, Minnie opened the door and took three fast steps out of the room before realizing Vince was there. In her left hand, half hidden behind her hip, was Deskil's collar.

"Hey, Minnie. You should probably give that to him before someone else walks in. Then again, Fes is on the front porch. She might be scaring away business," Vince said, offering Minnie a smile and a wave.

Frozen halfway between the back room and Deskil, she seemed at a loss.

Sighing, Meliae cleared her throat and then pulled off her collar when Minnie looked to her. Putting it back in place, the Dryad picked up the staff and started moving it around.

"I... we... well, shit," Minnie finished lamely.

"Anyways. So, I have a cart full of crap I want to sell you. I figure a few might be good for a resale and the rest for the materials," Vince explained, walking to the front door. "Got it in a cart out front. I'll meet you out there. If you see something you like, Meliae, grab it. You could do with some armor anyways. Leather would suit you."

Vince opened the front door and exited, closing it behind himself.

Fes looked up from the cart and gave him a broad smile. "Vince."

"Fes Berenga. Deskil will be right out. I figure after this, we hit the Ranger board. See if there's any work worth doing. Being a courier is easy and I do it at a run. Would need to drop Meliae off at home, though, on our way. I doubt she'd be able to keep up the entire way." Vince leaned up against the wall next to Fes.

Fes moved in close to him and took the patch of wall directly beside him. Her right hand slid up behind his thigh to grab his ass.

She'd gotten more forward after watching him with Meliae at night. The dynamics were changing.

"Don't want to stay here tonight. They look at me angrily. Camp in the field?" she accentuated her request with a firm squeeze.

"I, ah... yeah. That's a good idea. We'll take care of this, hit the board, and then get outta here. Sound like a plan?"

"Yes."

Vince felt a smirk slip over his features. Fes's hand didn't leave his ass, and she didn't offer up any more information, either.

Vince sighed and pulled down the only tag that was worth his time. A monster hunt. Up north in the Kingdom of Portland. It'd take them a while to get up there, but the price was significant. Two hundred standards.

He honestly didn't need the money, but what else was he supposed to do with his life? His father had been a Ranger. His mother as close to a Ranger as you could be without taking the tests.

What purpose do I have otherwise? Something has to stand between humanity and the Wastes. Humans are ugly, hideous things, and yet beautiful and caring at the same time.

With another sigh, he shook his head. Philosophy wasn't for him. He was a blade. Plain and simple.

"Monster hunt. Pretty far up north. Something's killing livestock one at a time spread out over a lot of farms. Little of the carcass is left afterwards. All the earmarks of a Wastelander who isn't confident enough to hunt humans and not skilled enough to hunt wild animals," Vince said, looking up at the two women in front of him.

Fes grinned, her left hand closing on the hilt of her sword. She'd never turn down a fight.

Meliae held up a finger on her left hand, her right hand casually holding her new iron shod staff. "Is the pay worth our time?"

"Two hundred standards. Pretty significant. Probably one of the largest I've ever seen. Which means someone is losing a lot of livestock up there."

"Did they happen to list anything else?" Meliae asked.

"No, it's... pretty bare on details. Then again, for it to show up all the way down here means every Ranger north of here has already turned it down. It's why the price is so high."

Vince let out a slow breath. "Let's do this one. We'll buy several horses with what we made selling to Deskil. A pack horse as well. I don't really want to head north on foot."

"Don't like horses," Fes complained, her smile dimming but not vanishing.

"Sorry. But it'll cut the travel time to a third, practically. Maybe even more. Let's do this job and that'll be it for a while.

"Do it, get our money, then we'll lay low till summer. We make a small stop here to do some banking. I'd feel better if we pulled out the majority of what I keep in the bank. Knight's Ferry is getting... uncomfortable, and I'm not sure when we'll be back. The bank here in Knight's Ferry is backed up by the Modesto bank, which is backed up by the Fresno bank, so we can go elsewhere, but... this would be our last stop before we headed home."

Fes said nothing further. Vince assumed she was still brooding about the horse but equally excited about doing a job.

Such a straightforward woman.

Meliae frowned, tapping the tip of her staff to her bottom lip. "At that point, is there somewhere else we can go to pick up your Ranger jobs and bank? Or shop? Why bother coming back here at all?"

Vince looked down in thought, his free hand coming up to rest behind his head.

"Blanchard, I guess. It's actually closer, but there's a lot more... a lot more slave trade going through there. It's on a bit of an intersection of rivers. Though they'd be less tolerant to someone damaging their merchandise, so maybe that's best. Good thought, Meliae."

Vince had another reason for not really wanting to go there. An ex who had never forgiven him for calling it off. It had been his only real foray into a relationship outside of sex.

In the end, he hadn't much cared for her personality.

"Let's get moving. I'd rather not be in Knight's Ferry when night falls."

"So eager to take a young Dryad out into the wild, husband? Beastly," Meliae said, her lips turning into a bright smile.

Vince closed his eyes and pressed a hand to his face.

Chapter 8

Fes dismounted and flipped the reins to a young boy. Vince hopped down easily from his saddle while Meliae gingerly got out of hers.

She wasn't the best rider, but definitely had improved after being forced into it every day.

"Two standards for all four for a day," quoted the boy.

"I'll give you two for the stabling, one more for you if you brush 'em," Vince countered. Leaning back, he stretched his muscles and felt a solid pop as things slid back into place.

"Done, sir! Uhm —"

"Here, up front." Vince pulled out several coins from the inside of a vest pocket and dropped them into the boy's cupped hands. "We'll be staying in the inn," Vince said, gesturing to the building attached to the stable.

"Great! I'll have everything ready for you in the morning, Mister...?"

"Vince."

Not saying another word, Vince pulled his saddlebag off the horse and flung it over his shoulder. Walking over to Meliae's horse, he grabbed hers as well.

"Thank you," murmured the Dryad, her hands pressing into the sides of her hips.

"Mm," Vince replied. Turning around, he made his way over to the inn. He heard Meliae's soft footfalls trail behind him, immediately followed by the loud clumps of Fes's boots.

Pushing open the door with his free hand, Vince stepped inside. It was a simple place, laid out cleanly and carefully. To his eye, it had the appearance of a place that catered to merchants rather than travelers.

That was fine with him. He didn't get saddle sore often, but having made such a long trek, he was willing to take a rest, even at a merchant cost.

A month and some odd on horseback to get here. When we get back, it'll only be a month or so before the summer market.

Shaking himself out of his thoughts, Vince stepped up to the counter and rang the service bell that was set out.

"Coming!" called a deep, gravelly voice from the back.

A handful of seconds later and an older Orc stepped out from a doorway and nodded his head at them.

"You and your... two companions, then?" asked the Orc, a finger surreptitiously touching the band around his neck.

The collars up here were simple things. Small. Barely more than a necklace.

Non-humanoid treatment differed the further north you went.

Vince nodded his head. He'd only been up this way once before and had admired the people and their customs. It wasn't home, though.

Even if home was a slave-fueled nightmare for many.

"Two rooms will be —"

"One room," Vince interrupted.

The Orc gave no reaction to that and continued on, "One room with one bed will—"

"Two beds, please," Vince interrupted once more.

The barest flicker of surprise registered on the Orc's face before he nodded his head.

"The room will be three standards; the extra cost is because it has a tub with heated plumbing. Will you be dining with us tonight?"

Vince nodded his head, his hand going into his vest to start pulling out coins.

"The rate for one normal meal is half a standard and for non-human meals is one fourth."

Vince dropped six standards into the Orc's outstretched hand. He'd rather pay more than the requested amount and earn it back in extras.

He knew without asking that Fes was tired of dry meat and Meliae was as fed up with dried fruit.

"Could you include fresh meat for one and fresh fruits or berries for the other? Between the three of us our diet is… spread out," Vince said with a grin.

Fes and Meliae both hummed their agreement and appreciation.

The Orc bowed his head once in acknowledgment, his face hidden in the movement. A snap of his fingers and a short whistle later and a young boy came out. "Jack here will lead you to your rooms. My name is Jerod. Please ask if you need anything."

"I'm sure I'll have questions later. I'm a Ranger on contract to a farm west of here in…" Vince paused, thinking about the name.

"Bellevue Farm," Meliae supplied from his side.

"Ah, yeah. Thanks," Vince said, smiling at the Dryad.

Jerod looked from the Dryad back to Vince and then nodded his head. "I heard the contract was moving south when none of the local Rangers could fulfill it."

"We'll fill it," Fes said firmly, a hand drifting to hilt at her waist.

Jerod only gave her a small smile in response to that.

"That we will, Fes. Lead on, Jack. We've been on the trail for… ever, it feels like."

With a small gesture, Vince indicated for Jack to continue.

Meliae made a chirping noise and skipped ahead a step. "A hot bath. I can get the dust out of my hair."

"Says the woman who regularly weaves twigs, leaves, and flowers into braids," Fes murmured, walking beside the Dryad.

"They smell nice," Meliae argued.

"The bees agreed," Fes said with a chuckle.

"Ugh. The bees were a problem."

Vince shook his head and fell in behind the two chatting women, adjusting the bags on his shoulder.

Jack led them quickly towards a room on the first floor near the back of the building. Opening the door, he handed Meliae a key and vanished before anyone could even think to tip him.

"Strange," muttered Vince. He watched the boy dart away even as his two companions entered the room.

Walking inside, Vince closed the door behind him and dropped the packs to one side.

A day of rest, a nice bed. Then off to work.

Fes and Meliae were all about the tub in the bathroom. Realizing he wouldn't be getting a shot at it any time soon, he opened the door again.

"Going to go see what I can find out about the farm. I'll be back. Take a bath, both of you. We'll head down to dinner together later," he called into the room.

Neither woman acknowledged him. Instead, they had discovered how to turn on the tub and were already determining who would go first.

Snickering, he slid the lock into position on the handle so the door would lock itself after he left.

Moving into the hallway, he closed the door behind him and headed back to talk to Jerod.

Catching the Orc as a new customer was whisked off by Jack, Vince gave the man a smile.

"Mind if I get that info from you now rather than later? I'm afraid I have no chance at that bath till they tell me so," Vince explained.

Jerod lifted one side of his mouth in a smirk.

"Uh-huh. What do you want to know? You said you were on the Bellevue Farm job?"

"Yep. Hired out of Modesto."

Jerod whistled at that. "South and then some."

Vince shrugged, leaning over the countertop. Pulling out a standard, he slid it across the wood towards Jerod. "Pay is pay. What can you tell me?"

"Same as most around here. Something killing the livestock. They send a few Rangers after it. Things die down. Go away. Nothing is ever actually found. Then it starts up all over again a few days later. Rangers had to refund the coin and no one was happy. Created some problems with the guild and their reputation."

Jerod slid the coin off the counter and dropped it into a pocket.

"I can imagine," Vince said with a shake of his head. The Rangers took their reputation very seriously. "Could you tell me more about the missing livestock and the attacks?"

Jerod mulled that over before nodding his head.

Standards don't go as far as they used to, lamented Vince.

"Every night, livestock would simply vanish. No trace of who took them, not a boot print, nothing. A little blood, sometimes a bone, nothing else. Not small livestock, either. Often enough it'd be a cow or a bull."

Something wrong there. No Waster would kill and eat an entire animal on the property without leaving a print. Leaving a bone and blood seems… strange as well.

"Any chance they kept those bones?" Vince asked, not believing for even a second they had hung on to it.

"No. Didn't keep the corpses when they started showing up, either."

"Corpses?" Vince prompted.

"About two weeks ago, they started taking two a night. Different locations. One would be eaten whole, tail to nose. The second always had leftovers. Not enough meat with one and too much with two, I guess."

The Orc shrugged his shoulders. It was supposition, but it helped Vince.

"Can you describe the corpses?"

"Eaten," described the Orc helpfully.

"Okay, then. Anything else of interest?"

"Well, they almost caught it up on the Sauter place. North of Bellevue. They got there in time to drive the creature off."

Interesting.

"They saved the lamb. It died ten minutes after that, though. No one wanted to touch it. They burned the corpse and then covered it with dirt."

Ugh, superstitious idiots. Any evidence at all would be helpful.

Vince forced a smile on his face. "And that was two weeks ago?"

"About."

Vince pulled out a scrap of paper from an interior pocket in his vest. Setting down another standard next to the pencil on the desk, Vince gave Jerod another smile. Picking up the pencil, he tapped the coin with it. "Mind listing off all the locations and dates of the attacks?"

Thirty minutes later and Vince was walking back to their room with a list. It'd taken some time to get the full accounting from the Orc, as he had had to help customers as they came in.

Grasping the knob, Vince stopped. With a smile at his own paranoia, he raised a hand and knocked gently on the door.

"It's Vince," he said aloud at the door after a few seconds.

Almost immediately after that, the door swung open and he was greeted by a wet-haired Dryad with a towel wrapped around her torso.

She gave him a smile and stepped aside to let him in.

Vince entered and looked around for a moment. The far bed had a lump in it that looked suspiciously like an Orc. Unmoving and likely sleeping.

Letting his eyes move back to Meliae, he watched as she slithered into the other bed. She pulled the covers up to her nose and then pointed at the bathroom.

"I'd invite you to share the bed… but you smell like horse and far too many miles under the sun. Go clean up, then come back and… dirty me," said the Dryad. Her eyes watched him over the sheets, a mischievous light glowing in them.

"Nymph."

Meliae made a musical sound and widened her eyes. It gave her an almost innocent look—if he didn't know better, that is.

She wasn't as combative as Fes, but she was more forward in their private moments. Especially when it came to the bedroom.

Chuckling, Vince stripped himself down to his birthday suit. Entering the bathroom, he felt a moment of confusion as he closed the door behind him.

Light came in through the slatted blinds to reveal that the bathroom was still in use. The tub, specifically.

It held a bathing green-skinned Orc. A lovely specimen of muscled athleticism. A towel was propped up under her neck and head. Next to the big tub on a stool was an empty cup, one hand resting nearby as if she'd finished it only recently.

The water had a faint pink color to it and Vince had to wonder if they'd scented and oiled it.

"The tea helped. The cramping stopped pretty fast. Hot water helps, oil smells great. Thank you," Fes murmured.

Oh. Her time for moonsickness.

A couple things clicked into place for him.

Fes had gone straight to bed the last few nights, leaving him alone with Meliae. He hadn't complained about the change. He had thought that perhaps they were merely shaking up the pattern to keep things lively.

Now it made sense. She hadn't felt clean, or in the mood. Sending her second out to take care of him in her place.

"While I'm glad to hear you're not in pain..." Vince said softly. Fes's shoulders tightened up at the sound of his voice. Her hands griped tightly to the sides of the tub. "I'm not Meliae. Forgive me, she sent me in here to bathe. Said I smelled like the wrong end of a horse."

Dark black eyes popped open and focused in on him. They then immediately fastened to his manhood before moving upwards to his face.

She always had a predatory look. He couldn't deny the fact that her bold and brazen looks always sped his heartrate up a bit.

"You do smell like the wrong end of a horse. Clean up. When you're done, you can have the tub." Closing her eyes and settling back into the towel, she pointed with her free hand to the corner. "Use the scrub brush and bucket. Soap smells like Meliae."

Vince interpreted that comment to mean that the soap was herbal in nature.

Smiling to himself, and pausing to get another eyeful of the bathing Orc, Vince went to the corner to begin scrubbing off their trip.

Fes and Meliae coming with him on this journey was a mile of a difference between his lonesome journeys. The fact that he wasn't alone, on its own merit, was an already amazing change. There was no possible way to put a value on someone watching your back, sharing watches with you. Splitting camp duties.

Then there were the nightly romps.

Grinning at the thought of it, he realized there was something he could do for his ailing Fes.

Taking himself to the task at hand, Vince scrubbed at his skin until it turned red. Then lathered himself to excess. Washing himself twice after refilling the bucket.

Soap came with the room. Paid for it. Use it all up. My soap.

Water splashed out of the bucket as he tossed the filthy wash rag into it. Standing up, he stretched his arms back over his head and then settled back down.

Fes opened her eyes as he turned around. A small furrow creased her brow for a moment and flashed away. She gripped the sides of the tub to brace herself to stand up.

"No, no. Stay seated, Fes," Vince said with a smile, holding out a palm to her.

Fes looked mildly annoyed but settled back into the tub.

"What are you doing?" asked the warrior.

Vince gave no response and instead moved towards the tub. Putting his hand in the water, he found that it was still quite warm. There was no need for him to change the water for her.

Sidling up beside her, he took the empty cup. Setting it to one side, he took the now empty stool and set it behind her. Taking a seat, he laid his hands on her shoulders and then began to work his thumbs and fingertips into her muscles.

"Mmmmpfffhhh." Fes relaxed immediately, her head resting back on the towel. Her dark hair hung limply over the edge of the tub.

Vince worked slowly and methodically over her shoulders and neck, rubbing and pressing at the iron stiff muscles and soft slippery skin.

Expanding the area he was working on, he reached up under her hair and started to work the base of her skull.

"Please. Yes," Fes murmured.

Grinning wide at the request, Vince pressed his thumbs to the back of her head and worked steadily at her. Fes's arms went slack and slid into the tub, her mouth hanging open, tusks in full view.

Rubbing and pressing firmly he worked his way around the base of her skull. Inching towards her ears, he continued to knead her skin.

Over her brow, down her cheekbones, along her jawbone, and down under her jaw.

Black eyes slid open and watched him from an upside position.

Smiling at her, he felt her jaw tighten up. Imagining she was going to say something, he slid his fingers just behind her jaw and waited.

"My tusks don't bother you." It was more of a statement than a question.

To answer her question, he teased her mouth open with his fingers and then dragged his thumbs along those very same tusks.

Hard, sharp, deadly.

"Nope. Why should they?" He was feeling a little flirty right now. Fes didn't tease him like Meliae did, which gave him the opportunity to do so himself.

Sure, she was physically aggressive, grabbing his ass or fondling him, but never flirty.

"Cood bi yu," Fes said nearly unintelligibly. Her teeth closing down on his fingers. Her teeth sank in but didn't break the skin. Her lips closed and she watched him, waiting for his response.

The sensation of her tender lips and strong teeth made his skin prickle. He was already at half mast from rubbing a beautiful naked woman. With the added sensations of her mouth, he wasn't surprised to feel himself go fully erect in a heartbeat.

"You could. You won't. Now let go of my fingers or I'll think terrible thoughts of what you can do with your mouth." Vince quirked a brow at her and gently pulled back on his fingers. She had a good grip on him; not enough to hurt him, but he couldn't get free without a little effort.

Both eyebrows went up at that and her teeth slid apart.

"You'd want that?" Fes asked, her eyes watching him.

"Why wouldn't I? A beautiful woman servicing me like that? Can't threaten me with a good time there. Not something for me to ask for, though." Vince leaned forward and brushed her lips with his own. "Now, shall I get you a towel, or would you like to soak a bit more?"

She turned her head partway to the side and studied him for a few seconds. Her cheeks became a very dark green as she stared. Her eyes flicked down to his erect self nearly pointing at her.

Fes turned over in the tub completely, splashing water over the lip. Before he could respond to that, her right hand reached out and gently cupped his privates. Her water-soaked skin was pliable and soft as she started to fondle him.

Her left hand gripped his hip and pulled him towards her.

Not wanting to risk stopping her, as who would ever say no to what he assumed she was about to do, he went with her pull.

Her fingers massaged and rubbed the family jewels as her soft lips parted and slid around his tip.

Not content with that, she pulled him closer until his thighs were pressed to the tub. In that one motion, she had buried his tip in the back of her throat.

Giving him a firm squeeze with her fingers, she moved her head back. Easing herself forward again, she then started to smoothly bob her head back and forth.

She kept her tongue writhing and swirling around him as her lips slid from tip to hilt and back again.

Laying one hand atop her head and the other on her shoulder, he balanced himself, but made no move to direct her in any way.

It was her show and her desire; who was he to dictate it for her?

She's really been paying attention to Meliae, shit.

Rolling her tongue and pushing his tip along the roof of her mouth and down her throat, she had him lost in the pleasure of it.

As she dragged her head back, she sucked firmly on him, her dark eyes moving up to watch him.

Fes's fingers slid up along the back of his sack to press and rub. He could feel her fingers pushing at him in a way that mimicked exactly what Meliae did.

She hadn't just been paying attention, but she'd clearly gotten pointers from Meliae.

She was eager and willing, if not confident. Where Meliae found out what he liked and then played to that, Fes seemed more willing to explore and try to find different things. New things.

Fes things.

She made a small, questioning noise as her left hand snuck up and circled his base with her thumb and forefinger. Her fingers pressed in as her right hand squeezed his sack firmly.

Between the vibration of her mouth and her fingers working him, Vince let out a rapid breath.

As if by magic, he was right at the cusp of losing the small bit of control he had.

"Fes, if you keep it up I'm going to cum," Vince whispered, his fingers curling in her hair.

As if it meant something entirely different to her, she made another small noise. Then she sped up.

What had been a caressing yet steady suction up to this point became mind-numbingly crushing between her cheeks and tongue.

Her right hand closed up on his balls tightly and pulled, squeezed, and massaged them. Not leaving all the work to her right hand, her left started to travel back and forth with her mouth, giving him another level of friction.

Grunting, he felt his hand close into her hair and his girth swell up in size.

Fes dove down to his hilt, pushing him deep into her throat, her left hand sliding away to grab his hip firmly. Keeping him there.

Shaking, he felt his seed spurt out, his toes curling at the way Fes manhandled him. Her grip on his jewels tightened further, milking him.

An audible gulp reached his ears as he felt Fes's throat constrict on him, swallowing him down. Another full spurt and another swallow could be heard as she contracted down on him, devouring him.

Then she pulled her head back rapidly as he felt a third shot leave him, followed by a final fourth ejection into her mouth, splashing her tongue and teeth liberally.

Coughing as he exited her mouth, Fes turned her head to the side and spat up a glob of thick seed and saliva. Coughing roughly, she got up another bit before taking a deep breath.

"Thick. So thick," Fes muttered, her hand stroking him back and forth as her eyes turned up to him.

Vince only nodded his head, her hand slowly working whatever he had left out.

"Damn, Fes, that was fantastic," Vince murmured, his breath fluttering at the continued attention she was giving his extremely sensitive manhood.

Fes gave him a smirk and kissed the tip, then dragged her tongue over it.

Vince shuddered from head to toe, wanting to curl up in on himself.

As if sensing his desire to pull away, she pulled on him, her hand tightening around him. Looking up at him, she kissed the side of his twitching member.

"Mine," Fes declared, her hand giving him a squeeze to emphasize her point.

Damn skippy it is.

Fes sauntered out of the bathroom without another word after that, not even casting an eye at him.

He wasn't sure what victory she had apparently claimed, either over him or Meliae, but it was clear she was feeling like she'd won.

Cleaning up quickly, Vince re-entered their room, only to find Fes fast asleep. She was sprawled out under the covers, taking up the entire breadth and width of the bed.

Apparently it's naptime.

Looking to the other bed, he found Meliae under the covers, watching him.

"Well. A couple hours till dinner. Maybe we —"

Meliae flipped the covers off of herself to reveal she was nude. Nude and spread eagle on the bed.

Giving him a brazen smile, she crooked a finger at him.

His soldier jumped to attention and pointed Vince onward towards the Nymph.

"What a fun day."

Chapter 9

Vince glanced at the map they'd purchased on their way out of town. Putting his hands on his knees, he shifted to get comfortable in the grass.

Meliae set a double handful of acorns on the corner of the laid-out paper. Squatting down next to it, she curled a lock of her hair around and ear, then turned her head and looked at the map in front of Vince.

Vince had been staring at the smooth neck of the Dryad. At the base of her throat was a purple bite mark that he'd given her the night previous. For whatever reason, she drew out the aggression in him. She seemed to be thrilled by it and wanted more of it every time they had a go of it.

Forcing his eyes back to the map, he pulled out a piece of paper. Flipping it open, he read over it. It was a list of all the places that had been attacked.

"Right, so if we start marking them out..." Vince's voice trailed off as he began setting the acorns down on each location.

He could feel Fes leaning over him, watching him as he worked.

"There," Vince said, leaning back from the map.

The acorns were spread out in a large area but were focused mostly around the farming area in the province of Salem. None of the attacks crossed north into Portland agriculture.

"Strange. It's all in Salem. There's only one beast I know of that would hunt one particular area over another when the only difference is a name," Vince said, waving a hand over the area.

"Humans," Fes muttered.

Meliae nodded her head in agreement.

"That seems like it to me. Suppose we'll find out. Matches up with the lack of tracks, strange leavings, and everything else. Well, up until..." Vince paused, checking his note. "Two weeks ago. Corpses started getting left behind."

"A difference in the pattern?" Fes asked.

"Different pattern. Different source," Meliae disagreed.

"Right. That makes even more sense if you check the last two attack locations," Vince said, pointing out two different acorns. "Same day, same night, too far apart for them to have been the same creature, person, or otherwise."

Fes grunted. "We take the pattern breaker first."

"Agreed. Take the random element out first, and then we can re-evaluate our pattern," Meliae said, nodding her head.

Standing up, she brushed her hands against her hips.

"Right." Vince gave the map a flip, sending acorns everywhere. Rolling up the map, he looked westward.

"Amusingly enough, that one seems to be hovering around Bellevue. It hasn't struck Bellevue yet, though, which makes it a likely target. That's the site of the original attack."

"We ambush it. Lay in wait. Then kill them." Fes clapped her hands together, her armor rattling a little at the movement.

"That very well could be, Fes. Though I'd like to see what we're facing first. Who knows, it could be someone who's hungry and starving. Maybe they're not quite as capable as they thought they were?" Vince asked with a straight face. His goal wasn't to demean or humiliate her, but to make sure she realized that extenuating circumstances could put people in difficult positions.

Like attacking a Ranger and his two charges.

Fes's shoulders bunched up, her brow creasing. She took in a breath as if to argue, held it, then let it out in a rush. Her body posture deflated immediately, her forehead smoothing.

Holding up a hand, she gave him a weary smile. "Thank you, husband. You prick me ever so gently."

Meliae scoffed at that. "No he doesn't, you scream louder than I do. Then again, that's your preference to wrestle with him, not mine. I'm all for being conquered, just not fighting for it."

Fes started laughing immediately, slapping a hand against her knee. Meliae gave the Orc a winsome smile as Fes lifted a hand in defeat. As the Orc met Vince's eyes, she ended up only going deeper into hysterics.

Chuckling to himself, Vince started walking over to his horse. He was glad they got along so well. Sometimes maybe a little too well. He feared the day they teamed up against him.

Night had fallen quickly without Vince noticing. A good number of creatures and Wasters were crepuscular. Active at dawn and dusk. Having been on high alert for dusk, the change to night had been almost sudden to him.

Now that the light had faded, the list of suspects had narrowed considerably. That or they were waiting at the wrong farm. There was always the possibility that Bellevue wouldn't get a visitor this night.

They'd baited the trap fairly well, though. Vince had convinced the farmer to leave out a cow as if it had escaped. To not be on guard or have guards out. To act as if everything were on a lower alert status but normal.

He'd even covered the assumptive cost that the animal would be lost and paid out in standards.

Vince was looking to collect his money back. The margin on this trip would be considerably smaller if he had to pay for the damn cow.

Fes shifted irritably, her hands opening and closing twice. Meliae opened one eye, then closed it again after realizing nothing had changed. Vince shook his head and kept himself aware as best as he could.

"This is stupid. There's no guarantee it'll even happen," Fes muttered. Again.

Vince didn't respond and instead only nodded his head. She knew what his answer would be. He didn't feel the need to voice it again.

Looking off towards the plains, he swept his gaze in one direction, then the other. His ability to see at night gave him a leg up. A big one.

Not too many humanoid species had developed night vision.

The few that had weren't the likely culprits here.

Then again, this is the outlier. Probably a wolf or something stupid. More likely —

A shadow flew towards him and his group. It'd simply popped up out of nowhere from a roll in the land he hadn't noticed. They had maybe ten seconds.

It was big. Big as a Centaur, if not bigger.

"Scatter!" Vince hissed, drawing his saber.

Meliae scurried off towards his right as Fes unsheathed her blade and took several steps to the left.

Armored, armed, and with a height that fluctuated somewhere between five feet to seven feet, Vince couldn't figure it out.

It wasn't until it was practically on top of him that he realized what it was. It had antennae and a human torso atop an ant's body.

A soldier ant, no less. A damn Waster soldier ant wandering around in a field.

The breastplate was flat and colorless, matching the color of the ant's abdomen. The head was covered in a helmet that covered everything and had two holes for the antennae. Shoulders, arms, and hands were also covered.

He'd have to work hard to get his saber through the armor. Really hard. Or find a joint.

Then the ant was on him, thrusting forward with a spear it had kept close to its side.

Flicking his saber to the side, he deflected the spear and sidestepped the charging ant soldier.

Spinning damn near in place, it turned and slashed at him with the spear.

Dodging the strike with only inches to spare, Vince closed in on the bastard. Looking to lop off an arm and end this quickly, he whipped his saber in a horizontal slash at the hand holding the spear.

Only to have it deflected by said spear.

Then the soldier ant leapt backwards, revealing Fes charging towards its last location.

"Damn him, I'll kill him!" Fes shouted turning to chase after the soldier.

Vince flanked out to the side of the ant, keeping his saber low and out in front of himself.

Reaching behind himself towards his abdomen, the ant dropped his spear into what looked like a holding cradle strapped to its body. Then withdrew a different weapon.

Fes was on him in a heartbeat, spinning her large blade in a wickedly fast slash.

The ant deflected it lightly and lashed out with a counter. Fes blocked it head on and stared up into the helmeted face.

Two scythe-like mandibles slid out of the helmet.

Realizing what was happening, Vince sprinted forward.

He knew the outcome, though, if he failed. The ant would bite Fes, effectively locking her in place. Then Fes would die, because that was when the stinger would come from below.

A normal every day, ant's poison wouldn't kill. Painful, to be sure, but not lethal. But a Waster ant? A Waster soldier ant? If that stinger landed, it'd be death.

The mandibles came down, snatching Fes's shoulder, and the abdomen of the ant curled slightly. Then the soldier started to stretch its six legs, giving it additional height and room to spear Fes with its stinger.

As the abdomen shot forward, Vince managed to wedge himself between it and Fes. It slammed into him with the force of a horse's kick. The stinger embedded itself in his side and he felt the venom as it was injected.

Fes freed herself from the ant's bite with a blow from her hilt, the mandibles vanishing back inside the helmet. Stumbling backwards, the soldier's stinger withdrew.

Standing up and charging forward, Vince slashed left, then right. Parrying both attacks, the ant focused in on him even as it was pushed backwards under his attacks.

Vince felt his heart hammer in his chest as the poison flooded his system.

Snarling, Vince went aggressively on the attack. Slashing, thrusting, and slicing at the ant, he kept it moving back.

He had to admit that the soldier was skilled. Very skilled. Vince was only a fraction faster, though the ant was considerably stronger.

Catching a lucky break, the soldier mistimed a parry by only a millisecond. It gave Vince a chance to slap the blade clean out of the soldier's hand.

The soldier leapt towards his weapon as it bounced over the grass. Vince followed and lunged forward, looking to drive his blade into its abdomen.

As if sensing his attack, the ant sidestepped and surrendered its chance to regain its blade. Instead, it pulled its spear back out and went on the defensive.

Using the spear as a prod, it kept Vince out of reach while continuously retreating.

"Why aren't you dead?" asked the soldier, his voice deep and hollow sounding from inside his helmet. There was a strange quality to the voice, like the words were being forced through a mouth wired shut.

"Welcome to your nightmare," Vince said with a grin, and swiped at the spear.

Fes and Meliae were trailing along the sides and a bit to the rear. They were trying to outflank the soldier, but the constant movement made the maneuver take longer and longer.

One of the antennae bobbed once, the other oddly still and hanging limp.

"This one yields," said the soldier. In one motion, it stabbed its spear into the ground and then held up its hands. With a slow motion, it lowered itself down to a height equal to Vince's.

"What?" Vince demanded in a heavy breath, his saber hovering point first in front of him.

"This one yields."

"I heard you the first time," Vince growled out, unsure.

"Then why do you ask for clarification?"

"I… because." Vince shook his head, his anger and adrenaline rapidly cooling.

"Because why?" the soldier asked. It settled itself down on the grass completely, its head now barely reaching five feet.

"Because you don't just yield after trying to kill me," Vince declared.

In his head, it had sounded better before he said it.

"This one tried. Failed. This one yields."

Fes came stomping nearby, her sword held at her side and ready to be swung around.

"Fes… hold. He yields. I guess," Vince said. Not quite willing to accept it, he kept his sword out.

Soft footsteps came up behind him. A soft hum of curiosity announced the person behind him as Meliae. "Yield? I don't understand."

"Nor I, but… here we are."

"This one yields."

"So you've said. What… what were you doing out here?" Vince asked, licking his lips.

"Hunting."

"Hunting? The cow?" That didn't seem quite right to him. A soldier ant was a ferocious thing that could tackle and eat a bear.

"Yes."

"Why a cow? That seems… below the worth of a soldier ant."

"One antenna is damaged. This one's ability to stalk, hunt, and track are… poor due to this," droned the soldier.

Vince digested that bit of information. Things started to make a bit more sense to him. He'd noticed that one antenna hadn't moved much.

Ants relied on them a great deal. It helped them scent out other ants, the situation, and those around them.

That was the least of what he could attribute to it. Based on what he was hearing now and what he'd seen, it sounded like they did considerably more.

"Don't you have a nest? Couldn't they patch you up? Pretty far afield for a single soldier ant," Vince said. Lowering his saber to his side, he watched the soldier intently.

"Dead."

"Dead? An ant colony? I've seen several. They're not easy to exterminate."

"Dead. Flood. Collapsed many tunnels. Elves came. Killed all remaining and the queen."

"Clearly not all. You're here," Meliae said, stepping up beside Vince. She had her staff out in front of her, the iron shod tip pointed towards the ant.

"Ordered to live. This one lives. This one yields to you. Likely you will kill this one. Order met, loss in battle. Death. Duty met."

Vince thought on that one. He was sure to the soldier it made sense.

To him, it didn't.

Then again, a few months ago, I'd have already killed him and moved on.

He could order it away and to harm no other humans. If it swore an oath, he'd believe it. They were notoriously rigid on duty and honor.

Such an oath would be a bit of a death sentence, though. A soldier in this condition without a nest wasn't likely to survive.

What if I order him to follow me instead?

This would be the test, then, he supposed. He couldn't stand the thought of putting a collar around the soldier. It would stand against everything Vince believed in. Even when he'd simply killed Wasters, he'd never liked the idea of enslaving them.

The alternative was again a death sentence.

"As the one who defeated you, what if I requested you to serve me?" Vince queried.

"This one would serve you who should be dead."

"What, your venom? There's very little in the way of poisons or venoms that would actually bother me. I'm sure I'll get a pretty bad case of hives and a rash in a bit, but... that's beside the point." Vince sheathed his sword and shook out his arms and shoulders.

"You are skilled," said the soldier ant.

"That tends to be the case when you practice often and live by your sword. Meliae, can you fix his antenna?" Vince asked the Dryad, turning his head to the side to regard her.

"Easily, but... is this wise?"

Vince turned back to the soldier ant.

"I would have you serve me. That, or I'll grant you mercy and send you on your way east, demanding that you trouble humans no more. I'll have your decision. Now," Vince demanded.

The ant's hands slowly fell to his side, the head bowing under an unforeseen weight.

Its options were clear and simple.

"This one will serve you loyally in whatever way you deem fit," whispered the ant.

"Glad to hear that. I'd rather not send you to what I consider a death sentence so... that's a load off my mind."

He meant it, too. It'd be nothing short of having taken the soldier's life himself.

"Take your helmet off so Meliae here can fix your antenna. Can't have you working at fifty percent. What's your name, by the way?" Vince gestured at the ant with one hand.

Reaching up the ant soldier pulled off his helmet and wedged it under his armpit.

Her armpit.

"This one is Petra, master," said the female ant soldier.

Blonde hair cut short stuck out in nearly every direction. Plastered with sweat and tangled from the helmet, it looked like threshed wheat.

Human-looking eyes watched him, haunted and a little glazed over.

Crystalline blue in color and utterly unreadable. Her face was remarkably human. She wouldn't be called pretty or beautiful by anyone anytime soon. She was no Meliae.

Her lips were slightly parted, her face slack and her eyes partially lidded.

Before anyone could say or do anything further, Meliae had stepped up and laid a hand on the damaged antenna. They came out from the soldier's temples, and this one hung low across her brow.

Several seconds later and the antenna started moving again.

The lack of focus in Petra's eyes cleared up as the antenna raised to the height of the other. Her brow smoothed and her lips pressed together in the barest of smiles.

Huh. She's cute when she doesn't look like a wax statue.

"Are you his servant?" Petra asked, her head swinging towards Meliae, the antennae dipping twice at her.

"Second wife, actually. Fes, the Orc over there, is his first," replied the Dryad, pointing to the warrior.

The blonde head turned around to regard the Orc. Blue eyes scrutinized and picked apart the Orc rapidly. In return, Fes gave Petra a smile that bordered on a sneer.

Petra dismissed her almost as quickly as she'd put her focus on her. Petra turned her head back to Vince.

"What would be your will at this time?" asked Petra.

Vince took a moment to collect his thoughts before responding.

"We're on a Ranger contract right now to stop the attacks here in the farmlands. How long have you been out here?"

"This one has been here for two weeks."

Vince nodded and scratched at his jaw. That left everything still up in the air with the other livestock deaths.

"Alright. We'll camp out for the night," Vince said, nodding his head. Turning to Meliae, he gave her a small smile. "Meliae, be a dear, would you please give me your collar? We didn't bring any extra. You're the one most likely to be confused with a human in comparison to Fes and Petra."

Meliae gave him a grin in return. "Oh? Does that mean I get to play the human wife accompanying her dashing Ranger husband? Perhaps I hail from an exotic location in the far northeast?"

Reaching up, she unbuckled her collar and then held it out to Vince.

Taking it from her hands, he turned to Petra again.

The soldier ant regarded him with a strange countenance.

Ignoring that, Vince stepped in close. With a few deft movements, and explaining as he went, he fitted the collar around her throat.

Lifting it once, he let it fall into a normal position.

"Keep it on whenever we're out and about. You can pull it off when we're at home," Vince clarified, stepping back from the soldier ant.

"This is a fake collar?" Petra asked, one hand raising to touch the item in question.

"No, it's a real collar. I've depowered it, though," Vince explained absently. "This location is good enough for a campsite," Vince said, looking around them.

Petra nodded at that.

"This one will collect her gear. After that, this one will be ready to serve her master," Petra said. Her legs extended and she powered straight upwards.

Vince had to look up at her as she now stood six and a half feet tall. Petra then clapped her helmet back onto her head.

Skirting around him, Petra quickly picked up speed and was off and moving away from them.

"Interesting. I hear that they have human anatomy downstairs as well," Meliae murmured. Vince looked over to her to catch a smile spreading over her face.

"Should kill her," Fes muttered.

Vince sighed and pressed a hand to the back of his neck.

Fes hadn't beaten Petra. If anything, she'd lost to her. Lost to her and Vince had put himself in a position to cover for her failure. He didn't have to think very hard on the fact that Fes probably felt angry at the situation.

He could only imagine the soldier ant being female would complicate things further.

"I wonder if it's true. Do be a dear, husband, and let me know if you find out," Meliae said with a humming noise. She lifted her staff up and lightly prodded his lower abdomen.

Fes's face cleared up a fraction, her eyes becoming thoughtful.

Dismissing all of it, Vince took a seat on the grass right there. Most of their gear was stabled with the horses in the farm owner's barn.

Which meant they'd be sleeping under the stars with nothing but the sky for a blanket.

Vince started to scratch at his forearm, then the backs of his hands.

He was breaking out in hives.

Chapter 10

Under the light of a new day, Vince's plan hadn't changed.

Vince set the map down on the grass and smoothed it out. With a grunt, he settled down in front of it.

"Removing Petra from the pattern..." Vince started. He began dropping small stones on each of the locations where attacks had occurred that hadn't been Petra. "We're left with the following."

Placing the final stone in place, the pattern was now very clear. Every location that had been hit was part of the Kingdom of Portland.

There wasn't a single farm hit in the Kingdom of Washington. There were multiple farms hit right across the border, but nothing in Washington.

In fact...

"If you look at it, it's almost as if it started at the border and worked its way south, then east, then back north," Vince said aloud, turning his head one way and then the other.

A Waster wouldn't care about boundaries. Nor would any normal beast.

"So?" Fes asked.

Meliae pointed at the line separating the two kingdoms. "This is the border?"

"Yeah. Portland and Washington. All part of the west, but separate kingdoms. I guess you could call the whole thing an empire, then," Vince said.

"Mother used to tell me stories of Orc clans that had problems with infighting. One warrior would fight the other for a wife, only to lose a different one to someone else. Could this be the same? Two kingdoms fighting without soldiers?" Meliae leaned her staff against her shoulder and turned her head, staring at the map.

"Very possible. Rangers don't get involved in internal affairs, but we'd have to prove it was an internal affair first. Which would probably put us directly in harm's way and make us the enemy of one kingdom of the other. I mean, who really wants to get their covert operations called out on the mat? Might also explain the Ranger disappearances and failed missions."

Vince frowned and rubbed his fingertips against his chin.

A long, pale finger pointed at the most recent attack site. Vince followed it up to find the unarmored Petra leaning over the map.

In direct sunlight, unarmored, and holding herself the way she did, he'd never figure her for a Waster.

She had an athlete's figure with just a hint of curve to her. Her hips were wider and her chest fuller than Fes's.

Her face had a definite cute quality to it, especially when she smiled. You could almost mistake her for a normal human.

Well, from the nether regions up, at least.

Below her private parts and beyond, her skin became dark, segmented, and firm. It was still warm flesh, soft, supple to the touch, but hard underneath. Hard like rock.

Her legs were only a touch thinner than a human's, though twice as long. Her ant abdomen came out behind her by only a few feet.

Her armor and weapons were self-made. Much to his chagrin, they were things she'd made from the carcasses of fallen ant soldiers, probably.

Vince didn't know it for certain, but he got the impression she had been among the fighting elite of her race. There was no distinction in job duties from males and females in ant colonies.

Only that there was a queen at the top.

Looking at her species differently, she had an almost Centaur look to her. Except the fact that her lady bits were human rather than a horse's.

Centaurs are strange like that.

He hadn't realized any of this about Petra until he'd woken up and found her splayed out on the grass, completely nude, inadvertently giving him an easy view of her genitalia.

Then again, the night previous had been mildly embarrassing for him. Smarting from her loss to Petra, Fes had claimed him roughly and mounted him in front of the ant soldier.

The ant soldier had watched before asking Meliae a question that he couldn't make out. After that, she seemed uninterested in the situation.

Petra was staring at him, her blue eyes flat, questioning.

Giving himself a small shake, Vince held up his hands.

"I apologize, I missed the question. One more time, please?" Vince pleaded, hoping no one had noticed his lapse in attention. The Dryad had. Meliae was looking at him with a tiny smile. Thankfully, Fes seemed wholly into the map and was glaring as if intimidation would make it give up its secrets.

"If this is a military organization, then this one would argue that they should have a staging area. Perhaps somewhere in the middle of this line of attacks. Sloppy to make such an easily distinguishable pattern, though," Petra said smoothly, her finger tracing the line of attacks.

Looking at it with that frame of mind, Vince looked towards the center area. There, near the center of it all, was an uninhabited area that was nothing more than trees and rocks.

So boring and ordinary that it probably got a handful of visitors every decade.

That being the case, Vince realized he'd have to investigate it, even if it was only in passing to the most recent attack site.

Pressing a finger to that spot, he looked around at his party. "This'd be the place if that theory holds up. Or around here. I think we'd be best served to at least canvass the area. Even if we're just passing through. We can make this trip today and still have time to make camp if nothing is there. I say we go for it. Now, even."

Meliae made a delicate frown, one finger pressing to her lower lip. "When we get closer, I'll speak with the trees. Most aren't willing to talk with me, but there's usually one that's chatty in every group."

Fes only grunted, turning her head away from the map and moving back to her mount.

Petra looked at him with a raised blonde eyebrow. "The plan is a good one. This one would ask why you require an opinion?"

"Because while this isn't a democracy, I do value your thoughts," Vince admitted, pulling the map free of the grass and shaking out the rocks. "No one rules alone. To believe so is to set yourself up for failure."

"The queen ruled alone," Petra defiantly said.

"And what happened when she died? Is there a nest left over? Did they even try to resist after that? To rebuild? To try again?" Vince asked, folding the map up.

"No. No, they... we... this one did not. This one will think on your words."

"I."

"What?"

"I will think on your words. Not this one. You are yourself, you're not an ant drone, soldier, whatever," Vince said, gesturing at her. Folding the map a final time, he slipped it into a saddlebag.

"This one... I... will think on your words," Petra said. Her legs straightened, and her head rose up to six feet.

Can you ride an ant soldier?

Vince's thoughts came out from under him as his eyes studied her abdomen. Between her ant rear end and human torso was a small stretch of what he would call her "waist." It'd probably require a custom saddle, but it might be possible to outfit her like that.

Petra was strapping on her armor and speaking to Meliae, and had not noticed his gaze, for which he was thankful.

His hearing caught on their conversation at the use of his name. His enhanced hearing could be dialed up or down at his need if he wasn't distracted.

It'd taken him time to get used to it—there were many noises in the night, after all—but it was worth it.

Checking a strap underneath his mount, Vince focused on their conversation. *Eavesdropping is only rude if you're caught or admit it.*

"—ot a queen. Fes is his first wife," Meliae said in a whisper to the ant woman.

"You hold his scent. As recently as a day old, perhaps," Petra said.

Vince hid his momentary embarrassment by climbing onto his horse.

Apparently, Petra could tell that he'd been with the Dryad before they'd set out.

"Yes. I'm his second wife, remember?"

"Second."

The women grew silent as they set on their way.

Vince settled in as the rear guard while Fes led the way. Petra and Meliae took up the middle. Petra, of course, was her own mount.

"Uh-huh, second. Fes believes it's her duty as his first wife to find more wives for him. Wives that will make him stronger. Women with talent or strength."

"Duty. This one understands duty. Is this one the third wife?"

- 85 -

Vince blinked at that.

Sex with an Orc is weird enough; how would one even go about that with an ant?

"No. If I had to guess the intentions of my silly tree, I'd say he didn't want to kill you and offered you the only other choice he could. He's quick to kill if he must, but slow to do so if he doesn't have to."

"This one would know more of this situation."

Vince decided that was enough for him and tuned the conversation out, focusing on the job he had to do as the tail end.

Getting ambushed now due to his lack of attention sounded pretty damn awful.

Meliae turned her head to Vince, her hand resting on a tree. "They're here. They move during the night and not during the day. They head straight north from here. Somewhere between ten and twenty. Trees don't count very well, but he shared his memories with me. They were jumbled, but I made some sense of it."

Vince opened his mouth to ask a question and stopped, watching Meliae.

The Dryad pressed a hand to her temple, taking in a breath. After a few seconds, she dropped her hand and gave her head a shake. "Sorry. Trees in human territory, that is, outside the Wastes, are... invariably loud or almost too quiet."

"Quite alright, take your time. Did you get an idea about what kind of weaponry they're carrying? Or what kind of armor they wear?" Vince asked.

"Swords, daggers, a couple of short bows. I think. Hard to tell, as they passed this way only during the night. Their armor was dark as well." The Dryad seemed far more weary than she was letting on. Or so Vince believed.

"Thanks, Meliae. Alright. I'd like to get closer and see if we can figure this out. If we can determine it's political without engaging, and slip out with proof, our job is done and will be paid out by the Ranger guild. Questions?"

Vince looked to Fes, who shook her head. She'd been quiet today. Vince wasn't going to pry at her about it, either. She'd talk to him about whatever was bothering her when she was ready.

Looking to Meliae, she also shook her head.

Next was Petra, whose head was once again covered by her helmet.

"This one would know what you wish of her, Master."

Vince took that as acceptance to his question.

"Protect Meliae and keep her in the rear. Stay something like... fifty feet off. She's our ace in the hole," Vince asked. Turning to Fes, he gave a slight inclination of his head towards the direction Meliae had indicated.

Out ahead of them was an open expanse of field, barren of trees and cover. Whoever had picked their location had done so with a mind for tactics.

To his eyes, it looked like a fairly solid wall of vegetation that'd hide whoever was in there while providing an easy view of the surrounding area.

Fes nodded and fell in behind Vince. Hunching his shoulders, he kept himself low and slunk along.

He didn't think they'd be able to make it in without being spotted, but he'd still make the attempt. After all, it was late afternoon and the sun was pitched fairly low in the west. They'd be fairly well highlighted to anyone curious enough to look south.

As if his thoughts had reached out and alerted their quarry, a shout came up to the north of them.

Seconds after that, bodies came boiling out of the trees and brush. Vince unsheathed his sword as he counted six charging them.

They were armed exactly as Meliae had warned they would be. Unfortunately, they were also very clearly military trained.

The six spread out to encircle them, slowing down from the run they'd started out at into a fast walk. Before they could settle in, he'd have to act. Beside him, he could practically feel Fes coming to the same realization.

Vince hissed between his teeth and then leapt forward with all the speed he could muster.

His saber snapped forward, the tip whistling through the air and cleaving through an unprotected wrist. Not letting the blow slow him, Vince took a half step to the right with his left foot while pulling his sword back.

He sprang forward again, his sword extending and skewering the second man in the lower abdomen.

Jerking his blade free as he passed the man who was crumpling in on himself, Vince spun on his heel.

Fes had chopped a third man nearly in half and ended up a few feet off to his left.

Before he could begin to celebrate the evening of the odds, Vince heard the crunch and clatter of more people coming from the camp.

They'd underestimated Vince and Fes and only sent some of their number. They'd paid a price for that, and Vince didn't doubt that now they were all coming.

Vince saw Petra's approach a fleeting moment before she arrived.

Petra's long, strange sword swept across in a horizontal blur. That one swipe took the lives of two men who had gotten close to one another. One lost their head while the other had the top half of their skull removed. The two dead bodies fell to the ground with a thump as their limbs spasmed.

Fes roared and leapt at the last man, her blade snapping a hastily raised broadsword in half. The weight of the attack drove the man to his knees as her weapon carved down through his shoulder and into his midsection.

Cruelly shoving a booted foot into his chest, Fes kicked him off the length of her sword.

Vince looked to the oncoming enemies. A quick count gave him eight combatants rapidly approaching. They were all wearing headdresses that covered their faces.

Eight of them, against three.

Meliae stepped up behind him, her staff held out at her side.

Four, I guess.

Vince felt his mouth turn into a thin line.

"Don't be angry. I can't sit back and watch you go into battle alone. A Dryad is supposed to protect her tree. Not hide in it."

"Stay beside me, then. Use the reach on your staff to keep people away. Look for openings, don't actually engage unless there's no other choice," Vince muttered.

Well, three and a half against eight.

Their foes were starting to slow on their approach. They seemed confused and angry at the same time.

Then Petra darted forward, her multi-jointed legs propelling her faster than he'd expected. Fes chased after her, yelling as she sprinted along. The two of them plowed into the six on the right and scattered them.

Vince moved forward to immediately engage the two who were turning to join their comrades. With a flick and twist of his wrist, his saber snapped out, slicing along the foe's shoulder and into their jaw with a crunch.

Turning his attention to the second, he had a moment to register the fact that they were leveling a revolver at him. Turning to the side to limit his profile, he did the only other thing he could think of. Fingering a throwing knife as he moved, he spun it off from his side with a flick of his wrist. His aim felt true and he watched as it flew towards the man's shoulder.

Spinning end over end, it sped onward towards the target. Then Vince lost sight of the blade as it passed the gun. Then it went off.

The boom of the pistol filled his ears and Vince tried to force himself forward to engage before they could fire another round.

The cylinder started to rotate as they began pulling the trigger again.

Green leaves and vines whipped up from the foliage at their feet. A mass of plant matter wrapped up around the cocked hammer and dragged the barrel towards the ground.

A sapling bent to the side and tilted towards Vince's attacker, then sprung outward. The tip of the small tree exploded as the green wood smashed through their unprotected throat.

Gurgling, the attacker dropped the gun and pressed their hands to their ravaged neck. Blood flowed over their gloves like a plastic bag with a slit in it.

Vince was stunned, his mind struggling to keep up with the situation.

He knew magic existed, had even seen a bit of it here and there. But not magic that could directly affect a fight.

From a Dryad, no less.

Only truly powerful Dryads could control nature like what had just happened.

Thoughts for later, fool. The fight goes on.

Returning his attention to the second person, Vince found them on their knees, a hand pressed to their shoulder. Apparently he'd struck truer than he'd originally believed.

Looking to Petra and Fes, he found the two finishing off the last attacker between them. Petra jabbed in a quick attack, forcing the man back a step. It gave Fes an opportunity to bring her big sword around in a slash that just about bisected the bastard in the middle.

Both Petra and Fes's eyes jumped over to him.

"Clear," Vince called out to them.

"Clear," Fes responded. Grunting, she leaned down and drew her blade across a corpse.

"Finish them off, don't leave them to suffer," Vince said, indicating the bodies at their feet. Getting cut in half wasn't always an immediate death, and the gasping agonal breaths he could hear only reinforced that.

Dying wasn't like the way stories described it. It could be swifter than a thought, and slow as ice in equal measure.

Looking to his own duty, he pushed his saber into the chest of the man with the missing throat.

There was no resistance as his blade slid into the spot the man's heart should be. Withdrawing his saber, Vince turned to the one with the shoulder wound.

"Wait, wait, I'm working for the kin—"

The statement ended as Vince shoved the tip of his sword into the man's chest and pushed straight into the heart. With a small twist, he made sure to dice the organ completely, giving the man only a few seconds to wait for his end.

"Why?" Meliae asked quietly from beside him.

"Because if I had heard him, we'd all be in an ugly situation between kingdoms. I'd be forced to give him aid, transfer him to the guild, and then sit idly by as two kingdoms probably went to war," Vince explained, his voice soft.

Wiping his blade on the now dead man, he sighed.

"There's always the possibility they'd try to claim you as repayment for their losses as well. I doubt it'd be upheld, but you three would end up in a 'warehouse' of sorts until this was finalized. Call me selfish, but I'd rather not let that happen. It'll be bad enough when I report what my suspicions are without proof."

Taking a few steps back to the other corpse, Vince rooted around in the ground till he found the revolver.

Squatting down, he eyed the piece with a frown.

"Is that a gun?" Fes asked. She'd come up behind him while he was looking for it. "Never seen one. Was loud."

"That it is. Expensive, to say the least. Ammunition isn't a readily available commodity. Especially for civilians. Or a bandit." Vince sighed and picked up the weapon. It was a double-action revolver. "One could argue ammo itself is a form of currency. Especially for something like this, which has specific needs. Very specific needs. We'll sell it to the guild. I already have a few at the house, but ammo is so expensive that… it's just not worth carrying around."

"This one would argue that your life is worth more than a bullet, Master. Perhaps it's time to carry one on the off chance something like this happens again," Petra intoned somberly.

"You're probably right. Speaking of, thanks for the save, Meliae," Vince said, looking up at the Dryad beside him. His eyes promised her a private conversation about her magic.

Blushing the Dryad nodded her head, not saying a word.

"Alright, loot all the bodies and stack 'em up. Leave 'em for the wild. It'll help obscure what happened here."

Chapter 11

They'd gotten lucky with the "spoils of war" from the dead and the camp they found after. Most of it was things they could pack easily and either take back home or sell without a problem to the guild.

Most especially fortuitous was that one of the combatants had been a female Elf in a slave collar.

That extra collar had immediately gone onto Meliae without any commands or requirements to put on it. It'd serve as a decent cover.

They'd have to break it when they got back home, but that was a problem for another time.

Right now, the situation was more of a political one. Vince would need to deal with what, to his mind at least, was a clear and obvious declaration of war between two kingdoms.

One that'd probably plunge the entire area into an ugly and bitter, drawn-out war.

The quickest way to undermine a country was to topple their economy or their ability to feed the population. In either of those situations, internal stability would usually fall to zero and bottom out rapidly.

This wasn't to say the country would immediately fall, but it would definitely put pressure on the government.

If the problem was severe enough, that government might not be able to cope with, say, a sudden and furious assault from a neighbor. One that promised the citizens of the other food at a reasonable price. Perhaps jobs to earn the coin to buy it, too.

At least, that was what Vince would've done. Destabilize, then attack.

Now he had to convey that point to everyone involved, without actually saying it.

The pop of a log shattering into flaming coal shook him from his thoughts.

Looking to the side, he saw Petra, Fes, and Meliae lined up against the wall. Staring straight ahead. Unmoving. Silent.

His license now had a third marker to denote Petra's ownership. It gave Petra protection, yet also could create a problem if people started asking questions about when he procured her.

Being forced to stand like statues was only the latest in the long list of slights they had to deal with.

The sooner they left for home, the better. This whole area was a powder keg and the population didn't seem to even realize it.

From the back of the room, Vince heard the doorknob rattle and the lock click. Facing forward, with his back uncomfortably towards the door, Vince waited for whoever it was to join him and proceed with his debriefing.

"Vince, thank you. Please remain seated," said an older voice. "My name is Al, and I'm the senior guild representative to the Kingdoms of Portland and Washington.

I've asked each kingdom to send a representative to join us based on your preliminary report. They have graciously acquiesced."

Vince said nothing and remained seated as requested. Stepping around his chair came three men. The first, dressed in a Ranger guild uniform, was who he assumed was Al.

The second man had a pinched face and looked the part of the elder statesmen. Dressed in resplendent clothes, he gave off the impression of someone who grubbed for coins from everyone who asked him for a favor, then had the gall to turn around and expense a lunch on his employer.

The third man was more interesting. Middle-aged, dressed in a military uniform, and... and familiar. Vince stared at the man, trying to place him.

It tickled at his mind like a cut on his lip. The kind you wanted to run your tongue over repeatedly, feeling the sweet tingle of pain with each pass.

On the edge of his awareness, he could feel everyone in the room. Each of the three felt like they were exactly who they should be to him.

The cursory analysis he did with his extra senses was a normal thing for him. Its range was a measly ten feet, but it provided him a window into a person's mind he had come to rely on.

This was all normal and expected by him. So when the familiar man's mind vanished from Vince's senses, he only barely managed to control his surprise.

The only people who had ever done that were his parents, who were well aware of his ability. More often than not when they wanted to hide something from him. Which only made it move obvious, really.

Trying to look the part of an eager guilder, Vince swung his eyes to his own representative, visibly dismissing the other men.

He knows I can sense him. Knows exactly what I can do with it and how to protect himself from me. How does he know? Does he know me? Did he know my parents?

"First. Why didn't you report in here once you were operating in the area?" Al queried. The question was said innocently enough, but it gave Vince a clue about the man's mindset.

"It isn't standard procedure to check in with the guild. Such a thing isn't mentioned in the handbook, guild rules, or even the lessons in polite behavior. I have no obligation to do so," Vince said bluntly. He wasn't going to beat around the bush. Technically, this man had no authority over him.

Only his personal guild handler had any type of control over him. And that person wasn't here.

In addition to that, Vince had a sneaking suspicion that the "bandits" might have been on high alert if Vince had checked in here first.

"Of course. Local custom would have Ranger's checking in first. This would be your first time up this way?"

"As a Ranger, yes."

Al nodded at that and seemed to set the matter aside.

"Now, Vince, you reported that you suspect there to be involvement from a government agency, yet you have no corroborating proof or evidence of that. Could you elaborate on that for me?" said Al with a slimy smile.

"Certainly. The crew we eliminated were very well armed, trained, and were conducting themselves in a fashion at odds with a bandit gang. We found a large number of tools, weapons, and other implements that were well beyond the means of what they were doing with those items.

"That leaves two options. They killed and robbed an elite detachment of military-trained operatives. Or they were the operatives."

"Yes. I understand you've already sold all of those items to the guild at standard rates?" Al asked.

It was a question he'd expected and had made sure to prep himself for it.

In order to better service their people, and make money, the guild bought any and all loot at a higher rate than what they could get selling it to a merchant.

"That's correct. I notified the clerk that they would likely be declared as evidence upon the sale so that they could be itemized correctly," Vince clarified. He didn't want it coming back to him later that he'd withheld anything, so they'd simply sold it to them with the intent that it was all accounted for up front.

"Good, good. You said they were well trained?" Al prompted.

"Very much so. They were well defended, had planned extensively, and were honestly tough to kill. They underestimated us, much to their detriment." Vince nodded, taking a sip of the tea he'd been offered earlier while he was waiting.

"After dispatching of them and searching through everything we could put our hands on, it was more of what we found missing than what we found. As I've already said, their possessions were in excess of what you'd expect a bandit to have. They also had nothing on them that would identify them in any way, shape, or form. Down to even the clothes they wore. Nothing that could be traced to anything on anyone."

Al and the familiar man frowned at that. The weasel-faced man made a harrumphing noise.

"Doesn't mean anything," said the familiar man.

"Ah, beg your pardon, Mister…?" Vince prompted.

"Seville. Seville will do fine."

"Beg your pardon, Seville, but it doesn't add up. Bandits that are attacking farms to simply butcher livestock and… what, sell the meat? There were no wagons, no wagon tracks, and no meat anywhere around the camp. Which means they didn't bring it back with them. Either they ate it or dumped it. If they ate it or dumped it, why bother?" Vince asked, holding up his hands in confusion.

"Why would well trained, military-specced, heavily armed bandits do little better than steal livestock?

"And to what end? To… eat it? No, a group like this would be raiding roads and merchants. Nothing about this makes sense. The only valid possibility then becomes that they were being paid by someone else to do these things."

Vince paused to take another sip from his tea. He'd said more than he'd wanted to, but they'd limited their responses to his statements.

The sinking feeling in his stomach warned him that not only were they aware of this, all of them, but that they all knew each other was aware of it as well.

"Is that all?" Al asked.

"All that I can report on. As you yourself said, there is no evidence to support any of this. This is all supposition."

Weasel face on the left peered at him suspiciously. "You're surprisingly well spoken for a Ranger."

Vince quirked his eyebrows at that yet said nothing, instead looking to Al to gauge his response at the implied insult.

Al waved a negligent hand at the comment and stood up.

"You're dismissed, Ranger Vincent. Please remain for a time so we may speak privately later. I'll seek you out in the next ten minutes or so," Al said brusquely.

Vince stood and nodded his head to Al. Turning without a word, Vince made his way to the exit. With a glance to his party, he gave them a slight tilt of his head toward the door.

Fes, Meliae, and Petra were already in motion, filing in behind him. Stepping out of the room, Vince held a finger to his lips.

Nodding in unison, his group said nothing.

They made their way up to their rooms in silence. Only the soft hiss of their boots on the wooden floor could be heard.

It was unsettling how quiet the building was. Eerie, even.

As the guild had provided them rooms inside of the compound, they'd only need to walk for a minute or two to reach their small bit of privacy. The rooms had been granted since their mission had taken a sudden and political turn.

It wasn't until Vince had closed and locked the door behind them that he felt anything bordering on "ease."

"Load of shit," Fes grumbled, flopping into a chair. "They knew. Wanted you to spell it all out for them."

"So it would seem," Vince murmured, walking over to the single table their room had. "This all… worries me."

"This one would agree. This place is built for the life of many, yet we are all that are here." Petra eased her abdomen down onto the bed. It was probably the closest she'd ever get to actually sitting down. A normal chair wouldn't accommodate her, after all.

"Yes. I asked one of the plants in the lobby. Apparently this lack of people is very out of the ordinary. There's no way to really get a sense of time from a plant, but if I had to guess, it's been like this for about a month." Meliae took the seat across from Fes, directly in front of Vince.

Peering down at the Dryad, he got a lovely view of her cleavage. It took him a second to realize she'd deliberately placed herself and arranged her posture in such a way to present him that view.

"I'll check the logbook, but I'd bet that everyone has been tasked with missions that are low risk, high pay, and for long periods of time, or very far away. Someone has singled out the Ranger guild," Vince admitted, tearing his eyes from Meliae's impressive assets.

"This one would remind her master that the first step to conquering a foe is limiting their ability to wage war. If the guild has no soldiers, they cannot fight. If they cannot fight, they are no longer a concern for one side, or the other." Petra rubbed one hand across her bare upper arm.

Since coming into the compound, she'd been forced to unequip her armor and wear normal clothing.

She still seemed rather ill at ease with her wardrobe.

For now, she was wearing Fes's clothes since she was the closest in approximate size to her. The vest she'd donned seemed stretched at the shoulders and across the front. It clearly didn't fit as well for Petra as it did Fes.

It almost looked like she was going to pop a button if she thrust her chest out.

Need to buy her clothes. Don't have time to dick around here in danger town. We'll just have to hit somewhere on the way home.

"You're right, Petra. That's the very reason I'd like to be gone as soon as possible. Let's pack up and get our shit together. The moment we're done with Al, I want to be on the road. Even if we're leaving at midnight. Can't get away from this place soon enough," Vince said with a nod of his head.

In the meantime, we can drop a few inquiries about Seville. He knew me. Or at least, knew what I could do.

Fes grunted and then folded her arms under her chest. "Can we use the training field? I can see it from the window. Petra and I should train. Spar, even."

Vince looked to Petra to make sure she was alright with the situation, though he had to admit to himself he didn't want to get between the two of them.

Since Petra had joined the group, Fes had been domineering and aggressive towards the ant-girl. He could probably fix the situation by pointing out the obvious and forcing them into the right roles.

Vince started to open his mouth to do that when Meliae kicked him in the shin under the table. Then did it again.

He wasn't stupid, nor was the Dryad. She was well aware of what was going on as he was, and she was clearly of the opinion that he shouldn't involve himself. At least not yet.

Smiling at Fes, he nodded his head.

"That should be fine. If anyone asks, tell them I told you to, but to not leave the compound, or with anyone else."

Giving Vince a feral grin, Fes left, Petra following along mutely.

No sooner had the door clicked shut than he looked to Meliae.

"Did you have to kick me? I admit I'm made of sterner stuff than most, but that felt hard enough that it might have actually left a bruise," Vince told the Dryad with a smile.

"No, I didn't. But then I wouldn't have an excuse to crawl under the table to wrap my lips around it and make it better," teased the Dryad.

Being a normal male, Vince felt his member leap upwards at the underlying suggestion. Nevertheless, he wanted to hear more.

"Don't you mean kiss it?" Vince asked, feeling his heart speed up a fraction.

Meliae tilted her head to one side, watching him with a smile instead of responding. She leaned forward instead, her top folding slightly in the front to expose herself more to his eyes.

Nymph. She'll eagerly perform in front of others, but she's the most bold when alone.

"A pity we'll have to wait for the guild mediator to leave for you to find out," said the Dryad, leaning back in her chair, closing up that view.

Not trusting himself to say anything, Vince nodded his head wordlessly.

Vince had no way to check, but he knew it'd been longer than twenty minutes since he'd left the meeting room.

He and Meliae had simply spent the time chatting about mundane things, which, while pleasant, didn't solve his growing irritation.

Make me wait much longer and we'll just leave. Politeness and pay be damned. Something isn't right here.

At that thought, the door shook under three rapid knocks and then swung open.

Mastering his expression before he could reveal anything, like the fact that the door had been locked, Vince watched Al enter the room.

The man seemed mildly disappointed, to Vince's eyes. He didn't even want to begin to guess what he could be possibly disappointed in.

"My apologies for making you wait. I'll keep this brief," Al said, coming to stand in front of the table.

"As you may have noticed, the vast majority of the Rangers who call this hub home are out on missions. I was hoping you'd be willing to stay on for a while until a few return," Al said smoothly.

"I'm afraid not. We'll need to be heading back immediately." Vince stated it as fact.

"I see. I'll be activating the emergency contingency of your Ranger contract, then. You'll receive pay equal to your average over a month's period for the last three months, broken out by day. Plus ten percent. As stipulated in the charter." Al reached into an inner fold of his clothes and flipped out a document in front of Vince.

Truth be told, Vince wasn't surprised. He'd thought of all the ways he could be forced into remaining here.

Which was why he'd spent a few hours reading through this particular section of the charter one night previous.

"My standard rate of pay, based on what you've stated, is two and a half standards per day. You can confirm this by pigeon, of course, or take my word for it," Vince said without a hint of emotion.

"What? That's... fine. After lodgings and meals—"

"Actually, as part of the same section in the charter, all meals and lodging are to be provided by the hub enacting the charter. In the next section, it details out that period of activation cannot be longer than a month. It also states you'll need to specify how long I'm to be on retainer." Vince picked up the document in front of him and read through it quickly.

Al stood up straighter, his mouth turning up in a small smile.

"The full month," he said immediately.

"Then I can request my entire pay up front, as the contract is pre-set for the maximum," Vince said. After a moment, he found the spot on the document that listed the time to be hired. Filling it out for a full month, Vince then signed the sheet. "Please have my pay ready for me tonight. I believe that works out to be seventy standards for twenty-eight days. You can have it delivered with my payment for the contract I've already settled."

Vince looked up at Al and gave him a pleasant smile.

Feeding and caring for four people, paying out his fee, and the contract completion all in the same month.

An expense line that heavy would get the main Ranger guild's attention. There was no doubt that Al would be getting a visit from an account manager after his finances were reported up for the month.

Al's skin had a faint sheen to it and had taken on the color of parchment.

Should have probably tried talking to me first rather than attempting to bully me, you fuckwit.

"Fine. I'd like you on patrol on the border between the two kingdoms. I expect to see your patrol route on my desk tomorrow morning," Al ground out between his teeth.

"Then I shall be on patrol on the border. Per the charter, I'm allowed to requisition anything I think I'll need during my mission," Vince said easily, already going through a mental checklist of the things he'd be taking with him.

"I'll requisition the appropriate supplies tomorrow morning before I depart. Should they be lost or damaged, you'll of course be responsible for them, as you're my employer. I'll be sure to earmark every item accordingly."

Al snapped his teeth together with an audible click.

Snatching the contract off the table, Al turned and fled the room.

"And you wanted him as an enemy because…?" Meliae asked after Al departed. The sound of his stomping boots echoed in the hallway.

"He already was one. For whatever reason, he signed off on every Ranger being gone. He's putting himself between two kingdoms. This mission is a suicide run meant to get us killed.

"No, he was already an enemy. I only made it obvious I was aware of it. Once we leave here, we won't be returning. We'll complete the mission as required and little more."

Vince sighed and leaned back in his chair, laying his hands flat on the table. "We'll need to hit the armory shortly. He'll figure he can get the more expensive things out before we get there."

"I see. Well, I better hurry up, then," Meliae murmured. With a smile, she slid out from her chair and under the table.

Before he could react, she'd already unhitched his belt, yanked open his trousers, and pulled his length free of his pants with soft fingertips.

Not being able to see what she was about to do definitely added to his arousal. In the few seconds it took her to engulf him with her mouth, he was already halfway to a full hard-on.

He could feel the soft wetness of her lips and tongue as she eagerly began to bob her head back and forth. There was a soft, rhythmic thump as the back of her skull tapped the underside of the table with each stroke of her mouth.

Tender fingers began to stroke his hilt as her tongue slid along the underside of his girth. Each time she got to the base of him, when he could feel his tip in her throat, her tongue slid out from the bottom to lick at the top of his sack.

"Damn, Meliae," Vince whispered. His fingers curled inward into his palms as her head came back up, bumping the table again.

"Mmmm?" murmured the Dryad, vibrating his length in her mouth.

Her fingers tightened up on him, her other hand cupping his jewels and giving him a playful squeeze.

"Never mind, just…" Vince trailed off as her head moved back down.

Vince leaned back as her head bumped the table once more. "That feels great."

"Mmm," Meliae cooed, sucking on him as her fingers playfully toyed at him.

Making a sudden decision, Vince pushed the table backwards.

He wanted to dominate her. To own her. To make her his. To claim her powerfully. Repeatedly.

Meliae's eyes opened slowly as the table skidded away; full and green, they lacked a pupil. She was hilt deep and her moist lips were melded to his flesh.

Reaching down, he curled his fingers into her hair with both hands. Getting a firm grip, he began pushing and pulling her head back and forth swiftly.

She gurgled, a cough stuck in her throat as her hands gently pushed at his hips. Her resistance was false, false and designed only to egg him on.

Her eyes begged him to destroy her in whatever way he saw fit, even as she pretended to fight him with her hands.

Grunting, he worked her head back and forth like it was his to do so. Her mouth pulled at him, sucking hard as he pushed her head back, and eagerly moving down when he pulled on her.

He wanted to just unload it into her mouth right then and there.

With a serious mental effort, he pulled her head back completely.

Gasping for air, Meliae gazed up at him with some emotion he couldn't identify. Precum and drool trailed from her mouth and down her chin. She ran her tongue over her full lips, making a show of it.

Grabbing her by the shoulders, he lifted her up and pushed her towards the bed.

Stumbling over her own feet, she flopped halfway onto the bed. She'd managed to bend herself over the bed. She turned her head and stared back at him, those full green glowing eyes demanding that he destroy her.

Even now, each movement was intentional. Designed to draw more and more ownership of her from him.

Lining up behind her, he yanked her pants down. His left hand pressed into the soft, luxurious skin of her hip as his right hand guided his tip into her small, narrow slit.

Pushing forward, he entered her in a single stroke. Her wet insides pulsed and clamped down on him as her body shuddered.

Reaching up, he tangled his right hand into her hair and pushed her into the bed as he began to hammer into her.

Meliae reached up and began to very gently tug at the hand on her head, as her other hand reached back to push ever so lightly on his hips.

Even as she pretended to fight him, she angled her hips and pushed back into him.

Vince plowed into her over and over, her small body rebounding each time. Her hands continued at their make-believe resistance as she moaned and thrust back at him.

There was nothing left in Vince at this point. He'd already been at his end back at the table. Only through wanting to break her had he made it this far.

His body tightened up as it prepared to climax.

A small movement at the window got his attention as his member expanded. Looking up, he found Petra watching him through the glass on the other side.

Meliae had noticed as well, her head turning under his hand to look up at the soldier-ant.

He felt Meliae tighten up underneath him, even as his seed spilled out, filling her.

Unable to break eye contact with Petra, or even stop himself at this point, he mechanically thrust into Meliae a few more times, pushing his seed deep into her.

Running out of genetic material, Vince stood there, looking at Petra, who stared back at him.

Untangling his hand from Meliae's hair, he set it on her other hip, holding her there.

Petra tilted her head to one side, and then disappeared from the window.

"We're on the second floor," Vince said.

Meliae nodded her head.

"She was there since Al came in. She was on guard, I think," Meliae murmured sleepily. Nuzzling her face into the blankets, she rolled her hips a little.

"I see. And... you wanted her to watch?" Vince asked cautiously.

"I want everyone to see me with my tree. I'm the luckiest Dryad ever."

Meliae started to grind her hips into him while her hands roamed down her body towards him. Her fingers grabbed a hold of his hips and pulled on him.

"We need to talk about this tree thing. Magic as well. And your eyes."

"Of course, Sweetling, anything for you. But... until then... again?" asked the Nymph.

Chapter 12

Vince dropped the bar in place, locking the armory door from the inside. The clerk who had escorted them here had left them alone. Probably to go run down Al and warn him about what was happening.

"Alright, first things first. Let's do a quick pass to see what's available first before making any decisions. Keep in mind we'll be wandering around the border. I don't plan on giving that ass an actual patrol route. Going to just give him a map with the border circled for miles on either side.

"While we're figuring out what to take with us, you can start teaching me about Dryads. Let's start with your tree," Vince said. He'd waited far too long to ask these questions before this point.

Meliae shrugged her shoulders as she began to walk down an aisle.

"I'm sure you've heard the tales. They're fairly accurate. A Dryad must remain near their tree. All Dryads are given a seed from their mother's tree as they reach adulthood. If the seed should remain unplanted for too long, the Dryad dies. If the planted seed becomes a tree and dies before it can make more seeds, the Dryad dies."

Vince nodded his head; that all matched what he knew.

A frown spread over his face as he skipped over a rack of weapons. They were all standard things, nothing out of the ordinary.

"Consider me vain, but I'm quite proud of my tree. It's singular and unique." Her tone was light and almost playful. She was leaning over a rack of spears.

"Your tree being... me," Vince said, supplying the unspoken answer.

"You're indeed my tree. I... can't remember what I was thinking when I did it. Not very well, at least. I was dying. I remember smelling blood. Blood everywhere. Your blood." Meliae wrinkled her nose at the weapons before her and moved on.

"I... remember the sweet stench of it. Can remember the taste of it in the air. Metallic and earthy. The scent of raw power, strength. Death. Not yours, but others'."

Vince began skipping entire racks of weapons, moving deeper into the guild armory. Meliae followed behind him though at a slower pace.

"My mother gave me all sorts of advice on where to plant my tree. Looking for places of power. Magic or life-soaked energy would be preferable. Something rich in the elements that could provide it with more than a normal tree would need. Obviously planting it in a human never came up, simply because a tree shouldn't be able to survive inside a living body."

"Makes sense. Why plant it in me, then?"

"The amount of power your blood carries is enormous. It's constantly refilling regardless of how much is sapped from you. My tree is embedded just inside your ribcage. Its very roots have spread throughout your body, mimicking your veins. In fact, it's even encased the vast majority of your arteries. It has not a single branch, leaf, or twig on it. It's a gnarled and twisted thing, stunted and never having tasted the light of day. Yet it already rivals my mother's in power. I begin to wonder if perhaps it would do better if it shrunk down to a smaller part of you."

That brought Vince up short. He scratched at himself where Meliae had pushed her seed in.

"Which leads us to the next question you had. Magic. Due to my tree's unprecedented growth, I can utilize magic. Not as well as those Dryads who developed it naturally over time, but pound for pound, I'm as strong. If not more so."

Vince grunted and passed over another set of weapons.

Makes sense. A little unnerving, but makes sense.

"And your eyes?" Vince asked.

"A little harder to explain. When I use magic, when I connect with my tree, or... when I let myself relax, that happens. I'm sure you've... noticed my nature?"

Vince chuckled at that. "That you want me to break you and treat you like a plaything? Yes, I've noticed. Shall I attach a nametag to your color? Maybe give you a new name? Something more befitting a pet? Walk you around town in a swimsuit made of string and a napkin?" Vince joked.

Looking back at the Dryad, he watched as her eyes rapidly shifted into a solid green, her skin flushing.

"Yes, please. Wait. No," Meliae huffed, placing a hand to her head. Her eyes changed back to normality. Slowly.

"Dryads can only be female. We need a male from another race to give us children. To that end, we... well, we end up with a need to be possessed. It's normally tied to our age and power. I'm constantly fighting with my own nature because I'm unbalanced."

"And is this something that will continue, or will it change as you get older? Not that I'm complaining, mind you. Rather fun. Not quite sure how I felt about the exhibition for Petra, though."

Vince returned his attention to the task at hand. They were quickly coming to the end of the room. Hopefully he'd find what he was looking for here. Everything up to this point had been a bust.

"I'm getting better at controlling it. Especially since becoming pregnant. It's been significantly easier to control. As to Petra, does it matter? She watches nightly anyways."

Not really wrong there, she does watch. Wait.

"Oh, is that what you call a rifle?" Meliae asked, her hand pointing to a series of glass cases.

Vince felt his mind split in two different directions. One side of his brain followed the word "pregnant" and the other half "rifle."

"Wait, wait, back up. Pregnant?" Vince asked, his voice trailing up an octave unintentionally.

"Hm? Yes. Don't worry, though. Dryads can control their pregnancy as easily as breathing. We'll not be having children anytime soon. Well, or at least until we're settled. The harder part will be deciding on which."

Meliae walked up to the glass case and flipped it open.

Inside were several single-shot rifles from the World War One period. The price for those alone would be substantial. The ammo would be costly, but providing one could retrieve the spent casings, they could be reloaded.

"What do you mean, deciding which?" Moving to the glass, Vince fetched out four of the rifles in total. He held up one to Meliae. "And yes, they're rifles. Springfield o-threes. Get familiar with it, you'll be holding one."

"Dryads can get pregnant multiple times. There's no limit. As an egg is impregnated, it's withdrawn into the lining for safety. The whole process is necessary since Dryads have such a long life. We outlive our partners with our lifespan. A full tree's lifespan, which can be very long. And what I mean by deciding which is your… ahem… genetic material is very efficient. I stopped counting after fifty. You seem to catch a few every time we couple."

"Do I have to use a rifle?" Meliae pressed her lips together, taking the rifle from Vince's hands.

Vince shook his head, trying to clear out what Meliae had explained to him. What had he expected? Unprotected sex would ultimately result in pregnancy.

He hadn't expected to be able to impregnate Wasters.

That's my own problem for not asking.

"Uh, is Fes…?" Vince asked cautiously. Reaching down, he opened the bottom of the case and found multiple cans of ammunition for the rifles.

"Once, so far. It wasn't viable. Impregnating an Orc in a few months is no mean feat. I'd consider it lucky to happen in a handful of years, let alone months. From what I can tell, though, Petra will be more likely to be fertilized with little difficulty. Physical differences aside, you two are simply more compatible as species."

Sighing, Vince knelt down and started pulling out the ammo cans.

Not something I really figured I'd have to start worrying about, getting enslaved Wastelanders pregnant.

"Don't worry, I can keep Petra infertile until Fes is pregnant. We've already discussed the situation between us, no need to be concerned."

"Seriously, Meliae? Why am I not part of this conversation? Maybe I don't want any of you pregnant?" Vince grumped, closing the cabinet after hauling out a total of four canisters.

"I admit I'm only partially informed of human culture, but I'm well aware of the fact you could take precautions to prevent pregnancy. Therefore, you're actively trying to impregnate us.

"Besides, I'm happy to have children with you. I can't wait to take you to my mother to show you off," Meliae said, her energy and excitement becoming increasingly apparent with every word.

"Huh? Why? After this, we need to head over to the messenger pigeons. I want to send a note off to our own guild hub about this whole thing. Things aren't right up here." Vince tied two of the lids together with one of the leather cords he kept wrapped around his belt. Giving it a tug he tied the second one and slung both over his shoulder. Grabbing the two rifles under his other arm he looked to Meliae.

"Because I'm a Dryad that can go anywhere. Dryads don't typically see their relatives. Ever. But me? My tree is special. Unique. I can go... wherever I can convince my tree to take me. Or simply go somewhere else to take me.

"I'm sure I can be convincing."

Meliae sighed and hefted the rifle to her shoulder, staring down the sight aperture.

"Besides, what other Dryad can claim their tree got them pregnant?"

Vince felt his mind starting to drift as they meandered along. They were ten miles north of the border, walking sedately through a forest of trees and leading their horses.

It'd been a quiet two weeks since their departure. Easiest money he'd ever earned at this rate.

At no time did Al ever instruct them on how long they should patrol the border. Nor did he ask for status updates, reports, or check-ins.

Which meant Vince was free to wander aimlessly on either side of the border, so long as he patrolled it. For a month.

Then he'd write up a letter to Al, send it from a town hub, and be off on the way to the south.

No fuss, no muss.

Petra lowered herself, bringing her head down to the same height as his own at his side.

Turning his head, he regarded the soldier ant. She'd neither said nor done anything out of the ordinary since she'd watched himself and Meliae.

"Something you need to say, Petra?" Vince asked her, his head turning to the front again.

Ranging out ahead of them, Fes was running point. Meliae was walking rear guide with a locked and loaded rifle.

"This one would know what your plans are with her," Petra asked quietly. Her helmet gave her voice a hollow echo.

"Not sure I understand your meaning. My plans are fairly simple. Take you home, get you situated, do the summer market, hunker down for winter. We'll be cutting it close at this rate, but we don't exactly have a choice."

Vince could see in the distance up ahead the trees were starting to thin out. They hadn't taken this route previously, so it was new territory.

By his request, they normally traveled at night and camped in as secluded a spot as possible during the day.

They were doing everything they could to limit the possibility of being spotted. By anyone.

Today, they'd changed it up so they could cross the expanse ahead of them during the night.

"But what of this one?" Her armored fist made a soft thump as she struck her torso.

"I don't understand. The same as Fes and Meliae. Live, be happy, try to survive in this shithole of a world," Vince said it offhandedly. He was distracted by the fact that up ahead the tree line wasn't just thinning, it was actually gone.

And there was a smell in the air that rose the hair on his neck.

"This one understands."

"Good, get your rifle out. We've got a change in landscape up ahead and I smell smoke. Too early to be cooking food."

Turning his head, Vince made eye contact with Meliae and motioned at his side.

Up ahead, Fes had stopped behind a large tree trunk.

Creeping up beside her, he watched as she lifted a hand.

Somewhere between two and three hundred yards distant, he could see what looked like a village. It was settled against a hillside. To his eyes, it had the look of something that splintered from a larger settlement.

Planned civilization.

Wooden buildings had been built and clustered closely together. A single avenue running from the main road in the distance brought them trade and traffic.

Truth be told, it looked like it could easily hold a hundred citizens. Vince could imagine it as a peaceful place.

If it weren't for the fighting in the streets and around the buildings.

Everywhere, there were groups of soldiers and villagers battling one another.

Vince frowned, his brow furrowing as he concentrated on the scene.

"This one thinks that this is... not correct," Petra said.

He spared the woman a glance before he turned his head back to the battle.

"In what way?" Vince asked. It hadn't looked quite right to him either, but he couldn't put a finger on it.

"They fight more aptly than the soldiers. They are also well armed, though without armor. They are not what they seem. At least to this one, that is how they appear."

Now that she'd said it, Vince couldn't help but see it too. The villagers weren't losing; they were systematically driving the soldiers apart. Losses weren't piling up, but it was obvious that the weapons were breaking through armor, and it was only a matter of time.

"Right. Executive decision time. Unsling rifles and keep ammo counts. I'd like to retrieve as much brass as we can. Start shooting at villagers when ready. Fire at will. We're in the Kingdom of Washington, so I'm going to assume these soldiers are lawful in their business here.

"Fes, I'd like you to remain vigilant and on watch. They could just as easily send someone our way to take care of us as ignore us," Vince explained, pulling his Springfield from the saddle holster.

Fes grunted while unhitching her blade. She took a few steps away from the rest of the group and rolled her shoulders.

Vince found himself thankful for the time they'd spent practicing shooting on the trip. It hadn't taken very long for everyone to get fairly acquainted with their new weapons.

"I'd mark it at something like two hundred yards. Petra?" Vince asked.

Of all of them, she'd proved to be the most versatile with the weapon, and seemed to have a good eye for distances.

"This one dislikes to correct her master, but she would put it at two hundred and fifty." Petra had already lifted her rifle to her eye and was staring down her iron sights.

Vince sat down and lifted his knee. Laying his elbow against the top of his knee, he folded his arm under the barrel of his rifle and gripped his other wrist.

Leaning into the iron sights, he let out a slow breath.

The crack of a rifle shot to his left gave him a jolt. Glancing over, he watched as Petra operated the bolt on her rifle and fired again.

Smothering a nervous smile, Vince lined up the iron sights again. He was no crack shot, but he'd do the best he could at this distance.

Throughout the town, the battle was instantly changing. The soldiers had caught on slower than the villagers, but both sides were aware fire was coming from the tree line.

Squeezing the trigger, he watched as a villager pitched over.

Cycling the bolt, he eased the barrel to the left. A rifle crack went off to his right, followed by another from his left.

Vince sent another bullet downrange and hunted for yet another target.

There were some shots he didn't feel comfortable taking due to the proximity of friendly soldiers.

The last thing he wanted to do was to go blue on blue.

Pulling the trigger, Vince pulled the bolt back to chamber another round.

Gunfire continued around him, and soon Vince lost himself in the simplicity of target finding and firing.

There was a brief period that the sound of swords clashing reached him, but he dismissed it. Fes would have called out if she needed assistance.

What felt like hours passed, and Vince found he couldn't identify any other targets.

"I've got a clear board. Anyone got eyes on?" Vince asked.

A crack of a rifle to his left was the only response.

"This one has no enemies in sight now."

"Nothing over here. I get the impression quite a few dove into buildings. Using them for cover."

"None stand in opposition of us," Fes growled.

She wasn't fond of the rifles. Vince was sure it went against her sensibilities. He imagined she'd rather have been charging down into the fray than what they had done.

The dead can't feel honor, and only the living care.

Looking to the Orc in question, he found a small cluster of corpses at her feet. Apparently four people had been sent against them and Vince hadn't even noticed.

"You alright, Fes?" Vince called.

The Orc woman bobbed her head, and waved a hand at him. She was moving to the back of the group to rest, he imagined. Putting down four by herself couldn't have been a fun experience.

"Petra, could you pull out the Washington banner and tie it to your spear? Would you mind being my flagbearer? Eventually they're going to send people this way. If we don't remain, they'll just send people after us, and I'd rather not have to be dodging people all day. Meliae, check on Fes?" Vince requested.

"Of course, Sweetling," Meliae purred at him.

"This one obeys."

Vince nodded his head and began cycling the bolt, the unspent ammo being ejected.

Looking to the right, he found a pile of brass casings. Doing a quick search and count, he was able to locate one for every shot he took.

Shouldering his rifle, he went about collecting the brass from everyone and putting them in the container they were using to hold them.

"Patrol. Three; two grunts, an officer," Fes called out.

Vince didn't react; he'd been expecting it. Soon enough, they'd get an idea on what had happened here and be able to continue on with their stupid patrol.

Three young men dressed in Washington colors closed within ten yards.

"Hail. Lieutenant Wallace, Washington army. F—"

"Vince. Ranger. What was going on down there, Wallace?" interrupted Vince.

"Oh. They were a forward operating base for Portland. They'd cleared the town, and moved an entire regiment in."

"Cleared the town?" Meliae asked.

"Eliminated all the inhabitants. One of the men had family here; it's how we found out there was a problem when we stopped in for a routine patrol. Became a real clusterfuck of street fighting from there. Honestly, I don't think we would have survived if you hadn't come along."

The lieutenant seemed ill at ease. Something was bothering him.

Vince scratched at his cheek.

Bold plan to take an entire village. Good plan, though. Having a village like this as an operating base would have provided critical information about troop movements coming down the main road.

"I take it war has been declared?" Vince asked.

"Yes. A week and a half ago. There've been no main engagements, but a series of raids and skirmishes. We didn't expect to see them so deep in our own territory," said Wallace, shaking his head.

Vince said nothing to that but waved at the soldier instead. "With that being said, I'll leave you to your work."

Turning, Vince started to turn away.

"A moment, Ranger. There's a standing order to tell all Rangers to report to the capital," Wallace said quickly.

"I'm on special dispensation by the Portland guild authority —"

"That's him, then," said one of the line soldiers.

"So it is. If you're the one who was sent on border patrol, I've received special orders for you. You're to report to the capital immediately. I'm to report having spoken with you directly about this matter immediately with the Portland guild authority," Wallace said, as if reading from an actual order sheet.

Vince grunted at that.

So much for getting out of here.

"Fine. Got it. We'll be heading there next," Vince said, completing his turn and walking back into the woods.

Petra fell in beside him. Just on the inside of the tree line, he found Fes with Meliae beside her. The Orc was slumped against the base of a tree and had one hand pressed to her bloody side.

"Damn it, Fes," Vince cursed, moving over to her quickly and kneeling down.

"Bad, but not life threatening. Not bleeding badly," Fes grumbled through clenched teeth.

Meliae looked from the Orc to Vince, but said nothing. She didn't need to.

"Alright. We camp here until you're able to ride. We'll hit the guild hub at the capital, then head for the castle."

"The guild hub first?" Meliae asked, her hands laying on top of Fes's. There was a soft glow playing back and forth between their hands.

"Yeah. There's something wrong with the whole situation and it's getting worse. Looks like this'll be a lot more work than I planned on. We'll check in with the hub, get an idea of their take on it, go from there," Vince said. He gestured at Fes. "What do you think?"

The Dryad pursed her lips and her eyes slowly became a solid green. A full minute passed before she responded.

"Deep. Pretty bad, actually. Thankfully it isn't fatal or even life threatening, and I've been working on it.

"She'll need rest. I can continue to help mend it, and keep it clean, but it'll take some work on my part. That and close proximity. Rest on her part," replied the Dryad.

"Right. We'll get to the guild hub, get a room elsewhere, bunker down to heal up, send a message to our own guild hub, and Petra and I will meet Al," Vince murmured, giving Fes a smile when her eyes met his own.

"We'll get you put to rights, Fes, then we'll get back home. I think I've adventured enough for a while."

Fes gave him a pained smile and a small nod of her head.

Chapter 13

Vince was pretty happy with their progress. They'd made it into the capital unchallenged. Getting into the Ranger hub wouldn't be as easy, though. The guild had taken the old regional airport as its base of operations.

Sitting smack dab in the middle of the airstrip was the guild hub, with a wide view of everything around it. It was a squat, ugly building made of heavy stone and arrow slits that a rifle could fire through.

It'd been built as the frontier hub, meant to be the end cap for the guild.

Of course, that was before Vancouver had been resettled in the north. Now it just served as a paranoid reminder of a darker period.

Walking down the road that led straight up to the main gate, Vince took it slow. Fes wasn't terribly mobile right now. Meliae was doing everything she could to keep the Orc warrior's wounds together and mending.

Her power had been far greater for him, since he was her tree. Fes was merely another humanoid.

Both she and the Fes looked worn from the effort.

Before they'd made it halfway down the approach, two things happened: the gates before him opened, and Petra rejoined him.

"This one has arranged accommodations per her master's orders. Does Master wish for the key?" Petra asked, sinking down to his own height.

"No. Thanks, though, Petra. Give it to Meliae. They'll need it more than we will. I'm sure we'll end up 'quartered' in the capital building. Guests," Vince muttered.

"This one complies. Armed men and a woman come this way. Does Master believe they are friendly?"

"I sure hope so. Here, Petra, help with Fes. I'll go greet our hosts," Vince said. Sliding his shoulder out from under Fes's arm, he waited for Petra to get into position.

Taking a glance at Fes and then Meliae before he moved off, he felt his guts squirm. She looked a sickly pale green. Her hair was lank and sweat soaked. Meliae had a wan appearance and the look of a plant left too long in the sun.

An older woman with short gray hair and armored in leather stood waiting for him at the entry. She was flanked by two helmeted Rangers with drawn weapons.

"Greetings from the south," Vince called as he approached them. "I'm Vincent, from the Modesto guild hub. May I approach and present my membership card?"

Vince kept walking and pulled out his card between two fingers. Holding it above his head in his right hand, he kept his left hand visible as well.

They looked pretty on edge, and he didn't really want to spook them anymore than he had to.

"Fine," grumped the woman.

Getting within arm's reach, Vince came to a stop and held out his card.

Miss Sourpuss took it from him and inspected it. Flipping it over, she ran her thumb over the markings and symbols that only guild hub leaders seemed to understand.

With a grunt, she handed it back to him. "Good to have you here, Vince. Took you southerners damn long enough to get here. It's been damn near half a year."

That's not right. That's not right at all. Something is seriously wrong here. Trained pigeons don't just... ah.

"Ah, no? I'm on a commission from Al, the hub leader for Portland. I've had my charter enacted and I've been told to report to the capital. Where he's staying with the king," Vince said as smoothly as he could.

It wouldn't do to panic her, and honestly, he wasn't sure how much he could say in their company right now. He glanced at the two Rangers behind her as if to make the point that they were there.

"I see." The iron-haired woman looked behind her and flicked her hand at the two guards. They walked off to one side out of earshot. The hub leader was looking to the side and seemed lost in contemplation.

"I was wondering if you could answer a question, hub leader?" Vince asked, sliding his membership card back into his vest.

"Name's Macy. What is it?" she asked, not taking her eyes from the ground beside her.

"In Portland, all the Rangers have been sent away on duties, missions, or long-range reconnaissance. The hub is all but deserted. Would you happen to be experiencing a similar problem, or something that has isolated you?"

It was a stretch, but Vince felt like he had a fairly solid grasp on the situation now. Al was the reason for this pit of shit up to his neck.

"What? I... yes. We've had no contact with the south for too long. Not even the normal requests for tax reports," said Macy. Her lips turned down into a severe frown.

"I see. I believe our situations are linked. You are of course aware that Portland and Washington are at war now?"

"What? That can't... no. Perhaps I've played right into their hands," whispered the woman. "I ordered the fort sealed up and only resources and members are allowed in or out. A few of our numbers left and never returned, so we stopped taking on commissions. I thought we were being hunted, but... I never thought they'd go to war."

"I am of course not a hub leader, Macy, but I would imagine you have a spy or two in your midst. I'd also wager, given the situation, that Al has surrendered control of the Portland hub over to Washington in a back-room deal.

"This is of course guesswork, but... it seems like the situation has been escalated. If I were in your shoes, I'd order the immediate withdrawal of all supplies, personnel, and anything of value. Tonight, even. Before troops can be brought in to surround the guild house after it's reported that I visited you."

Macy looked up and met his eyes with her own. Slowly, she nodded her head as she came to a conclusion.

"If you have anything you need, best you take care of it today," Macy said with finality.

"Only that you provide two of my number with a temporary room so they can rest for a time. That's all I would ask," Vince requested, gesturing towards the slow-moving trio coming up behind him.

The hub leader followed his gesture with her eyes and then looked back to him.

"Done. Now, if you'll excuse me," Macy said, turning on her heel. She marched back into the fort and disappeared.

Vince turned as the trio came abreast of him. "You have room and board. Petra, give them your sword and spear for safekeeping. I imagine they'll take our weapons anyways when we meet up. Better we don't let them fall into the wrong hands."

Vince unbuckled his saber and draped the belt over Meliae's shoulder.

"Sorry for turning you into a pack mule. Rest and sleep as best as you're able. Get out tonight and follow the plan. We'll meet up with you when we can. Questions?"

Meliae and Fes shook their heads as Petra handed over her weapons to Fes.

"Good, be safe. Petra, are you ready?"

"This one is prepared, Master."

Vince gave Fes a small smile and laid his hand on her shoulder.

The Orc woman's eyes focused on him for a second and she gave him a tired smile.

After a brief second to consider if he should even bother following through with this insanity, Vince set off.

It was several minutes later when Petra coughed into her hand. It was probably the singularly most unsubtle thing he'd ever seen or heard of.

"Yes?" Vince asked as they walked along the street.

"This one would ask you a question, if you would allow it, Master."

"Ask away, on the condition that you don't call me Master for at least fifteen minutes," Vince offered.

Petra's brows furrowed and her lips turned up in a small pout for a fraction of a second.

"This one accepts the terms... Vince."

"Good. Now, questions?"

"This one has watched you couple with the Dryad and the Orc repeatedly. This one understands your goal of impregnating them and finds that end good. Any growing colony has a queen laying eggs constantly.

"Yet there is no queen. No other males. You act the part of the mate, though. This one has very limited knowledge on your species and culture and would ask for information."

Vince could see the capital building of Washington in the distance. All around him was the hustle and bustle of civilians and soldiers.

No one would hear anything they said to each other in this madness. Just another conversation in a mob.

"Fes is... my first wife. Meliae is my second. There are no other males and never will be. There is only me. I'm afraid this isn't normal for human culture, either. We're kinda making this up as we go," Vince admitted, his eyes sweeping the crowd.

"This one thinks she understands. How did Vince take Fes and Meliae as wives?"

"I beat Fes in a fight and purchased Meliae."

"Yes. This one was also beaten and collared. This one is then your third wife. This one will strive to become your first wife. When would Vince like to couple and work towards a child?"

"I—" Vince started.

"Halt!" boomed a voice directly in front of him.

Vince turned his head and found himself looking at a patrol of guards.

Petra will have to wait a bit.

"Vince? Of the Ranger guild?" asked one of the helmeted soldiers.

"Yeah, that'd be me. I take it you're here to escort us to the throne room?" Vince asked.

A heartbeat passed before someone in the patrol responded. Vince was getting pretty tired of addressing faceless helmets.

"Yes. Please fall in with us and we'll escort you to the capital building immediately."

There was no arguing with that statement, and he honestly wasn't sure he could take an entire patrol without getting himself mobbed.

"Lead on," Vince said, walking into the middle of the patrol. Immediately the soldiers closed up around him and began "escorting" him to the building at the end of the main thoroughfare.

Their destination was a pre-Wastes government building that had gone through a number of conversions to turn it into a castle, complete with stone towers and wall.

Beside him, Petra stood up to her full height. With a grunt, she fastened her helmet, pulling the strap tight under her chin. She shrugged her shoulders and flexed her hands.

Petra began systematically cracking an open palm against each piece of her armor, seemingly checking the position and preparedness to receive a blow.

Vince couldn't help but grin at his soldier as she prepared for battle.

Subtle, she is not.

Vince let his eyes take in the room for a single heartbeat before focusing in on the trio of people seated at a table.

Al was easy to pick out with that smarmy grin and punchable face.

Next to him was an older man dressed in expensive pre-Wastes clothing. He looked like nothing out of the ordinary, and Vince felt like he'd be hard to recognize in a crowd with that mud-brown hair and those turd-colored eyes of his.

Which was amusing, since Vince expected him to be the king.

Across from them was a third man, dressed in leather armor and ill at ease. He was only a bit more memorable with blue eyes instead of brown.

Judging on the color of his uniform, as that was the only thing it could be, it was clear this man was a representative of the Kingdom of Portland.

No one rose from their seats, and all three men viewed Vince as if he were something to be scraped off a boot and tossed off the path.

"Reporting as requested, hub leader," Vince said, staring at a point between Al and who he was assuming was the king of Washington.

"Of course you are. Do you even realize… no, no, you don't. Because you're a fool. A stupid fool," Al seethed, his face turning a bright red as he spoke. "Running around the border without a proper route, doing nothing at all, I'm sure. Nothing other than fucking your little playthings."

Vince blinked, collecting his thoughts. Without meaning to, he began to reach out empathically to everyone in the room and just outside of it.

Behind him in the hall he could feel Petra, annoyed and nervous. The two guards with her were feeling the same damn way.

The three in the room with him were angry. Very angry. Murderously so.

Vince had to keep himself from turning his head to the left when he felt a fourth mind against the wall.

A shielded mind.

I see you, Seville.

"We were patrolling the border as you instructed. While I admit the majority of the duty was uneventful, we did come across a battle. As I'm sure you've already read the report, I feel it pointless to repeat the details," Vince said slowly. "Otherwise, we've followed your orders to the letter while maintaining the *neutrality* of the Ranger guild."

The last sentence Vince said while turning his head to stare directly into Al's eyes.

Al's spine straightened at that, taking in a slow, audible breath.

"We appreciate your services in that regard, Ranger," the king interrupted. "You're right of course, and we understand your wish to remain neutral while maintaining the peace at the same time."

Vince turned his eyes on the king and nodded his head slightly. "Just as I slew the bandits in Portland, I slew what I believed were unlawful townsfolk in Washington. The Ranger guild is to remain neutral."

The ambassador nodded his head once to that, nearly at the same time the king did. Al, on the other hand, looked like he'd wound himself up to a boiling point.

"I'll have you flogged and flayed —" Al started.

"Where in the charter do you have that authority? As I stated previously, I followed your orders to the best of my ability, within the stated orders I was given," Vince said without emotion.

Al slammed his hand down against the arm of his chair and lifted his other hand to point at Vince.

"Quite right, Ranger," the king boomed. Al said nothing, but Vince could clearly see his words were only restrained by his teeth.

Vince said nothing and waited. He'd need to be dismissed by either the king or the hub leader.

"You'll remain here in the capital for a time. I'd like to speak with you at length about your time on the border," Al said slowly.

As he spoke, Vince could feel the anger and hate oozing from Al's mind, and a slow-building sense of satisfaction and glee.

"We'll have a room arranged for you here in the castle." With that, Vince, felt the finality in the man's mind.

He's going to have us killed tonight. Fuck this. Being a Ranger isn't worth dying over. If they want to kick me out for not following the rules, fine.

"I'll—" Vince started, but was interrupted by the doors behind him swinging open.

Turning his head, Vince saw a squad of armed men lead Petra into the audience hall.

"These men will show you to your quarters. We'll speak more in the morning," the king explained. Turning his head to Al, the king started up a different conversation.

There was no point in resisting. Both he and Petra had been frisked and checked for weapons by the guards who had received them at the door.

Vince felt naked without his blade, but felt better that he'd given it to someone for safekeeping.

Even without it, though, he knew he was a match for any two men here, and Petra perhaps three.

Being unarmed didn't make a fight impossible, but it made it damned nearly so.

"This way... sir," muttered a helmeted guard.

Vince said nothing, but took his place next to Petra in the middle of the squad. They set off as soon as the guards closed around behind him.

Petra's helmeted head swiveled to peer down at him. Without any response from him, Petra turned her face back to the guards ahead of them.

Minutes ticked by as they walked onward, and upwards. They climbed quite a number of stairs until it felt like they were probably in the tallest tower in the keep.

The hell am I, a princess in need of rescue?

Reaching a floor that seemingly had no further stairs to take, they turned to a door on the left.

Cold iron covered most of the door in strips, giving it the appearance of being an iron door with wood, rather than a wooden door with banded iron.

"Invoke your slave collar and order your slave into this room and that she not leave it under any condition," came an echoing voice from inside of the guard's helmet.

"Petra, by the slave collar that binds you, I order you to stay in that room and not leave under any condition," Vince said immediately.

Vince hoped that Petra would be quick enough on the uptake to realize this wasn't what he wanted her to do at all, but that she needed to play along. He'd have to think of a plan so that they could escape.

Apparently he need not have worried, because Petra immediately turned around and marched into the room.

Closing the door behind her, the guards then dropped a bar into place that would keep the door well and truly shut. Then they led him down to the other end of the hallway. Another door greeted him; much like the last one, it had a security bar.

"Get in."

Vince didn't argue and slipped inside, taking a look around. Behind him, the door shut and he heard the bar drop into place.

"Nice cell," Vince muttered. All around him were rich furnishings the like he could only have imagined. The vast majority of it was pre-Wastes and beyond expensive.

He briefly considered lighting it aflame. If they were going to kill him in the night, he could at least make it expensive for them.

Noticing a window at the other end of the room, he walked over to it.

It was big enough to actually crawl out of, but that was where any escape plan would end.

There were no stones beneath the window or to either side. Directly above the window was a flat patch of stone that would prevent one from climbing up and out as well.

"Lovely unobstructed view. Oh, and look. A nice concrete stamp below me to catch me should I jump. Ah, how considerate. It's even located in a private area below me for quiet cleanup. I think I even see lovely red splotches down there. It appears I'm not the first resident."

Petra's helmet-free head swung into his view.

Vince blinked at her, too stunned to respond.

She reached up and tucked her hair behind her ears and then turned her head to the side to face him.

"This one assumed you desired her cooperation until such a time as she could escape," Petra murmured. "She has barricaded the door in such a way that no one will be enter for many hours, then escaped.

"This one would ask her master to move so she could enter to complete her task. While heights do not bother her, this one thinks that a soldier ant clinging to a wall looks out of place in a human settlement."

Vince nodded his head and quickly got out of the way. Petra filled the window as she maneuvered her legs through.

Suddenly breaking out in a smile, he shook his head. He'd forgotten that, much like an ant, she could climb nearly any surface.

"You're a beauty, Petra. I honestly hadn't even begun to think of a way for us to escape."

"This one thanks her master for the compliment to her appearance. Though she would like to ask you further about your preferences, she feels this is not the time."

"Quite right, quite right. Alright, let's see if there's anything small we want to steal, barricade the door, and then figure out what we do next.

"Personally, I'm done with this place. I figure we slip out once sunset comes, get out of town. Swing over to that village, pick up Fes and Meliae, head out to the deep countryside, and lay low for a while."

"This one thinks her master's plan lacks detail, but agrees that as an outline, it's a good start."

Vince scoffed at that, smiling once more. "Between the three of you, I'll never have to worry about being misled, will I?"

Petra merely shook her head.

Chapter 14

Guards had come to check on them. They had discovered quickly the door was blocked. Blocked by very expensive furniture and items that they didn't want to be responsible for. They were forced to retreat rather than earn their king's wrath.

Besides that, nothing happened. Vince spent the evening chitchatting with Petra.

Up to this point, apparently her life had been one of conflict. A neighboring ant colony had provided her with a daily war that had lasted for her entire life.

She described an endless conflict in which she had slain her enemies and watched her colony mates die. Daily.

Ants could repopulate quickly, and losses were absorbed with little difficulty.

Petra was a bit of an abnormality, though. She learned, adapted, survived. Most of those who'd fought with her, or against her, had been too young to know any different. Or too stupid to believe there could be a difference.

Which was why she had left the nest when it was apparent there would be no possibility of recovery. Even if there had been other survivors, they would have probably gone straight into another battle with their neighbor, only to be wiped out.

Vince had become so engrossed in her story that they'd talked about little else.

When the sudden explosion of orange sunlight beat through the open window, Vince was surprised. Sunset had come quickly.

"Dang. Time we got a leg on," Vince said, getting to his feet. "I know we didn't talk much about the plan, but I really can't think of what else I'd add to it. Trying to detail it out would achieve little since we're not sure what to expect."

Petra grunted and checked her helmet on her hip and her bundled armor on the other side. They'd decided that it would be better for them both if she made the descent in only her normal clothes. After a moment, she looked back to him. "This one dislikes it, but agrees."

"Well, with that being said... should I mount you like a horse, or do you carry me?" Vince asked. He wasn't quite sure how Petra planned on getting him down.

"Master will ride this one. She apologizes that this will not be comfortable, and asks that you hold on tightly to her with arms and legs."

"Right," Vince said under his breath.

Petra sidled over to him and lowered herself down. Her ant abdomen lay on the ground and her legs were arranged a little differently to accommodate him getting on.

Reaching out, he laid his hands on her segmented abdomen and leaned forward. Lifting a leg over her, he slid into the space Petra had indicated.

He wrapped his legs around her hips, then reached around and locked his arms around her middle just under her breasts.

"Master, could you please move your ankles higher or lower? This one must shamefully report that you have rested them directly atop an area that would not assist in climbing," Petra said, as she stood up slowly.

Thinking about it, Vince realized he had quite literally pressed his ankles into her nether region. "Sorry, Petra."

Easing up a bit, he managed to move his ankles down further till he found the point where her skin went from human to carapace.

"Better placement, this one thanks you."

Petra started to walk forward and Vince couldn't help but feel amazed. Petra's movement was smooth, her legs working around him as if he weren't even there.

Then they were outside the window and sideways.

Vince managed to keep himself seated and held on to the athletic ant-soldier as she glided along the wall to the back of the building.

Finding himself not enjoying the view, Vince pressed his face into Petra's shoulder blades and took slow breaths.

He could feel his center of gravity change as she maneuvered them along the wall. At times, he swore they were nearly upside down. As quick as could be believed, Vince felt the world right itself underneath him.

"This one reports that she has escaped with her master. Though, she would ask her master to remain seated. She can move more swiftly than he and can get him across the rooftops and out of the city quickly."

Vince nodded his head against Petra's back. "Done. Get us outside the city."

Petra didn't hesitate. They were off in a flash. Vince could feel the air parting around Petra from the speed she put on. His orientation to the world changed as she jumped from building to building.

Didn't even know Waste ants could jump. Normal ants can't.

"Master, this one sees the one called Seville," Petra said as they came to a sudden stop, breaking through his thoughts.

"What? Where?" Vince asked, peering out from around her back.

Lifting an arm, Petra indicated towards what looked like a man and a woman walking down the street.

From this distance, he could certainly believe it was Seville, but it was hard to really confirm that.

"Get us closer."

Petra bunched her legs and bolted. In seconds, they were around the front now and could see Seville's face easily.

It was indeed him, and walking beside him was an elven maiden. She wore a dainty slave collar of northern make, and they looked like they were engaged in a quiet but heated conversation.

The Elf gestured with her hands in short chopping motions while Seville made gentle waves with his own, seemingly soothing her.

They turned down a side street and paused, pulling items from a satchel the Elf had been carrying.

"Masks," Vince said softly as they pressed the items to their faces. It was the only thing it could be. "But why? Let's follow them. Discreetly."

Petra took them straight up the side of a building. Forcing himself not to close his eyes, Vince found they were following them from above.

"This one wonders why they wear a mask," Petra whispered.

"If I could answer that one, we wouldn't have to pretend to be the Hardy Boys," Vince replied.

"Who?"

"Never mind. Kids books my parents gave me."

Vince looked up towards the direction Seville was heading.

"Seems like they're heading to that mansion's rear gate, doesn't it?" Vince said, pointing down at the two below them and the gate ahead.

Beyond the gate was a large four-story mansion that sat squarely in the middle of a large green.

The building was massive in scale and looked like the definition of opulent.

"This one agrees. What does Master wish?" Petra asked.

Vince thought about it, and as he thought about it, he let his senses expand. Seville's mind was still locked up tight, but the Elf was wide open.

Apparently Seville didn't think to tell her about me and my tricks. Which means what he knows about me is a secret to everyone else. So far. Who knows how long that'll last.

The Elf was full of lust, fear, and excitement. Which made no sense. At all.

She was too far for him to pry into her actual thoughts, though.

"Let's... follow for now. If they go inside, maybe we can slip into a room on that fourth floor. Think you can manage it without being seen?"

"This one is not used to subterfuge, but believes she can succeed, Master."

"Right. Let's do it, then."

Vince and Petra watched their prey walk quietly to the gate.

Upon reaching it, a guard materialized at the entrance. Vince hadn't even noticed the dark-outfitted man.

Something changed hands and Seville was allowed to enter with his companion. The gate was surprisingly noiseless on its opening and closing.

Seville walked casually up to the nearest door and entered as if he knew what to expect.

Petra slipped away from the side of the house facing the gate. Moving around to a different side, with a higher wall and a lack of guards, Petra scaled it with ease.

Skittering forward, she carried them across the manicured grounds at a lightning speed. Straight up the side of the mansion she went and into a fourth-floor window.

Inside the room, they found it to be lit by electricity, and was decorated in a similar fashion to the king's "guest room" that they'd been in earlier.

A number of masks, gowns, and men's suits were laid out in various states of inspection across the furniture.

Seeing no enemies, Petra carried them inside.

Sliding off his impromptu mount, Vince moved to the door and pressed his ear to it.

The sound of murmuring voices, laughter, and an occasional high-pitched squeal reached him.

"Sounds like a party," Vince said.

"Master, this one believes we should leave. Whatever this is, it doesn't concern us."

"You're right, of course," Vince said, pulling his ear from the door. "And in the same breath... I need to know what's going on here. Seville knows me in some way. It may be foolish, but if this is a party, he might let his guard down. Enough that I can—well, maybe enough that I can get some answers out of him," Vince finished in a rush. He didn't want to admit that he could ravage a person's mind if he truly put the effort into it.

The one time he'd done it, though, he'd managed to stumble ten feet away and pass out under a bush only to wake up a day and a half later.

He'd killed the bandit he'd been dealing with, and nearly himself.

"As Master wishes. This one will defend you. How should we proceed?"

Vince sighed and looked at the clothes all around them. "I'd say we start by dressing accordingly. The only problem is that I'm pretty sure you're the only soldier ant in the entire state that is collared. Any ideas on how to disguise your race?"

Petra looked down at herself for a moment. Taking up a large ball gown-type of dress, she roughly pulled it down over her clothes. That of course didn't work, so she started to strip out of her clothes while arranging the dress.

While she was going about her business, Vince made short work of finding a suit that'd fit him and got into it.

Looking back to his soldier, he found her wrestling with the dress still.

She had begun to shove the fabric around with her hands. She managed to move it around and over her bundled armor, clothes, and helmet.

Letting go of the fabric, she had somehow managed to get the dress to settle around her in a reasonable fashion without making it obvious she had things hidden in the skirt.

Unfortunately, her ant parts managed to stick out behind her, which Petra noticed when she looked over her shoulder.

Shifting around in the large gown, Petra rose up in height until she was a few inches above six feet.

Her segmented rear end slid into the dress and was no longer visible.

"And what exactly did you do?" Vince asked.

"This one has raised her height to a point that she could pull her rear end in," Petra explained, gathering a vast amount of material in her hands. Then she lifted the dress up in the front.

As she had said, her "rear end," as it were, was now pointing downward towards the ground. Her legs were also closely pressed together, the tips of them creating a three-footed base.

Without meaning to, Petra was also giving him an eyeful.

Vince found himself staring into Petra's slit. It was no longer hidden by the strap of fabric she'd taken to tying across her private parts. Probably lost in the mad pushing and pulling of the dress.

It was interesting that she had a human female's genitals but no legs.

- 120 -

I wonder if it's angled differently for entry? Or childbirth? Wait, do they lay eggs or give live birth? Or are eggs a queen-only thing?

His pants started to get tight as his body reacted to the view.

Petra sniffed as if she were getting a cold, then apparently noticed his silent stare and leaned forward to see what he was seeing.

After a second, she finally noticed her error and dropped the dress down immediately.

Vince only detected the faintest blush color her cheeks. Other than that, she didn't show any outward signs of embarrassment.

Vince had to wonder at her self-control. If he'd been the one showcasing himself to someone, he doubted his response would have been that simple.

Is that true, though? How often do I end up having sex with Fes or Meliae right in front of her?

Becoming an amoral hedonistic savage there, Vince.

Petra smoothed the dress down with her hands. Vince could guess easily that she was trying to find her private parts band without looking like it.

"Can you keep that up? Is it uncomfortable? Can you move around like that? Best to try and test it all out here before we go in there," Vince said, diverting not only himself but what just happened.

Petra blinked and then nodded her head. Slowly, hesitantly, she started moving around the room. Her movements were awkward and robotic.

They'd stand out for sure.

She surprised him, though. Within half a minute since starting, she'd made remarkable progress. What started off as a newborn deer impression quickly became a tall elegant woman.

"Well done. What about backwards? Or bending down? Sitting?" Vince asked.

Petra nodded her head again and then pivoted in place and moved backwards. Oddly enough, it seemed that was easier than forward for her.

Moving over to a chair that had been placed against a wall, she lightly sat down.

"Sitting is not easy, but this one believes this looks as if she is sitting. Yes?" Petra asked, looking down at herself.

"It looks like you're sitting, sure. You're not?"

"No. This one will not show you, either."

"Of course. Okay, what about kneeling or sitting on the ground?"

"Shouldn't be a problem. The dress is long, and without the distance to the ground, it'll stretch considerably further. This one feels that she is ready to don a mask and will be unremarkable. She is excited to interact with humans on a human level. Though she believes that everyone here is accompanied by a slave, so she may need to play that role instead. What race should this one be if someone asks?"

"I... that's a good question. Good work with the dress as well, by the way. You're pretty tall right now and you've got an athletic build. We could try to pass you off as an Amazon? I've seen a few of them. They look fairly human but have increased strength and speed. Not to mention lifespan. Straight out of the fantasy books."

Petra nodded her head, her hands moving through all the masks laid out on a desk nearby.

She pulled a mask free that looked almost like a helmet. It was a single piece decorated in geometric patterns that covered from the nose to the back of the head, leaving the mouth and jaw completely free.

Pulling it over her head, being very careful to tuck her antennae in with her hair, she adjusted the strap and then looked to him.

"Very Petra-like choice," Vince said. Looking back to the masks, he picked up one that covered his eyes, nose, and forehead. It also had an attached wig of dark black curly hair that would help disguise him.

Pulling it down over his head, he looked to the tall soldier woman and smiled.

"Last but not least, you can call me Master, but you'll need to drop the whole 'this one' thing for a time. It's... a very noticeable speech pattern."

Petra's mouth turned into a frown before she nodded her head.

"I... will obey."

"Grand. Shall we?" Vince said, holding out his arm.

"Yes," Petra said, laying her hand on his forearm.

Opening the door, they stepped into a hallway and could already hear the distant sounds of merrymaking and the smell of food.

"Maybe we should use the window," Vince murmured.

Petra shook her head and then led him down the hallway. "Th—I could not have gotten us down in these clothes. This area back here has the strongest scent and sound coming from it."

As they turned the corner, they found a servant's stairwell.

"Just how good is your sense of smell, anyways?" Vince asked, peering down the dark stairwell.

"Very good. This one can tell that there is a significant number of people down there. All of them eager to engage in sex. It reeks of wanton desire."

Vince snorted at that and began walking down the stairs. "Stop saying, 'This one,' remember? And you're telling me you can tell when someone is horny?"

"All creatures put off scents when they desire sex. Even humans. It's just harder to detect with some species. Your scent is easier for me to track, as I know it well."

Vince didn't say anything to that. His thoughts were running around in an embarrassed flutter.

He couldn't help but wonder if she'd caught on to the fact that he'd be more than happy to take eyefuls of her when she changed or bathed.

"This one, that is, I am always very flattered at your attention. I wasn't sure if you could overlook my obvious non-humanoid body."

Vince grunted as they turned around into the next flight of stairs, ignoring the door, and heading down again.

"Your flesh is warm and soft to the touch. It's certainly firmer than human skin, but it's skin. It's... different, for sure, but at least you're not a Centaur. Not sure I could ever go down that road," Vince murmured, taking the steps slowly.

"I... do not understand."

"Ergh. Well, you have a human woman's genitalia."

"Correct. My caste can never be a queen. We reproduce too slowly."

"Yeah, well, a Centaur doesn't have a woman's anatomy. Horse."

They turned again down another stairwell. Lights, smells, and sounds were quite vibrant now. Vince was pretty sure they'd be entering the party at the end of these stairs.

"I see. I can understand how that could be off-putting. Your qualifying factor is human genitalia?"

"Not exactly, but I don't want to feel like I'm having sex with a horse, either."

"You're strange."

"Yeah, I know. Right, then. Let's do this." Vince stepped into a huge ballroom filled with men, women, and Wastelanders in masks.

Chapter 15

The gathering had the look of an elegant masquerade party. Conversations were ongoing everywhere as people ate and drank.

Both food and drinks were being shuttled around the room on platters as well as at tables laid strategically throughout the room.

Decorations were heavy but simple. Streamers, banners, and all sorts of things dangled from everything and anything.

Hanging from the wall opposite the main entry was a banner that read, "Stockholders and Board Members Sixty-Seventh Annual Meeting."

"Is this a company or...?" Vince let the question hang as his eyes swept down from the banners to the floor again.

Lining the walls were a strange and out of place collection of chairs, benches, pedestals, railings, and pillows.

A waiter passed by and offered them glasses of champagne, which they both accepted as to not seem further out of place.

"By the door," Petra said after the man had left.

Vince looked to where Petra had indicated. Understanding dawned on him.

The bright blood-red armor of slave auction guards stood watch at the door, checking everyone for weapons.

Every guest was handed a "gift box" as well. They were rectangular and a foot long by a half a foot wide, with only about three inches in height.

"Right. That explains that, then.

"I wonder where —" Vince stopped talking when he felt, more than saw, Seville and his closed mind. Trying to look in that direction as inconspicuously as he could, he found Seville and his Elf lounging in a set of chairs in the corner.

Neither had partaken of food or drink, and both seemed like they were waiting for something. They made no effort to join the party or to mingle in any way or form.

Whatever they were here for, it was business and only business.

"Goodness me, where ever did you get such a specimen like her?" slurred a man at Vince. He'd somehow managed to stumble his way over when Vince wasn't looking.

"Ah, no idea. I simply purchased her through an acquaintance. She hasn't deigned to tell me where the rest of her people are."

"And you br-uuuhhhggh-brought her here? You know the rrrrrrrules. You must have trained her hard." The drunk emphasized the word hard. "You renting her?"

"'Fraid not. Been training her diligently for myself alone."

"Pity. Here, you don't have a present. You can have mine, I'll go get another," mumbled the drunk, handing Vince his wrapped gift from the guards.

Turning around, the man trundled off towards a table filled with glassware. Trailing along behind him was a short woman in a toucan mask. She topped out at four feet tall.

"Short." Petra's comment was curt, her voice hard.

"Very short. Probably a gnome, dwarf, or something of that nature. Thinking maybe we should get out of here. This isn't what I was expecting, and I don't think we'll get anything useful out of it."

"Agreed. Let's—"

"Everyone, may I have your attention!" boomed a voice.

"We're leaving. Now," Vince said, and turned around, only to find the stairwell now guarded by slave auction guards.

In fact, looking around, he saw nothing but guards at every window and door. *And the trap closes?*

Vince forced a smile on his face as he led Petra forwards toward the voice.

"We're surrounded, Master."

"Yeah. No way out but pushing on. Now smile. We're supposed to be here, remember?"

"It's about time we get our first event underway," called the same voice from earlier. Vince now saw a man dressed in bright red finery standing atop a table.

"Now, you all received the rules prior to this. We'll be selecting contestants at random and proceeding from there. Once we've finished the events, we'll be proceeding to our strategy meeting."

A few people booed at that, which got a chuckle from the rest of the crowd.

"Now, now. I know we're here for fun and games, but we do have to conduct business. We'll be holding an auction after the meeting for those who remain. We've been collecting these specimens since the start of the year. I promise you, they'll be the finest you've seen."

At that, a general cheer went up around the room.

"Contestants will be randomly selected by the judges. Contestants who participate will receive a special voucher for a free purchase at any of the local or hub markets up to one thousand standards."

Another round of cheers came from the audience.

"Winners from each contest will receive a voucher for ten thousand standards at any local, hub, or guild markets. This can be used on multiple purchases or just one. Contestants may participate more than once, and win more than once."

A huge cheer went up at that.

"Back to the rules!" shouted the man energetically, holding up his arms. "As this is a demonstration of training, knowledge of your slave, and your slave's knowledge of you, all slaves who were brought with you must be here voluntarily. This will be authenticated when our handlers remove their collars to participate in the games. If they're not here of their own free will, we'll find that out during the removal process. You'll be fined five thousand standards, have your slave taken, and your membership revoked for three months."

They can remove collars? I thought they were permanent.

The crowd as a whole didn't react to that. Apparently these weren't new punishments for rule breakers.

"Everyone who isn't participating should please now wear their red button. You're welcome to remain as part of the audience, of course.

"Judges, please select the contestants for our first event."

Vince glanced around and noticed a good third of the audience had suddenly attached a red safety pin button to their clothes.

"I guess we're possible participants, then."

"This—I'm confident we could succeed. It would be good to have one of those vouchers. We could purchase a number of people and add them to our colony. If possible, we should participate in every event."

Vince checked himself mentally.

Meliae had been bought for sixty standards, if memory served. At that rate, with the prize money, he could buy something like a hundred and fifty of her.

Using his own money, both in the bank and buried, he could purchase three hundred Meliaes.

That didn't even include selling his trophy room.

Vince suddenly felt like the worst of the worst. He'd never even considered using his wealth to simply purchase the freedom of others.

"You're right. Let's hope it's something we can compete in without giving the game away. Even the participation money would go pretty far."

A woman in a bright red tuxedo sauntered past and then did a double take to look at Petra.

"You and your owner are in the first event. Head up to the front," drawled the masked judge.

"That was easy," Vince said to Petra as they made their way to the front.

Soon enough, thirty men and women and their slaves were brought up onto a stage. On that stage was one set of chairs. Vince hadn't noticed the stage earlier, much to his consternation.

What else had he missed?

"Slaves, please exit the stage to the rear to be checked by our handlers. Owners have a seat. While they're going through that mandatory check, I'll explain the event."

Vince took a seat and looked around him.

Apparently they'd selected fifteen men and fifteen women. All the women were in the chairs to the right, the men to the left.

He couldn't tell, but they all had the look of younger people as well.

"Our first event is straightforward. How well does your slave know you— without seeing you?

"That's right, ladies and gentlemen. Welcome to the exhibition round. We're starting it early this time since it took so long last year. Hopefully you've all brought better contestants this year.

"You know what that means. Men, unzip your flies and pull it out, ladies, hike up those dresses, and drop your panties."

Howls of laughter and cheers of encouragement came from the audience. Everyone on the stage started laughing as well as they did as instructed.

After a single heartbeat of hesitation, Vince undid his belt, unzipped his fly, and pulled himself free of his underwear.

His unhardened length lay against his thigh. Feeling his heart start to race, Vince felt like he wanted to run off the stage screaming.

Money to buy people. Money to buy people. Doing this for money to buy people who would be forced to do worse than this.

"As a reminder, no talking. This includes laughing, moaning, coughing, and all noise that you could think of. Your slaves are being instructed that they can use any means they want to distinguish who their owner is, providing that they're only allowed to touch your privates!"

Vince let out a slow breath as he tried to focus on anything other than the fact that a crowd full of people were going to watch at least fifteen women possibly fondle his junk.

A thousand standards could easily get thirty people if I kept the price low. Thirty people. Ten thousand would be even more.

"Okay! I've gotten word from our handlers all slaves have been checked out and they've all gotten the go-ahead. First up, contestant six!"

Being led up to the stage was a huge, hulking lion-man. He looked as if he'd been carved from stone rather than made of flesh and bone.

"Now remember, everyone, no noise at all. Our stage judge, the lovely lady in red here, will be keeping our time and rules enforcement."

The judge held up a hand and the room went silent. The lion-man's head swung back and forth as if he were trying to clear his head.

"Ready, set, go!" yelled the judge, dropping her hand, and with her other hand she clicked a stopwatch.

The lion-man was led to the first woman. Vince realized that the chairs the women had were different and could be reclined so that they could thrust their hips out easier.

For precisely what he imagined was happening now with the lion-man. The maned Wastelander had dropped down to all fours and shoved his head up between the woman's knees.

Vince couldn't see it very well from his spot, but he could hear it. A deep snuffling and sniffling could be heard. Apparently he was relying on his sense of smell to determine if this person was his owner.

In a room with this many people, though, and so many various scents, he wasn't sure how successful he'd be.

While a Beastman would have superior senses over a human, they weren't quite as good as an animal's.

A few seconds passed as the woman shook her head a bit back and forth to whatever else the lion-man was doing.

Apparently this wasn't his owner, as he pulled back and moved over to the next chair to repeat the process.

Vince watched without really paying attention, and let his gift fill his senses.

The lion-man was easy enough to pick out. He was eager to find his master. As fast as possible.

The contestants were a mixture of fear, excitement, and lust.

The crowd seemed full of mirth and desire.

And then there was Seville. With that closed mind of his, he was the easiest to pick out in this mob.

His elven companion was just as easy to pick out, as she was right next to him.

"There we have it, folks! Number six, you can't take her yet. We need her for the rest of the competition. Judge, what was our time?" called the announcer.

Looking back to the right, Vince found the lion-man had found his owner. Then apparently had nearly lifted her out of her chair upon doing so.

"Three minutes, thirty-two seconds."

"Folks, I think that's a record. This is usually one of our longer events, for you new attendees. Good job, contestant six."

The lion-man was led back off the stage, but anyone could tell he clearly felt proud of himself.

They're all here voluntarily. I wonder how that was managed.

"Next, contestant twenty-six."

A blindfolded beauty of a woman walked up on the stage, her heels clacking on the wood. She was brought to the men's side of the stage and she stood a few feet from the furthest man down.

Vince was much further down and only two seats from where the women's side started.

He started to feel an odd tickling at the base of his brain and his abdomen. In that moment, he knew exactly what type of Waster she was. As quickly as he could, he tightened up his control over his own mind with his gift.

Succubus.

Vince had only dealt with one once, and that had been from afar. They were straight out of horror stories and matched them perfectly.

Sex demons that only wanted to drain your life force away through sex. Not as terrifying as a Revenant or a Wraith, but certainly up there.

Not to mention that they had an unexplained yet well-documented effect.

They made men very horny. To the point of insanity, if they wanted. He could fight it fairly well with his gift, but he wasn't immune.

Vince felt the mad stirrings of primal lust pushing at his loins. His shaft hardened and stretched with need, demanding that he jump the Succubus and have his way with her.

"Ready, set, go!" yelled the judge when it was clear the announcer wouldn't be responding, enthralled like every other man in the audience.

The Succubus dropped down to her knees in front of the first man and inhaled his cock in one motion. Working her head back and forth furiously, she hummed and moaned in pleasure.

The man, on the other hand, was locked in place by her charms, both physical and metaphysical.

The Succubus slammed her face into him after what seemed like only seconds.

Cooing happily, the Succubus held him in place as he came into her mouth. Halfway through finishing she pulled her head back and pushed him back into his pants.

"Not him," said the Succubus, wiping her lips with a finger. Gliding over to the next man and latching onto his shaft with her mouth. Immediately she started to pump her head up and down.

Vince watched as she literally worked her way down towards him. Each man never took much longer than the first, and it seemed it would be more of a matter of luck if her owner was closer to the front or the back.

"Here he is!" she called, hopping up to her feet, her heels clacking loudly. Vince had actually started to space out while watching her.

She'd managed to make her way through ten men before she'd found her owner. As quickly as it had come on everyone, the Succubus's aura fell away.

"Uh... what? Ah, yeah. Yeah. Time, judge?" asked the announcer, somewhat at a loss.

"Three minutes, thirteen seconds," said the judge.

"There, there you have it, folks. Our curr-current leader. Good, good job, twenty-six."

Pressing a hand to his head, the announcer took a deep breath.

"Sorry, folks, I should have warned everyone about that one. I forget how powerful they are until they step up. Though this one was particularly strong, and well trained. Extremely well trained to get that level of control.

"My compliments to the trainer."

The owner waved a lazy hand at the narrator, the Succubus having returned to his crotch and needily slurping at him.

"Alright, let's uh, let's get her off the stage and get the next contestant."

Vince stopped paying attention as another Beastman stepped up onto the stage. Apparently this event was well known, and many had prepared particularly for this one.

Instead of watching, Vince stared at what was going on but didn't see it. He let his mind float through everyone around him and tried to learn what he could.

If he did it passively, and only encountered whatever a person was thinking, they'd never even know.

Most everyone he encountered were investors, or stockholders, in the "Auction House," as it was called in their minds. A few happened to be board members, but they were few and far between.

The event continued onward. Nothing as exciting as the Succubus happened again, but by wide margins, the dominant class of slaves selected for this event were all Beastmen and Beastwomen.

As he started to sift through another investor's thoughts and memories, he found himself staring at Petra.

Like every other contestant, she had a blindfold over the eye-holes of her mask. Blonde hair peeked out from the back of her mask. It was longer than he'd remembered. She'd been letting it grow out.

Vince really looked at her now. She'd been there with him all day, of course, but he really hadn't looked at her closely.

The dress she'd pulled on was a warm gray, with very thin straps, and emphasized her chest without putting it on display. She definitely had more to her figure than Fes did.

Her waist and hips weren't as much of an hourglass as Meliae was, but she definitely had a womanly curve to her.

Where Petra lacked a bit on her figure, she made up with it through how she carried herself and her demeanor. A predator's grace and a hunter's nature.

" — go!" said the stage judge.

Vince jumped at the suddenness of the shout. He'd been so busy eying Petra, he hadn't noticed her introduction.

Petra didn't bother turning to the man in front of her. Instead, her head swiveled around to face straight towards Vince.

Flowing down the line, she moved like a wolf tracking a target. Her head stayed focused on him with her even, steady strides carrying her on.

The judge and announcer both looked shocked as Petra closed in on him.

Turning her body towards him, she leaned forward over his lap, inadvertently giving him a deep view of her cleavage.

She took in a loud deep inhalation of him from an inch away. Not touching him, merely smelling him.

Dropping down to a kneeling position, she got in close to his member. Her nose bumped into the tip, causing her to jerk her head back.

Then she leaned in again and pressed her face to his hilt. Taking a slow deep breath through her nose, she pulled her head back, scenting all along his length.

In response, Vince couldn't help it when his entire shaft grew as hard as a rock and jerked against her face.

Petra set her hands to his hips and then leaned in again. Her lips nipped at the base and top of his balls.

Feeling those soft pink lips on him, his member jerked again, the tip pressing against her cheek for a second.

Vince watched in fascination, wondering what in the hell she was doing since it was clear she knew it was him.

Petra breathed out against him, her warm breath cascading down over his body. Opening her mouth, she pressed her lips to the side of him, moving upwards as her tongue trailed along from the inside.

Reaching the tip, she pulled back from him and let her tongue slide free. Using her tongue, she lightly lapped at the thick liquid drizzling out of him.

A particularly large glob oozed out. Finding it with her tongue, she deftly took it from his head and drew it into her mouth.

Turning her head to the side, she looked like she was trying to memorize the taste. Like she was savoring it.

Then she turned back to him and wrapped her lips around the head, her tongue pressing at the tip and then encircling it.

Slowly, deliberately, she moved her head forward. Vince watched as inch after inch passed through her lips. All the while her tongue moved slowly, slathering the underside of him as she did so.

Reaching the extent that she could go, her nose pressed to his lower stomach, his length down her throat, she began to pull herself back.

Her cheeks became hollow as she sucked hard on him, her lips tightening up as she pulled on him.

Vince shivered a little. This wasn't the hungry affair that Meliae's affection was. That incessant need to be dominated by him and used. Or the deliberate and aggressive battle that Fes made them, to fight and dominate him, only to blow him.

This was a blowjob meant for him and only his pleasure. That his pleasure would bring her pleasure.

She was aiming for his psyche as much as his physical need.

Her hands remained pressed to hips. Her breathing rate slowly picked up to match the speed of her mouth.

Every downward push was a little faster than the last, and every time she pulled back, she moved a touch quicker.

A minute in and she was moving at a smooth and steady pace, her tongue rolling and pressing to anything it could reach inside her mouth. Her lips reaching for his entire length every time, right up to the point that there was nothing left to take.

That unceasing rhythm was perfect, and Vince was so close to finishing in her mouth.

As if sensing the change in him, Petra began to pause once she'd gotten him down her throat and would purposefully swallow his length, her throat tightening up around the head as her muscles contracted.

Almost as if she were begging him to orgasm at that moment. To simply unload down her throat.

Unable to do anything else, and barely keeping quiet, Vince felt his body flex as he started to climax.

Petra slid him down her throat and held him there as his girth swelled, then spasmed.

After each spurt of his seed, Petra made a loud — deliberately so — gulping noise. As he finished with a final shot, her throat contracting with the motion of her devouring him, she lifted a hand above her head and indicated to Vince.

"Time! Two minutes, ten seconds."

Petra reached up with her other hand and unfastened her blindfold. Crystal blue eyes stared up at him through the eyeholes of her mask as she swallowed again.

She eased her head back, sucking roughly on him, causing him to shudder all over. Pushing him back down into the depths of her mouth, she swallowed once more. Her eyes watched him the entire time, boring into his own eyes. With a small smile curling the edges of her lips, she eased him out of her mouth and then stood up.

"Ah, that's... fantastic. I... well done. Could we get our next contestant up here?" the announced called.

Petra was swiftly led offstage like all the other slaves, leaving Vince alone in his chair to ride his climax.

Chapter 16

Vince missed the next two contestants as he sat in his chair. It wasn't that he didn't care; he was simply still enjoying the physical and mental benefits of what Petra had given him.

What man doesn't enjoy that sort of attention? A liar, that's who.

"And that's it, folks! We don't really even have to check the scores to know who won. Contestant thirteen, with two minutes and ten seconds. Congratulations to her owner.

"Ladies and gentlemen, we'll take a short break before we begin our next event," called the announcer.

Stepping over to Vince, the same man smiled and shook his head. "Impressive. You'll have to tell me how you did that later. Now, in a minute, some of our employees will escort you to collect your voucher. Personally, we recommend you leave it in our care until you leave, but most people still insist on taking it with them. As if we don't have anything better to do than rob them."

"If you don't mind me asking, why leave it with you?" Vince inquired, shifting in his seat.

"Never gotten a voucher before, huh? Must be new. Good for you.

"As to why, it's because it's unsigned. Since they're meant to be used anywhere, they're magically sealed, and little else. Which means whoever has it, owns it.

"Now, if you'll excuse me." The darkly dressed masked man walked away swiftly, leaving Vince still in his chair.

"She really took a toll on you. Sure she wasn't a Succubus too?" came a male voice from behind him. "Come on, let's get your voucher. Your slave is already there. We put her collar back on. Any previous commands you gave her will still be there."

Looking over his shoulder, Vince found a small group of red-uniformed guards.

Standing up, Vince realized he was hanging free. Tucking himself back in, he zipped up his fly and re-buckled his belt.

As he did so, Vince cast his mind about, trying to find Seville again.

Strangely enough, it felt like the man was behind him. Watching him, even.

The Elf was a bonfire of rage and hate, the emotions directed at everyone around her. With the briefest of touches, he looked into her mind and found she was no slave at all.

She was here with Seville voluntarily and wanted to be here.

Her mind started to shift as if she'd noticed his intrusion. Elves were sensitive to him probing a bit more deeply, it would seem.

Now why would they be here, of all places, if she isn't a slave?

Chuckling, the guards started off as soon as it looked like Vince had himself squared away.

Wordlessly, they walked him out of the great ballroom and into a side hallway. From there he was escorted through a few winding corridors and finally into the basement.

Two guards with automatic pre-Wastes weapons waited for them at the bottom of the stairs, in front of a locked and barred iron door.

Apparently they meant business, as those weapons were very rare, and very expensive.

The guards with him turned and immediately frisked him. One took the gift he'd forgotten he was carrying, while the others began checking him inside and out for anything that could be used as a weapon.

"Sorry, security this evening is on high alert. It isn't every day there's enough vouchers in one spot to bankrupt a country. Not to mention we've had reports that that damn terrorist group was planning to hit us tonight," said a guard quietly to him as he rifled through Vince's pockets.

"Not a problem," Vince replied, his mind speeding ahead. "Terrorist group?"

"That 'Free the Wastes' thing. Enslaving monsters is wrong and should be illegal, blah blah. Same song and dance. Next they'll be telling us we can't keep dogs or cats."

"I heard," said another guard as he lifted Vince's pant leg to check his socks and shoes, "that even the king is involved. Apparently he's a sympathizer. Him and that ambassador of his."

The man looking into Vince's jacket scoffed at that and took a step back. "All clean."

Vince could feel Seville and his Elf closing in on them from behind. Glancing over his shoulder, he saw no one.

No one was there. Nothing. Vince could feel them, though.

Could they have figured out it's me? That's farfetched, but... maybe?

Looking ahead again, Vince nodded to the guards and moved forward when they opened the door for him.

Stepping inside, he immediately found Petra waiting in the corner. Her head turned at his entrance and latched on to him. She made no move to join him, however, and merely watched from the corner.

His gift box was handed back over to him with a grunt.

The guards closed the door behind him and remained there on duty.

The room itself had several large black iron safes against a wall and little else other than a desk.

Sitting in front of that desk was a bald, fat man in muted browns with a sweaty face. Watery blue eyes peered at him from amongst the pudgy folds of his face.

"Welcome, welcome. I hear you're the owner. Apparently your lass here put on a show while breaking all previous records."

"That she did," Vince agreed with a plastered-on smile.

"So, here's your voucher, then." The fat man slid a rectangular piece of plastic towards him across the table.

Vince picked it up and flipped it over. The back of it was decorated with multiple authentication markings written in rune script.

There would be no counterfeiting this.

You'd have to have these to make them worthwhile. This single room seems more like a bank vault than...

They're here to rob them. They want the vouchers! They're unsigned and might as well be cash!

Smiling at the fat man, Vince did something he hadn't done in a long time. Instead of passively monitoring thoughts and memories, he pierced the man's mind with a heavy set of thoughts.

Vince's goal was simple. The location of the vouchers and for him to see nothing, hear nothing, and think nothing.

Immediately, the man's eyes glazed over. Then Vince had what he wanted. They were stored in a rectangular box just inside the left-hand drawer, meant to disguise their purpose by looking the part of a simple box that one would see filled with chocolates.

The safes behind him were filled with fake vouchers that would explode upon getting a certain distance from the mansion.

Fatty didn't move or twitch from his place.

"Petra, open the inner left desk drawer and pull out the box," Vince said. Looking down at the box in his hands, he realized it'd probably be wide enough, but not long enough.

As gently as he could, he fingered open the edge of the wrapping, doing his best not to destroy the shape the wrapping paper had taken on.

Tilting the present to one side, the contents slid out of the gift wrapping.

Cracking open the lid, he was smashed in the face with the heady aroma of chocolate. Expensive chocolate in a rather elaborate red box.

Opening it, he took two of the chocolates out and damn near swallowed them whole. Tilting the top of the container against it, he set it up to look like the paymaster had been given a box and had started to dip into them.

"Here, Master." Petra handed him the box he'd asked for.

Opening the top, he found a number of vouchers inside. All identical to the one he had in his hand.

Dropping his own into the pile, he closed it up again. As delicately as he could, he slipped the box into the wrapping paper. The height was almost too much for it, the width just right, and the length all wrong.

Setting it down on the table, Vince heard a subdued thump, grunts, and the crackle of electricity outside the door.

Time was running out.

Easing the box to the other side of the decorative paper, Vince managed to line up the edges and reseal it. So long as he held it right there, and never touched the other side of it, it'd look exactly as it should.

"Quick, in the corner," Vince said, gesturing behind himself.

Petra glided over there and looked to him for further instructions.

Vince pressed his back up into her and then held up his hands in front of him, the present quite visible in his left hand.

Petra's arms slowly closed around him and her chin pressed into the back of his head.

"Do nothing, say nothing," Vince murmured. Reaching out with his mind, he mentally flicked the switch on the paymaster to awaken.

The fat man jolted in his chair. Looking to Vince and Petra, and then to the commotion going on outside the door.

Shouting something unintelligible, the man clapped his hands together around what had looked like a pen holder on his desk. A deep, brassy alarm started to buzz all throughout the building.

Then the door exploded inward with screeching hinges and stinging smoke. Screaming across the room, it smashed into the paymaster and crushed his head against the wall. With a wet crunch, his skull popped and he collapsed on the floor as the door clattered and clanged in a different direction.

Seville and his Elf strode into the room. Both turned to regard Vince, assessed him, and then dismissed him.

Seville leapt over the desk and grabbed a hold of the twitching corpse. "Damn. Bust the safe doors open. As little damage as possible."

The Elf said nothing, but strode over to Seville and laid a hand on the closest safe. A single tick later and the door popped open with a muffled thump.

Seville traded places with her and started scooping out false vouchers by the handful while the Elf did the same thing to the second and third safes.

As soon as the Elf was done with the safes, she ripped half the tunic off the corpse, dunked it into the dead man's missing head, and began to scrawl on the wall.

"No time for that. Let's go," commanded Seville, bolting out of the room, a few vouchers fluttering behind him.

The Elf took a few moments more to finish what she was doing and then followed after him.

"Master?"

"Do nothing, we're guests. Guards will be here shortly. We simply explain exactly what we saw, minus what we did with the box."

"This one understands," Petra murmured, her hands pressing into his chest.

A minute crawled by before armed guards in bright red armor stormed through the broken door frame. Two marched right up to Vince and Petra and secured them while the rest scoured the room.

"A man and a woman did this. I think the woman was a Waster. They-they killed everyone, took something out of the desk, blew up the safes, then left.

"The woman wrote something on the wall," Vince explained, pointing with his right hand at the bloody whatever it was on the wall.

A guard with more decorations on his shoulder nodded at that and then stomped over to the desk. Opening the drawer that Vince knew would be empty, the man then checked the safes.

"You said they took what was in the safes?"

"Yeah. And a box," Vince affirmed.

Grunting, the officer turned and looked at the other guards.

"They… they mentioned something about the king. I don't think they noticed we were here. There was a lot of smoke from the magic they used to explode the door," Vince said in a voice that he tried to inject some fear into.

The guards in front of them looked to their officer. "Double time, down the boulevard. We can cut them off at the gate. You two," said the officer, looking at Vince and Petra. "Stay here for further questioning."

Then they took off at a dead sprint.

Apparently that had been the right thing to say. Reacquiring what had been lost took precedence in the man's head over securing any possible witnesses.

"Out we go. Let's not wait here any longer," Vince said with conviction, dropping his hands to his sides.

"This one knows of an exit. There are hidden corridors the handlers use," Petra said.

"Lead on, then. I'm afraid I'm the damsel in distress at this point, so I'll rely on my white knight," Vince quipped, stepping to the side for Petra to get by.

Petra set off, exiting the room and moving into the hall.

Splattered on the walls and ground were limbs, blood, and gore. There had been no fight here. It had been a slaughter.

Petra lifted the hem of her dress to step through the mess, which seemed odd to Vince, and guided him to the back of the stairwell.

Lifting both hands, she positioned them awkwardly on two different bricks that were a fair distance apart.

"What are you—"

"Shh. Listening, smelling."

Vince nodded and fell silent, watching.

Petra slid her hands across the bricks, her fingers pressing into the edges. Finding what she was seemingly looking for, she shoved her hands forward.

The two bricks she had pushed on sunk into the wall a fraction. The wall to their left swung away from them.

"My hero. Does this lead out?"

"This one believes so; she can smell and feel an outside current. Follow, Master."

Petra disappeared into the dark tunnel and Vince followed behind her, closing the wall behind himself.

Grateful for his night vision once again, Vince followed Petra easily as she led them down a maze of tunnels and forks.

She'd stop at times and scent the air, or touch the walls. Each time she did this, she came away more confident.

Vince could only assume they were making progress. To him, it felt like they were running endlessly and aimlessly.

Almost as if to clarify that thought, ahead of them Vince could see a man fumbling with something at his waist. He was standing in front of a wall and was attempting to push what looked like a small rod into a crack in the bricks.

Before Vince could see anything beyond that, Petra snapped the robed man up in both hands and leaned her head back. She also suddenly grew quite a bit taller as she clearly extended her legs.

Her jaw unhinged itself, and her mouth opened wide. Out snapped a pair of scythe-like mandibles. The last time he'd seen them, Petra had buried them in Fes.

In nearly the same second that they slid out, Petra closed them tightly around the man's throat.

A heartbeat later and her stinger was swinging forward from under her dress. It slammed into the man, piercing him easily.

Struggling in vain, the man squirmed and gibbered as Petra held him off the ground.

A minute ticked by as the man slowly stopped fighting. His hands no longer pushed at Petra's head, his feet no longer kicking the air futilely.

He hung there. Twitching.

Petra dropped the man to the ground and then stabbed him with her stinger again, this time in the chest. Right where his heart should be.

Turning her head to face him, he was struck by the sheer monstrous quality of her appearance. Her mouth was open, the bones clearly dislocated in her jaw to allow for those pincers to slide out.

From where, he had no idea. They looked like they'd simply retract back into her jaw itself. As if they simply retracted into the bone somewhere.

They'd flipped out in under a second, and the retraction had taken as little time as well previously.

She watched him, her eyes studying him. Drool pooled in her mouth and dripped from her lower lip.

It took Vince a second, but he finally realized she was waiting for him to react to her visage.

Truth be told, her previous comments had made him think about her situation earlier. She was the least human of his companions. The least human by far. This would be her most inhuman look.

Her most vulnerable.

It wasn't in his nature to flirt. Not really. But in this moment, she needed more than he could normally give.

Stepping in close to the extremely tall ant soldier, he reached up and grabbed the top of her dress and pulled her down to his height.

Planting a kiss on her cheek, he then patted it.

"Put your fangs away, Petra. You already showed me what you can do with your mouth earlier. We can experiment later, now's not that time."

Not waiting for an answer, Vince leaned down and started to rifle through the man's belongings and pockets.

Pulling free the metal rod the man had been fooling around with, Vince heard a solid pop behind him.

Glancing over his shoulder, he saw only Petra. She had a hand on her jaw as she watched him.

"Experiment?"

"Well, if your jaw opens that wide... an interesting thought, no?" Vince gave her a feral grin and turned back to the corpse.

"Ugh, I hate it when they do that," Vince grumbled as the corpse shat itself. Frowning, Vince found something cold and heavy in one of the pockets.

Pulling it free, it looked more like a metal stamp than anything.

"Collar," Petra hissed.

Looking back at her, he found her staring at the metal stamp in his hand.

"This thing?" Vince asked.

"Collar," Petra said through clenched teeth.

Shrugging, Vince stood up and then pressed the stamp to the front of her collar. It sizzled for a second and then nothing.

"This one thanks her master. The collar has no power now and she is free to discuss what she now knows."

"Handy. Seems we're not the only ones who can break a collar. Makes sense when you stop and think on it," Vince said. Pocketing the stamp, he turned back to the wall.

His eyesight was considerably better than this man's, as he could clearly see where this rod with teeth went.

Sliding it into the dark hole next to a point where three bricks joined, he smiled. Reaching the end of the keyhole, he rotated the rod around.

With a click, the wall parted and moonlight could be seen through the crack.

"Looks like we found our way out, then. Petra, I think it might be time to ditch the dress. If you're up for it, I think the best course of action is me riding you out of here."

Vince reached up and pulled off the mask he was wearing and dropped it.

"This one agrees, though regrets the loss of the dress. She felt more human in it. No one stared at her."

"They stared at you for other reasons while you were wearing the dress. With or without the dress, you're still Petra."

"Yes, Master." Petra reached down and shucked the dress over her head, and then dropped it lightly atop the corpse. Pulling the mask free, she dropped that as well. Her eyes stayed on the fabric before looking back to him.

A quick moment of rifling through her armor bag and she was wearing her normal clothes again.

"This one is ready."

Vince nodded and then slid up onto her as he had done previously.

Cautiously, Petra opened the door and peeked out. Then they were off into the night.

Chapter 17

Clambering over the wall, they made it into an adjacent alleyway without a problem.

"I should have known," came a soft voice.

Vince snapped his head around towards the voice, his senses scrambling to who was there.

Seville.

"Seville. Funny to see you here," Vince said casually, his eyes locking on to the man.

He was leaning up against a wall, his arms folded in front of him.

Searching out the Elf, Vince found her on top of the roof above him.

"Ask her to come down or we might go up to get her," Vince said, before there could be any misunderstandings.

Seville quirked a brow at that.

Petra lifted her left set of legs and placed them on the wall. She wasn't one for subtlety.

"Fine. Come on down," Seville called upwards. "Don't try anything. Just... come down."

A rush of air was all Vince heard before the Elf dropped near silently next to Seville.

Petra set her legs back down and then shifted from the left to the right. She was obviously considering things.

"Well, Seville? You wouldn't be chatting unless you wanted to ask something."

The Elf flared in an angry mental hue at his tone and words.

"Calm. If he wanted to kill us, he could."

Vince said nothing to that; instead, he took the time to slowly encase the Elf's mind in a vice.

She was the danger. Her magic would be swift and sure.

"My head feels funny," murmured the Elf, her hands coming up to her head.

"Seville?" Vince asked again, slowly increasing the pressure he had on the Elf.

The man who seemingly knew Vince and his secret said nothing. When his companion fell to a knee, both hands planted firmly to the ground to keep herself up, he held up his hands in front of him.

Vince's vision wavered for a moment as he continued to push in on her mind.

"Nothing. Merely curious as to who might come out. We were expecting someone else."

"Dead. Killed him to make our escape," Vince said, flipping the rod that was a key out to Seville.

"I see," Seville said, rotating the rod in his hands.

"Anything else?" Vince asked.

"No."

"Before I go, you know me. Know me and my parents. Yes?"

There was a brief flash of unadulterated hatred bleeding out from inside Seville's mind at the mention of his parents. Like a pan heated up to the point that it'd instantly sear meat on first contact.

Murderous, boiling hatred.

As quick as it had come, it vanished.

Then Seville smiled slowly at him and then shook his head.

"You can tell I'm guarding my thoughts, can't you? No matter. Yes. I did. I haven't seen them since they vanished. They visited often considering... considering that you were being corrupted by the Wastes. The Elves in the north have always been more willing to work with humans. You were brought there many times by your parents to consult with them."

Vince grunted. It was something he didn't know or couldn't remember. Releasing the Elf, he felt his mind clear.

Either way, if true, it was information. Information always had a price.

He would be in no man's debt. Especially this man.

"The vouchers you stole are fraudulent. The ones you have will explode after a certain distance. I'd recommend tossing them back over the wall.

"Knowledge for knowledge. Goodbye," Vince stated firmly.

Petra needed no instruction and took them straight up the wall they stood beside. In seconds, they were atop the roof and moving swiftly towards the south end of the city.

Gliding from rooftop to rooftop, Vince could hear a disturbance running throughout the city. From the brief snatches of conversation he picked up as they moved along, it seemed like the army had been deployed.

Looking back towards the castle, he could see the men and women of the military charging down a street. Squads broke off at intervals and entered houses with their weapons unsheathed.

Turning back to face forward, Vince rested his forehead on Petra's shoulder blades.

"This one senses fear. Fear everywhere. Something is happening," Petra said as she skittered along a rooftop.

"Yeah, I saw soldiers being deployed behind us and I could hear some of the conversation from below us. The army has been mobilized. No idea why."

"Master can see them? And hear them?"

"Yeah. I can. I think we'll need to have a long talk with everyone after this. Me keeping secrets won't be helpful."

Petra made a noncommittal noise as she leapt from the building they were on to one adjacent.

"...freeing any slave they find. The king's ruled that slavery is illegal!" Apparently they can neutralize orders on collars and are going from house to house."

"What? Quick, get—"

Vince felt the pieces click together in his head with that snippet of conversation.

Seville had been meant to rob the vault, so to speak. The king would then sweep through and confiscate all slaves.

It'd ruin the guild.

In one greedy swoop, Vince had hindered the plans of a group to free slaves everywhere. The Auction House would inevitably recover from this since the vouchers weren't in the hands of the king.

That would have been an awful amount of leverage he could have leveraged over the Auction House guild.

Seville seemed as if he was a ringleader of this operation. One who knew his parents and had deliberately said nothing to him.

Working with people who wanted to kill him.

Vince was torn, as he could easily support the cause, but not the people.

Deciding that he'd find no answer in this train of thought this night, he instead tightened his grip on Petra. That and he tried to desperately not look down or think about the height they were traveling at.

Dusk was closing in on the next day as the two wearily stumbled into the village Fes and Meliae were staying in.

Without horses, the journey had been exhausting. Petra had carried him an admirable distance, but even her stamina and strength flagged after a time.

She was no horse to be ridden unendingly.

Dragging his feet, Vince pathetically shambled up to the man behind the counter.

Vince barely recognized him as a man and didn't bother to catalog his features. "Man" would do well enough in his own head.

"Sir, what can I do for you this evening?"

"I believe you have accommodations set for the week under the name Vincent. Two of my companions should already be here," Vince mumbled.

Petra came to a stop beside him, wavering a little to and fro as she tried to find her balance.

They'd truly been on the run and had only stopped for a brief meal from a bush or tree and restroom breaks.

"Ah, yes. I'm afraid they couldn't remain and departed. They left a note for you should you come here." The man disappeared behind the counter then came back up, holding out a letter for him and a key.

Vince took the key and letter, blinking at them.

"Last door on the left on the second floor. Enjoy your stay."

Nodding his head, Vince set off for the indicated room, his steps heavy and plodding.

Unlocking, opening, then closing the door after Petra entered took what little energy he had.

He dropped the key and the voucher box onto the dresser top without a care for the noise it'd inevitably create. Then he slumped into the bed like an empty sack.

Holding the letter up above his head, he cracked open the wax seal and thumbed out the paper inside.

Focusing on the words, he began to read it.

Dear Sweetling,

People were paying too much attention to us. Perhaps because we were slaves, or simply because we were female.

In either case, we've moved on. It wasn't worth the risk depending on how long they'd keep you hostage.

Macy was quite kind and gave us more supplies than we could have ever needed, as well as some coin.

She also left a letter for you. I've put it in the dresser drawer. The key for it is stashed in your saddlebag with some prepared trail food.

Vince glanced to the right and found the indicated dresser did indeed have a drawer.

A few feet away, Petra was stripping off her clothes. Her armor was still tied together and neatly piled on the ground next to the door.

Before he could protest, or even speak, Petra was nude. Then she crumpled into the bed next to him, and promptly began snoring.

Smiling to himself, he returned to the letter.

We should now be on the trip back home. We'll be moving slowly and carefully off the beaten trail.

I know you have powers you have yet to disclose with us. Powers that may make it easier for you to find us. We'll stay to the eastern side of the road as we move, unless we have no choice.

We'll keep an eye out for you; be sure to do the same.

Do not fear or worry for us. With the power you've granted me, my beloved tree, I can guarantee we'll not come across anyone.

It is also why I'm able to travel so far from you. The amount of power you put into me is immense, and I should be more than able to survive for at least a month or two.

Beyond that, I admit I'm fearful of the consequences.

I stabled your horse at the corral a few streets away and made sure the saddlebags, which are in the armoire, are ready to go.

We left your weapons, two rifles, and a can of ammo as well.

If you end up having your way with Petra, please be sure to use protection. Or do it much closer to home so I can make sure to slow down the pregnancy. So long as it's within the first month, it shouldn't be an issue.

Fes is yet to become pregnant, after all.

In closing, Fes is healing well. I've sped it along as much as I possibly can, and we should reach home at a reasonable time. Perhaps only an additional week or two due to our caution.

Love you, Sweetling.

Yours alone,

Meliae

P.S. Fes is getting grumpier by the day without you. Be sure to give her lots of attention when you catch up with us, or meet us back at home.

Setting the letter down on the bedside dresser, Vince closed his eyes and immediately dropped off into sleep.

Muted shouting interrupted Vince's sleep. Opening his eyes, he blearily stared up at the ceiling above him.

Someone was having a pretty loud argument.

Beside him, Petra snorted in her sleep.

Everything was as it should be, other than the racket downstairs.

Focusing his hearing on it, he only had to listen for a second to realize what it was.

Soldiers were here. Searching for them in particular. The innkeeper had tried to play dumb, but apparently someone had ratted them out.

It was only a matter of time till they started checking each room.

Reaching over, he gripped Petra's shoulder and gave it a light shake.

The soldier-ant's eyes snapped open and her head whipped around to him.

Holding a finger in front of his mouth, he made a finger walking motion with his hand, and then pointed to the window.

Petra nodded and shimmied out of the bed, her breasts swaying as she maneuvered her ant body off the mattress.

Ripping his eyes from her unhidden and well-displayed features, Vince got out of the bed.

Snatching up the letter and the voucher box from the bedside dresser, he moved to the armoire. Pulling his saddlebag out, he shoved the letter and the box full of vouchers into the main flap. Then he fumbled around inside where he kept his food for the key Meliae mentioned.

Finding it quickly, he spun on his heel and went to the dresser. He popped it open quietly and snatched the letter.

Tossing both the room key and the dresser key on the bed, he went back to the armoire.

Petra grabbed him as he went by and pulled him in close.

"Help this one with her clothes and armor, Master," whispered the soldier.

Vince nodded his head at the request.

Petra picked up her bra and pulled it on, turning her back to him as she reached for her undershirt and padding.

Vince frowned as his fingers pulled the clasp shut. Pulling at the fabric, he adjusted it until it settled flatly across her back.

Her shirt and padding went next, and he had only a second to smooth it out before her chestplate and hip guards were being hauled on.

Vince immediately went to work on the buckles while she worked on something else. He couldn't quite see what she was doing with her back to him.

"This one can take it from here, Master. Please continue to prepare."

Vince shut the clasp he was working on and then moved back to the armoire. Picking up their weapons, the saddlebag, and slinging the rifles over his shoulder, he felt beyond encumbered.

Moving back to Petra, he hesitated for a moment and then put the saddlebag over Petra's abdomen. Giving it a quick cinch, and fitting it as best to her as he could, he then slid in her sword and spear into the appropriate racks.

He'd loaded her up like a pack horse.

The soldier-ant glanced at him, down at the bags, and then went back to her armor.

Pulling his sword and sheath into its place around his waist, Vince felt better immediately.

He pressed his hands to the side of the armoire and slowly began pushing it in front of the door.

Once he got it into place, with little to no noise at all, thankfully, he pulled the dresser over and pressed it against the armoire.

Then he slung both rifles over his shoulder and picked up the ammo can.

Looking to Petra, he found her cinching up a buckle under her chin for her helmet.

"This one is ready, Master."

"Out the window. Can you manage it with me riding you and all this weight?"

"This one will not fail her master. Though once she has reached the ground, her master will need to dismount."

"Agreed. After that, let's get my horse and go. I say southeast. The further we go into the Wastes, the better our chances are. Most will avoid it as much as they can.

"Once we get out of Washington, we can head back inward towards the main road. With any luck, we can link up with Meliae and Fes.

"They left a letter; you can read it when we get out of here."

"This one cannot read. She would ask her master to read it to her."

Vince blinked at that and then shook his head.

"Certainly. You need to learn to read later, though. I'll teach you myself."

"If Master wishes."

"I do," Vince said with a nod. Moving to the window, he unlatched the lock and pushed it open. With a deep breath, he then stepped out of the room and onto the roofing tiles.

Petra was beside him in an instant.

Looking out into the dark night, he realized it was still several hours before dawn.

Shaking his head, he mounted up on Petra, hooking his legs around her midsection. Reaching around her, he gripped onto her with his arms as well.

"This one would ask for a saddle. She enjoys being her master's mount, but this could be more comfortable, she believes."

Not being able to respond to her request, Vince could only hang on as Petra moved to the side of the building. In seconds, she'd shimmied them down the side of the building and into the street.

Rather than slowing down to let him get off, Petra sped up, dashing across the street and straight up a wall.

It wasn't until they slipped into the stables that she let him off.

Petra was gasping for air, her hands pressing to her sides as he dropped off her side.

"Soldiers... standing outside inn. Sorry, Master. Time... is short," gasped out Petra.

Vince tilted his head to the side and heard the stomping of boots in the distance.

Rushing down the line of stalls, he checked each as he made his way down the line.

Finally, he found his own and booted open the door.

His horse practically jumped at his sudden presence.

Not waiting, he reached out to the hook on the side of the wall and pulled free his saddle. Dropping it down on his horse, he went through the act of saddling his horse as quickly as possible.

Sliding one rifle into the holster for the saddle, he grabbed the reins and led it back out to Petra.

She was still huffing and puffing but sounded like she was recovering.

Pulling the saddlebags free from her, he put the second rifle into place in the receiver slot they'd made for it on her abdomen.

After he set the saddlebags in their rightful place, he vaulted into his seat. Then, pressing his heels to the sides of his horse, he careened wildly off for the gate.

Unsheathing his saber, he wheeled the horse around as they passed by and swung at the metal latch holding it shut.

With a crack, his blade broke the thin metal and the gate swung open.

That'll be a notch in the blade.

Petra gave the gate a shove and exited the corral. Vince was right behind her as they turned back onto the main street and headed east.

Eventually, the only thing Vince heard was the sound of his horse's hooves pounding the grass as they exited the city.

Looking rearward, he could see a multitude of lights. Torches, buildings being searched, people being roused.

They'd gotten out just in time. He wouldn't squander this reprieve, though.

Speed was the name of the game until they got the hell out of Washington.

Looking towards the path they were traveling, Vince leaned forward over his horse's head and hung on.

Chapter 18

Vince entered their camp as quietly as he'd left it. Petra sat, as she was able to, at least, on a nearby tree trunk. She was quietly inspecting her weapons and gear for any damage.

He eyed her for a second as he made his way over.

Not looking up at him, she continued to work field stripping her Springfield. "This one would like to know what her master has seen."

"How do you always know, exactly?" Vince asked, taking a seat across from her in the grass. He pushed his back up to a log and let himself relax.

Running scout duties never did any good for his nerves.

Between them was the stacked wood for their next evening's fire, if they could afford to light one. To one side, and within reach if they had to flee, were their packs, saddle, and saddlebag.

Their lone horse was staked a bit to their east so it could graze, and act as a sentry as well.

They'd taken refuge in a forest on the east side of Washington. Vince always felt more at home with trees surrounding him, so it hadn't been a question if they'd venture into it or not. It didn't hurt that the further east you went, the fewer people you'd encounter.

Directly to the south of their location was the Columbia River and the front line. Washington had failed their initial push into the south and had been sent tumbling back north. Now trenches were being dug along both sides of the river. Machine guns from the pre-Wastes era were being brought in and set up to cover the river.

For all intents and purposes, the two countries were locked in a struggle that would only end in a bloodbath, and a crushing defeat for one side or the other.

That or never-ending war.

Which left them on the wrong side of the river and wondering if Fes and Meliae had been able to make it across themselves before this situation developed.

Knowing them, they're fine. Meliae probably went further east until they could find a gap to slip through.

"This one can sense Master through her antennae. It is harder with more humans around, but not impossible." Petra's fingers pushed the bolt through its action, testing it while she had it pulled apart.

"Ah, is that how you found me in the party?" Vince asked, shifting his weight around.

Petra's face screwed up in a scowl, before turning into a smirk. Heat colored her cheeks as she clearly relived some of that night in her head.

"Not quite. This one couldn't sense Master as well with her antennae trapped in her mask. She was worried at first that it wouldn't be easy to find Master."

Sliding the trigger assembly back into the stock, she hesitated, clearly ill at ease.

"This one must admit she couldn't find Master until she felt… him… wanting… her. The strength of Master's desire was palpable. It was like being struck with it.

"That's why this one regrets losing the dress. She is sure that it was partly that she looked human in it that you were so interested in her. She has not felt the same level of desire from her master since, though she wishes it."

Vince sighed and brought a hand up and rubbed his jaw. "I'm not really sure how to answer that, Petra. I can tell you that I honestly haven't exactly been feeling... randy. We're kind of on the lam, and my mind has been more attuned to getting us home."

Petra nodded her head an inch, her fingers frozen on the stock.

Grunting, Vince knew that wasn't what she wanted to hear. "Petra, you're very attractive. Even if you're not completely human. The dress didn't change anything for me because I'm well aware of who and what you are. Everything you felt from me was directed at you for being you.

"If the situation were different and this were more of a scenic trip... well, yeah. I think you're as pretty and sexy as Meliae or Fes. Don't doubt yourself, just... be you. You be you."

Petra pulled her chin in further, her head tilting downward. Her bangs slid down to cover her face from his view.

"As to what I saw, we could do the river crossing, but it'll have to be at night. It's dusk now, but in an hour or so it should be dark enough, I imagine," Vince said, pushing the hair out of his eyes. He'd been meaning to get it cut, but things kept happening that prevented that.

"They've got it all crosshatched with spotlights and machine guns. The area I was looking at is a little deeper, and we should probably be able to cross if we can keep ourselves submerged most of the time."

Petra didn't say anything to that but bobbed her head. He got the impression she was watching him from the corner of her eyes.

"The alternative is skirting way out to the east, but I'm not confident it'd be any better over there. Might actually be worse. People seemed rather lazy at the river. No one has attempted to make the crossing as of yet, so... that helps."

Vince gave his head a shake, trying to get his hair to settle better.

"This one would like to cut her master's hair," Petra whispered.

Thinking about it for a moment, Vince shrugged. At this point, anything would be better than this. "I'll take you up on that, actually. It's just damn unmanageable right now. Do you want to do it now, or...?"

"This one would prefer to take care of it now. If Master can't see in the water, it will be a problem."

Vince couldn't fault the logic. He got up, walked over to her position, and sat down in front of her. "Want my knife or do you have yours?"

"This one has her knife."

Petra immediately combed her fingers through his hair, drawing it backwards. "This one would know her master's preference."

"Uhm, I don't know. Short? Whatever you think will look good. I can't exactly see my own hair without a mirror, and we don't have one of those."

Petra's fingers were warm as they brushed through his hair. Her nails were short with only the smallest bit of length to them.

She folded his hair one way, and then another. "This one regrets to tell her master that his hair is tangled. Does master have a comb?"

"In my saddlebags. I can get it —"

"No, remain seated. This one can reach from here. She will also be wetting your hair to get it untangled."

Out of the corner of his eye, he saw one of Petra's legs reach out to hook the saddlebag and bring it over.

"Alright." Vince wasn't quite sure what to say. Fes and Meliae shared his bed often, and there was genuine affection with both of them. Nothing like this, though.

This felt more like budding romance from one of those terrible novels his mother used to read. He didn't doubt Meliae would offer to do something like this and would spoil him, if given the chance.

Problem was, they really hadn't been given a chance for anything like this. Their time had been spent working or getting to the next place to work. There was little to no downtime.

Ever.

"Forgive this one, Master, the water will be cold," Petra murmured from beside his ear. She'd leaned in close to him while his mind wandered off. Her warm breath tickled his ear and made his skin prickle.

A trickle of water splashed into his hair. Before it could run down his back, her hands were there, rubbing the water into his scalp. Twice more Petra ran water into his hair and helped it to soak in with her hands.

Her left hand pressed into his brow with a light touch as the comb began to work through his hair.

Closing his eyes, Vince focused on Petra and what she was doing.

With gentle yet insistent work, she untangled his hair. Her careful fingers worked the knots out tenderly one by one. Then she'd work the comb through the area she'd cleared.

Petra worked until it felt like she'd conducted an intense survey of his head, mapping out every bump, tangle, scar, and pulling out every bit of vegetation he'd inadvertently picked up.

Vince felt Petra shift as she reached around behind him and laid the comb down. She gathered up his hair in one hand and pulled it away from his head.

The swish and hiss of a blade cutting through hair was the only indication that she'd begun the task she'd set out to do.

Vince remained still as Petra worked, her fingers sliding through his hair, followed by a pause as she gathered it up in one hand. Then the soft sibilant sound of hair being cut.

At length, Petra seemed satisfied with her work. She hadn't run the knife through his hair for at least a minute. Now she was merely brushing her fingertips through it as if to see how it would lay on his head.

"This one would ask her master to please open his eyes," Petra said softly.

Vince opened his eyes and blinked twice. He'd honestly gotten lost in the tender touches and warmth Petra has bestowed on him.

There was a kernel of disappointment in him that it was over.

Her bright blue eyes stared down at him when he turned his face up to hers.

A flash of a smile burst across her face and fled as quickly as it had come.

Leaning in close to him, she gently pressed a hand to his jaw and tilted it to one side.

He could see her eyes as they roamed over his face, inspecting him for what, he had no clue.

Slowly, she tilted his head the other way and proceeded to do the same thing again.

Holding his chin steady, she came a touch closer and brought the knife up to the side of his face.

A soft prickling in his sideburns was all he felt, and a single swish of the blade. Pulling back, she turned his head again and the same act was repeated to the other side.

Her thumb and forefinger of one hand carefully peeled his ear down. The knife tip grazed along the skin behind his ear. A few brushes of the edge to his flesh and it withdrew.

Moving his head back the other way, she did the same thing to the other side.

Petra eased back from him and seemed to admire her work. The hand on his jaw guided his head into different positions but with only the barest whisper of direction.

Petra's eyes slowly focused on his own.

He gave her a small smile and quirked a brow at her.

Wetting her lips with her tongue, she then parted them.

To the west and south of them was a blast the likes of which Vince had never heard before. A fireball lit up the night sky in every direction, shattering the peace of the night.

The noise from it felt more akin to a lightning bolt from directly overhead than anything.

As if to settle the matter on what it could be, the pop and crackle of gunfire made its way to him.

"They're attacking. Or pushing. Something. Everyone will be distracted. We should do this. Now, even. Whatever they're doing, it's big," Vince said, standing up. Turning around, he pocketed the comb Petra had set on a rock.

Listening intently, Vince was trying to discern anything he could about the weapons behind used.

Behind him, he heard Petra getting up to her feet. She took a deep breath and then blurted everything out in a rush. "Master, this one must confess she cannot swim."

Vince pressed his lips together to keep himself from saying anything in response to that.

It wasn't her fault she couldn't swim. He doubted soldier ants could swim even if they could be taught how or wanted to.

Not a whole lot to paddle with below, after all.

"Alright. Do you trust me?" Vince asked.

"Of course, Master. This one's life is yours."

"Good. Cut the horse loose after you strip everything off it. Then gather everything up and load yourself with as much as you can. I'll take care of the rest."

Turning his head to the river south of them, Vince set off at quick pace. Sooner than he could believe, he found the point where the trees thinned and the shore began.

Even the soldiers on this side were entirely focused on the west. This would be their best shot to make this work.

Dodging back into the woods, he moved east while keeping his eyes open for logs. Big, dry logs.

He found two of what he was looking for, and a third that would do, by the time he found the spot he wanted. It was between two lookout points, but he'd selected his entry point closer to the one to his west.

They would be less likely to look east, and the ones further east would have a harder time distinguishing them from the gloom.

Working quickly, Vince dropped down to the ground and pulled the logs closer together.

The show to the west had been timed with night falling. The temperature was dropping quickly, and what little light there was came mostly from the stars now, which was rudely interrupted by the blasts of whatever was happening to the west.

This really couldn't have been more in their favor unless Vince had been a part of the planning.

Petra came up behind him, everything packed and stored and carried on her ant abdomen. "This one has freed our animal. She is... she is ready."

Vince reached out, flipped open his bag draped over her rear end, and pulled out several cords. With swift pulls, Vince lashed the logs together into a makeshift raft.

A final cord was used to tie the whole thing to his belt loop and they were ready.

"Load everything up on this. Some things will get wet, that's just the way it is. We'll have to dry and clean everything after.

"What I want from you, Petra, is to get under the raft. Use your legs to hold on to it and just keep your head above the water. Can you do that?"

Petra let out a slow breath and then straightened her shoulders. "This one would die for you, Master."

"Not quite what I was asking for, but that'll do. Alright, let's go. Keep low, keep quiet."

Vince looked to the east, then the west, and set off. Waiting wouldn't benefit anyone.

When they reached the water, Vince kept going, slithering into it as quietly as he could. Even as he dragged the raft into the water, Petra loaded it up with their belongings and crawled into the water beside him.

Once the water got to his waist, Vince launched forward into a breaststroke. The cord pulled at his pants as he felt the whole thing shudder, then stabilize.

Quick, quiet pants for breath behind him, with the occasional sputter, told him Petra had done as he'd asked.

He didn't dare turn around to check. His eyes were on the point of the shore he wanted to land on.

From the across the river, that single point looked like it might have a blind spot for the group to the east.

Angling himself against the current, Vince swam onward through the cold water. Halfway across, Vince started to get nervous. There wasn't as much gunfire from the west anymore. Their diversion had managed to even keep the spotlights off for some reason, but the continued fighting had helped.

Maybe the generator was hit?

On top of that, his muscles were trembling. Swimming against the current, dragging Petra behind him, and doing so in water that wanted to kill through the cold was sapping his strength.

And quicker than he'd anticipated.

Gritting his teeth, Vince pushed himself, pulled at his dwindling reserves and demanded more of his strength.

His body started to heat up; his heart started to pound in his chest. Onward he swam.

When his foot touched the muddy bottom, he wanted to collapse right there. His body thrummed and burned with the exertion, only to clash with the bitingly cold wind.

The temperature had really dropped. Weather patterns had changed since the Wastes were created. Unnatural weather could strike at any time.

In this case, the air felt like it was bordering on freezing, and the wind only made it a hundred times worse.

The cord at his waist shifted and he knew Petra had disentangled herself from the raft and gotten her legs back onto the ground.

A shout went up to the east of them, and before he could think to respond, the cord around his waist snapped, Petra scooped him up in her arms, and they were off like a shot.

The cold air tore at him, and the sounds of rifles being fired echoed on both sides of them as they passed into the tree line.

Petra didn't stop for anything. She sailed through the undergrowth, her legs clicking as she carried them forward.

She used tree trunks, bushes, anything to push off of and keep them moving.

Several minutes went by before Petra slowed down, and finally came to a stop.

The blonde was panting heavily, her lips were blue, and her teeth chattered incessantly.

Vince tumbled from her arms as her legs gave out from under her.

He didn't have much time. For himself, or for her. Looking around, he realized that by sheer luck, she'd taken them right into a small gulley between the trees. He could start a fire and there'd be a good chance they'd be overlooked.

Even if they were caught, at this point, it'd be better than the alternative. Dying of the cold.

Pulling the saddlebags, baggage, and weapons from Petra's back and rear, he dropped it all to one side. The brilliant woman had taken the time to gather everything before grabbing him.

He stripped her quickly, pulling her clothes off until she was nude.

Her gaze was empty and her eyes glassy. Her teeth clattered like screws in a coffee can.

Pulling off his own soaking-wet clothes, he dropped them atop hers and then reached into the bags.

Ripping out a handful of rounds from the ammo tin, he then pulled out his fire starter kit.

Sweeping off an area of leaves and twigs, Vince pulled out a batch of tinder he'd set aside for fire making.

Vince put a cartridge between his teeth and bit down. He pulled the bullet free of the jacket with a tug and then dumped the powder into a small pile at the base of the tinder.

Biting another cartridge, he rushed to one side and quickly began gathering branches.

Dumping an armful down, he tore another bullet out of the jacket with his teeth, pouring the powder atop the first pile.

After two more armfuls of branches, a chunk of dead log, and another bullet pulled free, Vince felt like he could start the fire and be able to feed it for a bit.

Kneeling down in front of the tinder, he pulled out his sparker. It was just a piece of flint attached to a rod that would be dragged across a textured bit of steel.

He snapped the tool thrice in rapid succession, and the powder caught and went up in a puff of flame.

Pushing the miniature inferno underneath the tinder, he looked to Petra.

She was drooping all the way over to one side, like a wilted flower. Her arms hung limply at her sides.

By the time he looked back to his fire, it had gone up quick. The tinder was aflame and burning. Dropping the dried-out dead log straight into the fire, he waited for a second to make sure it went up in flame, and then crawled over to Petra.

Wrapping his hands around one of her arms, he winced. Her skin was ice cold.

"Petra, come with me. Just a little closer to the fire."

"Cold, M-m-m-m-master."

"I know." Vince pulled on her arm and the soldier shifted forward sluggishly, her legs pushing at the dirt beside her.

Pushing a large stack of wood atop the log with a hand, he returned his attention to his companion since the fire was happily throwing out heat now.

Vince pulled Petra down into the ground beside it. Putting her back to it, he then pushed himself up into the front of her, and pulled her head down into his shoulder.

Her shivering was intense, and her skin sucked what little heat he had right out of him.

After a second, her abdomen curled forward, her legs stretching out behind him.

Then she contracted everything, and he was pressed into her bodily.

She turned her head slightly, her frozen face pressing into his throat.

Unwilling to fight her, since it seemed more like she was seeking comfort, he relented, wrapping his arms around her in return.

Slowly, the insane shivering went away, and her skin gradually picked up some heat.

Feeling like the worst was over for the moment, Vince closed his eyes and let out a breath as Petra continued to clutch at him with every bit of strength she had left in her.

Chapter 19

Slowly, Vince cracked open his eyes as light stabbed at him through the branches and leaves.

Sleep had been scarce and hard won, and he didn't really appreciate the early-morning wake-up call.

He'd been forced to feed the fire several times, and had to even gather more wood at one point during the night.

The air was cold but not unbearable. The fire he'd set the previous night was coals and embers now but still putting off a good amount of heat on his arms.

Which were wrapped around Petra, who in turn had wrapped her arms and legs around him.

Blinking a few times, Vince tilted his head to the side to get a view of their surroundings during the day.

In shifting his body, he found he was suffering the age-old problem of all men.

A raging hard-on.

That happened to be buried in Petra's abdomen.

Heat rushed into his face at the situation. At the same time, he realized he could feel Petra's nipples crammed into his chest.

Petra nuzzled her face in his neck, his skin prickling wildly at the touch of her lips and memories of the party.

"This one feels her master's desire," Petra murmured against his skin.

Vince didn't respond immediately. He was trying to focus his mind as rapidly as he could. They needed to get moving. Start heading south again for home.

And not thinking about a nude blonde who had devoured him with what seemed like a desperate devotion and —

No, no, no, no.

"That you do, Petra. As I said previously, it isn't you, or a lack of you being attractive.

"We should get moving," Vince said firmly.

Petra ignored him, her mouth moving against his shoulder. He felt her teeth sink into his skin and her tongue brush along his flesh.

Below, he felt her legs pull at him, shifting his body around. She was positioning his hips to be parallel to her own. As she moved him, the tip of his member dragged down across her navel.

Vince had a better sense of smell than others. He could smell her moist womanhood and its obvious need without being close at all.

"Petra," Vince said huskily, leaning in close to her ear. "As your master, I command you to stop. Not because I don't want to, but because this isn't the time or place."

At his words, he could practically feel the war within Petra's head. Her willpower versus her desire.

Her legs pushed and pulled him up and down at the same time. His member had gotten stuck in the pearl of her entrance. After several seconds where he had to wonder if she'd simply mount him as the others had, she relented.

Her legs shook almost imperceptibly as she eased him back from herself. Her blue eyes caught him and manhandled him with the need there.

"Thank you, Petra," Vince started. Getting to his knees, and angling his soldier, who was at full attention, away from her, he continued, "We should get dressed and probably head west. I'd like to see if we can take a peek at what happened last night."

Her eyes tracked his nether parts, her tongue wetting her lips.

She was always duty strict, ramrod straight. Except apparently when it came to her master.

She nodded and then turned her eyes up to meet his own. "Yes, Master. This one would agree that a proper scout is in order. She will conduct this duty and return shortly."

"Petra, I think —" She was off before he could finish. She'd snatched up her clothes with one arm and dashed off into the trees.

She'd left behind her armor and weaponry, so it didn't seem like she was expecting trouble.

Vince shook his head, watching the soldier ant weave through the trees as she dressed.

"Maybe she wants to be alone," Vince muttered to no one. Shrugging his shoulders, he decided to relieve himself of some stress and then get to cleaning up the campsite.

"So to sum it up, Washington has established a bridge head and an encampment on the southern shore," Vince summarized as they walked along a game trail through the woods.

Petra had reported back and they'd set off as she started to explain what she'd seen.

"This one agrees with that summation. Al was there, as was Seville. The soldiers were busy constructing a fort manned with mechanical gun positions."

"Machine guns, you mean," Vince corrected.

"Yes."

Vince whistled through his teeth. "And you said they were building a bridge as well?"

"Yes. This one saw that they had engineers using cement to lay what looked like walls. They looked like they would be quite high. They'd also set up a temporary floating wooden bridge as well."

"Right. Well, Portland is in trouble. I hope they've secretly stashed some weaponry aside for an occasion like this. They'll need an armored vehicle or some explosives, it sounds like."

"This one saw nothing like that."

"No, probably not. They're expensive. Insanely so. Especially to maintain and hire the appropriate people. They might keep that kind of stuff in an armory. I doubt it was on the front line.

"Whatever, not our problem."

The trees began to thin all around them. Slowly, almost without meaning to, they stepped out of the forest and onto a road side.

Directly across from them was an overly convenient small village.

Seated in the middle of that, in a prominent and obvious position, was an inn.

"A road town." Vince looked up at the sky above them. They could continue on. There was still a number of hours before it even got into the afternoon.

Petra had taken her time at the river and collected quite a bit of solid information, but not enough to damage their travel speed.

"Let's stop here for a moment. We can see if they have supplies we can pick up, maybe a mount."

"This one agrees with her master's sentiment. This one would like to discuss more of what happened at the party. She has yet been able to discuss that metal stamp in Master's belongings and what they ordered this one to do."

Vince grunted and set them on a straight course to the inn.

"Take the road and hide. I'll take care of this and head out down the road here as soon as I'm done. Better if they don't see you. At all, if possible. Besides being pretty of face, your body is fairly distinct."

Petra looked to him and then set off down the road. Within moments, she'd managed to get herself to the side of the road and hidden in the brush. She was barely visible to his eye, but only if he looked directly at that spot.

Leaving her to it, he entered the inn.

A brief round of haggling, a small bit of info, and Vince was already back on the road, Petra at his side.

"This one would like to know what Master wishes to do next?"

"Head south," Vince said, holding out a strip of jerky to the woman. "Supposedly there's a stream south of here. Apparently it's not mountain runoff, either, so there's a chance it won't be as cold as an Ice Fairy's ass."

"Any news, Master?"

"None we didn't know."

The conversation died after that and they trudged onward.

Vince was sitting on the bank of the stream they'd found. At this moment, he was content.

Washing all the grit off from sleeping on the dirt had given him a blessedly refreshed feeling.

The air had warmed enough that sitting in his wet underwear on a grassy bank didn't bother him. He'd even worn his favorite pair of boxers for it.

Petra was in the process of scrubbing herself in the same manner as he just had. Her hands were working at one of the creases in her chitin-like skin on her rear end.

Growling, the soldier slapped the washcloth she was using in her hands.

"Problem there, Petra?" Vince asked, shading his eyes with one hand.

She was nude except for the small strip of fabric she'd tied around her waist and nether region.

Vince was doing his best to ignore her chest, even if his eyes continued to roam over her the moment his concentration slipped.

"Yes, Master. This one would ask you to assist her in washing. Unfortunately, she cannot take care of her own needs," Petra said darkly.

Vince nodded at that and then stood up, walking over to the woman.

"This one apologies, Master. She is worthless as a woman. Her only use is as a soldier to be tossed into combat." Petra turned her head to one side as she said it, holding out the washcloth to him.

"Now, now. None of that. You're not the emotional, Negative Nancy type. What's really bothering you?" Vince asked, taking the cloth from her hand.

Laying his hands on her warm body, he began running his fingers along the firm chitin.

"This one doesn't know. She is… she is frustrated. She wants to stab something with her stinger and then eat the creature."

Vince raised his eyebrows at that. Shrugging, he splashed water up onto Petra. As the water cascaded down, he began to scrub at the dirt and grit lodged in the crevices.

Taking his time, since they had plenty of that, he worked diligently on her. Silence reigned supreme for a time as he systematically worked over her abdomen, cleaning, dislodging things, and scrubbing her.

"Master, the metal stamp you took from the dead man. This one had been ordered not to mention it at all. It can unlock any slave collar, break any order, and force any slave to accept new orders."

Vince had figured it was something like that. It didn't surprise him that the slavers had a contingency plan put into place.

"This one was scared they would ask her questions about Master. Instead, they only ordered this one to not to speak of the stamp. Then they asked if she was there voluntarily and wanted to be."

Dunking the cloth into the water, Vince then shook it out. Reaching around to the back of Petra, he started working at the area where he knew her stinger was.

Keeping his fingers mindful, he did his best to clean her up without aggravating her.

"While they didn't ask other questions, they did reveal that every auction house location has at least one stamp in case of emergencies."

"Makes sense." Vince carefully pressed his fingers into the crevices of her chitinous plate, pulling free grit and grunge.

"This one thanks her master. His touch is calming."

He wondered for a moment. Her venom seemed rather strong and could kill in minutes.

"Petra, possibly awkward question for you." Vince stood up and gave her abdomen one last look before feeling like he'd completed his task.

"Ask this one anything, Master, she is yours."

"Your venom seems... extremely strong. Does it survive outside of you for long?"

"This one has never tested that, but she knows it is still effective after a number of days."

"Would you mind if I milked you? I've done it before with snakes. I'd like to see if I can use your venom for anything."

Petra eyed him warily, her brows coming together.

"How would this be done?" she asked neutrally.

"It's rather simple. I imagine you need to put your stinger into something that gives resistance to be able to inject your poison. I happen to have a mason jar with me with nothing in it. I put some fabric over the top, angle your stinger, and put it in. Hopefully your venom comes right out."

"This one is willing," she said slowly.

"Great. After me, then." Vince made his way over to his saddlebags. After a moment, he fished out a strip of leather and a mason jar.

Taking a seat on the grass, he patted the area next to him.

Petra came over and then stood up to angle her stinger towards him.

Reaching out, he took hold of the rear of her abdomen. With a careful hand, he guided the stinger into the leather that was wrapped around the mason jar.

The stinger pierced the leather easily and almost immediately venom began pumping out.

Petra managed to ease herself down into a semi-sitting position as she watched.

Reaching around the base of her stinger, Vince began to gently push on it, trying to simulate prey for her.

Her response was automatic, and she pushed her abdomen forward against the jar.

Vince couldn't look away. Her venom was freely flowing, a watery, sticky-looking substance that had filled a fifth of the jar already.

Petra made a soft noise that shook his concentration. It had almost sounded like a moan of discomfort.

Looking up to the soldier ant to make sure she was okay, he was mildly surprised.

Her eyelids were fluttering, her breath unsteady, and her cheeks a rosy red.

"Are you alright, Petra?"

"Master, it feels... very good. Though she thinks she must stop."

Vince then noticed the smell of her. It was the same as from the forest. Maybe even a little more intense.

He looked to her underwear strap as if he could peer through it. The way she looked, the sound of her breath, the very smell of her, and the memories of her from that morning clouded his mind.

Petra must have caught where he was looking, as her hands immediately dipped down to her underwear band. With quick fingers, she unfastened it and pulled it away, revealing her glistening privates to him.

Her fingers pressed to those moist lips and her thumbs stroked the hood of her pearl.

Vince almost lost the grip on his mason jar. Pulling it back, it made a soft pop as her stinger came free of the leather.

Turning his head, he found a flat rock to gently set the glass container down on.

Petra's hands hadn't remained idle in his momentary distraction. As he turned his head back to her, she'd changed positions.

Her abdomen was out behind her, and she was hunched over his boxers.

Deftly, she maneuvered her mouth into the hole in the front and fished him out with her lips.

A quick inhale from her and Vince was buried to the hilt in that warm, hungry mouth.

She made a soft mewling noise as she bobbed her head up and down. Her fingers had tracked down his jewels and were massaging them tenderly.

"Damn," Vince said with a hitched breath.

Petra's eyes flicked up to him and she seemed to come to herself in that look.

Letting him slide out of her mouth, she backed up, her hands coming free of his boxers. "Master, this one apologizes, she knows she's not humanoid, but—"

"Petra, shut up." Vince pushed his boxers down quickly. Reaching over, he slid a hand behind her neck as the other pushed up into the mound above her nether region.

The soldier ant cooed into his mouth when his lips met hers.

Moving with his original intent, he pushed her back into the grass, settling atop her as his tongue snaked out into her mouth.

Petra let out a rough breath through her nose against his cheek, her hands alighting all over him. As if his skin were fire and she couldn't touch him for long.

His own hands went to work immediately. One hand cupped one of her breasts and gave it a gentle squeeze as his other hand reached further down beyond her mound.

Finding her wet entry was easy; the problem was the moment he touched it, she ground herself into his palm.

Whimpering excitedly, Petra threw her head back, exposing her neck as she thrust her hips at his hand.

Taking the invitation, Vince turned his head and sunk his teeth into her white neck. Biting down hard, he felt her buck against him. Hanging on to her, he sunk his teeth as deeply as he could without causing her to bleed.

Her whimpers had turned into panting moans, her fingers hooking into his shoulders and digging in.

Releasing her throat, Vince resettled himself, his hands coming up to rest just under her armpits, pressing to the ground.

She looked at him then, blue eyes wide with hopeless devotion and yearning.

And fear.

Using his knees, he pinned the top pair of her legs against her sides. When he concentrated on the feel of it, the position felt identical to Fes or Meliae. The skin of her legs felt more firm and were thinner, but there wasn't much difference.

Then he reached down with one hand. Grasping a hold of his shaft, he guided himself to her entrance, and then pushed into her.

Petra's moans were choked off as he entered her. Her hands pulled at him roughly, her body shuddering underneath him. Inch by inch he filled her, pushing deep into her.

Once there was nothing left to put inside her, he stopped, his eyes drinking in the sight of her.

Her eyes were a touch glassy and her mouth turned up in a small smile. "It hurts, Master."

"My apologies, Petra. The first time normally isn't the most pleasant."

"It feels good already, though, Master. The brief pain was when this one lost her maidenhead. She will be fine. Use her for your pleasure. Your pleasure is hers. Use her." Petra accentuated her demands by pulling her hips back and then thrusting up at him, effectively forcing him in and out of her an inch or two.

Vince shook his head with a smile. Her attitude towards his pleasure seemed broken to him, but who was he to complain.

Closing the distance between them, he kissed her tenderly and then drew his hips back.

Coming up for air, he watched her as he thrust himself back in. She mewled once, and then eagerly pushed up at him with her whole body as if to get to him quicker.

Satisfied she wasn't in pain, Vince began to work himself back and forth through her channel. His head dipped down to sneak kisses and licks of her face and neck.

Petra's hands trailed up and down his back as her other four legs occasionally pressed to his shoulders or hips. As if wanting him to thrust into her harder.

"Use this one. Use her for everything. Use her," Petra murmured. "Use her. Use her. Make her moan. Break her. Fill her. Use her till she can't stand. Dirty her. Own her."

The rapid descent into dirty talk with her soft, charming voice was a surprise. Reaching up, he captured her wrists and then pinned them above her head with one of his hands. His other hand pressed more deeply into her side as he started to thrust into harder.

Leaning his head down, he bit down viciously into her neck, the soft flesh filing his mouth.

"Yes, yes! Use her, fill her. Make her yours. Tell her what you want. Anything. Anything. Fill her with seed!" Petra called out, not fighting him in the least, struggling to raise her hips with each thrust.

The sweet sound of her begging voice, the way she wanted to be dominated by him without a hint of a game, the way she screamed it at him made him drunk on the power of it.

This wasn't anything like the way Meliae wanted to be broken. To be used extremely and in a humiliating way. Meliae wanted to be forced, for him to break her, to show her off in a way that would shame her.

Petra just wanted to be used. To be used for his pleasure.

Her legs settled onto his back and pushed into him wildly when he entered her.

The force of the impact of his hips started to knock the wind out of Petra, her breath coming out in groans and gasps. The clap of her flesh with each entry echoed through the trees.

"Seed me," she begged as she gasped for breath, his hips having sped up further and pounding her into the grass.

Vince released her dark, bruising flesh and lifted his head. Then kissed her savagely, his shaft tightening as seed slammed through his member. Filling her.

Petra whimpered happily into his mouth, her legs closing tightly around his hips and pulling him in as close as possible.

At the height of each spurt, he ground himself against her, eliciting a fresh batch of whimpered moans.

As he came down from his orgasm, Petra squirmed under him, her hips pushing at him, her legs pulling at his waist still.

Surrendering her lips, he watched her from an inch or two away.

"Master cannot pull out until all his seed is claimed. Please wait to pull out. Please," Petra pleaded with him, watching him wide blue eyes.

Vince smiled at the crazed soldier ant and laid his head own on her shoulder, releasing her wrists above her head.

As if they were made of magnets and his back iron, her arms slammed down around his shoulders, pressing him tightly to herself.

"You seeded this one. Seeded her fully."

"Yes, I did. Damn, were you sexy about it, too."

"This one lives to serve you, Master. Seeding her was a gift to her from you. Master need only ask for anything else. Anything. Only ask. She will do anything. Anything you want."

Vince didn't respond to that. Instead, he closed his eyes and snuggled his head to her shoulder. He enjoyed the warmth and comfort that she offered.

Chapter 20

"Sweetling, I missed you!"

Vince's eyes popped open as Meliae pressed herself bodily against him. She nuzzled her head under his chin. Then she rubbed her body against his, her fingers digging into his clothes.

Vince and Petra had fallen asleep on the stream bank rather than keep traveling. Of course, that was after having their second time right there on the stream bed.

A glance at the sky told him it was early morning. The sun was barely up.

Petra was beside him, still snoring despite Meliae's entrance.

Her clothes were rumpled but she was dressed. He knew for a fact she was missing her underwear band, though. They'd pushed her shirt up out of the way the second time and stripped the band off.

Smiling at the warm and cuddly Dryad, he wrapped his arms around her in a hug.

"Well hello there. How'd you find us? I would have thought you'd be further south than us," Vince admitted.

Meliae scoffed, lifting her head up to meet his eyes. "As if I wouldn't know where my tree was. I can always feel you. Always know where you are."

"Good to know." Vince grinned and kissed her once.

Looking up, he found Fes a few steps beyond where he lay. She had one hand pressed to her midsection, the other holding on to her mount. She looked ragged, but on the mend. A wide smile was plastered on her face as his eyes met hers. "You're looking better, Berenga. I'm glad. I was worried for you."

"I'm well, husband. In pain, but well. Our seed grower has tended to me expertly," the Orc said. Her shoulders had looked stiff at first, but she seemed to droop as she spoke.

Meliae nodded her head, pressing her face into his chest. "You smell like Petra," she murmured.

"I don't doubt that. Alright, get up, my little nymph. I need to go hug that grumpy Orc Fes of mine," Vince said teasingly, patting the Dryad on the back.

"Only because you called me yours," Meliae said, freeing him. She rolled over and curled up against Petra, resting her head on the soldier ant's shoulder.

Petra's eyes opened, her head tilting down to find Meliae.

The Dryad gave her a grin and then whispered something to her.

Ignoring them both, Vince stood up and then walked over to Fes.

Meliae mentioned in her letter that Fes needed some attention. This would be a good opportunity for that.

Trying to stand up straight, Fes let go of the horse and held her arms open to him.

That alone was out of the ordinary for Fes. Pulling her into a tight hug, he held her. Laying his head to hers, he tenderly ran his hands up and down her back.

"You okay, Fes?" Vince whispered in her ear.

"I hurt. Our seed grower saved me from death, I'm sure of it. I think she understated how badly I was injured. She spends much energy to heal me every hour."

Vince let out a shallow breath and hugged Fes tighter.

"She takes care of everything for me as I heal. I owe her. How can I be Fes if I can't protect her, Petra, or you?"

"Because you gained these injuries while being Fes, Fes. No one will slight you for being wounded tending to your duty. You just need to heal now."

"You've claimed Petra," Fes said. It really wasn't much of a question, since it did look rather obvious.

"Yeah, I did." Vince leaned back and gave Fes a smile. "And you're Fes."

Fes nodded her head at that. She didn't seem upset in any way, shape, or form at that. If anything, there was the slightest bit of relief in her eyes.

"I was angry."

"Angry?" Vince parroted back, not quite understanding.

"When fighting the soldiers at the village. They fought like Petra. They tried to separate me from you all. So they could flank you.

"Was very angry. Everywhere, I lose ground. Meliae warmed more than your bed, and she has your seed. Petra now shares your bed. I don't think I can join your bed in my current condition. Petra fights me to a standstill and I can't beat her. My aim with the rifles isn't as good as everyone else.

"I'm losing my place." Fes's eyes looked clouded to him. Lost.

Vince frowned at that and thought about his answer. What he'd have said to a human woman wouldn't work with Berenga. She was a strong, proud Orc woman. One who didn't need any of them and chose to be here.

Behind him, he could hear Petra and Meliae whispering back and forth. He did his best to ignore it and tune it out; he didn't really want to listen in to what they were saying right now.

"That doesn't sound like my Fes at all," Vince said finally, having come to the answer he wanted to give her. "My Fes would learn from her enemies and how to beat them. My Fes would claim her place in my bed even if she could not claim me as violently as she normally would. My Fes would practice until she's better than everyone else with the rifle. My Fes wouldn't cower and whimper," Vince said firmly.

Fes's eyes were wide and locked on to his face. Her mouth hung open and her breathing stopped.

"My Fes is having a tough time right now, though. She's trying to hold on to her beliefs, to get what she wants, and to remain who she is.

"I'm sure she'll come to a decision once she recovers. Berenga is still my Fes, after all. Isn't she?"

Fes's mouth closed and her jaw muscles bunched. Her shoulders straightened and her tired dark eyes looked like they were lit from the inside with anger.

A ghost of who she had been before their journey north was coming back. The woman he'd met in the wilderness who wouldn't bow down to anyone.

Her hands pressed into his back for a second more, then she let go of him. Her hands drifted to the front of his chest. Trailing her fingers down for a second, she then curled her fingers into his clothes. With a jerk on his clothes, she pulled him forward bodily towards herself.

Then she kissed him. Roughly, wantonly, and very much in Fes fashion.

Pulling back from him, she pressed her forehead to his. "Your seed is mine tonight," growled the Orc warrior.

They made good time on their way back south. They made a brief stop in Salem to pick up supplies and another horse.

The time on the road was spent mostly in rest. Conversation flowed easily between the four of them.

Fes seemed as if she'd woken up. Each time they stopped, she demanded that Petra, as her subordinate, instruct her in her fighting style.

Fes couldn't put everything to full speed, but she seemed apt in her lessons. Often, Meliae would have to halt the lesson when Fes was close to hurting herself or reopening her wounds.

The Dryad doted on Fes as if she were an older sister to her. She brooked no nonsense from her once it was clear she'd overdone it. In everything else, she submitted to Fes immediately.

The Orc warrior had also decided she need to re-stake her claim, or so it seemed to Vince. She'd claimed his bed for a week straight. It wasn't as rough and tumble as it had been before she was injured, but it was still rather violent, all things considered.

Suffice it to say, Vince tried to go easy on her, though he did allow her to come out on top once or twice.

As if she'd re-solidified something in her own thinking, she returned him to a rotation. Petra had moved into the second night position and Meliae the third.

He didn't question it, and didn't really want to. Whatever they were working out between themselves didn't need him butting in right now.

It wasn't until they reached Sacramento that they'd stopped for longer than a night.

Sacramento had a very large Ranger guild hub, a central banking site, and one of the largest news networks available.

Which meant it was probably the best place for them to hunker down for a few days and get their bearings.

Vince was alone as he exited the Ranger guild hall. He'd relayed everything he knew to his superiors, had gotten paid for his work, with a considerable bonus, and was asked to not speak of this incident to anyone. At which point they'd paid him another bonus.

Buying my silence. No one wants it known that a Ranger guild not only fell, but fell internally.

Vince shook his head and looked around at his surroundings.

The mood had certainly changed since the last time he'd been here.

Slaves were being walked on leashes instead of being allowed to walk free. Almost on every corner, men and women were denouncing Washington for being in league with the Wastes. There was a considerable amount of fear and anger coursing throughout the streets.

On top of that, the militia forces had been called to active duty, then told to assist the police in their work.

Soldiers and anyone who could be useful in a war had been sent north.

The Empire was responding to Washington's break with the government. The slave guild was funding a huge portion of the war as well.

Everything was going to shit.

Under his arm was the box of vouchers. He'd planned on heading to the bank after this and negotiating a transfer to standards at a loss.

Standards could be spent anywhere; the vouchers could not.

Giving himself a quick onceover, he found he looked the part of an everyday citizen. He didn't want to stand out in case the slave guild started to ask questions about those vouchers.

With a steady pace and a wary eye, Vince made his way to the bank. He seated himself sedately in the lobby after having asked to speak with the branch manager.

The branch manager at a location like this would be a rather influential person, he was sure. It'd also be the best person to work with on this deal.

Vince surreptitiously studied the bank. Guards were in every corner, armed with rifles and fixed bayonets. On top of that, the bank employed two machine guns. They were both on raised platforms in opposite corners, enclosed except for a narrow slit they could see out of.

Security here was no joke.

A woman stepped in front of him and held out her hand to him.

"Hi there, I'm Nancy, Nancy Lu," said the woman in clear tones. "I'm the bank manager. I believe you asked to speak with me, Mister…?"

She was an attractive woman of Asian origin. She dressed like someone in her mid-thirties, but her face and body skewed his perceived age of her.

Long black hair fell down her back and her large dark brown eyes flowed over him.

Standing up, he immediately took her hand and gave it a firm handshake.

"Name's Smith," Vince lied smoothly, giving her the brightest smile he could.

Her handshake was strong, her skin soft. Then Vince gently caressed her mind with his extra senses. She was a vulture, a wolf, a buzzard, a lion, a shark. Everything she was was predatory. Everything had a price in her mind, and there was no end to the lengths she would go to make money.

Raising her eyebrows at him, she gave him a warm smile. "Would you accompany me to my office?"

"Of course, Miss Lu. After you," Vince said, releasing her hand.

"Please, call me Nancy."

She turned and walked off towards an office door that was in line with the teller windows.

Holding the door open for him, Nancy closed it as soon as he crossed the threshold.

"What can I do for you today, Mr. Smith?" she asked.

Vince smiled at her and took a seat in front of the large wooden desk. Opening the box, he removed the vouchers and laid them down in front of her as she took her seat.

"I'm afraid I don't quite have the confidence I used to in the Auction House. What with the war and all. I'd like to convert these to standards."

Nancy picked up one of the vouchers. She tapped a long finger against one of the seals and flipped it over to look at the back.

"These appear authentic. Would you mind if I had someone inspect them?"

"Be my guest. I was hoping to get ninety-five percent of their value in standards. The remainder being a service fee of sorts."

Nancy thumbed a button on a small plastic square in front of her. "Could you please have Andy come in here? I need him to authenticate a voucher."

"Right away, ma'am," replied someone on the other end.

"Well, Mr. Smith, I can certainly agree to cash these out for standards. We deal with the guild for many services and often."

"I'm not sure I could do it at ninety-five, though."

She gave him an underwear-melting smile and leaned forward over her desk. While she was dressed modestly, her movement had revealed some cleavage. Belatedly, he realized she had a body similar to Meliae's.

And there's where it starts. The beautiful bank manager who gets a better cut because she uses her advantages.

"I'm willing to negotiate. Many things have a price you wouldn't normally think to offer," Vince replied with a grin.

In this case, he was the one with an upper hand. There were other banks he could go to. He also had a small harem that took care of his appetites.

At that moment, a knock came at the office door. Nancy sat back in her desk. "Come!"

A soldier walked in, dressed out in dark brown fatigues with a helmet covering his head.

"Ah, Andy, good. Here, please check this to confirm it's authentic," Nancy said, holding out the voucher she'd been handling.

The man, who looked as ordinary as dirt, took the paper from her. Ten seconds of intense scrutiny later, he handed it back to her.

"Authentic." Without waiting to be dismissed, the man known as Andy walked back out the door and was gone. As the door closed behind him, Vince finally noticed the slave collar around the man's neck.

Nancy huffed at the rude departure and put the voucher back into the pile. "His work is excellent, but his manners are awful."

The bank manager tapped a finger onto the vouchers in thought. Then she picked up the stack and began counting them.

"There's eighty there. All at ten thousand marks."

Nancy nodded her head but kept counting. When she was done, she realigned the stack and looked at him again. Putting her chin in one hand, supporting it with her elbow on the desk, she smiled at him.

"You mentioned things that didn't normally have a price. What'd you have in mind?" Her eyes had an inviting look to him that he was sure she'd practiced for hours.

"Ninety-five percent of the value, in bank notes. No documentation other than 'Smith.' I believe I'd like to tip you five percent of the value. So I'd need ninety percent for me, five percent for your lovely self, and five percent for the bank.

Personal greed always did nicely. She might be willing to sleep with him, but that wouldn't help him in the long run.

Not to mention Petra had kept him awake late into the night the previous evening. Nancy was beautiful, but Vince was still spent.

Nancy's eyebrows shot up at that, her flirty demeanor lost in an instant. She was more than likely well paid. Few without morals would willingly turn down forty thousand standards.

Considering it seemed like she was willing to sleep with him to knock down a few percentages, he doubted she'd be able to walk from a deal like that.

Nancy thumbed the electronic square of plastic on her desk into an off position. Then she got up and went to the door. With a turn of her wrist, she locked it.

She gave him a truly radiant smile then. "Done. Let's get you taken care of immediately. Maybe we can talk more later tonight as well?"

Thirty minutes later and Vince was at large with seven hundred and twenty thousand standards in bank notes in a wooden box tucked under an arm. They were all in various denominations of ten, twenty, and fifty thousand standards.

Standing there, he took a minute to collect his thoughts. Nancy would do whatever she felt would further her goals. And he doubted she was above having someone assaulted who had left the bank with more than half a million standards.

Now he was glad he'd taken the time to think of an escape route if he was followed from the bank.

He had no proof he was, or was going to be, but there wasn't a reason to take a chance.

For all he knew, she was genuinely interested in him as a person and nothing to do with his money.

A healthy dose of paranoia keeps one alive.

Taking a breath, he set off on a direct route for an inn he wasn't staying at. Stepping in through the front doors, he didn't pause or hesitate. He acted as if he owned the place and went right up the stairs.

At the end of the second-floor hallway was a window. That window had been open when he'd been planning his alternate escape route. Feeling quite lucky indeed, he found it was still open.

Hopping through the open frame, he dropped down to the alley behind with a dull thud.

Hightailing it through the alley, he kept himself to the back streets until he made it back to the Ranger guild.

A flash of his card, a smile for the receptionist, and he was inside. Safe from prying eyes.

As part of the services rendered to all its members, the Ranger guild offered key-operated lockboxes in a private vault.

Vince paid the admin the minor fee and entered the vault. Walking up to the wall of lockboxes, he selected one with its key inserted.

Forty-two.

All the boxes were bolted to the wall and came out on a shelf welded to a giant steel frame. These weren't going anywhere.

Pulling his choice out of its tray, he flipped open the steel lid. A cursory glance and he'd confirmed it was empty except for the owner's tag, which he fished out quickly.

Opening the wooden box under his arm, he pulled out two bank notes for fifty thousand standards. Then he closed and dumped the wooden box into the lockbox.

Dropping the lid in place, he shoved the whole thing back into the wall, then locked it back up and pulled the key out.

No one would be able to open his box without the key, and there were no duplicates.

Only the guild had the master key, and they only did an annual sweep to make sure boxes were paid for and working as intended.

Hiding away the bank notes and the key, Vince went back to the admin. Handing over the owner's token and his Ranger ID, he waited.

Identity recorded, ownership logged, he was free to go.

Vince slipped back into the common room and started towards the room he was sharing with the girls.

He needed to pick up Meliae and then head over to the slave market. Fes would be resting, and Petra could stand guard.

The market would be opening up in an hour, and supposedly it was going to be a big one. Many slaves were being sold in the south since the northern market was not completely accessible.

He had a plan. It would take a huge chunk of his newfound wealth, but so be it.

Petra's earlier comment still rang inside his head. He could buy many, many slaves. Put many men and women to work in an area that no one would bother them. Give them a chance to live a life that was denied to them.

That, or they could simply go back to whatever life they wanted in the Wastes. He wouldn't keep them if they didn't wish to be kept.

And with the possibility of that many mouths to feed, he'd need far more in the way of tools and supplies.

He was only just starting. And time was already against him.

Soon both sides would realize that slavery was the economical lynch pin for some areas. The military would turn to purchasing them for military recruits, and Washington would do their best to get them to join their cause.

Vince only had so much time before that happened.

Time to get to work.

Chapter 21

Vince settled into the recliner near the rear of the theater. The slaver guild had converted it after a number of their big auctions had been rained out one too many times in the past.

Regardless of weather, this auction could continue.

"A bit upscale for a dungeon," Meliae whispered from beside him. She'd slunk into the empty recliner and adjusted herself.

"I'm sure it's easier to sell people if they feel like it's professionally done."

Meliae harrumphed at that and then snuck her hand over the arms of the recliners to clasp his own. "They stare," she said by way of explanation.

Vince looked around at the few people who were seating in seats nearby. Quite a few men immediately turned their gaze elsewhere as Vince met their eyes.

"You can't blame them. You're beautiful and you're showing off a little," Vince said, indicating with a finger the tight clothes she'd put on.

"Fair enough. And yes, I am showing off. Everyone should admire me and my tree. I was hoping there'd be another Dryad here so I could gloat."

"That's surprisingly petty of you," Vince said with a grin.

"We all have our hang-ups. Mine is wanting to show you off to everyone. Besides, you love me for it," Meliae purred at him, pressing herself up into the arm of her recliner and giving him an eyeful.

Love her for it? Do I?

That wasn't something he was quite prepared to answer. Sure, he liked her. Impregnated her. Spent every third night with her.

But did he love her?

Seemed like a silly thing to ask himself at this point, in the whole scheme of things.

Instead, he gave her a sincere smile. "Be good and I'll humiliate you terribly tonight."

Meliae's eyes flashed to a full green. She barely managed a nod with her head, her eyes slowly going back to normal.

"Promise?" she whispered softly.

"You'll feel shame for days."

Meliae blinked rapidly, clearly battling for control of her emotions. Turning, she settled back into her recliner, and crossed her legs. Her left hand still remained in his, her fingers slowly intertwining through his own.

With Meliae, rewards always went further than punishments. Because her rewards were punishments.

From her actions, he could guess she had been planning on ramping up the pressure on him until he had to do something.

Rather than wait, he'd cut to the heart of the matter.

"Good afternoon, everyone!" called a voice from the stage at the front of the theater.

"What are we looking for, Sweetling? I understand the plan in general. I'm not a planner like Petra, though. Even Fes might be better than me for this."

"We're looking for good-hearted people we can welcome aboard. It would do us no good bringing people who would be poison for us. I trust your instincts, my little Dryad. Put them to work for your tree, would you?"

Meliae blushed so heavily it looked more like she was holding her breath. Her thumbnail grazed up along the inside of his palm.

Vince turned back to the front as the auction started.

"Our first item. A lot sale for two families of Elves. They're generational slaves at this point and well trained. We're offering them as a group sale today, but we can negotiate a separate contract if the buyer wishes only a partial purchase."

Vince looked at the group of twenty-three that walked in from the right side of the stage.

What the auctioneer hadn't said was that they were Dark Elves. Of the many sub species of Elfin-kind, many distrusted the Dark Elves on a superstitious level. Whatever fool that decided to sell them as a group would only exacerbate that superstitious belief.

"Opening bid is ten standards, do I have ten?" That was a low price. A very low price. Not even a full standard per person.

The group ranged in ages and sexes, from small children to the elderly.

All were nude, as was the custom with slaves.

"I have ten, do I have fifteen?"

Vince carefully brushed the mind of each and found they were all uniformly terrified. Terrified and resigned. Whatever home they came from had been warm and kind. They had no illusions to where they'd be going from here.

Especially the women.

"You will buy them. All of them," Meliae said, her voice hard.

"I'll buy them," Vince agreed, giving Meliae's hand a squeeze. The Dryad shot him a look, and then gave him a bashful smile.

"Thank you…" Meliae said softly, turning her face back to the stage.

"Ten going twice —" called the auctioneer.

Vince held up his placard in his left hand.

"I have fifteen, do I have twenty?"

There were no higher bids.

"Once, twice, thrice, sold to the gentleman in the back."

Vince looked to his side and found an usher coming his way. Waving the man in, Vince set his left hand on the man's shoulder.

"I'm going to be purchasing a good number of people today. I'd like you to arrange a storage facility so my purchases remain undamaged. Do a good job and I'll tip you one hundred standards. Questions?"

"No, sir, I'm your man. I'll take care of it," enthused the young man.

"Good. Go."

Vince turned back to the stage.

The next two sales were gladiators. They had hatred in their hearts and had been born and raised for nothing but death. They wouldn't do well with his plan. Their battle experience would be useful, but only so long as they had an enemy he could throw them at.

Lost in a thought, he missed the next introduction and looked to the stage to find a group of Ogres and Trolls. Seven in total.

They were regarded as slow and stupid creatures, but when Vince peeked into their minds, he found they were of an average intelligence. Though their thoughts were ponderous things.

Of the seven, six were of a mind that he could work with. The big Troll on the end was a nasty thing, though. She'd been abusing the others up to this point and regarded them as trash.

"I want six of them, skipping the big female on the end," Vince said.

"You clearly see something I don't," Meliae said with a confused sound.

Vince hesitated, then came clean. "I'm empathic, to a degree. I can sift through their thoughts and feelings. If I push it, I can read their memories, but it takes a lot out of me. It's why I need you here. I need you to bounce my gift off of and confirm it so I don't waste energy. Let's discuss this more in depth elsewhere."

Meliae nodded her head vigorously at that. "Buy all seven. She's a brute, but I'll speak with her. Trolls listen to us Dryads. They're more like plants than people."

Vince thought on that but then held up his placard. He trusted Meliae. This was him showing that trust.

"Sold to the gentleman who looks like he prefers buying in bulk for seventy standards."

The auction proceeded in that way, Vince buying up anyone who looked like they'd suit his purposes.

In the end, he picked up a family of Wood Elves, several Goblins, an entire colony of Beaver Beastmen, two Dryads whose trees had been found and sold with them, a group of Bearmen, an entire village of Dwarves, and a vast array of one-offs.

The final count was well over two hundred and sixty people and a mite shy of three thousand standards. The costs had been cheap in his eyes.

At this rate, it'd take him forever to run out of money.

Meliae and Vince were escorted to a warehouse in the back of the theater.

"I'm so sorry, sir, I had to put most of them here, but the rest of them are in another room," apologized the usher.

"Not a problem. You've done fantastic. Could you fetch the manager for me?" Vince asked, surveying the room of milling life that he was now responsible for.

"He's already on his way, sir."

Vince nodded at that. Meliae was already pushing her way through the crowd, making her way straight for the big Troll at the back.

"Ah, forgive me for keeping you waiting," panted a fat man with sweat-plastered hair and weak blue eyes.

Vince looked to the man and then held out his hand.

"Pleasure doing business with you. I assume you'll waive the registration fees and simply write them all to my account. In addition, the return of their clothes, of course?" Vince asked.

The fat man froze as he placed his hand within Vince's.

"I'll be in town for three more days. I do hope you were planning on holding an auction each day as well? I have a great deal of time on my hands and I'm purchasing as many as I can before I head back to the East Coast."

The manager took that in and then smiled broadly at Vince. "Yes, we can handle the collars, registration, and clothes easily.

"We were actually only this morning talking about having more sales tomorrow. I guarantee we'll have much more available tomorrow and the day after."

"Great. I'll also need to purchase wagons from you to transport them. If you can get me reasonable rates on food for them for a journey of two weeks, I'll do business with you on that matter as well."

The manager smiled even wider and bobbed his head. "Of course, of course. I'll take care of everything. Would you like to open a line of credit—"

"No. I'm giving this to you for safekeeping. I expect an exact account of everything at the end of this. If you even think of taking advantage of me, I'll buy this building from the bank and lodge a complaint with the guild.

"My accountant will be combing through this for every single standard spent," Vince threatened, handing over one of his bank notes.

"I'd never dreaaaeeeuuuhhhh…" the manager said lamely, looking at the amount on the note. "Sir, this is—"

"It's not enough? Here. Another, then," Vince said, handing over the second note. He was deliberately being vague and stupid with his money. "If you need more than that, I'll need to stop at the bank first. And if you breathe a word of this to anyone, or my presence here, well, please refer to my earlier statement about your building and the guild."

The manager had gone from a happy, red-faced fat man to a fearful, white-faced fat man scurrying away to get everything in order.

Looking back out to the crowd of faces looking up to him on the platform, he tried to pick out Meliae.

"Of course she is," Vince murmured on seeing her. She was with the other two Dryads, happily chatting away with them.

"Many apologies, Lord, for interrupting your grace as you surveyed your merchandise, but I would beg a word with you," came a soft, breathy voice.

Turning his head to the side, he found his entire purchase of Dark Elves watching him.

At the forefront was a young Dark Elf woman, naked as the day she was born. She did her best to hide her shame at her situation.

"What can I do for you…?" Vince asked, deliberately ignoring her nakedness.

"I am called Thera, my lord. I would offer myself to you as concubine to assure my friends and family of good placement. My previous master had sought to sell me off when I reached my full maturity, so I am, as of yet, unsoiled."

Pretty sure she just told me she was a virgin.

"No, I'm afraid—"

Another young Dark Elf woman rushed forward and prostrated herself in front of him.

"Please, lord, take my sister and I as concubines, if only to guarantee our families proper treatment. We have never experienced the touch of a man; we were to be sold as needed," pleaded Thera.

"Listen—"

"Lord, please," begged the group in unison.

Vince sighed and pressed a hand to his eyes.

Accept them, never touch them. They'll shut up and work hard for you.

"Fine. Consider yourself so chosen, Thera, but not your sister, I'm—"

At that moment, the big family of Wood Elves made an appearance, pushing in amongst the Dark Elves. Two young Wood Elf women prostrated themselves next to their Dark Elf kin.

"Master, my name is Eva—" started the wood Elf next to Thera in a musical voice.

"Fine! Stop, no more. Thera and Eva are now concubines. I order you and your families to stop anyone else from attempting the same thing. Consider your families as my house servants and chamberlain."

Vince was losing his temper. He wanted none of them and they'd die virgins before he touched them.

"The manager is coming back with clothes. Distribute them to their owners. Be fair, be diligent, take no sides.

"Tonight, everyone is going to be loaded into wagons. I need you all to arrange it and get everyone properly ordered. You'll be leaving as soon as night falls with a companion of mine.

"She will lead you to a point where we'll be camping until we move."

Vince ground out the words between his teeth as he stared at the Elves. "Any questions?"

"My lord, which of us should service your bed tonight?" Thera asked in a voice bordering on breaking.

"Neither of you. Now go, shoo."

The two he'd "chosen" as concubines convened with their cohorts. The Dark and Wood Elves put any differences they had aside and merged into one group. After a rapid exchange in a language he didn't know, they broke apart, splintering into the crowd.

His two "concubines" took up positions on each side of him, watching the crowd with him.

Eying the women critically, he quirked a brow. "And what are you two up to?"

"Following your orders," Thera said immediately.

"We shall prevent anyone else from approaching," Eva concluded.

"I see. Well, don't stop the Dryads. I have business with them," Vince said, turning his eye to the three Dryads shuffling their way over with two trees between the three of them.

The three Dryads resembled each other vaguely, though they had different heights, and vastly different appearances. Though each had the same green eyes that Meliae did.

The first Dryad was several inches taller than Meliae. Though her body type was similar to Meliae, her hips were a touch narrower, though her chest was larger. Her hair was a dark brown with lighter brown streaks throughout. Like everyone else he'd purchased, her hair had been hacked dreadfully short in the slave fashion.

Beside her stood the other new Dryad. She was significantly taller, coming close to Vince's own height. She was closer to Meliae in having an hourglass body, but her shoulders looked broader to him. Straight blonde hair hung short and ragged at the level of her ears.

"Sweetling, this is Karya. She's a walnut," Meliae said, indicating the one with dark brown hair.

Then she pointed to the blonde. "And Daphnaie," Meliae said, uttering a name that sounded strange to his ear. "Who's a laurel. She also goes by Daphne."

Definitely easier to pronounce.

Vince nodded his head to the two women. Both of them eyed him speculatively, before looking back to Meliae.

"See? A tree. Overflowing with power, even though my tree drinks all it can."

Daphne opened her mouth and pointed at his chest. "Your tree is entirely in his chest?" Her voice was eerily similar to Meliae's in its musical quality, though deeper.

"It started to spread, but then retracted. It was being overfed. Even now, it's overfed." Meliae said that with a touch of pride, and maybe a hint of fear.

Karya moved before he realized and had her nose pressed to his chest. "He reeks of sex and power."

"Yes. Yes, he does," Thera agreed from beside him. Eva nodded her head at the same time Thera spoke.

"I'm glad we all agree on that," Vince said, pressing his hands to Karya's shoulders and eased her away.

Getting her to move back a few steps, Vince looked to Meliae.

"So?" he asked her. She was supposed to find out if they could move freely and if their trees would handle the journey.

"I'm afraid not. Neither is carrying the seed of a man, though they both have a seed from their tree."

"I don't —"

"If they were pregnant, they could go further without their tree," Meliae explained.

"Ah," Vince said.

That makes an odd sort of sense.

"Definitely explains why you were able to practically be an entire state away without a problem."

"Yes. Yes, it does," Meliae said, ducking her head as her cheeks flushed.

The other two Dryads, and the two Elves, all eyed Meliae.

"So, what do you want to do?" Vince verbally prodded Meliae. She was his Dryad expert, after all.

"Ah, about that. I... can they plant their trees in you?" Meliae asked, her eyes coming up to meet his own. They'd gone to a completely green color without a hint of iris or even whites.

"I don't understand. You want... me to be their tree, too? Is that even possible?" Vince asked slowly.

Meliae nodded her head woodenly. Looking to Daphne and Karya, he found their eyes to be the same completely greened-out version of Meliae's.

"Would I suffer any ill effects or anything?" Vince asked to any of the three of them.

All three shook their heads.

This is going nowhere.

"Meliae, if you explain this to me, and why you're reacting like this, I'll humiliate you in front of everyone here."

Meliae shuddered and lifted her hands to her face. "Sharing a tree with two other Dryads would shame me until the day I die. I could never look at another Dryad without them knowing. It's unheard of."

Vince frowned and scratched at his jaw. He noticed that the Elves were quickly distributing clothes, rations, and instructions to everyone in the room.

"In other words, all three of you would be shamed eternally for sharing a tree, which has knocked these two on their ass," Vince said, pointing a thumb at the two wooden Dryads.

"Yes, Sweetling. It's... a bit easier for me since I'm carrying your seed."

"And they can't travel otherwise?"

"They won't last a week. Their trees didn't survive their uprooting; it's taking a good portion of their power so they die slowly instead of immediately."

Vince grunted and pulled out his belt knife. Then he stripped off the tunic he'd worn into town.

"Fine. I'm assuming I need to cut myself open again?" Vince resolved himself to this action. He couldn't condemn them to die just because he didn't want to be a traveling flowerpot.

"Yes. Same spot, if possible. I can keep you from bleeding or feeling pain."

"This is until they plant their trees later," Vince said, pushing the knife into his chest right on top of the same place from the previous incident.

True to her word, he felt no pain. The knife parted his flesh smoothly and easily, the wound popping open into a gaping maw.

It was eerie, staring into the same exact wound that had nearly taken his life.

"They won't be able to replant elsewhere. No seeds will grow inside you," Meliae admitted.

At the same time she said that, Karya pushed a walnut into his chest, while Daphne shoved a black seed in.

"Meliae, what—"

Meliae pressed her hand over the wound, and it closed itself in an instant. As she pulled her hand away, he looked down and found the flesh looked undamaged as ever.

A single streak of blood was the only evidence he'd ever cut himself open.

Both Thera and Eva kept their eyes moving, but their noses were twitching.

Strange.

Vince let his thoughts go back to Meliae and he growled at her.

"I'm sorry, Sweetling. I couldn't let them die. Not when we could all survive together."

"Goddammit, Meliae," Vince huffed.

"You'll never even know. I promise. Only benefits. Pure benefits. Strongest tree ever," Meliae said excitedly, her hands rubbing up and down his biceps.

"So much," Daphne muttered.

"Too strong," Karya said.

A second later, both of them dropped to the ground as if someone had hit their power switch.

"They're okay. Only transferring their bond to their new tree. You're much stronger now than when I planted in you," Meliae said, waving a hand at the two unconscious women.

Thera and Eva were there immediately. They were joined by two of their coworkers, who all worked together to carefully bring the Dryads to one side.

"Thank you," Vince murmured to the Elves.

Then he closed his eyes and shook his head. He wasn't cut out for this. He was a Ranger.

"Can... can I get my reward tonight? Other than the other Dryads, I was very good. Reward me?" Meliae asked, her tongue sliding over her lips.

Vince groaned into his hands and wanted the day to end.

Chapter 22

Vince had spent the following two days in the auction house of Sacramento, purchasing a vast array of Wasters.

None were as unique or interesting as the first day. The next two days were little more than leftovers from other auctions nearby.

He purchased those would fit in and not rock the boat and wanted a chance at a new life. Unfortunately, many were bitter, angry, and resentful. They'd murdered others or done worse in their hatred.

While the ones he'd purchased wouldn't be as useful as some, they'd be part of the labor force for his plan. That, and they'd be free.

He'd take a happy Waster with no skills over a skilled individual with nothing but hate in their heart.

Vince felt like he was losing himself as they journeyed south with over four hundred pairs of eyes watching him.

What regret he'd had for taking Eva and Thera as concubines vanished as their families went to work with a single-minded determination.

They'd increased their numbers as well. He doubted there were very many Elves left in the purchased population that weren't included now.

Not that he could complain about them only bringing in Elfin-kind. Everything was neat. Orderly. Planned.

He found that when he felt like he was about to be overrun, Eva and Thera were there to pick up the slack with exactly what he needed.

He'd decided to skip Modesto after he found out that it'd been stripped clean of slaves to purchase. They'd all been sent north for him to look over.

Knight's Ferry would be too hard to remain anonymous, so that was out.

Which left him with Blanchard as the best place to spend money.

Blanchard had originally been not much more than a stain on a map. Now it compared to Modesto or even Fresno in size and scope.

All thanks to its slave trade.

Vince looked at the truly massive building that served as the local auction for Blanchard. The sale would be starting in about an hour, and Vince was ready.

He'd sent everyone east to begin settling into their new home.

Everyone except Daphne, Karya, Thera, and Eva. The two Dryads were too weak to be separated from him yet. Thera and Eva simply wouldn't listen to him when he told them to keep moving.

"Lord, I believe everything is in order," Thera said from his right.

"Master, all is as it should be," Eva concurred from his left.

"You sure you two aren't related?" Vince said to the two Elves. They were drastic opposites in skin tone, yet so very similar in every other way.

Looking to Eva, she was the picture of a Wood Elf. Tousled brown hair, brown eyes, delicate features, exquisite looks, tanned skin, full lips, and an athletic body. She topped out at a paltry five foot two.

Thera was similar in nearly every way to Thera. So much so that despite their skin tones, you couldn't mistake them as anything other than the same species.

She shared her "cousin's" build exactly, though she had several inches on her in height. With dark eyes and long, dark hair the color of a raven's wing, she was nearly like a shadow. Her pearl-gray skin only added to that impression.

Both of them were dressed in a fashion that turned the head of everyone they crossed, though for very different reasons.

Thera had donned a set of black painted brigandine armor. The metal plates were tight around her chest, but not prohibitively so. Her arms and legs were coated in hardened leather.

Belted to her hip and slung low was a long sword, and a matching dagger on the other side.

Eva, on the other hand, was dressed in dark brown leather armor, with a slim blade at her waist. On her back was a strung recurve bow.

He doubted either was anything less than proficient in each weapon, though they clearly had their preferences.

"Beyond a doubt, Master," Eva assured him.

Vince looked to the building again.

He'd only managed to spend a hundred thousand standards so far. Most of that had been on supplies. Slaves were cheaper than he'd imagined.

This would be the best spot to pick up more. Then he'd have to wait for them to replenish their stock, so to speak.

Taking a deep breath, Vince put one foot in front of the other.

"No time like the present."

He was greeted at the door by a clerk.

"I'm sorry, sir, we don't allo—"

"Get your manager," Vince said simply. Turning his back to the clerk, Vince walked over to a chair and sat down with a sigh. Thera and Eva flanked each side of the chair while Daphne and Karya took the chairs to each side of him.

"I don—"

"Get your manager," Vince repeated, with a flick of his fingers.

This time, both Thera and Eva turned their heads in unison to stare at the clerk.

As the clerk hustled off down a corridor, Karya leaned in close to him.

"Why do you act like that?"

"Because that's what they expect from someone with money. If I act the part, they'll accept the part, then forget the part when we leave," Vince explained

"That sounds stupid," Daphne replied. Of the three Dryads, she was very no-nonsense.

"Yet here we are. And here's the manager now. Good morning."

A slender man in his forties approached Vince as he finished speaking. He was as nondescript as anyone else and barely registered as average.

"Good morning to you as well, sir. How may I assist you?"

"I need a private booth. Here is a letter of recommendation from your offices in Sacramento, as well as several notes to act as collateral for the time being." Vince reached into his vest and pulled out an envelope and handed it over.

Inside was two hundred thousand standards in notes.

The manager flipped it open and read over the letter the manager from Sacramento had written. Then he looked to the bank notes.

Everything went back into the envelope and disappeared into the man's coat. "I understand. Please, follow me this way, good sir. I believe we can take care of everything for you."

Vince nodded and then stood up. A walk and an elevator ride later and Vince sat himself down in a comfortable recliner overlooking a vast stage.

"Will there be anything else at this time, sir?" the manager asked from the doorway.

"No, but I'll be in town for tomorrow. Will you be holding a sale then?" Vince asked without looking back.

"Ah, I can arrange one. We don't always hold them back to back, but it can be lucrative at times."

Vince only nodded his head.

Thera ushered the manager out the door while Eva closed it, then locked it.

Daphne took the chair to Vince's right, Karya his left.

"Do you really need more?" Daphne asked.

"Yes, and yet no. I need people with skills. In particular, fighters with the right attitude, farmers, lots of those, teachers, and if we can manage it, some accountants."

"Farmers? Accountants?" Daphne asked, her voice tinged with disbelief.

"Can't run a city without someone counting the coins. We can't afford to not be profitable. And that means being self-sufficient. Hence, farmers."

"Can I get you anything, Lord?" Thera asked.

"No. If anything, take a break," Vince said, looking to the Elves. Then he pointed to the side table where fresh fruits and pastries had been laid out. They looked fresh and as if they'd been carted in only a minute or two before they came in. "Get some food, relax."

"We couldn't eat before the master."

"Eating isn't done without our lord."

"I order you to eat, then. Please follow those orders," Vince said. Turning back to the stage, he sighed.

Daphne was there, her lips pressed to his ear. "They wish to please you."

Tilting his head away from Daphne, he eyed her. "I know. They'll do that by listening."

Karya's breath steamed over the skin of his neck, her lips brushing up against it briefly.

In moving away from Daphne, he'd put himself quite a bit closer to Karya. Her fingers dug into his shoulders and pulled. "I want to please you too."

Standing up, Vince folded his arms across his chest.

Meliae had told him that the two would be like this for a while. He'd have to wait it out till then.

"I can't wait to get home," Vince muttered. "Thera, Eva, did the suppliers confirm their meeting times?"

"Yes, Master," Eva confirmed.

"They did, Lord," Thera agreed.

"Great. After this, we can hit them up. If they can meet our needs, we'll be done here. Long gone before the military paymasters realize we've robbed them blind."

Down below on the stage, an auctioneer swaggered up to the stage. Vince watched the heavyset woman as she settled into a chair behind the podium.

"Master, will we truly be living in a forest?" the Wood Elf asked.

Vince nodded his head. "That we will. There's a large cave system nearby — quite mountainous, to boot — a wide river, and a few smaller streams. It's more than what we need for our people."

"I'm glad to hear of this, Lord. Will the manor fit the entire household?"

He couldn't help but chuckle. "Not at all. We'll have to build separate housing units."

"Unacceptable, Master. We'll make arrangements."

"Not possible, Lord. Leave it to us."

Vince pressed his thumb and forefinger to the bridge of his nose. "For concubines, you really don't listen."

"No," they said in unison.

"First up on auction, by special request of our manager, is a lot sale."

Vince raised his eyebrows. Apparently that letter he'd handed over had conveyed more than the text of it had let on. He'd been polite enough to not break the seal and read the letter himself.

"This is more of an assortment than by type," continued the woman. To one side, several men pushed a large tank of water onto the stage. "Inside are four Nereids, nine Nixies, and at least two water elementals. Forgive us the improper count. It's hard to distinguish them from the water at times. The elementals, of course, cannot be collared, but the rest are already taken care of."

"Daphne, Karya, Nereids would be cousins of yours, yes? Would they listen to you if they needed encouragement?" Vince asked.

He could use them. They could help maintain the river and keep it healthy.

"Yes. Much in the same way Thera and Eva are cousins. They breed with any other humanoid race, just as we do. Nixies can be male or female. I do believe they'd listen to us, though, yes," Karya said.

"Let's start the opening bid at one hundred standards," declared the auctioneer.

Vince pressed the small button set into the recliner that indicated he would bid.

"I have one hundred, do I have one ten? Please keep in mind you're responsible for transport. The tank is of course yours.

"I have one ten, do I —"

Vince pressed the button.

"I have one twenty, do I have one thirty?

"I have one thirty, do I—"

Using his thumb, Vince pushed the button again. Then two more times.

"I... I have one sixty."

Vince pressed the button another time.

"Make that one seventy."

As if to demonstrate the point, Vince then pushed the button three more times.

"I... I now have two hundred from the same person," said the woman. She looked flustered at Vince's heavy-handed tactics.

"Master, do you need them that badly?"

"Is the river in that bad of a condition, Lord?"

For a brief second, Vince wondered if they were doing that on purpose. Dismissing it, he realized it didn't matter if they were or weren't.

They got the job done rather well, and Vince would rather measure throughput.

"No, no, the river is fine. But I want it to remain fine. Those will do the work that hundreds couldn't do on land. Between them, and the Dryads, we should have the entire ecosystem on track.

"I'd rather not stand out, but that should shut down whoever else it was."

"Sold to private booth number forty-two for two hundred standards."

Vince took his seat again and slunk down into it. He didn't enjoy this, and the only thing that kept him positive about the whole thing was the end goal.

It wasn't until the end of the auction that Vince found something to catch his interest.

Up to this point, it had required little more than a cursory inspection to determine if they were mentally prepared for what he wanted. If they met his requirements, he bought them. Most were merely laborers, or unskilled.

What took the stage was an old Centaur, gray of hair and with a weathered face. This ancient Centaur was well beyond its prime.

It was the mind behind those eyes that had brought Vince from his stupor. It was a mind filled with thoughts and an education. One who had taught generations for innumerable years.

"Our final item for sale is a household auction. Per an agreement with the previous owner, we're selling them as a group."

A group of fourteen or fifteen fair-haired Wasters surrounded the Centaur. Vince wasn't interested in them, but he figured he'd have to purchase them all to get the Centaur.

"Not them, Master," Eva said, stepping up to the window.

"Definitely not those, Lord," Thera said, stepping up beside Eva.

"What? Why?" Vince asked as the auctioneer continued. Vince took a closer look at those surrounding the Centaur.

"High Elves," Daphne said simply.

They were indeed High Elves. Where Eva was tanned, and Thera grayer skinned, these were all pale. Pale to the point of being like snow. The blue eyes that peered out from their ragged haircuts were a stark contrast.

They were also rather tall, from what he could tell from here. Otherwise, they shared all the same features as Thera and Eva. Beautiful, ethereal, sharp-eared, and graceful-looking.

Now after having seen three races of them, he could tell that the Dark Elves were more muscular, the Wood Elves shorter of stature and more graceful, and the High Elves were far taller.

"Do I have an opening bid of a hundred standards?"

"And? You two are traditionally enemies to the death, and yet I see your families working hand in hand daily." Vince pressed the button to signal a bid on his part.

"Yes, Lord. We do, and are, but that's…" Thera trailed off, looking to Eva.

"Master, High Elves are the reason Elfin-kind is here on your world. They're no good. Thera's family and my own are not foolish enough to ruin a good thing, so we combined our families."

Vince listened to them, but didn't really care. In a heartbeat, he'd combed through the High Elves' minds and found all the same emotions Thera and Eva's had experienced.

No, they were no different.

" —standards. Do I have three hundred?" called the auctioneer.

"And? Last I heard, Dark Elves ate human children, and Wood Elves would castrate men they found in the woods.

"Both of those actions only cemented the early relationship between humanity and the Wastes. Should I blame you for your ancestors' actions? I doubt these High Elves here had any hand in the event." Vince triggered another bid on his part.

Three hundred is cheap for the Centaur.

Karya and Daphne exchanged a look but said nothing. Vince wondered what that was about, but didn't inquire.

Both Thera and Eva were silent at that. Mostly because he was right. Early encounters between Humans and Elves had not gone over very well.

"We will… strive to be as openminded as you are, Lord," Thera said with a sigh.

"Master, we'll not fail your confidence."

"Good. Make sure you pick out the right person for me —" Vince paused and focused on the auction again. Someone had once again outbid him.

"I wonder what a High Elf, Wood Elf, Dark Elf family can accomplish," Vince said under his breath.

Pressing the button twice rapidly, he raised his bid to six hundred standards.

Thera and Eva nodded their heads, saying nothing more.

"Sold, once again to forty-two. That concludes our auction for the day. I hope to see you all return tomorrow for our back-to-back special two-day sale."

"Good. Thera, Eva, go round them up like last time. I'll take care of the bill and meet you in the back with the wagons," Vince said.

The Elves bowed in unison to him and left.

"We're alone," Daphne stated the obvious. Karya nodded her head sharply at that.

"And we're leaving." Vince opened the door and left the booth before the two Dryads could work their magic.

Vince sent a clerk scurrying to find the manager with the simple message that he'd be back tomorrow. Hopefully the manager would have everything taken care of without Vince's name being written down on a single piece of paper. Another clerk directed him to a back office where his purchases were being given back their clothes and the paperwork was being taken care of. It was a small office overlooking a warehouse floor.

But it was in plain view of anyone who might look up here, which suited Vince perfectly right now. He hoped it would keep Daphne and Karya on their best behavior.

"Hiding is pointless," Daphne said, annoyance discernible on her face.

"As is running," Karya added.

"Too bad. I already have a Dryad who hits me with her sex magic. Don't need all three of you hitting me with mystic mojo," Vince complained, sitting on the desk.

Daphne glared at him from under her brows while Karya smiled impishly at him.

A young man popped his head in quickly, handed Vince a letter, and bolted out the door.

"Wait! For fuck's sake. It'd be nice if they waited for a minute," Vince complained. Flipping over the paper, he broke the seal and pulled out the letter inside.

He read it over once and then read it again more slowly.

"You're afraid," Karya said slowly. "And angry."

Vince glanced up at the Dryad and nodded his head. "A problem is coming back to haunt me, apparently. A friend of mine is in town. A blacksmith and his wife. They were chased out of the village they live in. In addition to that, it seems the village itself is becoming a mob. They want to head east and burn my house down."

"Why?" Daphne asked, a confused look on their face.

"If I had to guess, it's because I bought slaves, then killed a number of bandits who attacked me. Seems the bandits were more friendly with the town than I thought. And that they told someone they were going to rob me."

Vince crumpled the letter in his hand.

Thera and Eva entered the office at that moment, escorting a young High Elf woman. Her pale blonde hair was shorn in the slave fashion, of course. Bright blue eyes stared straight into him. Unwavering.

Her face was as beautiful as Thera's and Eva's, all three of them sharing that strange alien beauty of the Elves.

His two concubine bodyguards had managed to get the High Elf into a long-sleeved, silky-looking pale blue dress. It hugged her from her shoulders to her hips in an intoxicating way without showing an inch of skin.

"Master, this is Elysia." Eva gestured to the High Elf.

"We believe her suitable, Lord." Thera had the look of someone who'd been forced to do something, but wasn't upset with the outcome.

"Elysia. I assume you're the one selected for your family?" Vince asked her.

"That remains to be seen, my liege." Her voice was clinical. "I lack critical experience for the role. I do believe my unique skills will make up for that, however."

"Oh?" Vince asked curiously. Hopefully. "Can you show me one of those skills?"

Elysia pointed at the paper in his hand. "Do you need that?"

Vince shook his head and held it out to her. "Was in the middle throwing it away, actually."

The High Elf narrowed her eyes at the paper. A second later and it burst into a sky-blue flame.

Vince held on to the paper until it licked his fingers. Interestingly to him, there was only the barest twinge of heat on his fingers.

Vince found himself smiling as the flame guttered around his thumb and forefinger and then went out.

"I'm well versed at magic, my liege. As High Elves usually are, I'm the most proficient at combat magic. There was some thought to training me as a gladiator."

Containing his excitement was tough, considering the circumstances. He remembered distinctly what Seville's Elf had done, and she had been a Wood Elf, if he remembered it right.

"Impressive. Consider yourself chosen. You can show me everything else later."

"Of course, my liege. I live to serve as your concubine. I have no experience in the affairs of the bedroom, but hope you will treat me kindly," Elysia said, a small smile curling her lips before she dropped down and prostrated herself to him.

Chapter 23

The second day of the auction never occurred. The military brass swooped in and purchased everyone. They'd be joining an army that had been brought up from the old Mexican border that no longer existed.

Of course, the manager apologized profusely while saying "business is business." Vince had no doubt the manager had been paid grossly for his part.

That meant time was up. There would be no further sales until the military decided to stop buying everyone.

In the north, Washington had broken through the lines even further, an entire mounted division slashing their way through the lines and disappearing.

Here at home, the letter he'd received from Deskil was already out of date. It wasn't Knight's Ferry who was turning into a mob, but Knight's Ferry and all of the surrounding towns and villages.

Stories flooded the streets of the evil man who lived in the woods with his slaves, carving up poor human travelers for their body parts.

It was the fact that he cavorted with Wasters that truly sparked the masses, though. He dared to treat them as humans. Feed them and clothe them equally.

Mainly an Orc and a Dryad, or so the stories went.

The name was never right, and they simply called him the Woodsman in the east.

Vince felt a growing anxiety gnawing at his mind. He hadn't gotten what he wanted. He'd never found his accountant, or his farmers. He was also woefully undermanned for actual combatants.

Maybe less than one hundred and fifty would be useful in a fight.

The rest would only be good for dying, unless he got them trained up. Time wasn't on his side for that option, though.

Train, or build. Not both.

"Train or build…" Vince mused aloud. Drumming his fingers along his father's desk, he looked down at the paperwork he'd put together.

He hadn't expected to have to choose. Maybe naively he'd believed he'd have time to build up and then train.

In the end, he still had damn near half a million standards. There simply hadn't been enough time or people. It had cost more to buy the supplies to get them through until they could be self-sufficient than it had to get the people.

At least he'd managed to secure everything they'd need. Tools, food, daily life things.

Closing the ledger, he leaned back and stretched his arms above his head.

They'd gotten in late last night. A peck on the cheek and a hug was about all he'd been good for when he had collapsed into the bed with Fes.

Looking out the window, he saw the early-morning gloom clearing up, and sunlight breaking through.

Time to start to the day and get everyone moving. First were the collars.

Picking up the metal stamp and the battery, he meandered out of his office.

Thera materialized out of the shadows as he closed the door behind him.

Nodding his head to the Dark Elf, he moved to the front door and popped it open. Elysia and Eva stood up from the deck chairs on the porch.

The High Elf had found a staff at some point during the night. To his eyes, it even had a subtle shimmer to it.

"Going to be popping collars today, and giving out orders. Might be best to get whoever is best with infrastructure work out here," Vince said, walking over to a deck chair and its accompanying table.

Elysia, the ever-clinical robot of the three, gave him a blazing smile and was off at a jog.

"Such an eager beaver today," Vince murmured, setting down the stamp on the table.

"Master, our family is still adjusting to our new brothers and sisters. She is... excited to be in so large a family clan."

"Yes, Lord. Though we resented it at first, we've found we are much more able already."

"I imagine. That's kinda the thing with evolution, isn't it? You each develop traits best suited for your environment. Put it all back together and you've got a better product, the sum of the whole being greater than its individual parts."

Vince held up the battery with a shit-eating grin. "Who wants to go first? You're about to watch three Dryads get hit by a lightning bolt."

Thera and Eva eyed him speculatively. Thera stepped forward and put herself in front of him. "As the oldest, I'll submit first. Give me your commands."

She held herself ramrod straight and burned him with her eyes, her hands proffering her collar to him.

"Okay? Hold tight to your collar, and when you feel tired, winded, and like everything is on fire, pull as hard and fast as you can. It'll be obvious."

Before she could question the command, Vince tapped the battery to the collar and activated it.

Thera's hands moved and the collar came undone, hanging loosely in her hands.

"There we are," Vince said with a smile. Taking the collar from her nerveless fingers, he set it down on the table. "Time to make your choice, Thera. Remain here and build with me, or leave here, and live your own life."

Thera blinked twice, her dark eyes moving from him to the collar.

"You think on that. Let's wake up the Dryads." Sticking the battery to his forearm, he discharged it.

From inside the house, he heard a yelp and what sounded as if someone had fallen out of bed and hit the floor.

"Ha. That's what you get. Tease me the entire trip, eh?" Vince said viciously. "Alright, come over here, Eva. Let's get you taken care of while Thera thinks."

"Master, I—"

"Stop, come here, grab your collar, and hold it up. Same instructions," Vince said commandingly. Eva went silent, obeying his orders as she had to. She held up the collar.

Touching the battery to it, he activated it.

Eva lost her grip on the collar as soon as it came free. It clattered to the ground as the Wood Elf stood there panting.

"You alright, Eva?" Vince asked her, turning the battery on his forearm and discharging it again.

He vaguely felt the tree in his chest shifting, but only a touch. The real difference was what felt like two other trees. Both in his abdomen, but one reaching into his arms, and the other his legs.

This time there were no shrieks, but he definitely heard another thud.

"Ha," Vince gloated. Elysia came back at a swift pace. He noticed she'd taken the time to modify her dress for mobility rather than looks. It no longer reached her feet, but stopped an inch above her ankles.

"Perfect timing. Come here, Elysia." Vince pointed at the place to his side. Thera and Eva were still on his other side. "Yep, stand right there. Now grab your collar tight and hold it up. Good. You're going to suddenly feel tired and like you're on fire. I need you pull at your collar as hard as you can when it happens."

"Wait—" Thera said breathlessly.

Vince pressed the battery to the collar and hit the switch. Elysia looked startled as the collar came off with a crack. Her face was flushed and she was taking slow, deep breaths.

Turning the battery on himself, Vince chuckled evilly, then activated it again.

Something slammed into the door, followed by a yelp, then a curse.

"Vince, stop. We need a break between," Meliae called through the door.

"You're in luck, then. Next up is Karya and Daphne." Vince couldn't stop from smiling and took a seat in one of the deck chairs.

"Elysia, I'm afraid you'll need to make a choice now. The same one Thera and Eva are thinking on. Do you remain here and help me build, or leave and go elsewhere?"

Setting the battery down on the table, he eased comfortably into the chair. He'd spent countless evenings simply watching the woods around his home in this chair.

"Keep in mind I'll be freeing everyone from their collars. So everyone will be given the choice. If you want to discuss it with your family, I understand. If you remain, we'll need to put the collar back on, but it'll be depowered. No one will be able to give you commands.

"You three can discuss it elsewhere if you like. I'd understand," Vince said, looking up at the three Elves.

Thera, Eva, and Elysia looked at one another.

The door opened and out came the three Dryads. All three looked like they'd dressed in a hurry. Normally they spent a decent amount of time to dress when given the chance.

Meliae was in front, walking slowly but determinedly to him. Daphne and Karya were hanging off each other and shuffling their feet forward.

"Aww, you poor ducklings. All torn up after three? We still have hundreds to do. Maybe you should take seats," Vince said with a feral grin.

"You wouldn't," Meliae said, her eyes a full, shimmering green.

"Oh, but I would, and will. You're going to like it. You're going to say thank you after every single one. Then you're going to ask for more, for another one. All sweet like, 'Please, may I have another?' And when we're all done and I've stuffed the three of you with as much as I can... well, then I'm going to personally destroy you in our bed, Meliae, while you two watch. In fact, I might even invite the Elves here to watch.

"Consider it payback. Now say thank you for the first three."

All three Dryads were watching him with three pairs of eyes that were green through and through.

"Thank you," they said in unison. "Please, may I have another?"

"Of course, of course. Please, have a seat. The Elf family should be coming soon. We'll be popping their collars next."

The Dryads dropped into the empty chairs, their wide green eyes fastened to him.

Thera stepped in front of Vince and looked down at him. Her collar was held in front of her between her hands.

"I pledged myself as your concubine. I will abide by that pledge. Please re-collar me. My family will agree with my decision and remain as well," said the Dark Elf, holding out the collar to him.

Eva and Elysia both stepped up beside their "sister" and held out their collars.

"I understand. Glad to have you officially on board. As to your collar, merely put it back on. It'll simply be a piece of jewelry from here on out.

"Besides, it's not like much has changed. You had no orders or commands from me to begin with.

"Ah, and here's your family now. Let's get started; this'll take me a while. As we go, I'll start dispensing orders. Please make sure they're carried out. Whoever has the best head for writing and memory should get a ledger." Vince stood up and laid a hand on Thera's shoulder.

Her head bobbed up and down as she reattached her unpowered collar. Eva and Elysia following suit.

"Lord."

"Master."

"My liege."

Vince waved them off and started in on their rather large family.

Elysia's handwriting was meticulous. Flowing evenly and precisely through each line of her ledger, she copied the names of slaves and the jobs Vince assigned. She added her own notes and had divided sections in her ledger for various things.

Vince wasn't quite interested in this tedium and was more than happy she'd taken it upon herself to do all the work.

The front door to his home opened and Fes walked out, Petra close behind her. Whatever discussion they were having immediately stopped on seeing him.

Fes looked to the Dryads, who were nearly comatose in their chairs, then to the Elves cloistered around him.

"Husband, did you claim the other two Dryads?" Fes asked, a green hand indicating the corpse-like Dryads.

"No. They're drunk on power. They'll be fine by tomorrow."

Fes's mouth turned into a grimace. "Why not? They—no. You'll do what you do in your own time. You're like the boulder atop a hill. I can shove you, but unless you're ready to move, you won't budge."

Vince snorted at that and then waved a Dwarf in. "You want me to claim more wives?" he asked, picking up the battery.

"Yes. As your Fes, the more power you have, the more power I have. We need much more power. You will conquer all."

"We will return later. Going to go train and spar."

"This one—" Petra started.

"We train," Fes said firmly.

Petra glared at the Orc but relented when she realized Vince was watching the exchange.

"Hold on tightly to your collar, and pull when you feel tired," Vince said. He felt as if he'd turned into a machine. Activating the battery, the Dwarf wasted no time in pulling off the collar.

Then put it back on immediately and turned to Elysia to give her his name.

Tuning them out for a moment, Vince felt his lips turn up into a foul grin and looked to the Dryads.

They watched him with the barest signs of life. Their eyes glowing green and glittering.

They waited. Knowing what was to happen. As his thumb moved up to the stud, he could feel their trees inside him quiver in dreaded eager anticipation.

Thumbing the stud, the battery discharged into his arm.

Each Dryad locked up, their teeth bared, toes curling, fingers clenching into the arms of the chairs as they stiffened up. Then they relaxed just as suddenly as the power filled their trees.

"Thank you. Please, may I have another?" the Dryads woodenly murmured in chorus. They'd gotten much better about saying it together by the tenth discharge.

Karya started panting audibly, her mouth hanging open. Daphne had the look of a woman so drunk she no longer knew if she lived.

Meliae was the only one who had enough awareness to take a sip of the water he had put out for each of them. Looking to her left and right, she helped her Dryad sisters each get a drink as well.

"Of course I'll give you another," Vince said, and turned to Fes. "I'm punishing them. They actually love it. Part of that 'destroy me' Dryad thing. Trust me on that one. But you're sparring in the woods? Don't get lost, or I'll have to come find you. All kidding aside, I don't want to worry over you, Fes Berenga."

Fes gave him a wide smile, her tusks becoming evident. "You're enjoying yourself a bit too much, I think, with those poor Dryads. As to the woods, yes, husband. I will listen."

"Course I am. They tease and mock. Rile me up. They want this, and they know I'll eventually lash out if they keep it up. Admittedly, I'm being trained and they're being trained, but that's the way it goes.

"I don't think they expected this, though. Heh."

Vince looked to Petra, who had been staring at him. "Petra."

"This one awaits orders, Master."

"Be safe. Come home alive."

"This one will do as her master instructs."

Vince nodded and turned back to the Dwarf he'd collar-popped. "Stone or metal?"

"Stone," came the gravelly response.

"Rock quarry or the wall, Elysia?"

Vince stood bolt upright as the shock of Fes's firm hand slapping him on the ass caught him unaware. Then she stepped off the decking and set off for the woods.

Petra lingered for a moment, her eyes moving from him to Fes and back. Then the ant soldier darted in and kissed him hungrily. Before he could respond, she scuttled off the deck to catch up with Fes.

The Dwarf stumped off to whatever work assignment Elysia had given him.

"Where are we at, then?"

"The quarry needs more hands right now, my liege. That's because the early reports from the wall are that they're going through the bricks faster than we're making them."

Vince leaned over Elysia's shoulder and looked at the figures she was pointing to. It was a summary with every work type listed and current count in tallies.

"Blacksmiths are short in supply. More so than the quarry, even. Can't help what their background is."

"No, my liege."

Vince laid his left hand on her shoulder and began tracing the entries with his right hand.

Lumberjacks, all the Beavers. Of course.

Wall defense, Trolls and Ogres.

Siege weaponry, Gnomes.

Library, Centaur, couple Elves.

Scouts, whole lot of Ratfolk, Brownies, and Pixies.

He'd bought those by the dozen in Blanchard.

Front line warriors, Bearmen, Wolfmen, Orcs, Kobolds, Gnolls, and... Vince didn't bother to read the rest, as there were too many.

River defenses and upkeep, Nereid, Nixies, Water Elementals.

Farming, handful of Halflings. Not nearly enough.

Carpentry...

Vince couldn't make heads or tails of it. They were spread across all the races. They had quite a number of them, though, thankfully.

Miscellaneous, Goblins.

He still didn't understand that one. Elysia had asked him to trust her, so he did. Didn't mean he understood it.

"What do we really need right now?" Vince asked to himself.

"My liege," Elysia said, turning her head. She seemed unperturbed by the fact that they were inches from each other.

Vince realized at that point he was practically hanging on the poor woman. "We need weapons, traps, and fortifications. Once the Beavermen finish clearing the immediate area and approaches, we should have them begin working on a wooden stake wall facing out, opposite to the side we have our wall going up."

Vince nodded and leaned away from Elysia.

"Oi, there you are, Vinny," called a Dwarven voice. Looking up, Vince saw Deskil stomping up the deck. He marched right up to Vince.

"Ha, Deskil. Good to see you. Didn't expect to see you here, though," Vince said, holding out a hand to the Dwarven blacksmith. Looking over Deskil's shoulder, he saw Minnie approaching, too.

"Minnie, a pleasure as always." Deskil took Vince's hand and shook it firmly. "What do I owe the pleasure to?"

"I'm afraid I've come calling, cap in hand, Vinny. I've lost my forge, my tools, and my home. I can work. I'll work hard. Just give me—"

"Done. We have precious few metalworkers. They're over there right now." Vince indicated to the large roped-off area in the distance. Visible even from here were the crates stacked one on top of the other. "We've got all the tools, equipment, and ore for a team of blacksmiths. I don't know the exact counts of everything, but there should be an Elf over there who has all the details.

"As for pay, well, that's the rub. We're more of a commune at this point than a city. Everyone here is working for our mutual benefit with one goal. I can guarantee you a home for free. Eventually. And more than you could eat or drink right now."

"Vinny, were you the bastard who bought out several months' worth of ore in Sacramento and then again in Blanchard? Damn near ran the entire guild under for a month till they found another supplier?" Deskil asked, his bearded face splitting in a wide grin.

"That'd be me. So, up for the job? Also, is your collar depowered? No powered collars allowed here."

"Aye, and aye. We'll catch up later, Vinny. Work to do," Deskil said, rolling up his sleeves. The Dwarf trundled off at a walk, and soon was off at a run.

Minnie walked up to Vince and then hugged him. "Thank you, Vince. We... weren't really sure what to do."

"Of course. My pleasure. Though I'm surprised you found us. Was it that easy to follow the trail?" Vince asked her. He knew they'd left a pretty easy trail with all those wagons and supplies.

"Very. Deskil tracked you, if you can believe it." The woman pulled back and glanced over at her husband, who looked to be sprinting towards the blacksmith's area.

Minnie sobbed once and then started to laugh as she rubbed at her eyes. "They took everything. Claimed I was a Waster-lover. We got out while they were trying to find the safe.

"We could see the fire even as we left. They burnt it all down. He looked shattered. Lost."

Minnie laughed harder now and rubbed at her nose. "Now the stupid fool is running faster than I've ever seen. How much ore did you buy?"

"Something like eighty thousand standards' worth? Round there."

Minnie shook her head, sniffling. "Thank you and curse you at the same time, then. I won't be able to pull him out of there for weeks. He'll look at this as a blessing for the simple fact that he can make whatever he feels like without a care for me nagging him about the cost of ore for his pet projects."

She ran the books?

"Well, what will you have me do, then? I'll be needing a job as well."

"You any good at accounting?"

Minnie smiled warmly at that. "I am. Though it sounds like you need a professional, and I'm—"

"Better than me. So, congratulations. You're the accountant. For now, go get some sleep. A meal. We'll tackle the ledgers tomorrow night.

"For now, all I can offer is a patch of grass. Warehouse has plenty of beds and blankets. Weather should be good this week, according to Meliae, but we should have several dormitories put up by the end of the week. Once everyone is under a roof, we'll start working on homes."

Minnie let out a slow breath and nodded her head. "I'm sure you know that they're talking about you in nearly every town. And what to do about you."

Vince agreed with a nod of his head.

"I'm betting they'll be coming to pay us a visit eventually. We'll be ready."

Vince looked up to the next person in line, and waved them on.

Chapter 24

Vince closed the door to his manor with a soft click. It'd been two weeks since he'd broken everyone's collar.

Not one single person had left after being given their choice. They all remained. Which left him with something like six hundred and fifty pairs of hands to work with.

And work those hands did.

The forest clearing had gone impressively. The Dryads had worked quickly to get all the spirits out of the area they needed to clear and moved into other trees or given a promised residence over a home.

With no resistance and trees that seemed eager to fall, the Beavermen had cleared more than enough of an area for a large city, including the surrounding approachable areas. Many trees had been left alone if they had a locational significance, or held a truly obstinate spirit, which gave the whole thing a forested feeling, without being a forest.

Goblins had run rampant over everything, picking it clean of debris, rocks, and anything else that could impede building or farming. All for the simple fact that Vince had asked them specifically. Because it was a task no one else could do as quickly as they could.

Halflings had taken over the farm work from there. Vast tracks of farmland were already being cultivated.

His contingent of carpenters had descended on all that readily available wood and thrown up dormitories. Faster than any human carpenter he'd seen, that's for sure. Half of them had then started in on the workshops and factories, while the remaining half began on actual housing.

Vince had originally been concerned about that aspect of the project. It sounded like his carpenters wanted to build each house to specifications. Then he realized that with so many different races, they had to.

More surprising was how quickly the camp had sprouted up families and pairings. The number of houses they'd need dropped a few every day as more and more of his people got married or joined families.

Nodding at a passing Hobgoblin who gave him a gap-toothed grin, Vince set off for the walls. He didn't want to panic anyone, but the walls needed to be up. Soon.

Eva, Thera, and Elysia glided into place around him before he'd made it ten steps.

None of them had changed their duties after he'd freed them, despite him telling them to stop.

They'd even gone ahead and coaxed some of the carpenters to work on his manor. Which would now be fit to call a mansion, since it had rapidly been expanded to three times its original size. Taller than he wanted, and bigger than he needed, he felt lost in it at times.

At least someone had the presence of mind to take all my existing rooms and move them item by item. Converting the new rooms into duplicates of the old, just with new walls and elsewhere in the house.

He imagined it was probably painstaking work, moving a room item by item.

Probably Elysia.

Even his messy and horribly cluttered trophy room, which had been raided the next day by Deskil when he'd heard about it.

"Inspecting the wall, my liege?" Elysia asked, taking the position just behind him and to the left.

"Yeah. Why? Is my attention drawing attention?" Vince asked.

Thera nodded her head from directly on his right and a step ahead.

On his left at his side was Eva. "Yes, Master. You are."

"Damn." Vince stopped dead in his tracks and slipped one hand into another. His Elven trio circled up in front of him, facing him. "Well, how are they doing?"

"Very good, Master."

"Yes, Lord. Completion isn't far off."

"Perhaps even next week, my liege."

Vince looked from one Elf to the next. "Alright. What does need to be inspected, then? Anything?"

Thera's brow furrowed and she looked to Elysia at the same time Eva did.

"My liege, I would suggest that you relax today. Perhaps look to your own inner circle. Maybe train," said the High Elf neutrally.

Okay, so there's a problem and they're being cautious.

"One of you can explain that statement to me." Vince lifted a finger and waved it between the three of them.

Elysia looked pained and wouldn't meet his eyes.

Eva sighed and pressed a hand to her brow. "Master, Petra and Fes fight. Every day."

Thera closed her eyes and bowed her head. "It's true, Lord. The only discontent is in your own home."

Vince grunted and looked to one side. "Got it. I'll take care of it."

The problem here was that Fes was acting within her rights as Fes to dictate Petra's actions to a certain degree. Petra, having not actually been beaten, or beaten Fes, didn't respect the situation. Her chain of command was fuzzy.

Fes, on the other hand, needed a strong hand guiding her in the same way. While her issue wasn't one of chain of command, it was of leadership through trial of arms.

It wasn't his way, but if he wanted to keep Fes happy, and in turn Petra, this was his answer.

"Thera," Vince said, turning his head to the Dark Elf.

The Dark Elf's shoulders straightened, her head snapping up.

"Get the Dryads. I'd like to meet them in the training field behind the manor.

"Elysia, could you please fetch Petra and Fes?

"Eva, I need training weapons for anything that could come up.

"I'll meet you out behind the house. Promise."

The Elves regarded him suspiciously. There'd been times where he'd tried to send them off on errands so he could be alone. At once, they decided without speaking that the requests were legitimate and moved off to their appointed tasks.

Vince was annoyed. He'd known there was a problem but had deliberately ignored it. Ignored it to the point that his Elven council had to tell him that it was no longer a private problem.

Heading back to the manor, he went through it to the back to the fenced-in private back yard. It wasn't something he'd asked for, and no one told him who'd done it, but he was suddenly grateful for whoever had requested it.

In the center of what once was an empty field of grass and trees was now a cleared circle of dirt with a wooden lip encircling it. Walking to the center of that, Vince started going through warmup stretches.

He was sure he didn't need to, never had, but he always felt better in doing it.

As he worked his waist muscles into what he hoped was a more limber state, the Dryads and Thera walked over to him.

"Ah, good. Meliae, can we talk for a minute?" He smiled at the Dryad in question and motioned at her as he walked to one edge of the ring.

Meliae grinned at him and bounced her way over to him. "What can I do for you, Sweetling?"

Vince decided to dive right in. "I get the impression you're rather good at fertility and sex magic. Is that you personally, or you as a Dryad?"

Meliae blushed deeply at that and nodded at him. "In general, Dryads have an affinity. Mine is… yes, it's fertility and sex. Daphne is better at direct intervention with flora. Combat, you could say. Karya is very in tune with the land and animals. People."

"Good. Can you keep me… er… can you make it so I can perform repeatedly? One after the other? Three times, preferably."

"Easily. Any of us could do that," purred the Dryad, her eyes starting to green over. Her hands gripped her staff and wrung it back and forth.

"Good, hang on to that until later." Vince had to hurry it along since Fes, Petra, and Elysia were arriving. Right behind them was Eva with an armful of practice weapons.

Vince worked to school his face into neutrality. Once he'd done that, he moved to intercept Fes and Petra.

Both of them watched his approach warily. Gesturing to Eva, he indicated the grass at the edge of the ring. "Right there is great, Eva. Thank you. Elysia, Thera, thank you as well for getting this put together so quickly."

The Elves nodded their heads, smiles flashing and disappearing quickly.

Vince turned to face Fes, then Petra, giving them both a hard look.

"New rules. I'm tired of the bickering and the infighting. That ends today.

"Title of Fes is only able to be challenged for once every thirty days. Current Fes dictates a date within three days of the challenge. Thirty days counts from the initial challenge date.

"Winner is Fes and will be respected and regarded as Fes. I'll personally fight the Fes three days after each challenge to maintain proper etiquette.

"To start this correctly, I'll now fight each one of you."

Vince walked over to the pile of training weapons and picked up a wooden saber, then walked to the center of the ring.

"You may determine your order. Please be swift."

Before anyone could argue, Meliae leaped into the ring and lifted her staff, pointing it at him.

Vince grinned at the spunky Dryad. Holding out his training saber, he waited.

Faster than he expected, her staff thrust out at his head.

Taking a single step to the side, he couldn't help but laugh.

All that plant food!

"Meliae! My chipper little Dryad wife, I'm surprised. That was well done. Are you ready, though?"

Her eyes were greening over again, her lips fighting a smile. "Give it to me, Sweetling. Hard and fast."

Acting counter to her request, her staff spun out low towards the back of his feet. It was even faster than her thrust.

In the middle of his chest, he could feel the burning ache again. That strange sensation he'd felt back in the river. This time, he couldn't claim it was exhaustion. This was different.

It was coming all throughout him now, though. A little weaker than the feeling in his chest, but there.

Begging to be used. To be forced to do his bidding. Be given direction and made to do so.

Shaking off that feeling, he focused on Meliae.

Vince dodged back and then launched forward, his training sword whipping around with as much speed as he could put into it.

The flat of the blade slapped into the front of Meliae's shoulders and sent her tumbling into the dirt.

The busty Dryad lay on her back, breathing heavily. "Ow…"

Walking over, Vince offered her a hand up and a lopsided smile. "Much improved since previously, my little warrior Dryad."

She gave him a goofy grin and got to her feet. Walking off to the side, she slumped into the grass.

"Next."

Daphne and Karya looked like they would enter the ring.

Vince pointed at them with his sword. "This is reserved for those who share my bed. Watching doesn't count."

Moving his sword laterally, he pointed it at Fes and Petra. "Next."

Fes entered the ring while Petra dug through the training weapons. Fes had already retrieved a training sword that looked akin to her near great sword.

"Husband, are you sure? If I win, I can't look at you the same way."

Vince tilted his head to one side and regarded her.

He wasn't the same man he'd been when he defeated her the first time. Sure, he wasn't what a human could reasonably do even then. After everything that had happened now, though... he wasn't sure where he rated anymore. The passive power the Dryads' trees gave him was immense.

Vince had the feeling he could pull deeply on them as well if he wanted. That the ache begging to be used would push him well beyond limits a human body could support.

"Come, wife Berenga. Know your match and hearken back to our first meeting."

Fes wasted no time and slashed at him, her sword moving quick. Before she completed the attack, she'd changed her footwork to bring herself around for whatever he might do.

She'd trained with Petra for quite a while, and he could see clearly how her form had improved. Previous to this, she'd been more of an experience fighter. Now she was a trained fighter that thought of the possibilities.

She was incredibly dangerous.

Vince slipped in close and blocked her attack outright. Stopping it dead in its tracks.

Fes stared at him, not quite believing it. Vince took another step and slammed the hilt of his sword into her stomach.

The only sound that came next was the sudden exhalation of breath as Fes had the wind knocked proverbially out of her.

Crumpling to her knees, she dropped her blade, her head hanging.

Vince waited patiently, giving her the minute she needed to get her breath back under control.

Finally, she lifted her head, gazing up at him.

Vince gave her a loving smile and leaned down to kiss her lips tenderly.

"Much better, wife Berenga. You've improved. Are you well?" he asked gently.

Fes nodded her head, and got to her feet.

"So strong," she said. There was a tiny change in her tone. One he hadn't heard since they'd first bonded.

Desperate admiration.

"Have to be. I have such strong wives. They keep me on my toes. Off with you now, I need to tend to Petra now."

Fes picked up her blade and walked off towards Meliae. All three Dryads turned to the Orc and immediately bent to the task of fixing her.

Turning to Petra, he pointed the blade at her. "Come, Petra."

"Master." Petra entered the ring, angling her spear at him. She made no move to engage him.

"Playing hard to get, Petra?"

"Master is well aware this one would do anything he asked. But if she can defeat Master, she will be Fes."

Vince couldn't argue the fault in logic.

Petra relied on her whole being when fighting. Having lived on a war front her whole life, that counted for a lot.

Leaning forward, Vince then darted in. His left hand grabbed the spear and yanked with all everything he had as he swung around with his blade.

Petra released the spear and leapt to one side.

His sword stroke passed through the empty air.

Vince chased after her, catching her only a second after she landed. Swinging his blade up in an underhanded blow, he caught her under the armpit.

The strike was so strong that the heavy ant soldier was surprisingly knocked flat on her side.

The sharp crack of the blade breaking in half was audible over everything. Vince looked at the split blade with a frown.

Falling into a neutral stance, Vince laid his blade on his shoulder. "Good adaptation."

Petra was on her side. Three of her legs twitched as she righted herself, getting up to her feet.

The ant soldier stared at him, her antennae twitching slowly. "Master," Petra whispered, and then moved to the edge of the ring.

Having finished with Fes, the Dryads leapt into action on Petra.

"Good. Now that that's settled, I recognize Berenga as my Fes. Do any challenge her?"

Petra looked at the Orc, and Fes looked at the ant soldier.

"This one does." Petra turned and looked to him as she said it.

"Great, the Elf sisters will act as referee since they're a neutral party. Once the Dryads clear you for action, you two may begin."

Vince walked over to the Dryads and sat down next to them, motioning to the Elves. "I appreciate your assistance."

Elysia, Eva, and Thera couldn't hide the way they looked at him. Awe, fear, and a bit of what looked like adoration.

"My liege."

"Lord."

"Master."

The Dryads collectively shooed Petra onward, having found nothing wrong with her. She was rather tough, after all.

Petra and Fes went to the center of the ring as the Elves fanned out around the two of them. "Winner is the first to score what would be classified as a fatal attack. No targeting the head," Vince called, and then turned to Meliae.

"You alright?"

The Dryad nodded her head and gave him a bright smile. "It went as I expected, but I surprised you."

"That you did. Have you been practicing?"

Meliae pointed at Karya and Daphne. "They're far more martial than I am. I'm sure they'll be better able to fend you off."

The other two Dryads didn't respond to that, but he could see the green of their eyes threatening to overtake the pupils.

Vince ignored the implied requirement of them being part of his bedroom routine and turned to watch Petra and Fes.

They squared off slowly, each wielding a sword.

"Who do you think will win?" Karya asked him.

"I'm not sure. Nor do I think it matters. Half of the problem was my own fault for not asserting dominance. Berenga needs it from a cultural perspective. Petra from a societal and class perspective."

"I just need it. I like it when you break me," Meliae mewled, pressing into his arm.

"You like being forced, not broken. Though one does usually dictate the other."

Meliae made happy sounds of agreement and then released his arm, patting his shoulder.

"After that power display of yours, I don't think Fes will want to wrestle for a while," Meliae said as her eyes turned back to the fight. "You didn't even pull on our trees. I'm sure you felt it, calling out to you."

Vince knew exactly what she was talking about in regards to the trees.

As if on command, the feeling returned, though much subtler now.

Carefully, he "pulled" on it with his thoughts and then let go.

All three Dryads shimmered a faint green hue for a second and faded.

Meliae, Daphne, and Karya had given him their full attention.

"Ah, I see. What did you mean about the wrestle thing, though?"

Meliae cocked her head to one side. "Berenga is a playful Orc. She willingly took on the role of your Fes, but she got rid of a good portion of the ritual of it.

"As Mother told it, the Fes is frequently mounted from behind as a form of subjugation.

"Berenga prefers to wrestle for dominance or mock fight with you for it. I've seen you let her win on occasion, and how she lets you win as well. If she didn't want to, you'd have to kill her for it, probably."

"Interesting." Vince thought on that for a bit. Maybe it'd be good to reinforce that one today.

She was certainly different now than how she'd been when they'd first started off on this journey. The rigidity of her mind and actions had softened. She'd even become tender towards him.

Loved him.

And I love them.

Vince sighed, a smile flickering over his face. Draping an arm around Meliae, he pulled her in close and kissed the top of her head.

"Thanks for the hint. Love you."

Meliae froze up, her body becoming rigid in his embrace. Then she melted into him, nuzzling her head up under his jaw.

On the sand, Fes and Petra were slow to engage each other. Small attacks and efficient parries were all that were exchanged.

Slowly, it became the inexorable fight of wills he had somewhat expected. Fes and her indomitable spirit and Petra with her near tireless endurance.

Wooden blades clacked back and forth as they attacked and defended, their footwork looking expertly done to Vince's eye. Their movements clean and efficient.

"They really are quite good," he murmured.

Then it was suddenly over. Fes's blade was wedged into Petra's side.

Fes had welcomed a blow and diverted it. She had taken Petra's blade high on her arm and let it graze over her shoulder as she brought around her own weapon into Petra.

The Elves conferred for a moment and then Thera motioned to Fes.

"Berenga is the winner by virtue of the fact that her attack would have slain her opponent. Petra's would only have disabled her. This is our finding, Lord."

Vince clapped his hands. "Great. Fes, Petra, Meliae, Daphne, Karya, into the house. Thera, Eva, Elysia, please tidy up here and then take whatever duty you see fit. I'll be retiring for a while."

Standing up, Vince didn't wait for replies or acknowledgments and made his way into the manor.

Entering through the rear door, he started unstrapping his leather armor. He never left without it and felt naked if he wasn't wearing it.

Moving up the stairs, he peeled off his armor from his chest.

A boot nudge and he'd entered his bedroom. Vince began piling his armor and clothes in a messy pile on the dresser.

Standing nude, he turned and waited.

One by one, the summoned women trooped into the bedroom. Including the Elves who weren't invited.

Once they'd all entered, he pointed to the door. "Shut it."

Petra lifted one long leg and closed the door with a click.

Vince now pointed to the ground. "Clothes." The demand was simple without any room to argue.

A moment later, there were eight piles of fabric on the ground, and eight naked women.

Vince didn't bother to correct the Elves. Instead, he deliberately looked them over. Eying their chests, hips, and privates. Then met their eyes.

They came willingly. Let's give them a show behind the curtains. They can decide after.

Deciding to move this along, Vince lifted his hand and gestured to the naked Orc woman and then indicated the bed wordlessly.

Chapter 25

Fes's dark eyes followed the movement of his hand. There was no fear in her, no disagreement, or anger. A gentle sweep of her thoughts and he'd gotten his answer.

Overwhelming acceptance, lust, desire, and a sense of wanting to know her place.

She has more in common with Meliae than she'd ever admit. This isn't all for them, of course; what man doesn't fantasize about something like this?

The Orc woman crawled onto the bed, facing the wall, and settled down on her forearms and knees.

"Other way," Vince said softly, moving to the side of the bed. He laid one hand to her hip and gave her a nudge.

Fes blinked and then slowly turned around, facing the rest of the women. Her skin darkened in a flush as she tried in vain to meet their eyes.

Vince leaned in and nipped her pointed ear with his teeth, then whispered for her alone.

"You are my Fes. Tonight, you will be treated as Fes. I expect you to make eye contact with everyone. To stare into their eyes as they watch you being mounted. Do you understand?"

Fes gave a tiny bow of her head.

"Good. Know that I love you, Berenga."

The Orc's eyes widened, her skin prickling along the length of her body. Vince took a step up onto the bed and then settled in behind the Orc.

Using his hands, he forced her knees a bit further apart, her hips lower, her stomach down towards the bed, and her shoulders up.

Then he carefully sunk his fingers into her hair and then gripped into it.

Looking down, he angled himself until the tip rested against her moist entry. Then he pushed forward into his Fes roughly. Pulling back on her hair, he didn't stop until his hilt was flush with her lips.

Drawing his hips back, he looked up from their joining and set his eyes on Thera. He watched the Dark Elf intently as he began to thrust in and out of Fes. Thera met his eyes for a second before looking to Fes instead.

Reaching out with his gift, he penetrated her mind and then forced her to meet his gaze. Then he prodded at her thoughts with lust and desire. Staring into her.

Fes moaned, pushing her hips back into him, her neck straining as his hold on her bent her inexorably towards him.

He wormed thoughts of sex into Thera's mind. Thought of her trading places with Fes. Being moved into different positions.

It was then that he felt Thera reach the cusp of what she could tolerate. He released her mind and looked to Elysia. Blue eyes met his and skittered away immediately.

Pinning her mind as easily as Thera's, he began to dump everything into her. Suggestions, desires, implications. The sounds she'd make instead. Forcing her to meet his eyes just as he had Thera.

Elysia began panting heavily, her hands pressing into her stomach.

The Orc warrior started to grunt with every heavy thrust of Vince's. He'd kept his speed low, but his strength up. Vince only plowed his hips into hers harder and harder, while pulling back on her hair.

Elysia hit her breaking point faster than Thera. She started to hunch over herself, her hands pressing into her lower abdomen firmly.

Vince was forced to exit her mind and leap into Eva's.

Eva was the easiest to spread out and pin inside her own mind. She was already full of desire and he flamed it. Flamed it hard and breathed burning life into it. He yanked hard on her mentally, forcing her eyes to meet his own as he loaded her full of thoughts and ideas.

And simple, unadulterated lust.

His lap smacked into Fes with loud cracks, his tip driving deep into her. What had been building for several minutes was coming up to a climax.

Releasing Eva, who collapsed to her knees and leaned into Elysia's side, he then slipped into Daphne, Karya, and Meliae at the same time.

Using them as a font, he channeled the worst lust, domination, and ownership he could into their minds.

At the same time, he pushed forward, forcing Fes to collapse into the bed, her face being pressed into the comforter. He set his knees in to the back of hers, gripped her shoulders with one hand, his other buried in her hair, and began thrusting into her with reckless abandon.

Reaching inside of her mind, he found what he could only describe as her pleasure center.

Then he lit it up like lightning bolt going through a tree.

Moments later, he hit his peak, pushing hard into her as deeply as he could. At the same time, he tried to boil the minds of his Dryads with his climax.

Fes moaned each time as he drove deep into her, pushing his seed as deeply as possible. The quivering Orc moaned into the bed while clenching and unclenching her hands in the comforter.

Pulling himself out of Fes, and mentally disengaging from her, Vince shuffled back on his knees. Taking a seat on his shins, Vince surveyed his work.

Fes's knees went out from under her and she lay in the bed. A moaning, gasping mess. She shook from head to toe. Her legs spasmed once or twice, her eyes distant as she gazed out at nothing.

Then he released the Dryads from his mental domination and looked to Karya.

"Clean it," Vince said, pointing at his stained member. It oozed seed and was liberally coated in Fes's own liquid.

The demand was heavy in tone. There was no room for argument. Only obeisance.

Karya leapt forward, her hands pressing to his knees as her mouth engulfed him hungrily. She pushed him down her throat and closed her eyes as her lips wrapped around his hilt.

Soft suckling noises could be heard as she did her best to obey. Inside her mouth, her tongue spun crazily, wildly, around his length. Scrubbing him with it.

"Thank you, Karya," Vince said, petting Karya's head as she worked diligently.

"Daphne, please take our Fes and set her down so she can watch."

Daphne moved forward, her gaze locked on Karya's head as she lifted Fes from the bed. Gathering up the Orc like a child, she set her down on the ground with her back against the wall.

He patted Karya on the brow. "That's enough."

Karya slid her head back and her lips came free with a pop. She gave him a cat-who-got-the-canary smile and watched him from under her brows as she slithered back towards her original spot. Slowly, she got to her feet and leaned up against the wall.

Vince tugged gently on the trees inside him as he lifted a hand to Petra.

Immediately, he could feel the trees revitalize him, pushing energy into him so he could perform again.

The soldier ant came forward slowly, concern written on her features. Vince realized the reason for her hesitation. He could never bend her over as he had Fes.

Crooking a finger to her, he waited with a smile.

Petra sidled up beside the bed and then moved in close.

He pressed his lips to her ear.

"Lay on your back, my soldier. I want you to make eye contact with everyone, make sure you watch them, as they watch you. I want you to feel their eyes on you. To know that you're being watched. That is my desire of you, my desire of my second. I love you."

Vince pulled back from her ear and waited.

Petra's face turned a deep scarlet. Then she lifted herself up, and carefully laid herself down on the bed, her torso and abdomen facing the ceiling. Then she spread her six legs and laid her arms down beside her head.

Shifting forward, Vince took himself in his right hand. His tip caught in her lips and he pushed the head into her. Hitching his knees up under her topmost pair of legs, he set his knees into her sides.

Pinning her wrists together with his left hand, he clenched his hand shut.

Reaching up with his right hand, he casually thumbed a nipple and fondled her breasts. Then he sunk the full length of himself into her with one smooth movement.

Petra inhaled quickly and laid her head back on the edge of the bed. With his free right hand, he grabbed a fistful of her blonde hair and pulled her head back and to the side, forcing her eyes up to the others.

Where he'd started hard and slow with Fes, with Petra he went fast and deliberate.

Wet sloshing noises could be heard under Petra's high-pitched whining moans. Gripping tight into the flesh of her forearms, Vince linked back into Thera's mind.

Looking up, he snared her with his eyes and devoured her mentally again. He turned loose on her all the feelings of his previous climax and enjoying Petra right here and now. The feeling of her, and how it would feel if it was her.

Her soft Elven body being broken beneath him.

She lasted almost as long as the first time before he was forced to turn her loose. Her knees buckled as he did so, but she regained her balance and kept standing. Her eyes were glazed over and her mouth hung open.

Petra was whimpering and moaning beneath him, her hips bucking wildly as he pummeled her.

Instead of taking Elysia and Eva separately, after seeing how little Thera could handle, he grabbed them both together with his thoughts.

Encouraged by Petra's wild abandon, he drowned Elysia and Eva in the dark part of his mind. The part that had been waking up from his Dryads. The part that wanted to bend and break them to his will.

To break his Elves and demean them as the concubines they called themselves.

He dumped an endless stream of thoughts and desires into them. Most specifically, he forced their own perspectives into what was being done to Petra. To make them live it out as if it were them.

Elysia crumpled immediately, dropping down to her bottom and sitting on the floor. Eva slumped over and lay in Elysia's lap as they stared at Vince, and he stared back at them.

Petra's legs shot up and pressed into the ceiling above them as she cried out. Vince lifted her arms further above her head, pulling harder at her hair. Her head was twisted further, bending her like the plaything she wanted to be.

Vince felt his climax spiral out rapidly, and he had to cut Elysia and Eva loose a touch rougher than he'd wanted.

Then he smashed his way into the minds of all three Dryads again. Winding them rapidly into his orgasm, he dragged them mentally through his wants and emotions.

Slipping into Petra's mind, he burned up the part of her mind that he now recognized as her pleasure center from his experience with Berenga.

Petra made a hiccup-like noise that turned into a gurgling moan as her body went rigid.

Vince ground himself up against his soldier ant as he unloaded his hot seed into her. Holding his breath as his body shuddered, Vince pumped into her twice more.

He grunted as he finished. Easing himself back from her, his eyes fell on her slit. It pulsed and quivered, a small trickle of what he'd left behind seeping out.

Taking a seat on his backside, he put his knees out in front of himself. Finally, he released the three Dryads from his mental chokehold after he calmed down.

Meeting Daphne's eyes, he started to lift his hand to point to his crotch. It was once more slick with thick seed and whatever Petra had left on him.

He hadn't even opened his mouth to give her the order before she practically appeared in front of him, her hands pushing his knees apart to get more access to him.

She buried his tip in her throat and moaned lewdly, pressing her face hard against his lower stomach as if to get more. Her hands gripped his nuts and began to knead them, as if she could milk him directly.

Wrapping his hand into her hair, he pushed her head in closer, making sure she kept deepthroating him. He was almost sure she couldn't even breathe at this point.

"That's great, Daphne. Just like that," Vince murmured, fingers curling in her hair tighter. Daphne mewled and sucked harder on him in response.

"Karya, pick up our second and settle her. Just like Fes, please."

Responding immediately, Karya slid her arms under Petra and lifted her easily. She carried her to the corner and set her down, propping her head up on Fes's shoulder.

They're so strong now. All that magical energy straight into their trees clearly changed them.

Letting go of Daphne's head, he pulled on the trees inside him again. Once more he felt his sex drive surge, his energy skyrocket.

"Daphne, Karya, bring me Meliae. Put her on her back. One of you hold her left arm and leg, the other her right arm and leg. Keep her splayed and open for me.

"Do well, and I'll reward you both later."

As if they were wolves on a scent, Daphne peeled herself off Vince as Karya's head whipped around. Meliae blinked and took a step back before the other two Dryads attacked her.

They wrapped her up with strong arms and hands, lifting her bodily from the ground. Then dropped her onto the bed in front of Vince like a sacrifice. Daphne and Karya then cranked her arms and legs back, spreading her wide for him.

The view was lovely. He admired the full-chested and curvy little Dryad.

Vince crawled atop her, set the tip to her entrance, and slammed himself into her dripping channel.

Meliae let out a gasp that turned into a deep moan. Her arms and legs spasmed against Daphne and Karya. Vince bit her ear fiercely, almost to the point of drawing blood.

"My precious Dryad. Time to show everyone what you Dryads want. I've been pulling in the Elves for part of this. This time, I'm going to let everyone dwell in your mind. To share all those nasty thoughts and wants that pop up in there," Vince promised.

He knew her mind. She couldn't help herself. She'd have thoughts that would burn her with shame. Shame that would burn hot and fierce, in turn making her want more, and then burn even deeper with shame.

Meliae made a soft squeak as she thought on his words.

"From you, my third, I want your eggs. All of them. I want you to make as many of them available as you can. We're going to see how many I can seed in one load. Your eggs are mine, I might as well fertilize them all. Right?"

"Yes," whispered Meliae. He couldn't mistake the excitement, mind-crushing shame, and want in her voice. "Yours. All yours. Every one."

"Good."

Meliae's eyes were fully green, and glowing now.

To start, Vince gently cupped the minds of Fes and Petra, then opened a window into Meliae's from their own.

Then he grabbed the minds of his Elves, Daphne, and Karya, then linked them to Meliae's directly. Then he opened up the floodgates to Meliae and let it crash over them all with every single memory of what he'd ever done to Meliae.

And then showed them every one of her desires of him.

Easing her head to the side with his brow, he bit deep into her neck, sucking hard. He was intent to mark her visibly.

He rocked his hips back and forth as hard and fast as he could, driving his shaft through her like a hammer pounding on a nail.

The tiny Dryad shuddered with each blow of his hips, her voice coming out in gasps and grunting moans.

Reaching up with his left hand, he grabbed a handful of her hair and pulled back, forcing her to meet the eyes of all three Elves, along with Petra and Fes. It also forced her to bare more of her neck to him.

Letting go with his teeth, he drove them back into a different stretch of unblemished pale skin. For a moment, he swore he tasted blood in his mouth.

Meliae cried out, her body flexing. Daphne and Karya held her in place, forcing her to accept everything.

Vince glanced up to find the three Elves, Fes, and Petra all staring at Meliae as they were flooded with sexual scenes, emotions, needs, and the twisted desires of a Dryad.

Thera finally succumbed and sunk slowly to her knees to lean up against Elysia.

Meliae, lost in her own world, cried out between hip-shaking, breathtaking thrusts.

"More! Harder! Harder! Break me!"

As she always managed, she spurred him on. That strange magic that she held over his libido.

"Defile me! Own me! Fill me with your seed," she cried out, only to be silenced with a grunt as he hammered his member home into her. "Your personal flowerpot!" She grunted, then moaned as his hips crashed into her over and over. "All of your seed into me!"

Releasing the bruised flesh in his teeth, he bit down where her neck met her shoulder.

Meliae whimpered, deliberately turning her head further, offering up more flesh to him.

The pounding she was taking was audible. Each and every slap of flesh punctuated with filthy demands from the Dryad's sweet mouth and full lips between growling grunts and moans.

Vince gave in to the need and pumped her as hard as he could, his member rapidly expanding and flexing as he unloaded syrupy seed into her.

As he'd done with the other two, he sent enough stimulation through her pleasure center to even melt a Dryad's wanton nature.

"Yes! Yes! Give me it!" Meliae cried, her voice breaking as it became a wordless scream. Her thighs and arms pulled hard at her Dryad handlers, desperately trying to wrap herself around Vince so he couldn't pull away if he tried.

Then, he pushed the Elves, both Dryads, Fes, and Petra's minds into Meliae's hip-breaking orgasm.

Gasping out a breath, Vince pushed hard against Meliae, who ground her hips into him, squeezing the walls of her channel for all she was worth. Her breath was caught as her scream ended, unable to even breathe.

As the last burst left him, he collapsed atop his Dryad.

His eyes focused on the naked Elves against the wall, who looked dazed. He unclipped everyone from Meliae and closed the window into her mind. As everyone was released from the communal orgasm, Meliae finally took a breath.

As one, the Elves sat taking gulping breaths against one another.

Looking to the used and naked Fes and Petra, he found they looked wiped out.

Daphne and Karya let go of Meliae's limbs and then started to bicker quietly about something over his head.

The now released Meliae slumped into the bed, her arms and legs too heavy to lift.

"I love it," she gasped. "When you break me." Meliae took another deep breath. "Sweetling."

Vince chuckled once at that.

Four hands promptly eased him onto his back, away from Meliae. He slid out of her, the tip dripping with seed and smeared with fluid from hilt to head.

Daphne and Karya's heads appeared by his groin. Vince was tired but realized what they'd been arguing about. Laying a hand on each of their heads, he eased them towards his shaft.

They each took a side, starting at the base. Their lips pressed against each other's around his girth. Each ran their tongues over him greedily and inched their way to the top.

Their tongues battled back and forth when they reached the end. Before they could get into trouble, Vince tightened his hands in their hair.

Then he pulled Daphne's head down along his length. He forced her head up and down twice slowly. Leisurely.

After that, he pulled her back and forced Karya to deepthroat him next. Pushing her head down an extra third time, he then released them both and let out an exhausted sigh.

Both Dryads went back to taking turns downing him. Licking and slurping at him. Four hands squeezed and fondled his jewels as they chattered back and forth quietly.

Vince didn't care. A cursory sweep of everyone's mind told him he'd done what he set out to do. All knew their place, or what it would be.

All were content.

Chapter 26

Vince dragged a sleeve across his brow and then stood up. He'd never had a green thumb, but even he could help to prepare soil.

Putting one hand on his hip, he looked up into the sky and wished for a breeze that wasn't coming.

He was on the eastern outskirts of the city that would be. Buildings were going up rapidly, roads were being paved, industries being kicked into high gear and churning out products.

Things were on track.

"Den master!" called a high-pitched voice.

Looking around, Vince finally identified who was calling out to him. It was one of his Ratfolk.

Vince waved at the two-foot creature as it scurried towards him. It was flanked by several of its den mates. Waiting patiently, Vince slung the hoe he'd been using up on his shoulder.

"Den master," said the one in the lead. They came to a sliding halt in front of him. Dirt sprayed across his boots and a pebble rattled off his shin. "We sighted humans. Coming this way from the west. Many. Unmounted. They follow the tracks. Here in a sun and a half."

They weren't the brightest, but they'd proved insanely loyal to him and good scouts.

"Good work. Get your den mates into the warren and sleep. I'll need you tonight. As a reward for your excellent service, you can claim an extra item from the depot," Vince said with a grin. He fished out a circular token from his pocket, checked that it had a number one on it, then handed it over.

"Den master, thank you. We go." The Ratfolk looked pleased. After a quick confirmation with each other, they took off at a sprint.

They hadn't been given much in the way of respect previously, he gathered. Rewards and positive affirmation went a long way for them because of that.

Elysia had been beyond wise to recommend them as scouts.

Thinking of the High Elf, he turned his head to find her sitting not far from him. She had found a large rock and floated it over, turning it into a seat. She was reading over some book she'd dug out of his library.

Thera and Eva were some fifty feet behind her. Engaged in some light sparring. They'd started working with Fes, Petra, Daphne, and Karya to up their martial prowess.

Elysia's style of combat didn't lend itself to sparring. Things were either on fire or not.

The High Elf's blue eyes flicked up to him over the top of the page she was on. If his eyesight weren't as good as it was, he probably wouldn't have noticed.

She'd developed a habit of watching him. He'd politely ignored it most of the time. Her eyes remained glued to him when she realized he was watching her.

Tilting his head to one side, he wondered if it would be better to see the Fairies himself or send Elysia.

Slowly, the High Elf lowered the book down, as if to make sure he knew she was aware of his gaze.

He set the handle of the hoe against his thigh, then brushed his hands against the work tunic he was wearing.

No, we're done here.

Vince grimaced and then pulled the work tunic off over his head. Picking up the hoe, he set off for Elysia.

Elysia stood up from the rock and looked back to her sisters, then to him. Closing the book in her hand, she smoothed out her dress with the other.

"My liege, what may I do for you?" Elysia asked him when he got within range.

Instead of responding, he smiled at her and closed in.

After he'd dragged them through the quagmire of what was Meliae's mind, the Elves had changed. They were more aware of him. Nervous. Bashful, even.

Of course, that only provoked Vince as a predator. Teasing them had quickly become a favorite thing to do.

"I'm not sure, what are you offering?" Vince asked, closing in on her until a single foot separated them.

Elysia's cheeks turned a faint red, glowering at him from under blonde eyebrows. Then, unexpectedly, she gently smacked his chest with the book. "Stop it."

"As you like," Vince said amicably. "I need to meet with the Fairies. Ratfolk reported a sighting. Need to confirm it with them. No word from the Brownies."

Elysia's eyes drifted off as she took her thoughts inward. After several seconds, she came out of whatever thought she'd fallen into.

"Agreed. We'll meet you there," Elysia said, turning to go get her sisters. She stopped and then glanced over her shoulder at him. Deliberately, she set her eyes to his waist and then trailed upwards along his bare torso. "Put a shirt on as well. You're distracting."

Then she was off.

Vince smirked at that. Of the three of them, Elysia was the most honest. He liked it.

Dropping the tunic and hoe off at the farming shed, he retrieved his clothes and armor. Then he veered off for the tree of the Fairies.

They didn't go out on scouting missions. They were to be used as scouting confirmations. They could keep themselves aloft in the low sky while being nearly invisible.

Their stamina was the only thing that kept them on standby missions.

One of the trees they'd left alone was a large and looming black oak tree. The spirit inside was old. It had said it would prefer to die with the tree if that was what it came down to.

Instead, Vince had made arrangements with it. Protect and nurture his Fairies, and he'd leave the tree alone and protect it in turn.

Managing to get the last strap in place as he neared the tree, he glanced up into the foliage.

Nothing moved.

Stepping up to the base of the tree, he looked up into the branches above.

"Scouts have reported a sighting. West by about a day and a half, and they're on their way here. I need confirmation and then oversight," Vince said to what looked like nobody and nothing.

Then they appeared. Winged humanoids the size of a small bird. They had shimmering wings on their back that could carry them at incredible speed.

"Master!" they cried at him, landing all along his shoulders and head.

Male and female Fairies chattered at him, all trying to get his attention. The overwhelming demand made was that he visit soon for a meal.

"Yes, I promise to come by and have lunch sometime. I really do need that scouting mission taken care of, though."

As one, they grumped about promises that could be broken. Eventually, through repeated promises that he really would have lunch with them, they started to flit off, only a few remaining in their tree.

Turning from the tree, he realized he needed to call a council meeting. Rather than by race, every function, job, building, or department had someone in charge of it.

They had others below them in charge of other things, and so on and so forth. Very, very military, and very efficient.

Thera, Eva, and Elysia were all standing behind him, waiting.

"Ah, good timing, ladies. We need to hold a council. Preferably in an hour or so. Can you put that together for me?" Vince asked, his eyes sweeping from one Elf to the next.

"Consider it done," they said in unison.

"You ladies sure are in sync lately. You should stop fighting it when I call you sisters," Vince said, waving a finger back and forth at the three. "Besides, you spend more time with each other than you do anyone else. I've never even seen you argue with each other. For all that 'all Elves hate other Elves' nonsense, you sure don't act like it. As far as I can tell, every Elf here is working hand in hand with the others. All in your family, no less."

"Probably the most put-together faction I have."

The three regarded each other, then looked back to him. Elysia looked thoughtful, Thera annoyed, and Eva a little lost.

"What, is that a problem? If you want a better example, have you looked around our city lately?" Vince asked, and then indicated everything around them.

The Elves started to look around them when he said that.

Ogres were holding carpenters aloft in the air as they worked on buildings. Orcs and Dwarves were doing inventory checks on ore from a wagon. Goblins were busily working to insert paving stones into the road as a couple of High Elves created them. A mixed unit of Wolfmen, Bearmen, and Ratfolk were sparring against a team made up of Dwarves, Orcs, and Hobgoblins in a field nearby.

"You can't tell me you don't see it. You're intelligent and beautiful women. Can you honestly tell me you don't see it?" Vince said.

Eva turned back to him and cast her eyes down at her feet. "I see it, Master."

Thera looked back at him and smiled slowly, then wrapped an arm around Elysia's waist. "My Lord is ever wise," she proclaimed, wrapping her other arm around Eva's middle. "My sisters and I will get the council together."

Elysia smiled shyly, before setting her arm around Thera's shoulders.

As one they walked off, their heads turning to each other in a conversation Vince deliberately blocked out.

The swift and deadly Eva, the intellectual Elysia, the warrior Thera. Between the three of them, if they worked together, they couldn't fail.

Careening in at full speed from the side of his vision was a Fairy.

"Master! They're already here," cried the Fairy in despair. "They're minutes from the walls.

Turning from the fairy, Vince walked up to an Ogre. He didn't recognize it by name. Smacking it on the hip, he stared up at it. It took some oomph for an Ogre to recognize something had hit it.

Slowly, the big head swiveled down to peer at him, then grinned when it recognized him.

"Lord?" it asked slowly.

"Remember how to sound an alarm?"

The Ogre nodded its head ponderously.

"Sound the alarm for the wall."

A second later, the Ogre gently set down the Elven carpenter he'd been holding up to work on a roof and then placed his hands to his mouth.

He sucked in a deep breath and began to let out a single thunderous bellow.

All around the growing city, everyone stopped and listened. As the Ogre finished, he set off for whatever job he had for a wall alarm.

Then everyone else took off in every direction.

There was no sound except for the pounding of feet, boots, and claws. Everyone knew their task.

Vince was glad he'd made it a habit of going out armed and armored. He had to get to the wall.

Heading out at a swift jog, Vince fell in with the mass of bodies moving that way. The dormitories had been converted to barracks and armories as more and more of the citizens had been given a home. Men and women of every species streamed in one side of those buildings and came out the other with arms and armor.

It went smooth, swift, assured.

Daily drills had given everyone a plan and confidence.

As the walls came into view, Vince felt better.

The entire western expanse was done. All the way to the point that it bordered with impassable rock that went far to the north, then west. He'd build walls in that direction eventually, but for today, nature would be his shield there.

The southern wall was also complete. If one were to pencil in the eastern and northern wall based on those two, they'd realize it encompassed an area five times what the original plan for the city was.

"Room to grow" was the phrase he'd heard passed around when they'd unveiled the plans.

The eastern wall was only a fourth done, the remainder being open to whatever might come. Hopefully they'd be too stupid to bother checking that it went all the way around.

One can hope.

It was a pity the wall wasn't done, but that was life.

Taking the fortifications in seconds, Vince immediately moved up into a tower that overlooked the front gate. They'd been built every so often in the wall to reinforce it, and provide a place to view everything.

Looking out to the west, he could see them. They were walking in on the plains his people had created all around the walls. They'd needed a clear line of fire and had it now.

A mass of men and women with weapons from all walks of life, from personal to professional.

Here and there, he could see city guard, militia, even the occasional soldier. He counted as best as he could, but gave up when he realized they were all shifting around.

Beyond them were wagons and carts that he'd bet were loaded with foodstuffs and other things.

"Around seven hundred heartbeats," Karya said from his side. One hand pressed into his hip as the other slithered into his pants.

Vince didn't fight her since it would only encourage her. Attention was attention, after all.

"Quite a number. Well, it's within what we prepared for." Vince shifted to one side as Karya's hand worked its way into his privates and gripped him firmly. "Are they all humans? Is this everyone right here? No one sneaking around?"

Karya shook her head, pressing her face into his side and taking a deep inhale. "Not that I can detect."

Her warm hand stroked him tenderly, hungrily. Karya and Daphne remained untouched by him. As did the Elves.

They'd been starved of all sexual contact since challenge night. He didn't fight the Dryads off, but he didn't let it get out of hand or cooperate, either.

Their reward that night had been the allowance that they could watch any of his nightly encounters they wanted at any time. They were happy for it, though they thought they'd get to participate.

"Where's Daphne?" he asked, rubbing Karya's head.

"She's down at the gate, darling. You don't need her, you have me," Karya complained.

"I do have you, but I do need her. Sorry, Karya." Vince carefully extracted her hand. It wasn't that she had no effect on him, because she did. Quite a bit, actually.

The fact that every night he was taken care of by someone who cared for him deeply, though, made it easier to resist.

Leaning out of the tower window, he looked down to the gate.

There stood the tall Dryad, watching through the open gate.

"Daphne," Vince called down. The buxom woman turned her head up and saw him, then gave him a ferocious smile. "Can you get ready? They don't look like they have siege equipment, but you never know."

"Yes, dearest." The big Dryad moved to stand on the inside gate of the wall and then became motionless.

Karya grabbed his ass and squeezed it, her other hand tickling his neck with her fingertips.

"Are you really that insatiable that you want me to plow you while we're being attacked?" Vince asked, only mildly irritated. Part of him was flattered.

"Yes. Push me out the window facing the enemy and fuck me. I don't fight as much as Meliae does. Seed me. I've been practicing. I can get thousands of eggs ready for you to fertilize in under a minute," Karya said huskily at him.

"Tell you what. Be good for the rest of this week. On top of that, if you can get me my Elves, Fes, Petra, and Meliae, I'll let you and Daphne start having a turn next week. Promise," Vince said, looking out to the enemy approaching.

"Prepare to pay up, darling," Karya said, already on her way out of the tower.

"Gladly." Vince wasn't against expanding his number of "wives," as it were. Fes was already encouraging him to take both Dryads and all three Elves.

The Dryads were stuck with him, though. When he died, so would they. They hadn't been giving themselves to other men, either. In fact, they seemed to hate other men.

They desired only him.

It made it easier on him to accept them.

Looking back into the mustering lane that was set up against the wall, he saw his Ogres and Trolls were armored up. Armored up and waiting for orders.

Hanging on each waist in a gigantic sheath was a massive broadsword. Clutched in each hand was a spear with tree-like proportions and a banded tower shield that looked more like a drawbridge.

They were already a hardy species. Putting them in Dwarven-made plate mail increased that survivability tenfold. Then give them a proper weapon, and train them like soldiers while putting a shield on their other arm, and he expected great things.

Let's see how well they do.

The big, feisty Troll he hadn't wanted to purchase waited below the tower. After her talk with Meliae, she'd changed.

She'd taken control of the large species and ruled over them sternly. All respected their "Lord" and his "Big Commander," in both word and action. Rule breaking or dishonor was immediately punished. There were no repeat offenders.

Military law and courtesy rang well with the whole group.

He'd had no problems with them. At all.

"Kitch!" Vince called out the name of the Troll.

Her misshapen and beastly face swung up to meet his.

"Take your people into the field. Tell our foes to leave. If they don't... lay into them. Show me how well your people learned their trade. Show me Kitch and her warriors," Vince said evenly.

Kitch grinned evilly at him, then crossed her arms against her shoulders in salute. She then cracked her massive mitts into each other and bellowed a short grunt.

Her people fell into a marching formation.

Then the group of thirty-some odd Ogres and Trolls exited through the gate that had been built specifically to accommodate their size. They marched in formation.

They moved in sync, their arms and legs pumping to an unspoken cadence.

It was terrifying to Vince.

Stopping out in front of the wall, Kitch quickly lined up her people into two rows and took several steps out ahead of the line.

"By order of Lord, you leave!" shouted the Troll. "Leave, or die. One minute to turn around. Then you die!" The armored Troll turned back into her line and slid into the center rank in the second row.

At a glance, he could tell that these people wouldn't be leaving. They looked like they were shouting at each other with some sort of fervor.

He couldn't figure out what was driving them, but it didn't matter. Moving to the back of the tower, he leaned out again.

"Frit!"

Waiting below in the mustering lane were a number of his captains. A Bearman lifted a shaggy head. This was his mixed units captain. A Wolfman and Ratfolk stood beside him.

"Get yourself in position as reserves for Kitch. They're going to end up surrounded. We might need you to harass the flanks so they can get out or at least evacuate wounded if they have them. I don't imagine you'll need to completely engage, but use your discretion."

Frit saluted and barked his orders to his lieutenants. All three were off at a jog. A company's worth of soldiers in Dwarven armor and weapons lumbered out the gate and fanned out in reserve for Kitch.

Ratfolk rode their compatriots like mounts in specially built slots for them. They could scamper up or down with each and without impeding their comrades.

Armed with tough, long spears made specifically for them, they looked unimpressive.

Vince knew better. He'd seen what Frit had been practicing. They were his mischief makers.

Ratfolk could flank a unit from below and escape before they were caught.

The humans gave their reply to Kitch's demand.

They charged.

Chapter 27

Kitch bellowed an order and her people reorganized themselves. They made a quick circle of twenty with ten in the center. Those in the outer ring handed their spears to the center, and then joined their shields together with those at their sides. Then they unlimbered their swords, sliding them into the spaces between the shields.

Those on the interior stacked their shields in the middle and then got ready with their spears, positioning them so they could work in concert with the outer ring.

Vince nodded in approval. Kitch had certainly been studying. He was no commander himself, but he could appreciate her orders.

Moving to the entrance, he looked out to the wall.

"Sivir!" he called to the siege ballistae atop the gates.

They were large crossbows that fired huge bolts. An enclosed and armored seat and loading bay had been added to each one. They'd been built on simple gears, levers, and bearings with Gnome ingenuity.

Loading had been taken up by Hobgoblins. They could set in a new bolt and cock it as if it were nothing more than a kid's toy. These ballistae had an insane rate of fire because of that.

A crazy-haired gnome popped out from around the side of one of them.

"Hold your fire unless you see a real target of opportunity. I'd rather not give away your range quite yet if we don't have to."

Sivir saluted and disappeared around the side of a ballista. Shouted commands traveled up and down the length of the wall.

Fes stepped up beside him and peered out the viewing port ahead of them.

A soft scuttling on the stones told him that Petra was clinging to the outside of the tower.

Taking a quick peek down, he found his three Elves waiting at the base of the tower where it met the wall. They were facing the human wave of trash.

"Kitch has this. Why deploy Frit?" Fes asked. She pressed her arm into his. She'd gotten subtle with her desires.

Grinning, he gave her a quick hug and then indicated Frit.

"I trust Kitch. I won't risk her life with that trust, though. He's just there in case."

"This one agrees with Master after hearing his reasoning, Fes," Petra said, her voice coming from outside the tower.

Fes considered that and nodded her head. "As do I, Second."

Since he'd put everyone in their place, they'd actually become rather friendly with each other.

Nothing like knowing the chain of command.

The humans reached the range of spears and began dying. Then the swords began flashing out.

Finally, that fleshy wave hit the shields… and stopped dead. They flowed around his heavy metal group as if they were an ocean.

Then the dying truly started in earnest.

The Ogres and Trolls kept to their formation, remained in their solid shield wall, and simply killed.

It was their first true battle as a unit. Vince hadn't been sure how it'd turn out or if they'd be able to maintain discipline.

He'd worried for nothing.

As if realizing the same thing, he saw what nerves his heavy group had vanish. They became machine-like. Stabilize, stab, retract, stabilize, stab, retract.

Bodies started to pile up at the foot of the shields.

A bugle call came from somewhere he couldn't see, and the wave of humanity started to retreat. Retreating at a run.

Who made that call?

Vince's mind flipped over on that thought. It meant that this was planned. He needed to inflict more losses.

"Elysia," Vince called, moving to the ladder.

The High Elf looked up to his summons. "My liege."

"Signal Frit to harass and return as able. Once they're clear to do so, signal Kitch to head in."

The High Elf nodded and then moved off to one side.

A crack split the air. Elysia had said it was the sound of her depleting a space of air and letting it fill in rapidly.

Apparently some of the books his parents owned had given her the idea.

Her magic gave her control of the elements, which included the air. This mastery gave her an impressive ability to conduct sound. Much akin to a bugler.

She followed the original boom with three rapid-fire cracks, and then a low humming note, then another single crack.

They'd developed a few means of communicating in the field, this being one of them.

Frit knew his designation, the low humming note. As one, they set off in a loping stride.

They could cover distance like cavalry without being winded. Before the humans had even gotten out of the kill circle of Kitch and her troop, Frit and his soldiers fell upon the retreating humans.

"Can't let them leave as they please. They didn't come with any gifts or anything. Terrible neighbors. The least they can do is water our grass for us," Vince murmured.

Fes gave him a wide, toothy smile. "My brutal husband."

"When needs must. An enemy I leave alive today is another one I must face tomorrow. None of these fools will become allies."

Another crack split the air, followed by two low notes, then a rumbling, grinding noise.

Kitch and her people reorganized themselves into a marching column, collected their gear, and quit the field in proper order.

Frit and his forces ran down the humans as they fled. Clawing them, biting, stabbing. The Ratfolk slipped free to finish off wounded or maimed combatants rather than keep riding. They wouldn't be much good running down fleeing humans.

Frit was on the edge where Vince was starting to get nervous when they started to wheel around.

Vince nodded and then left the tower. Kitch could use encouragement for a job well done.

The Elves fell in behind him as he passed, all three looking more the part of bodyguards today, their heads on a swivel and inspecting everyone and everything around him.

He reached the gate as Kitch came back in.

"Kitch!"

The Troll turned her head and found him. She pulled off her helmet and gestured for her troops to continue.

"Well done, Kitch. I'm extremely proud of you and your soldiers. Give them my regards, and please come by later. Each will need to collect a token from me for that exemplary demonstration. Well done indeed."

Kitch looked confused, then gave him a slow smile. She gave him a partial salute, as her arms were full, and followed her troops.

"Master, she has never received praise."

"Lord, she has probably been shunned her whole life."

"My liege is kind."

Vince snorted and turned back and looked out to the fields. "She did exceptionally well in training her folks. They performed perfectly. Look, you can see a circle of grass where they stood, and all around them the bodies of their foes."

A warm and soft body pressed into his back. Quick fingers played along his sides. "Two hundred fewer heartbeats, darling."

"Fantastic. Thank you for checking," Vince said, catching Karya's right hand and kissing her wrist.

"Alright, they've got their nose bloodied. Hopefully that'll keep them from deciding for further stupidity. They'll probably wait for that second group."

"Second group?" Karya asked.

"The Ratfolk said there was another force beyond this one still en route. The Fairies are out scouting and hopefully getting me a count.

"All we can do for now is wait."

Vince spent most of each day on the wall, or nearby.

The Fairies had returned the same day he'd sent them out. They'd confirmed there was indeed a second force still coming. And that force had roughly six hundred men, except they were apparently "soldiers" this time.

They even had a baggage train with camp followers.

Someone was funding this throwdown to actually purchase an entire merc company contract. With an actual war being fought in the north, there'd be more merc companies available, too.

His Fairies had reported that the two groups had merged together last night. On top of that, at least two hundred of those civilians had started to move south around the wall as well.

The situation was starting to deteriorate.

He'd had his Beavermen work on reinforcing the stake wall to the east. They'd completed it previously, but were now making it much denser.

It wouldn't hold out a determined enemy forever, but it'd provide enough cover that they couldn't simply swarm into the budding city.

His siege crews had been told to fire as fast as the Hobgoblin loading crews could swing it during the next engagement.

Assigned along the wall were his magic users as well, spread out to help hold the wall in whatever fashion they could. Each section they inhabited had been reinforced with a raised lip they could fall back behind.

The last of the defenses were archers with short swords. Anyone who couldn't fight in the front line had been trained with a bow and taught how to fire over the wall in volleys.

Then to do their best if there was a breach of the wall or gate.

It wasn't pretty, but it'd take numbers out of the enemy.

"Master, the humans in the south have found where the wall is incomplete," reported a Fairy, floating above his head.

Vince sighed and rubbed at his eyes with his hands. "Of course."

"The Ratfolk are still out causing mischief, but they succeeded. All of the food stores are… ruined." The Fairy sounded sickened with her own statement.

"Good. I hope they like eating and drinking Ratfolk shit. Anything else?"

"No."

"Stay here on the west gate. I'll head out to the east. Spread that info along."

Vince turned to his Elves, who were never far from him.

"Eva, remain here. Thera, Elysia, stick on me. We've got a party to host on the eastern flank."

Vince turned to where Fes, Petra, Meliae, Daphne, and Karya stood. They'd been talking quietly right up until he'd started giving orders.

"Fes, Petra, Meliae, Karya, you're in charge here. Daphne, with me."

Moving towards his captains, Vince picked up his pace.

"Kitch, you're on gate duty. Let none pass." The Troll looked to him and nodded.

"Frit, with me, get your unit together. We're on the east side."

"Henry," Vince said to the Dwarf in charge of the Orc, Hobgoblin, Dwarven unit. "You too. Consider yourselves co-captains."

Vince set off at a jog for the east. Behind him, he could hear the lieutenants getting people put together.

Elysia, Thera, and Daphne fell in with him.

"Dearest, are we not leaving too many here?" Daphne asked.

Vince glanced over his shoulder and shook his head. "Meliae and Karya aren't front line soldiers. I'd leave Elysia here if I could as well, but I need her. Sorry, Elysia."

"I live to serve you, my liege. I'm grateful to be needed."

As they left the small city in its massive walled enclosure, Vince had to wonder what was about to happen. Things weren't adding up right. He was missing something. Something that would cost lives, he was sure.

Vince pulled up on the inside of the wooden stake wall.

"Daphne," Vince said without turning his head. "Fill the field with brambles and thorns. Elysia, dry the stake wall out. I want it so bereft of moisture that it'd catch fire from someone thinking warm thoughts at it."

Both women said nothing, but he felt the magic being poured out of both. Daphne's was like a torrent of rushing wild energy, where Elysia had a tight control over everything she did.

"All done, dearest."

"I as well, my liege."

Vince turned and found Frit and Henry waiting behind him. Both saluted him, waiting for orders.

"Take up defensive postures behind the stake wall. Arrange yourselves in whatever way you see fit. It'll be set aflame once the enemy commits and cannot backtrack. Turn this into a fiery bottleneck of death," Vince explained, jerking a thumb to the twenty-foot gap left in the stake wall for his people to come and go.

Frit and Henry nodded and then turned to each other to work out their interpretation of his orders.

Looking to Daphne and Elysia, he gave them a small smile. "Forgive me for turning your work into nothing more than a bonfire, but it'll help greatly. When the time comes, can you get everything going at the same time?"

It was a tall order. The stake wall went all the way down to the actual stone wall in the south.

"Yes, dearest."

"I believe so, my liege." Elysia sounded winded to him. Thera had slipped an arm around her waist, holding her close to her side. It looked like a friendly gesture, but he was sure that the Dark Elf was holding her sister up to a degree.

Elysia had used a good deal of magic to dry out such a large stretch. He didn't doubt that she could do what would come next; what he doubted was her ability to do anything after that.

"Alright. Daphne, can I give any of this energy to Elysia? I'm not... I can't use magic. Never been taught, but I know I'm full of energy."

Daphne tilted her head to one side and then nodded at him. The tall Dryad grabbed his hand and then put it on Elysia's chest, right above her heart.

"Push into her from where the trees are. They will understand," Daphne said, holding his hand in place on the High Elf's chest. "Do it gently or I will hurt you later, dearest."

Of his Dryads, Daphne was the one most likely to put up a good fight. Added to the fact that he'd dumped hundreds of collars' worth of power into her tree, she was the one person who might actually be able to give him a fight.

"Of course," Vince agreed easily.

Focusing on his trees, he tried to will energy from him into Elysia.

Nothing happened at first, of course. His trees were confused and not quite sure to make of his request. Then at once, all three began to rush energy forward into the High Elf.

Vince looked up into Elysia's face as her eyes started to widen. He pulled back with all the internal mental power he could, trying to slow it down. Overwhelming the poor thing wouldn't do him any good.

It'd piss off Daphne as well.

After a tsunami-like initial wave, his trees picked up on the context and throttled it all the way down to a manageable level.

Standing there with his hand on the beautiful High Elf's chest, he felt a touch self-conscious. Minutes had rolled by and it seemed as if there was no end in sight to how much he could put into Elysia.

Daphne was the image of confidence and merely smiled at both of them, looking back and forth between them.

"Daphne." Vince frowned, looking to the Dryad.

"Yes, dearest?"

"Will this hurt our trees?"

"No, no. If anything, this is good for them. They normally push out large amounts of power when you make waste. There's only so much that they can process or use."

"Elysia, is this hurting you? How much can you or Thera hold, exactly?" Vince asked gently. The High Elf had said nothing and done nothing. Merely stared at him, her pink lips parted.

The High Elf blinked once and focused on him. "My liege, an Elf's capacity is endless. It is part of our life essence. Thera uses her pool to strengthen blows and heal wounds. Eva to guide shots and cling to the shadows, as well as for her woodsmanship. I use it for my magic."

"Oh. I suppose that's why you're all so long-lived, then. Wait, does using magic age you?"

"We build up reserves and use that rather than what we need to survive," Elysia said dreamily.

"Okay. Is that enough to do what we need to?"

"My liege, you've given me more than even the strongest of our kind hold after years of meditation. I have enough to work endlessly for years, never meditating again. And still live a millennium."

Thera had been watching from the side. She'd had a concerned look originally, though now she looked only jealous.

Vince smirked at that and then lifted his hand from Elysia's chest. "We'll leave it at that, then. I mark that at about... five minutes. We'll have to charge Eva at the same level later. Should get to work on Thera next, since she uses it for combat."

Elysia gave him a strange smile and nodded her head.

"You sure that did no harm to the trees, Daphne?"

Vince looked to everyone around him. Frit and Henry had placed their units accordingly and were ready.

"If anything, dearest, they're healthier at this moment than they've been in a long time. Be sure to charge Eva today if you can. It'll give the trees more room to grow.

"In fact, charge them regularly. Perhaps daily, if you can manage it."

Then Daphne gave him a feral grin and came in closer to him. Of the three Dryads, her attention was subtle, flirting, suggestive. She wasn't as blatant as Karya or as needy as Meliae.

"To really get the most out of it, you should claim them and put all of that energy into your seed," Daphne said clearly. She tapped a finger to his sternum. "It'd empower them greatly. As if you'd charged them for hours."

Thera and Elysia's sudden attention was like a physical slap to his forehead.

Elven hearing was no joke.

Letting out a small sigh, Vince turned and faced to the east. Everyone kept pushing him to claim the Elves.

Claiming the Dryads was one thing, but the Elves were an entirely different matter. He'd bought them, and they'd sworn to him under false pretenses. Thinking it would get them better treatment.

No. He'd not be claiming them.

Frit's shaggy head turned one way, then the other. He took a deep snuff of the air. "Lord. Humans near. Horses near."

"What?" Vince asked, his eyes scouring the landscape. He pushed his limits and senses. He demanded to know where these horses were.

There.

He hadn't noticed them. They were blended into the backdrop of the distant woods and were motionless. To his eyes, he could count at least two hundred horsemen.

"Confirmed," Vince said, the word tasting like ash in his mouth. "Two hundred, give or take. In the tree line. Damn it. Send a runner back, we'll need spears."

Frit barked at one of his men and a Wolfman sprinted off.

"Elysia, how much can you do with that big dose of magic we put in you?"

"My liege, I can slay many. The problem, though, is that I sense someone in their midst who can counter me. I hadn't noticed it until you pointed them out. I apologize for my failure."

"Fuck that. Can you overwhelm them?"

"Yes, my liege. But it would take time."

"Okay. Make passive traps, then, things that they can't counter, and make sure they don't throw anything back at us."

Vince thought on that for a moment. "Can you heal wounds at all?"

"Not well, but with this surplus, even I can mend flesh."

"Frit, Henry, bring the wounded here. Faster, the better. Elysia is going to be our medic. Daphne, would the trees stop me from handing out too much? If they felt it wouldn't be wise?"

"Immediately, dearest. They want what's best for all of us, but they must protect their lives first."

Without looking away from the distant enemy, Vince reached up and laid his hand on Elysia's chest again. "Forgive me, Elysia. But you need to tell me the limit of what you can handle. We need you at the level of an Elven goddess."

Vince opened up the flow into her again, turning his head to face her. He didn't control it at first, and let that massive tidal wave flow right into her.

Elysia squealed, her hands balling up into fists, but she kept herself upright. She stared into his eyes as magic roiled through her.

"More, my liege," she grunted, her blue eyes sparking with lightning.

Vince prodded the trees to push more. Faster.

"More," came the response, the static of electricity coloring the single word.

Chapter 28

Vince was watching when both groups fell in together and set off for his position. They were coordinated to a degree.

He'd gotten lucky this time. They'd underestimated what they'd need to take the east side and overestimated the west side.

Had this been more of the merc company, he'd have been in serious trouble.

Elysia stood on one side of him, Daphne the other.

In front of him was a smoldering Thera. Her entire body was shuddering under the onslaught of magic he was unleashing in her. Steam was actually rising from her head. She stood there, panting, gasping, fighting to remain upright as he filled her. She'd subjected herself to a faster flow than what Elysia had been able to handle.

There was no time left.

"Elysia, grab your sister," Vince said, and then brought the flow down to a trickle.

The High Elf was there instantly, supporting the Dark Elf. Vince ended the flow completely and removed his hand from Thera's chest.

"Lord. So much power," Thera said through chattering teeth.

"You did better than Daphne did. Remember? She fainted the first time."

Daphne snorted at that.

Vince looked back out to the rapidly approaching enemy.

Then he saw who this enemy was.

Al. Al and everyone he'd broken out of the north with.

But why? It doesn't make any sense.

Vince thought on that, his thoughts chasing it round and round. Thera was rapidly recovering, probably using some of that energy to repair whatever damage the transfer had caused.

Then it hit him.

If he was dead, he couldn't be present to give evidence of Al's culpability in the events up north.

Frit and Henry had reorganized their lines when the spears arrived, with Bearmen and Hobgoblins being in the front row, Wolfmen and Orcs in the second, and the Dwarves taking the third row.

The spears in front would take the bulk of a charge, and normal doctrine would have a horse charge before a rabble of infantry hit. He imagined they'd try to punch a hole in his defense and then split it.

A lightning bolt from the clear sky appeared above them. It was met in midair by... nothing. It simply ceased to be. There wasn't even the crack of thunder. It was just gone.

Then another lightning bolt flashed above the enemy line. Then another, and a third, then a fourth.

Each one was met and vanished.

Looking to Elysia, he found the High Elf standing with her hand up. A small smile had blossomed on her face. "I almost had them. They're strong. I think there might be four of them. I'll show them the strength of my liege."

Lightning bolts began falling uninterrupted onto the enemy ranks, one after another.

Each was invisibly countered. Until it suddenly wasn't.

Three lightning strikes blasted into the enemy line, the thunderclap deafening. Men, women, and horses went down and dirt sprayed up from the strikes.

Then the bolts were being countered again.

Elysia growled, grinning with her teeth. "I got one."

Vince watched as the cavalry separated from the men on foot, distancing themselves. Al was in the middle of that cavalry charge somewhere.

"Spears up!" Vince called.

The cavalry had nowhere to go but straight into Vince. There'd be no wheeling around, no disengage. It was here and here alone.

"Light the bulwark," Vince called out.

Two balls of fire, having formed from the center of Elysia's hand, launched out and hit the dried stakes. One fireball for each side of the gap, and suddenly the wood was a raging inferno.

The cavalry was committed; the infantry would be forced to follow.

A roar came up from the lines of his men in front of him. The cavalry roared back. Then everything was screaming horses and men being flung from saddles. Spears splintering, the crash of weapons.

His much smaller force did the impossible. They held the line. Here and there, horses and men broke through the line. Too many jammed into one spot had created fractures, though they sealed quickly.

Thera hadn't waited for instructions. She was a blur of death, flickering into the line and taking any who came in her range and spitting them on her sword.

Vince played bodyguard for Elysia as she simultaneously fended off magical attacks and healed those who were brought before her.

Daphne stayed at his side, her staff held like a spear and ready for anyone to come close.

Ratfolk, now being able to go about their business, jumped free of their hosts and began an ugly task—killing all those who fell to the grass in that charge. Then they started working on thighs, knees, and calves of horse and man alike.

They used the corpses of the fallen humans as bunkers and worked their spears deftly, killing in concert with their larger counterparts.

Swords were drawn as the spears were no longer necessary.

The battle became a slog between cavalry with nowhere to go, infantry pressing into them from behind, and Vince's line holding their own.

A Hobgoblin went down in a spray of blood, followed quickly by an Orc. In the center of his line, something was going wrong.

Both the Hobgoblin and Orc were dragged from the line and passed backwards rapidly to Elysia.

Vince chose to act and began shouldering his way to the front.

"Dearest, no!" Daphne called out, unable to keep up with him.

Scooping up the shield of the Hobgoblin, Vince pushed into the front. Dwarves continued to work hurriedly to retrieve the wounded behind him as Vince personally plugged the hole.

Vince found the problem. An Elf. Vince didn't care what sub-race he was, or even what he was doing here. Only that he had to go before he did more damage to his people.

Stabbing out with his saber, Vince forced the Elf to back up. To Vince's left and right, the shield wall held.

The Elf leapt forward, fast as could be. Vince deflected the strike and returned another stab.

Caught off guard, the Elf hadn't expected his strike to be blocked. Vince's saber caught him low in the hip and slid off.

The Elf stared death at him even as he reevaluated his position.

Vince could swear he saw the exact moment the Elf decided to back up and try somewhere else in the line. It was the same moment Vince decided the Elf had to die.

Pulling on his trees, Vince slid forward two steps and lashed out with his saber in an overhead horizontal swipe.

Fast as the Elf was, he didn't even see it coming. The blade separated his head from his neck, and the left foreleg of a horse.

Stepping backward, Vince slipped in the field and fell heavily on his backside.

A sword leapt into the space his shield had been and skewered his hand.

Screaming in pain, Vince lashed out with his saber.

His shield didn't feel right in his hand as Vince clambered upright. The shield wouldn't move exactly as he wanted it to.

He managed to get it around in time to block an overhead chop from a woodsman's ax.

Except that when Vince tried to bring the shield back in, he couldn't get it up. He couldn't hold the shield up, and his hand wouldn't close tight enough to hold it firm.

He'd made it back to the line, but his shield was worthless. A faceless cavalryman with a sword realized it at about the same time Vince did.

The soldier was pushing his sword forward in an ugly stab that would skewer Vince. Struggling to get his saber around for a deflection, Vince realized he wouldn't make it in time.

Even with the speed and strength offered to him by his trees, it wouldn't be enough.

Then Daphne was there, shoving him deeper into the line as she spun forward with her staff. The Dryad glowed with an earthy green aura as she bulldozed into the cavalry man.

Smashing into the man's face, the staff rebounded backwards, and Daphne brought it back around in the other direction to club a second man down.

With a flick of her wrist, her staff came backwards towards a third, then down and around towards a fourth.

A spear exploded out of her stomach as it was driven through her back. The shaft snapped off when Daphne completed her next turn.

Her feet tripped over themselves and she stumbled forward into the press of the front line. Then she disappeared under the mass of boots and feet.

"Daphne!" Vince screamed, trying to get forward into the line again.

He was violently shoved back, then pulled backwards as everyone realized who he was, and that he had no business in the line.

Coming free of the press of the line with a suddenness that was jarring, Vince collapsed on his backside.

"My liege!" Elysia was there, pulling the shield from his arm as Thera disarmed him of his saber.

Vince looked from Elysia to Thera. "Daphne's in there, we need to get to her."

Thera looked back to the press of bodies in the gap of the flaming stake wall.

"Thera, it's my fault," Vince said softly to the Dark Elf.

The Dark Elf stared at him for a moment and then set off at a blinding speed.

Vince slumped onto his back as Elysia pushed on his shoulder. She gripped his left forearm in both hands. Looking at her face, he saw it was a picture of concentration. Desperate concentration as she murmured under her breath.

Something's wrong.

Looking to his left hand, he saw that half of it was missing. His ring finger, pinky, and half his palm weren't there. Simply gone.

"No wonder I couldn't hold a shield." Looking to said shield, he found a chunk of meat that looked like his palm still mashed into the grip.

Elysia stood up and looked back to the battle ahead of them. A lightning bolt crashing down from above into the enemy ranks at the rear.

Vince looked down to his left hand and found that, while it wasn't whole, it was no longer bleeding. He now only had three fingers on his left hand.

Standing up slowly, Vince looked around for Daphne or Thera.

Before he could decide to head back in to find her, Thera popped back into view, dragging an unmoving Daphne behind her.

The spear had been lost somewhere, though it was apparent to anyone who looked where Daphne had been struck. Blood pumped out of the gaping wound with every beat of her heart.

She looked like she'd been dipped into a vat of blood.

"Elysia, do... do what you have to." Vince paused. She'd been using energy nonstop. She might not even have enough to do this. And he couldn't channel into her at the same time she was trying to use her magic.

"If I dump energy into Daphne, can you use that instead of me pumping it into you?" Vince asked, squatting down next to Daphne as Thera dragged her over.

"Yes, but... but my liege, this is... this is grave. I'm not sure I can—" Elysia made a fluttering motion with her hands.

"Do all that you can."

Vince looked into Daphne's face. Her green eyes were staring up at him. She gave him a bloody smile, her teeth coated in the red liquid.

"Sorry, dearest," Daphne said, trailing into a coughing fit.

"Hush. No more talking. Only healing. No dying," Vince said gruffly.

Placing his hands on her chest, he opened himself up to his trees and begged their assistance.

Their response was what he'd hoped for. Overwhelming and instinctive.

Elysia had sat down across from him. She tore off Daphne's tunic, exposing her entire torso, then laid her hands on top of the wound site. Blood seeped up between her fingers, spreading rapidly over Daphne's stomach.

Her eyes started to glow faintly at the sheer magnitude of the power being emptied into her. Then the color began to fade away.

"Daphne, damn it. No. You have to focus and stay with me here. Karya managed to get me to agree to spend time with just you and her next week. You can't leave yet," Vince said glaring down at her.

Daphne gave him a bit wider of a grin, the glow in her eyes slowly fading to nothing.

She's bleeding out. She needs more blood. Elysia can fix the wound, but without blood, it's pointless.

Mom's biology books. Blood. What makes blood? No, not blood. Plasma. Bone marrow.

Vince grabbed hold of his mental gift, latched on to his trees, and tried to drown himself in the power in his own body.

Then he tried to focus that raw, unadulterated maelstrom of energy into Daphne's dying body.

Specifically, he targeted the bone marrow throughout her body. Demanding that it ramp up blood production.

Daphne's eyes lost what little color they had in them, her eyelids fluttering.

"I can't stop the bleeding," Elysia said.

Damn it, no, damn it, no, damn it, NO!

Vince felt something break inside himself, and then all the power he'd been bathing himself in rushed out of him. Into nothing.

"I'll hold this here," Thera replied.

"It won't stop. I can't stop it," Elysia said in a panicked voice.

Vince felt winded. Then exhausted. Like the river that was his life had run dry.

Hanging his head, Vince looked to the battle lines. His troops were pushing forward now. The humans were giving ground steadily. Then they broke and started to run.

"It's over," Elysia said with a soft sigh, standing up. Blood dripped from her fingers and stained her dress terribly.

Vince watched as Frit and Henry chased the humans off for a short distance before returning to the gap. Wounded were gathered up and brought to Elysia, who immediately triaged the situation and set to work.

"She's a good healer, dearest." A warm hand pressed to his cheek, a thumb brushing over his eyebrow.

Vince looked down to find Daphne smiling at him. Bloody teeth and all. Looking down, he saw her stomach was a twisted mass of scar tissue. It didn't look like it would hinder her much, but it looked awful.

Daphne looked down and saw the same thing he did. "Guess I won't be wearing anything showing off my stomach again."

Vince snorted, then started to laugh in between a few choked-off sobs.

"Idiot. Like I care about scars. I mean, they'll be calling me lefty here soon," Vince said, holding up his mangled hand.

"Maybe you have me beat," said the Dryad, laying her head down on the grass. "You bound our trees into one."

"I what now?" Vince asked, reaching up to brush the hair back from Daphne's brow.

"Meliae's tree, Karya's tree, and my tree are now connected in a grove-like situation. Beneficial, but dangerous. More for you than us."

"Don't care," Vince said, and then laid his forehead to hers. "You're okay?"

"I'm okay, dearest. Don't do that again. It hurt," Daphne complained.

"I won't." Vince gave her a quick peck and then stood up, walking over to Elysia, Thera, Frit, and Henry.

The High Elf was hunched over a Hobgoblin she'd just put back together. His chest was a mass of scar tissue, but he lived, and looked to be in no pain.

Elysia glanced up at him as he approached, a pained look in her eyes.

Frit gave him a salute at the same time Henry did.

"Lord, minimal losses," growled Frit. "Perhaps one in twenty slain."

Vince didn't respond, but instead, fell down on his knees next to Elysia.

"My liege, I'm sorry. I couldn't save your hand comp—"

Wrapping her up in his arms, he silenced her. He pulled her in close and tight. Hugging her roughly.

"Thank you, Elysia. You did more than I could have asked for. Any favor I can grant you is yours. Merely ask," Vince whispered huskily into the long, pale ear of the woman.

And he meant it, too. He'd truly believed Daphne had paid the price for his foolishness. He should have let his men do their job.

The High Elf mage relaxed in his grasp, laying her head on his shoulder.

"My liege, I have no requests. You've given me a home, a family far beyond what I originally had, and a purpose. If I had to ask for anything, it would be to fill me up with your power again when you're recovered. It was a pleasant experience. I had more power than any other Elf in legend. You only asked me to heal and fight for you. I'll reward that trust in me. I swear it.

"Oh, Thera and Eva, too. I have to watch out for my sisters, after all."

"Done."

Al wasn't in the mass of corpses. He'd lost half his cavalry here, and most of his infantry. But he himself wasn't among them.

Elysia had gotten creative when given time to think on the situation. She used a major portion of the power left to her to raise a stone wall from the south all the way to the north, effectively completing the city wall project.

It was something no one would have thought of simply due to the power restrictions it had.

They'd have to add a gate later, and towers, but this was no longer a way in.

Vince had sent Frit and Henry west to assist with whatever needed to be done there.

Upon reaching the western wall, he found that they'd fared a little worse than he had, but not terribly.

Fes, Petra, Meliae, Karya, and Eva had worked together and taken control of the wall and operated it better than he could have.

There were no wilting heroines here. No princesses needing to be saved.

He'd been the only one who had needed saving.

The losses here were one in fourteen. A fraction of the numbers the humans had left behind.

A member of Kitch's band by the name of Renzig had fallen. He had held the gate after it'd been blown open with a bomb. The Troll and her crew had been working to clear the wall of ladders and men alike.

During the performance of his duty, Renzig ended up being struck by another bomb that had been tossed in after the first. It'd been enough to tear through armor and Ogre skin alike.

Realizing he was going to die, Renzig had wedged themselves against the ruins of the gate, and died there. An Ogre was not something easily moved or shifted. In laying himself out the way he had, he'd bought the time Kitch needed to arrive to block the entrance.

With no food, as the Ratfolk had taken the order of "use the enemy's food as a damn toilet" seriously, and wounded to care for, the rabble army fled.

Goblins cleared the fields on both sides, securing everything and anything usable, and disposing of the rest.

Vince didn't ask how they'd disposed of it. He didn't want to know.

The battle for Yosemite City ended in victory.

Epilogue

Vince walked alongside the wagon as it trundled toward the city. It was hard to believe that these fields had been flooded with blood six weeks past.

He could see his Gnomish siege engineers watching the horizon from the wall. Their Hobgoblin loaders stood at their side, ready and chatting amiably. Partnerships forged in the furnace of battle.

An Ogre stood up and could just barely be seen over the wall. It set down a High Elf at the base of a tower and then wandered off as the mage set off in the opposite direction.

All his Elves were mages at this point. Even the Dark Elves, who were such physical creatures that they had to be retaught how to use the magic.

Of course, this would happen when you spent a portion of every day charging those very same Elves with all the excess magic you could.

Apparently his Dryads approved wholeheartedly of the practice, as did the trees. Meliae had made an analogue to "pruning" a tree of its excess.

The small snippets of conversation and hushed whispers behind him died away.

"I think they finally believe, Lord," Thera whispered from his side.

"My liege, don't hold their doubt against them," Elysia agreed.

"Yes, Master, they didn't know," Eva pleaded.

Vince chuckled and shook his head, casting a glance over his shoulder.

He'd been four weeks from home. The military had stopped purchasing slaves as army recruits when they'd realized that the enemy in the north would simply capture them, pop their collar off, and turn them back on the Empire.

So Vince had headed west to purchase supplies, new citizens, and sell products and loot.

There'd been quite a bit of armor and arms left over from the attack on Yosemite City. Deskil had rejected all of it when Vince asked if he wanted to smelt it down for material. Told him to sell it. It all had a "taint" to it, he said.

Even including purchasing new citizens, they'd made fifty thousand standards in profit. Apparently Dwarven-made equipment was in high demand by the Empire's armed forces. Many of the blacksmiths they normally went to in the local area had been killed in the anti-Wastes riots.

Of course, Vince had only sold them the castoffs that Deskil felt weren't up to the quality he wanted to give to Vince's military.

All told, he was returning with two hundred new citizens of various walks of life. He'd even managed to pick up twenty more Ogres and Trolls. Kitch would be delighted. They were much harder to find, let alone get in such numbers.

Frit would be happy as well. A new batch of Beastmen tribes to add to his mixed units. Only Henry wouldn't be quite pleased. He'd specifically asked for more Ratfolk, but there hadn't been any available.

Apparently those tiny warriors had impressed their compatriots.

Vince would be heading out again in four weeks to purchase more citizens, sell more stock, and check in with the Ranger guild.

He'd given them all the information on the attack on the city, including that he'd seen Al leading it.

The guild was in a mess right now. They'd lost two outposts in the north, a great deal of trust from the populace, and were being pressured by the Empire.

They needed more news from Vince like a hole in the head. So they paid him to go on "vacation" for a month.

"No, I won't hold it against them. But I will mock them for it later, if the situation arises."

"Of course, dearest," Daphne said amiably. She and Karya rarely left his side now.

Meliae had remained at home with Fes and Petra. They'd all declined coming with him on the journey and said they'd remain and keep watch over the city.

He suspected something was afoot but couldn't put a finger on it.

As he got closer to the gate, he realized there was a likeness carved into the interior of the archway.

"Renzig's Stand," Vince said aloud, reading the plaque below the magically carved likeness of Renzig. With a nod of his head, Vince approved of it completely.

Reaching out as he passed, he laid his mangled left hand on Renzig's shoulder. "Thanks," Vince murmured.

Then Vince realized that small plaques had been affixed next to Renzig's. Each held a name. A name of someone who had fallen in defense of the city.

"My doing, Sweetling," Meliae called from the interior exit. "I didn't think you'd mind." She gave him a bright smile, holding up her hands to him. "You can punish me if you like it. Or punish me less if you don't."

Vince grinned back at her and hugged her tightly when he got close enough.

"Good to see you. We're adding two hundred, give or take. Made money, too."

"Mm, my breadwinner," Meliae purred at him, planting a heavy kiss on his lips.

Daphne and Karya snickered as they fell in behind Meliae. They still deferred to her in all things.

The Elves in turn fanned out behind Vince to the side of the road.

Frit, Henry, and Kitch walked up to him, giving him a crisp salute.

Vince set Meliae down and returned the salute.

"Two hundred recruits," Vince said loudly. "We'll be popping collars later today. Then assigning dormitories and units. Please come with your lieutenants so we can process them into your units quickly.

"In your case, Kitch, I got you twenty-three Ogres and Trolls. You're welcome to attend the collar popping, but I imagine you'll want to square your people away immediately."

"Yes, Lord," rumbled the big Troll woman. Then she gave him a toothy grin. "Will speak with Master Deskil for equipment. You approve?"

"I do, Kitch. You and your troop have earned all that I can give and more. And speaking of that, I purchased a gryphon from the beast masters. I want you to see what you can do about turning it into a mount for your people. They're big enough to carry an Ogre off for a meal, so I figure you can ride them as mounts. If this one works, we'll buy more."

Kitch clapped her big mitts together and rubbed them eagerly. "Lord is good to us. Too good."

"Dwarven steel armed and armored, mounted, flying Ogres and Trolls," Thera said quietly.

"Should be fun. We'll have our heavy cavalry unit after all."

His captains saluted again and then left, talking between themselves.

"Husband," Fes said from behind him.

Vince managed to turn around before Fes wrapped him up in a bone-crushing hug.

"Oh, hello to you too, Fes. Miss me?" Vince said, hugging her back.

"Yes. We did," Fes said, pressing her forehead into his cheek. She lipped his ear once. "Challenge tomorrow?"

"Yes, challenge tomorrow. As we agreed," Vince confirmed, rubbing Fes's back.

"Good. Petra claims she can win this time. We shall see," Fes said. Vince was astounded when Fes turned her head and grinned at the big soldier ant above her.

They'd grown considerably closer since the night of the challenge, then more after the battle.

Then Fes turned Vince loose and shoved him towards Petra.

"This one is eager for the challenge," claimed Petra, folding herself around Vince with both arms and four of her legs. She was practically hanging on him. "This one missed her master desperately."

"You were welcome to come with me. I did offer," Vince said.

Petra ducked her head in next to his and stole a kiss from his lips.

"Pregnant women shouldn't travel. They also shouldn't be sparring," Meliae huffed. "Which is why challenges tomorrow will not be by martial combat."

"Mel—"

"This o—"

"No! I'll not have it. End of discussion," Meliae said firmly, crossing her arms across her chest.

Fes and Petra both fell silent, but nodded agreement.

Vince had to replay that exchange in his head once. Meliae was the third of three, yet Fes and Petra deferred to her. She had also said they were pregnant.

"Ah, I see. Does that mean...?" Vince asked curiously.

"Yes, Fes has a viable pregnancy. So I've allowed Petra's to begin to grow. Mine as well. Daphne and Karya are holding on to theirs for now. Congratulations, you'll be a father of three relatively soon," Meliae said in a clinical tone.

Fes blinked at that and then turned to Karya and Daphne with a feral grin. "Tomorrow is challenge day. As claimed wives, you will fight for your position. Come, we will discuss this and how you represent our husband and your Fes."

Petra fell in beside Fes and the two led Daphne and Karya off.

"Hm. I'll make sure nothing funny happens," Meliae said with a sigh. "See you later, my love. You're mine tonight. I already paid Fes off to get bumped up in the order," Meliae admitted. She darted in to kiss him deeply, then patted his chest as she started to pull away.

"Oh, and did you ever read this?" Meliae asked, fishing an envelope out of her tunic and holding it out to him. "It's still sealed, so I assumed you hadn't yet." Then Meliae was off after the others.

Eva peered at the envelope. "What's that, Master?"

"A letter. From a Ranger in the north. It slipped my mind."

Vince flipped over the envelope and broke the seal, then pulled the sheet of paper free.

Dear Vince,

I hope this letter finds you well. I'm a woman of short words and shorter time, so I'll make this brief.

I knew your parents. They were good people. A little odd, but good. I even met you once when you were nothing bit a tyke.

I hate to call them liars when they cannot defend themselves, but I must. They didn't head east.

As you know, the Ranger guild had an outpost up in the north there once. That was actually where your parents met.

After they left, it fell to the Wastes and no one bothered to try and reclaim it.

They met with Seville, then headed north into the Wastes up there. I had been there on a business trip when they came through.

I'm not sure if this helps or not, but it might not hurt to head north and check out the old Ranger outpost up there.

Because knowing your parents, they probably went there first.

Sincerely,
Macy

"Lord?"

"Master?"

"My liege, are you well?"

"Ah, yeah. I'm fine. Just… interesting news." Vince folded the letter carefully and slid it back into the envelope, then handed it over to Elysia. "Please put this with my important correspondence. You can read it later if you like and share with the rest."

"Yes, my liege," said the High Elf, stashing the letter away immediately on her person.

Wagons kept moving past them as they stood to the side. His new citizens couldn't keep their eyes in any spot. They looked around in every direction. From person to person. Waster to Waster.

All moving about with jobs and tasks. Wearing collars but having no humans around. They were all very confused-looking.

Behind Eva and her sisters were his newest Elves. They were a common commodity in the markets. Hunted, bred, and valued for their magical abilities and intelligence.

It was fairly horrific.

Amusingly enough, with this new group, the number of Elves in his employ was in the nineties. Doubly amusing was the fact that by sheer luck they were relatively balanced in numbers as far as subspecies.

The clatter of talons on stone got his attention as a Wolfman slid to a stop in front of him.

"Lord, from the east. People approach."

"East?" Vince asked. Shaking his head, he gestured at the messenger. "Right behind you. Lead on."

Vince turned back to his Elves.

"Take your new family members aside and teach them the ropes," Vince said, looking at the three sisters. "Not much left to do today until later."

Elysia and Eva looked to Thera. She shook her head and then pointed at the Elves.

"Ask for directions to the Manor. You'll be sorted out," Thera explained.

All three Elves turned back to him.

A sigh slipped out as he turned to head east at a fast walk.

When he got there, the gate was open and he could see a small group of people heading his way.

They couldn't have been more than a hundred feet out at this point.

At such a short distance, he was fairly certain they were Elves. Their hair coloring would indicate High Elves or Wood Elves.

Vince passed through the gate and continued right on through to the other side.

Behind him trailed a mixed unit of Frit's. Beyond that, he could hear the heavy clatter of metal distantly.

Stopping thirty feet outside of his wall, Vince waited.

They were indeed High Elves, with a few Wood Elves mixed in for good measure.

"Summon your slave master, I would speak with this abomination's leader," grumped a High Elf male who epitomized the clichés. Arrogant, handsome, and graceful.

"You're looking at him. What can I do for you?" Vince asked, his eyes sorting through the twenty-some odd guests.

"Die."

A ball of fire skipped across the distance between them and vanished. Then a lightning bolt vanished above Vince's head.

Two more fireballs hurtled towards him and a rather large boulder that was ripped from the ground — only for the fireballs to vanish and the boulder to be sent spinning southeast, rolling away on the grass.

"Your pet did well. I don't think she can handle another round. Surrender and she need not suffer."

Vince held up a hand towards the High Elves as Elysia stepped forward.

She was a bookworm until provoked. Then she made Fes look timid.

"I think you have a false impression of what's going on here — "

"Do you not own everyone here? That's the tale we heard."

Behind him, he could hear Kitch getting closer. She wouldn't tolerate this if she was here. He'd have to finish this up quick.

"I am indeed the master here. I purchased everyone here and th — "

"Then die."

Another slew of magic disintegrated as if nothing happened.

Elysia's eyes had started to crackle with lightning. She had a preference for electricity.

"I-I don't understand."

Vince glanced backwards as Kitch exited the gate. "Well, I recommend you act like a dignitary from here on out. My Troll captain doesn't take kindly to people who are rude."

"Rude?" said the man.

"Yes. Rude. Now. As I was saying. Elysia, would you be so kind?"

"My liege, I will gladly smite them in your name," said the High Elf. She stepped forward and brought her hand up.

Everyone in the opposing party had a bolt of lightning reach out for them. Then a second as the first was stopped. Then a third.

"Stop! Elysia, stop. I was going to ask you to show them your collar. They think you're bound," Vince said, laying a hand on her forearm.

In the time it took him to get her to stop, half of the High Elves had collapsed or fallen to their knees.

Elysia looked to Vince, then the High Elf who had spoken so haughtily to them.

"My liege is merciful. You should die," Elysia said as if she were looking at a worm.

Deftly, she removed her collar and waggled it at the other group. As if to confirm the point, Eva and Thera did the same.

"As you see. Everyone here wears a false collar. Yes, I purchased everyone here. Then freed them and gave them jobs and a home."

Kitch stomped up to him, sword unsheathed and glaring murder at the visitors.

"It's alright, Kitch. Elysia gave them a lesson in manners. We're merely talking now."

Kitch growled deeply, menacingly. Then she turned her head to Elysia and ducked her head.

"Now, what can Yosemite City do for you today?" Vince asked the High Elf male he'd been conversing with. "And if you say die again, I'm going to tell Kitch to eat you." He paused. "Wait, would you eat him, Kitch?"

"For you, Lord. Sometimes upset stomach. Magic."

"Ah, makes sense. So? Are you lunch, or a polite dignitary of an Elven tribe come to seek something of Yosemite City?"

The High Elf looked from Elysia, who was re-buckling her collar, on to Kitch. "Even the Troll?"

Vince looked up at Kitch and smiled for her. "Who, Kitch? Yes. Even her collar is for show. She doesn't like taking it off, though."

"No. Lord's collar."

"I would like to request the gift of guest rights," said the humbled High Elf.

"Granted. Thera, could you see they're taken care of?"

"A Dark Elf?!" the High Elf said, as if only now noticing her.

"Hm? Yes. She, Elysia, and Eva — she's the Wood Elf there — are my bodyguards, companions, and chamberlains. They manage everything here, really. Be lucky it wasn't one of them I asked to help out. I don't think I can reattach limbs and things."

Thera and Eva were simply next to the High Elves in the next instant.

"We will take care of your needs for our lord," Thera said gravely.

Eva nodded her head, circling around behind the group.

Vince shook his head and turned to Elysia. "Anything you need to do?"

Elysia looked at him and then slowly smiled at him. Then she reached out to tap his chest with the ledger she carried with her at all times. "I shall remain. You can't function without me."

"True enough. Alright, notetaker, let's see how good you really are. I need to find the dresses we bought for Petra, Fes's new armor, and Meliae's plants. Which wagon is that all on?" Vince asked, gesturing vaguely back at the city.

"I know exactly which one it's one, my liege. It's with the other presents you purchased."

"I purchased other presents?"

"Of course. I bought them for you on your behalf," Elysia said, flipping open her ledger. Thera and Eva trooped by with their new charges. Kitch eyed them balefully as her troop did the same.

"That's great. Did I buy anything for you?" Vince asked, grateful for the High Elf.

"You did. A beautiful chess set and a silver tea service. You were very kind."

"Oh, those do sound pretty nice. Would you like to get all these presents and then go play a match? Have some tea? I'm sure you'll stomp me out, but it'll be fun, I hope."

"I will indeed beat you, my liege, and I'm sure it'll be fun. I promise to still respect you in the morning, though," Elysia said, looking up at him from her ledger.

Vince blinked at that and then grinned. *They're all getting so much more lively.*

Thanks for reading.

I hoped you liked Wild Wastes.
If you did, please leave a review.
Reviews never hurt to bring in more readers

Drop me an email at: RandiWDarren@gmail.com
You can also reach me on Facebook: https://www.facebook.com/RandiDarren

Made in the USA
San Bernardino, CA
05 July 2017